Praise for *Deadly Little Secrets*

"Jeanne Adams has done it again with *Deadly Little Secrets*. Excellent and thrilling! *Deadly Little Secrets* is fast-paced, riveting and highly entertaining."—*New York Times* bestselling suspense author Carla Neggers

"An evocative and explosive thriller! Jeanne Adams delivers another electrifying read in *Deadly Little Secrets*."—Roxanne St. Claire, internationally bestselling author

"ANA, YOU ARE GOING TO INVITE ME IN, AREN'T YOU?"

He held her hand, his thumb making restless circles on her palm. Her imagination was in overdrive, thinking of having his hands on her body.

Part of her, the part that was so afraid of screwing up again, wanted to say no. That part wanted to scoot away to the other side of the seat.

The rest of her, the part that was more truly Ana, agreed. "Yes," she said, forcing herself to meet his dark gaze. "I am. I'm not sure it's smart, but I'm going to do it anyway."

"Smart?" Gates asked, knowing it was a rhetorical question. "Hmmm. I'm not sure I'd call it that, either. Ana—" He started to tell her that this wasn't something he did on a whim. He didn't get to finish.

The window next to her crackled, and there was a sharp snapping sound as the bulletproof glass buckled, but held.

"Get down!" he shouted.

More by Jeanne Adams

Dark and Dangerous

Dark and Deadly

Published by Zebra Books

Deadly Little Secrets

Jeanne Adams

ZEBRA BOOKS
KENSINGTON PUBLISHING CORP.
http://www.kensingtonbooks.com

ZEBRA BOOKS are published by

Kensington Publishing Corp.
119 West 40th Street
New York, NY 10018

All Kensington titles, imprints, and distributed lines are available at special quantity discounts for bulk purchases for sales promotion, premiums, fund-raising, educational, or institutional use.

Special book excerpts or customized printings can also be created to fit specific needs. For details, write or phone the office of the Kensington Special Sales Manager: Attn. Special Sales Department. Kensington Publishing Corp., 119 West 40th Street, New York, NY 10018. Phone: 1-800-221-2647.

ISBN-13: 978-1-4201-0882-8
ISBN-10: 1-4201-0882-4

First Printing: September 2010

10 9 8 7 6 5 4 3 2 1

Printed in the United States of America

This book is dedicated to two dear people who graced my life.

The first was a courtly gentleman,
a man of principle,
honor and laughter:
my father, James Pickering.
He passed away before this book went to print,
but he was supportive of me in all ways from the beginning of my life to the end of his.
This one's for you, Dad-bear!

The second was one of the most interesting, challenging, funny, sarcastic women in the publishing business,
my late editor, Kate Duffy.
Kate, you said you couldn't wait to read this one,
and see me pull it off.
I hope I did you proud.

Acknowledgments

Every book brings different challenges as you write it, and this one is no exception. I love the Greek culture, but alas I don't speak Greek. To my dear friend Contos for her assistance with all things Greek, *efharisto,* thank you! The same could be said of Italy, so *mille grazie* to my dear friends Mr. and Mrs. Claudio Debenedetti for tea, cookies, and their assistance with the Italian idiom. I also had wonderful help from my Italian/Australian pal, Josephine Caporetto. *Mille grazie* to you as well, Josie!

My life is richer, fuller, and more productive as a writer thanks to the wonderful support of the Romance Bandits (*www.RomanceBandits.blogspot.com*). Thank you, Banditas! You rock! To my plotting group, Avocat Noir, I bow in your general direction with great humility and thanks. To my friends, Cassondra, Donna G., and Susan W. who read drafts and tell me about big, huge plot holes, bless you.

To fellow Romance Bandit, New York Times bestselling author Kate Carlisle, thank you for all the fabulous details about San Francisco, the Opera House, and the geography and weather in your part of California.

To my agent, Laurie McLean, you're brilliant and I'm so glad to be associated with you. Thanks as well for making sure I got the Bay Area details right.

To my editor, Alicia Condon, and to Megan Records and all the fabulous staff at Kensington, a huge thank you!

Last but never least, to my family, you are the best blessing in my life. Many thanks and much love, always.

Chapter One

The bodies lay before her. Five sets of staring eyes, five gruesome deaths mocked her from the shocking clarity of the police photos.

"Five dead," the gravelly voice rumbled in Ana's ear. "A completely cold case, and one fat headache. That's what I got, Agent Burton." Even the noise in the background didn't disguise the irritation in Agent McGuire's voice. "Whoever they were, they were slick, professional, and cold as hell. They left us nuthin' to work with, ya' know?"

Ana Burton scanned the photos, fighting her own horrified reaction. The three meticulous professional, execution-style hits juxtaposed with the tortured bodies of two of the victims. Her stomach clenched. The pictures were painfully graphic; no angle was left to the imagination. In one, the sheer volume of blood pooling around the body made the dead woman look like she was haloed in red. In another photo, a young man lay with arms akimbo, his body ribboned with slashes and his remaining clothing so covered in red that its pattern was obliterated.

"I do know," she replied, pulling herself back from the brink. Her own losses were too fresh, too close to the surface to be looking at this kind of thing. She cleared her throat and refocused on McGuire. "You and Agent Hines, you were all over it," Ana told the retired agent, and meant the compliment. The notes on the cold case—a nine-year-old investigation of art fraud—were meticulous. They also led absolutely nowhere. "I'm hoping new technologies might shake something loose."

McGuire hollered at his grandkids to keep it down before he continued. "Gotta say that it would be good to get those bastards. You saw the case files—two of those people were killed slow. Mean. The art fraud part, that's stealing. Stealin's one thing. Good to catch them for that too, but the killing part? They need to go down, way down, for that."

"Couldn't have said it better, Agent McGuire. I talked to Agent Hines this morning, and he feels the same. Okay if I tap you again, if I come up with something new?"

"I'd be pissed if you didn't, get me?" McGuire's growl was part hopeful, part order this time.

"Got it. I'll be in touch."

They hung up, and Ana noted the conversation in her case log. She'd opened this cold case file two days ago, the second case in her four-month exile to the CIA's San Francisco office and the Cold Case Division. With this one, however, she'd felt the gut-level excitement she got from a real case, a hot one. Much as she didn't want to get involved—she was only on cold cases until her probation hearing—this one had her instincts perking up. Between her art degree, computer expertise, and Agency experience, this one would challenge her every skill set.

Don't get cocky. The self-caution was new. A painful reminder that she'd been tested in Rome and people had died because she was wrong. As horrific as the photos were, at least these people were already dead and buried. Her lips twisted in a grimace. She couldn't kill anyone on a cold case.

She'd already talked to the other agent, the very impatient Agent Hines. He'd handled the legwork on the original crime. Hines was a Senior Special Agent now, covering Oregon, Washington, Montana, and Wyoming. McGuire, on the other hand, had retired to New Orleans. They'd each given her a personal rundown, suggested some new areas to check, and been generally cordial. Neither recognized her name, which was a relief. To them, she was just another agent doing grunt work on a cold-as-ice case.

Her cell phone beeped an incoming text. She read about her best friend's latest scheme, some matchmaker deal. "Jenny," she muttered to the phone as she returned the text. "I don't want to go to some cattle call. Nice men? I don't think so. How many times do I have to tell you those Maximillionaire Matchmaker cocktail parties are a straight-up booty call?"

The image of some millionaire stalking up and down a line of scantily clad models, Jen included, popped into her brain.

Not in the market, she texted back. **Remember the migraine?**

The headache had actually come from gritting her teeth and resisting the urge to shoot the self-important moron who'd bored her to tears the last time Jen talked her into a social event.

She decided not to mention that part.

Jen was on a mission to get her out of her apartment and into the land of the living, if not the dating pool. She kept saying, "Hey, you used to love it, you were the life of the party."

That much was true. Before Rome, before probation, Ana had loved dressing up, going out, hanging out. Now?

"Not so much," she said, pondering the changes in her life. She had good reasons for holing up at home. The cat needed her. And she needed the cat. And to organize her shoes by color. And to rearrange the spices she didn't cook with. Life outside the apartment was work, and she didn't want to do it. Not right now.

Besides, no one wanted a brooding, gun-toting washed-up CIA Agent for a date.

Through the glass top of her cubicle, she saw Special

Agent Pretzky change directions and stalk her way. Ana winced, which increased her self-disgust. Cold-case duty, a safe place for a dangerous, potentially weak link in the Central Intelligence Agency's strong chains, wasn't fun, but working for Pretzky was even less so. Everyone walked on eggshells around her and avoided direct contact. Pretzky had made it obvious she didn't trust Ana Burton, agent-under-scrutiny.

Hell, Ana thought, resigned to another difficult encounter. *She didn't trust herself, why would anyone else trust her?* Really, the stone-cold silence from the other agents was okay. Some days, Ana didn't even want to talk to herself, which was a sad state of affairs since she was notorious for constantly talking scenarios through out loud.

Pretzky, however, insisted on talking, but she used it as a whip, the way the others used their silence. Neither was pleasant.

"Agent Burton." The woman rounded the corner of Ana's cubicle and stood, hands on hips, glowering her disapproval at the new stack of boxes on Ana's desktop. "That isn't the arms dealer's file." Trust Pretzky to know which files were in the dump truck load of cold files on her desk. She probably had them microbugged.

"An art fraud case from mid-2000. The arms dealer is finished. Here's the report," Ana said as she handed over a file folder with a neatly printed report, in triplicate, enclosed. Since Pretzky expected it, Ana gave her a rundown. "The prime suspect from the old notes didn't do it. I tracked down the guy who did pull the trigger, via DNA, to Nevada. He died in prison. The man confessed to our case, even gave evidentiary proof and signed a confession, but no one bothered to cross the t's and let us know."

A ferocious frown creased Pretzky's brow. "They didn't see fit to notify us?"

"No. It's in my report," Ana said. She'd been waiting for Pretzky to appear so she could hand it over. She'd sent everything else to Closed Files. It would be held there till Pretzky signed off, but it was off her desk.

One cold case down, eight million to go.

Pretzky's "Hmmmm" was more of a growl, but Ana ignored it. She ignored most things these days, except the job, and the cat. And Jen, who refused to be ignored. Withdrawing, of course, was exactly what the department shrink wanted her to admit to, and Jen regularly accused her of.

She practiced the Company line on that one: Deny, deny, deny.

Ana crossed her arms and waited as Pretzky read through the data. It was good, thorough work, and Ana knew it. Not that Pretzky, or anyone else, would admit it, but it was. Ana knew there weren't many agents who could have unearthed the data she had, thought of the angles, pulled the case files, and made the intuitive leaps that got more info and closed the case in two months of digging through old dirt. It was her gift. Or at least it had been.

"Have you sent everything to Closed Files?" Pretzky demanded. It was damned if you do, damned if you don't with her.

"They've got everything, but I sent it with the proviso that you had to sign off." Per regulations. Ana didn't add the last bit.

"What's next?" Pretzky demanded, pointing at the notes next to Ana's computer.

"Like I said, art fraud. Glacier cold, after almost a decade. About ten high-profile victims. Each victim was selling paintings from their collections through various galleries." Ana held up a photo of one of the real paintings. "Real painting leaves one gallery, but a forgery arrives at the buyer's gallery or directly to the buyer. In most cases, the forgery was undetected until the new owner was appraising for insurance. Or on a secondary sale, the forgery was tracked back through the sales to the original owner. The Agency got involved because it was international, and because there were possible international mob connections." She held up the photos of the corpses. "Torture slayings on the East Coast, execution-style killings out here in the Bay Area. Five dead."

"Any DNA or soft evidence to run?"

Ana shook her head. "Professional all the way, probably with inside help. No DNA, no prints." She wouldn't give any of her theories, as she might once have, nor would she speculate or brainstorm. People took that, ran with it, and got hurt. The only thing she added was, "Two or three new databases that may yield leads. We'll see."

"Want to discuss it?" Pretzky said, brusquely. The offer was pro forma; Pretzky didn't want her to agree.

"Not yet." Ana tried not to wince, knowing she was lying. The discussion, the brainstorming, was her favorite part of solving cases, and God knew she loved it; lived for it. Now, though, with the cloud of suspicion hanging over her, she didn't want anyone depending on it. Besides, everyone from Pretzky, to the shrink, to Jen was waiting for her to go back to the old way, the cocky, my-data-analysis-is-gold Ana.

"Hmmm," Pretzky continued to look over the old case notes and Ana's new inquiries. "No connection between the East and West Coast galleries?"

"A couple, but the original team checked them out. Problem is, several of the principals at the galleries disappeared."

"Disappeared?"

"In the wind," Ana agreed. She also agreed with Pretzky's next comment.

"Nobody just disappears. You're going to start there?"

"Yes." It was one of her specialties. Finding the unfindable. Nothing made her feel as alive or as worthy of her paycheck as the data mining, the just-in-time analysis she did for field agents. There was right and wrong. Helping find the data that unraveled the puzzles or led to the sources was what she lived for, no matter how much dreck she had to sort through to find the key. In fact, the thrill of the hunt, sorting the wheat from chaff was a rush. And sometimes the nature of the dreck made the find that much more interesting.

The job was everything to her. She just had to hang on and believe in herself and defend her actions. She prayed daily that the final Inquiry Panel cleared her to go back to her real work. If they didn't, she had no idea what she would do.

Pretzky continued to hum in her throat as she read. Finally, after a few more pointed questions about the new project, Pretzky took the closed-case report and stalked away, hunting for other agents to annoy.

"Thanks so much," Ana muttered sarcastically, turning back to her terminal. This case wasn't online, but the data she needed for cross-referencing were. She continued reading the extensive, well-written notes in the original file. The fraud had been perpetrated on a number of Bay Area dealers and collectors, as well as dealers and collectors in a variety of other US and international cities. Rome leapt off the page, but she fought down her immediate reaction to even seeing the word.

The images in her mind were harder to suppress: a bomb designated for the Italian Parliament, the fiery explosion, two agents dead.

When her incoming e-mail alert pinged four times in a row, she almost kissed the monitor, she was so happy for the distraction.

"What have we here?" she wondered, opening the first, only to find a slew of unrelated Italian phrases. The subject box said *Please Translate*. "Uh-huh, right. For whom?" She was officially out of hard data analysis until she was cleared, so she shouldn't be getting this kind of e-mail. Scrolling through the Italian, she winced at the note at the bottom.

> Hey gorgeous! How's the dead zone? Sending this to you 'cause you're the best. Help! It may be Italian, but it's all Greek to me. HaHa. Seriously. Stumped on this one. Literal, it ain't. Luv ya, TJ.

"TJ, why do you keep coming to me?" She nearly whimpered the words. "I almost got you killed and you love me? Why do you do this to me?"

TJ had been one of the additional agents in Rome. He'd nearly gotten killed with the others because of her faulty data assessment. Instead, he'd helped her pick up the pieces, clean up the mess. They'd had a relationship, once upon a time until he accused her of never being willing to open up. She'd accused him of cheating on her. She'd been hurt too much to tolerate that.

They'd both been right, so they stayed friends. A minor miracle.

Once she was back in the States, on probation, he'd continued to send her questions, to publicly note her help in reports, and to praise her work to all and sundry. It was as if he wanted to turn the screws. He said it was to help her remember who she'd been, all the good she'd done.

Sighing, she hit PRINT. She needed to see it in hard copy sometimes, to make sense of it.

The second one was from him as well. It was titled *More Greek.* It contained one phrase only, which, in this case, was actually in Greek.

The third e-mail was from Pretzky. She'd signed off and sent the report.

The fourth was from Jen.

"Damn it, Jen," she hissed, printing and deleting the e-mail. "Who has a cattle-call date with millionaires at four-thirty on a frickin' Wednesday?" She then backtracked through the coded system, which she'd long ago deciphered, and deleted the e-mail off the delivery server. Personal e-mails were frowned upon even in Cold Cases. She wasn't rocking the boat over another of Jen's goofy plans to get her out of the house.

Obviously Jen was taking personal time off to try out the millionaire dating pool. Pulling out her phone, Ana sent her a text.

> **Can't go. Translations to do. Calls to make. No time for cattle calls.**

It would make Jen laugh, at least. It wouldn't deter her, but nothing did. Within days she'd be after Ana again to try something else in the way of dating or getting out, or taking a class or something. Ana's back still hurt from the yoga experiment.

She slipped the Italian work into her briefcase. She'd look at that tonight.

Her phone rang, and this time, she checked the incoming number. Not Jen. Hmmm.

"Agent Burton," she answered. "To whom am I speaking?"

"Agent Burton, this is Gates Bromley, special assistant to Mr. Davros Gianikopolis." The man's rich, luscious voice filled her ear. "You had called regarding a follow-up on an old case."

She was so mesmerized by the voice, it took Ana a heartbeat to make sense of the words. "Yes. I'd like to make an appointment with Mr. Gianikopolis to discuss his losses in the incident. I'm following up on some new leads."

"I'll be happy to meet with you, get the information, and assess if there's any new data we can add." Holy cow, the man's voice was pure, liquid sex.

For a second, all she could think about was the image of liquid sex. Jeeez, she had to get out more. Jen was right, and she hated to admit it. In the next second, she processed what he'd said and bristled at the high-handed phrasing. *Assess the data, my ass.* Fabulous voice or not, this guy needed a set-down.

"Mr. Gianikopolis is the insured." She kept her voice brisk, impersonal. "I'll need to speak with him. You are welcome to be present, Mr. Bromley." She put all the *I Am An Agent Of The Law* insistence she could in her voice. "Which day this week is he available?"

There was a momentary pause, and when Gates Bromley replied, he sounded amused. "Mr. Gianikopolis is in town, but unavailable for the next several days."

"Fine. Tuesday then?" she pushed.

"Ten a.m. at his estate" was the still amused but clipped reply. He rattled off the address.

"I'll be there. Thank you," she added, remembering her manners. She'd gotten her way—didn't hurt to sugar things up. "I won't take much of his time."

"I'll see to that, Agent. Good day."

Ana clicked off. "I'll see to that? I'll see to that? What a snotty thing to say," she accused the now-humming phone. "You can bite my ass, *Mister* Gates Bromley."

"Oh, man, and here I was hoping to do that," a male voice responded over the cubicle walls and Jim Davis leaned on the opening to her cubicle. Ana cursed under her breath. Just what she needed. The only other person in the San Francisco office who would speak to her was Davis, and he was a slimeball.

"Shut up, Jim," Pearson called. "And get over here. I need that file." Davis blew Ana a smarmy kiss and obeyed. Pearson, the one other female agent besides Pretzky, had filed a complaint against Davis. Though not particularly friendly, Pearson had warned her about him.

"Thanks, Pearson," she muttered as Davis disappeared. She noted the appointment with Mr. Gianikopolis on her PDA, on her paper calendar, and in the file. Checking Gianikopolis off the list, she picked up the phone for the next call.

It was all downhill from there, which made for a bitch of a headache and a long afternoon. At least she had a full Thursday to look forward to, and Friday. She hated the weekends now, with nothing to do but think, which was why she'd gone along with some of Jen's crazier schemes.

"No more yoga, though," she promised herself.

Dragging into her apartment several hours later, she picked up the plaintively meowing cat.

"There now, Lancelot, we'll have a nice dinner and a glass of wine," she said. "Well, wine for me, some cream for you. We'll read some strange Greek and Italian phrases and pop off to bed, perchance to dream." She grimaced. *No. No dreams.* "Strike that, Lancie, let's just stick with a good night's sleep."

The cat wiggled, and she let him jump down. She followed him into the bedroom and changed into sweats. It felt good to get out of the dramatic black pantsuit. She'd stopped wearing the flamboyant Italian silks, the colorful scarves from the Milan markets. Now she stuck to what she thought of as her going-to-court suits for work. Somehow the formality of them helped her feel stable, serious, on the job. It gave her control of *something* in her life, no matter how small.

That was important right about now.

Dinner in hand, Ana dragged her briefcase to the coffee table. "God I'm tired, Lancie. The job used to energize me, you know?" she said, gesturing with her fork. The cat was far more interested in following the path of the tidbit on the fork than listening to her words. "Here," she slid the bite onto a napkin and put it on the table next to the cat.

"Not like you haven't heard this all before, cat," she sighed, ruffling his ears. "I'm like an effin' broken record."

They sat in companionable silence as the news rolled by, and a sitcom came on. Somehow, it didn't really seem all that funny but it was better than a crime show or a drama. She avoided them like the plague.

"My own demons are enough, thanks," she told the TV as she switched channels away from a cop show. Finally, at eleven, when the news came on, she picked up the folder with the e-mails from TJ. Pulling her long dark hair into a tail, she got to work.

She smiled over his note, then read the phrases from both pages and laughed out loud, seeing why TJ had been concerned. Then she translated them and sent them to him with a note:

> **TJ – out of context and literally translated, these could be disturbing. But they're idioms, so you can't take them literally. Send me the context if you can.**

> *Ti hanno tagliato la lingua?* loosely translates as "cat got your tongue?"
>
> *Acqua un bocca* is literally, "water in your mouth," but it means you can't tell anyone, or you have to keep something a secret.
>
> *Scopa un altra* means someone is playing the field. This usually refers to an affair outside of marriage.
>
> As to the Greek, *me keratose* is literally "he horned me," but it's a euphemism for being cheated on, as in "he cheated on me."

She hit SEND, then doubted herself and pulled up the sent e-mail to double-check it. No. It was right. She had to quit checking everything to the point of obsession. She took her dishes to the kitchen and stuffed the files in her briefcase.

As she sat back down, a program started itself on her computer, and a soft tone sounded an alert.

"What? Why would someone be searching me?"

She opened the alert, noting that a superficial search had already shown up and that whoever was looking at her had initiated a deeper, more intensive search, which included databases one had to pay for and register with. She grinned.

"If you had to register . . ." She hummed the two-tone *Jaws* theme. "I can find you."

Cracking her knuckles and taking a big swig of wine, she set to work.

"Damn, whoever this is, he's good," she muttered, yanking her dark hair off her face and tying it into a knot. The tracer had used a series of cross-referencing search engines, with ISPs that bounced back and forth as he searched first one and then the other in an attempt either to move faster or to deflect notice.

The clock on her computer chimed midnight. That was her signal to shut it down and go to bed. She'd gotten pills to help her sleep. Problem was, she absolutely had to go to bed by midnight or they wouldn't wear off before her alarm buzzed, which meant she would be worthless at work. Of course, if she didn't take the pills and she had one of those nights when she couldn't get to sleep or stay asleep, she'd be worthless anyway.

She wanted to keep going. It was killing her. "What is he looking for?" The search was deep and thorough, but it wasn't for financial data or data about the inquests or Rome.

"My college? Why Marshall?" she wondered. The chime sounded again. Twelve-fifteen. Now or never.

"Gah, I hate this. I hate pills," she complained to the cat as she reluctantly shut down her laptop. Damn. She wanted to know what this guy was up to.

"I can check in the morning. I can check in the morning," she chanted as she went to her bedside and got the pill bottle. "I have to have sleep."

"I told you, someone's looking at the files, calling people from the list," the voice whispered on the phone. "It's that new woman, Agent Burton. I haven't been able to get in touch with Agent—"

The man on the other end of the line cut him off before he could name anyone. "Someone? You call me again, without a name of *who* is doing this checking? Shoddy work, Perkins. Very shoddy work."

"Don't use my name."

"What, you think the Agency could have possibly made the connection between us?" He laughed when he heard Perkins draw in a frightened breath at his more menacing tone. "You had better hope not, Perkins." He used the man's name over and over, just to irritate. "Now, don't call me again until you have a name. And not even then until you know there's something about which to be concerned. Calling old contacts on an old list of victims means nothing. You knew the files would eventually come up for review, which is why you set the alert. They had nothing nine years ago. They have nothing now." He paused for a long, cool moment designed to unnerve his worthless snitch. "And if they begin to have anything, you will see that it's taken care of. I assume that's understood?"

"Yes, yes, of course," Perkins stuttered. "Certainly."

"Monitor it. Nothing more. Let me know if anything changes." There was resignation in his voice as if he was sure Perkins would screw it up, which was quite true.

"I think," Perkins began, then stopped.

"You think?" He began drumming his fingers on the mahogany desk.

Perkins sighed. Most annoying. When Perkins finally spoke, it was with a quaver. "I have a bad feeling about this."

He clicked off, hanging up on the still-whining Perkins, and sat looking at the disposable cell phone in his hand. How irksome. Perkins had his uses, but he was a nervous little shit and it was risky to continue using him. He was prone to panic, and that panic could easily turn to ass-saving. Perkins, in order to save his own ass, wouldn't think twice about giving anyone up. He'd have to be eliminated. Soon.

"Weak tools," he muttered, wiping the phone with a cloth. He cleaned it thoroughly, then put it in a plastic bag and used the heavy bronze bust of Shakespeare on his desk to pulverize the pieces. Slipping on a pair of latex gloves, he left his office and climbed the stairs to pick a diaper out of the holder on his son's changing table. In the bathroom, he poured water into the diaper so it swelled, as if it were full. Opening the bag, he dropped half the pieces in, then repeated the process with a second diaper.

Sealing them both in a large plastic freezer bag, he carried them to the garage. Popping the trunk, he dropped it in. He'd deposit the diapers in separate trash cans on his route to the office the next day. It was time consuming, but it had saved his ass so many times he never even thought about it anymore. He just did it.

"Honey?" his wife called out, as he closed the garage door. "Are you coming up to bed?"

He smiled. Caroline was a wonderful woman, a great wife for a man in his position. Always eager, always on the ball, and very seldom curious about his work or his travel schedule. "In a moment, dear. I just want to check on Jeremiah."

He heard the smile in her voice as she told him not to be long. She thought him a doting father, and in that, at least, she was right. Most of what she knew about him, about his business, was a lie. That he loved her and their son, however, was true.

Slipping back into the nursery, he touched his son's damp curls. The boy was a sweaty sleeper, and his curling blond hair looked as honey colored as his mother's in the dim glow from the night-light. He tucked the blanket in and pressed a kiss to his fingers, and then to Jeremiah's cheek.

"Daddy loves you, little man."

Chapter Two

It took most of Thursday morning to wade through the calls and paperwork she'd already generated, before Ana found time to dig into her alert. When she finally managed it, she was thwarted at every turn. It was frustrating as hell. Whoever had done the deep search had bounced the ISP all over God's green creation and back again. She wasted the last two hours of the morning and most of what should have been her lunch hour trying to track it down, to no avail.

"Why would it bounce through the Bay Area Cisco facility?" she grumbled. The Agency contracted with Cisco for equipment, most people did these days, but to have one of the bounces go *through* Cisco? That was just weird.

Another search had turned up, but that she'd been able to track. Bromley had checked her credentials, tried to go a bit deeper, but the Agency had those files blocked. The CIA frowned on people knowing too much about their employees. Frowning, she wondered if he'd done the illegal search as well. She didn't have enough probable cause to dig that out.

"Why?" she wondered, scribbling more notes. Bromley hadn't worked for his boss during the art fraud case. There was a note in the file that he'd asked to review the case when he came to work for Davros Gianikopolis, but nothing else.

She spent the rest of Thursday digging at the search and

fielding return calls. Postponing being in her quiet apartment, she got dinner sent in and continued to work. She left late and was back in the office Friday morning before anyone got there.

"A great life if you don't weaken," she quoted to herself, thinking that in the old days, she'd have had at least a dinner with friends or something besides hearing about Jen's date to look forward to over the weekend. Now, well, too much time to think and brood was her enemy, not her friend.

She started Friday by following up on the Moroni Gallery in New York. It was an exercise in futility and frustration. No one who'd been there for the case was still in the same precinct, or even still on the police force.

"Where the hell is he?" she muttered, opening yet another search on the New York detective listed in the notes. It took her till well after noon to find him. His obituary popped up in one of her searches. The listing was five years old.

Instead of pounding her head on the desk, she went to lunch. She was walking back from the deli when her phone rang. One look at the caller I.D. and she answered it.

"Hey, Jen."

"Oh, my God, you should have gone with me last night," Jen gushed. "There were the most gorgeous men, two of them. I'm going on a date with one of them." Ana could visualize her friend bouncing up and down in her seat.

"Whoa, whoa, wait a minute. I thought you said this was a meet and greet, not a date." Ana stopped outside her office building, stepping behind a planter so she could continue the conversation.

"It wasn't a date, but one of the millionaires chose me for a date," Jen hurried on, "and he's really nice. I really like him."

"What's his name? What does he do?" Ana set her lunch on the planter and fumbled a notepad and pen from her purse.

"You are not going to run him and tell me horrible things about him," Jen insisted. "You always do that, and I'm not telling you. I don't care if he's an ax murderer at this point.

We're going to dinner at Quatra Quilla up in the hills tomorrow night. Just us in the restaurant, no one else. Everyone waiting on us." Jen sighed. "I'm going to feel like a princess."

"Oh Jen, don't get your hopes up, honey."

Jen groaned. "Don't be a buzzkill, Ana. I know he may be a total wipeout, but the experience will be a freakin' Cinderella ride. What the hell, you know? You have to live full out."

Ana rolled her eyes. Herein lay the difference in their dating philosophies. Jen believed that you dated anyone who asked and enjoyed The Experience, no matter if it was a bust or if the guy was an ass, or ax murderer. She believed you learned something or got something even if there was absolutely nothing to it beyond one date. Ana, on the other hand, believed there should be at least one damn good reason to go, and preferably seven damn good reasons, including a background check that turned up single status.

Not that she didn't like men; she did. She just didn't trust them after her run-in with a married man in Italy. Getting your heart broken by someone eligible was one thing. Being lied to and led on, when you were a data geek who should know better, was another.

Resigned, Ana moved to a bench at the side of the building. "Sounds fun. So, tell me about him."

"Seriously?" Jen sounded suspicious.

"You don't want me to run him, I won't. Seriously." It was a little lie, and unless he *was* an ax murderer, Jen wouldn't have to know what Ana had done.

"Okay," Jen said and plunged into a description of the guy and what he was like and how well they'd gotten along. Peppered throughout her monologue were the guy's name—Jack D'Onofrio—and his business—magazine distribution—so Ana would easily be able to do a quick background check on the guy.

"So, what was the dating service like? Tell me about it."

Jen skated over the question, continuing to detail Jack D'Onofrio's sterling qualities.

That bore checking out. Avoidance was Jen's modus operandi of choice when something bothered her, and she had yet to learn that it would put Ana's radar up quicker than anything.

"So, if you enjoy your date with this Millionaire Jack, what happens then?"

"No telling," Jen said cheerfully. "Like any guy, if we hit it off, we hit it off. This service, they've got a lot of rules and stuff. They want to set me up with someone else too, so that the guys kinda compete, you know?"

Ah, there's the rub, Ana decided. Jen didn't like to do more than one at a time.

"Anyway," Jen rattled on, "the other guy wasn't my thing so I'm not keen." Jen said it offhandedly, as if it were as simple as saying "no thanks," but again Ana sensed there had been a whole lot more to it. "But Jack—" Jen was quickly back on track with tales of her new beau.

Knowing it might take a while for the litany to run down, Ana headed into the building and back to her desk. "And then Jack said . . ."

Ana finally got off the phone by agreeing to meet for lunch on Saturday to hear all about the dinner. She swiveled to her personal laptop, booting it up and setting a series of searches to run on Mr. D'Onofrio. The primary search didn't take long. Nothing but his magazine businesses popped, which surprised her, but she decided that maybe, for once, Jen might have pulled a decent card from the deck.

"And now for my own aces and kings," she muttered, beginning background checks on the two men she would be meeting on Monday. Nothing like a little legwork to pass the afternoon.

"Well, well, well," she muttered several hours later as she began the run on Gates Bromley. The initial run on Davros Gianikopolis had been extensive. The man had holdings all over the world, from Singapore to Bangalore to a plant in Bisonsville, Kansas. Wading through the listing of the business holdings bought and sold in the last year alone had taken an hour and a half. She'd saved and logged the rest of the search for reading later.

As the pings and bings notified her that her first search was done, she opened files and began to read. "Look what we have here, a rap sheet. Hmmm," she mused, vaguely disappointed that it was short. She really wanted a reason to dislike Mr. Velvet Voice.

The sheet was fairly mild for someone in security work. Bromley's title might be special assistant, but she'd read between the lines when she got to the real data. He'd been rapped on the knuckles for assault, a frequent charge when keeping the hoi polloi from a public figure like "Mr. G," as the media had dubbed Bromley's boss. Bromley had beat all the charges or had them dismissed, but there were quite a few. A second search finished with a beep, and she opened that file on top of the other.

"Yeah, yeah, where's the good stuff?" she groused, scanning the pages rapidly onscreen. There were several notations in the CIA files. Not surprising given the international nature of his boss's business. Again, though, it was really mild stuff, nothing that she could pull out and wave in his face as leverage for cooperation. "Damn. Nuthin' here. Can't anyone dig anymore?"

She opened another new window, more searches.

"Iraqi veteran," she read, and frowned. The picture of him in the files, both the publicity shots for Gianikopolis's businesses and some candids at various functions, didn't say military to her. "Really? Didn't see that one coming."

She made some notes and scanned the recent stuff, then switched to the military database. Bromley's file had a classified tag, which she didn't tamper with. She didn't want to explain her need to check it, so she stuck to the accessible, surface stuff.

"Went in as a lieutenant, came out as a captain, three-year tour. Saw some action despite that geek rating, didn't you,

Mr. Bromley?" she muttered as she read about his technology ratings, and the fact that his unit had been ambushed at least twice. She made more notes. He'd gotten some of the highest marksmanship scores in his class year at the academy and had at least three Military Police markers in his file. There may have been more; from the data she could access, there seemed to be hints of it. "Came out combat-seasoned with those commendations." She whistled at the listing. "And decorated, too. Wonder what made a," she checked his education, "Harvard MBA take to soldiering?"

Digging deeper, she found some old hits for drunk and disorderly in police files. "Hmmm, tied a few on, did you, young master Gates? That probably explains the MPs. Didn't do any of that once you went to work for the man, I see," she said, tapping the pen on the desk as she double-checked his matriculation dates. There was a five-year gap between college and the military. Mr. Velvet Voice sure had been busy.

"So, where were you? Hmmmm?" she asked the screen as her fingers flew over the keys. In two separate windows, she opened search engines and entered relevant terms. She hit ENTER and caught her paper notes up to date while the computer processed.

It was the LexisNexis search that turned up the obituary. It also unearthed the heartbreaking story of Gates losing nearly his entire family to a killer, the bodies burned in an attempt to cover the murders with fire.

"Oh, crap," Ana managed, her voice choking with emotion as she read about the arsonist's fire that had consumed the family's warehousing business. Rifle shots had killed both Gates Bromley's parents and his brother, all because of a woman scorned. The notes section of the report said Gates and his sister were only alive because they'd been away at a trade show, marketing the family's business services.

Two arrests after the fire, one a woman, the other the arsonist she'd hired. Reading between the lines, Ana figured out that the woman had had a romantic interest in Gates's father. When he turned her down and fired her from her job as his secretary, she hired someone to kill the family and burn down the warehouse.

"And for what?" Ana asked the photo of the killer. "He didn't want to be with you. Big deal. Other fish in the sea." She'd never understand why people killed for the illusion of love. Had she been hurt by lovers? Of course, but once they'd betrayed her, she didn't want them back. It baffled her why anyone would pursue someone who didn't want them.

Extreme cases like the Bromleys creeped her out. It wasn't as if Bromley's dad had dated the woman, then shoved her off. She'd never had him, but killed him for not wanting her.

Losing family was never easy, nor did the hurt of it ever fade. If anyone knew that, Ana did. She didn't want to feel any sympathy for Bromley, but she did. She'd lost her own parents to a terrorist's bomb. "Damn it. I need to keep that filed away, not let it affect me."

"Something new, Burton?" Pretzky had crept up behind her as she worked, and Ana shrieked as she spun in her chair.

"Jesus, you nearly gave me a heart attack," she said, without thinking about whom she was speaking to.

To her surprise, Pretzky grinned, though it was more akin to a malicious smirk. "You were talking to yourself."

"Bad habit."

"It is," Pretzky snapped, the smirk still in place. "Break it. It'll get you killed." Letting that unpleasant thought dangle for a moment, she added, "What's up?"

"Nothing substantial," Ana managed, still trying to slow her heart rate.

"LexisNexis?" Pretzky crossed her arms, her expression dubious as she scanned the open windows on Ana's monitor and on her laptop. "*Entertainment Weekly*?"

Ana sighed when she felt her eyelid begin to twitch. She'd never had tics or twitches before Rome. Since then . . .

She hated having to explain her somewhat unorthodox research methods. Of course, she'd hate it even more if Pretzky figured out she was doing a run on Jen's new guy, so she went with the bullshit.

"The high-net-worth individuals noted in the files on this case are all either business moguls or celebrities. In order to cross-reference the vectors . . ." she said, deliberately making her voice more monotonous as she rattled off technical search terms. "Anyway, these vectors, when managed properly with a broad spectrum matching logarithm can frequently yield a substantial data mine for cross-referencing active searches."

She could actually see Pretzky trying to follow her methodology, and was relieved to note her temporary boss getting lost on the way. Pretzky liked to believe she understood every facet of the Agency's work, especially computer crimes. In reality, she didn't understand what Ana did at all. Then again, most people didn't, which was why Ana got superior results and, until Rome, plum assignments and grade and pay increases.

Pointing to a field on the second screen Ana was utilizing for her multiple searches, Pretzky snapped, "That entry is in Italian. Your translation skills aren't an issue here, Burton."

"I'm aware of that." Ana winced, and took a breath so she wouldn't sound so God-awful defensive. It was all she could do to keep her voice level and unemotional. "It's a pertinent entry on one of the individuals in the file who lost more than five million dollars in the art fraud case." It was a big fat lie, of course. That entry involved Gates Bromley and an Italian supermodel on the Riviera, not his boss's art. She said a little prayer of thanks that the open window detailing Jen's boyfriend's financial data was decently covered by the photograph of the model.

Fortunately, Pretzky didn't read, or speak, Italian. Nor had she checked the names on the file.

The woman stood for a moment longer, trying, Ana guessed, to figure out a way to find fault. Hoping to get out of it with better grace, Ana offered, "Did you want a listing of the sites and the individuals I'm searching?"

"No need," Pretzky said, but didn't bother to hide the annoyance this time. "Carry on."

It took her a few minutes to settle her heart rate, but Anna did go on. She printed out several of the searches, then wiped them from her search list, from the history, and from her hard drive. A dedicated effort would bring them up, but no one else in the building, especially IT, had that kind of time.

She packed up for the day, and faced the prospect of an empty Friday night with a grimace. At least she'd have something to look forward to on Saturday, and there was always work she could do from home.

Saturday was full of Jen and her doings. Jen positively glowed and couldn't say enough about what a gentleman her Millionaire Jack had been. By the time they'd gotten through lunch, Ana was thinking longingly of her quiet apartment. Instead, Jen dragged her shopping and out to dinner.

By Sunday's solo dinner of leftovers, she'd seesawed back to actually being grateful that she'd had Jen's antics for a distraction. Monday was full of phone calls and meetings, and she was grateful for the distraction, working late again just to avoid her empty apartment.

On Tuesday, finally on the road to Mr. G's estate in the hills north of San Francisco, she was pleased with all the background work she'd been able to plow through on the defrauded victims. The thorough understanding she had of Mr. G's losses should make today's meeting interesting.

Ana drove up to the speaker at the edge of the driveway into the compound. Several workers bustled around a landscaping truck on the other side of the driveway, and there were workers cutting grass beyond the ornate fencing. By habit, she made a note of the license plate, counted the number of workers, noted the lone woman working the crew.

"State your business, please," the voice said, a second time since she hadn't answered the first hail. Embarrassed, she briskly stated her business.

"You're expected, Agent Burton," the man said, and directed her to drive through the first set of gates.

To her surprise, the gates shut behind her, trapping her between them and the next set. "What the hell?" she muttered, noting the openings in the second wall. "Huh, the modern version of arrow slits and murder holes," she decided, seeing the shadow of movement behind one of the gaps.

The sharp-eyed and well-armed guard asked for her identification and, unsmiling, took it into the guardhouse. He was apparently reading the contents to someone who approved, because he nodded and put down the phone with a smile. He was far more pleasant when he returned her documents.

"Thank you for your cooperation, Agent Burton. As I said, you're expected, but we double-check everything."

As an answer, she took her identification and put it away before she spoke. "I hope no one would attempt to impersonate an agent."

The man grimaced. "They try everything," he muttered, glancing beyond her car to the outer gates. "Really."

She moved through the estate at an easy pace, appreciating the peace, quiet, and beauty that money could buy so close to the city. The estate was a huge, well-manicured fortress.

She arrived at the front portico, and a man was waiting for her. It was a bright day, but the area shaded by the overhanging canopy left the man standing there in shadow. Her dark glasses made it worse. All she could tell was that he was above average height. Judging by the dramatic doors behind him, he was at least six feet tall, probably a little over that. A dark gray, well-tailored suit emphasized his height, and showed off impressive shoulders. His hair was a medium brown; his eyes probably were too.

She tugged down her suit coat, making sure it and her skirt were straight, before she went around the car. She arrived at the hood ornament just as he came down the last step to meet her.

"Agent Burton?"

"Mr. Bromley?" They both spoke at once, and he smiled.

Fortunately, it wasn't a Hollywood, blinding white smile, otherwise she might have thought he was a god. The voice was just as luscious in person, but a crooked eyetooth and a scar over his eyebrow kept him from being too perfect.

"Please, come in. I regret that Mr. Gianikopolis won't be able to join us today," he began.

"Wait. What?" Jeez, all that reading for nothing? Any warmth she'd felt for the man in front of her evaporated. A spurt of anger surfaced as well. "You didn't call to reschedule?"

"My assistant did, yes, but you were already on your way. As I'm sure you know, cell service is spotty coming up the hills. This was . . . unavoidable, I'm afraid. A family matter."

Annoyed, Ana managed to overlook the physical attraction and focus on the irritation. A feat of pure determination, because Gates Bromley was one fabulously attractive man.

"Then I guess my trip is a waste."

"No," he said, motioning her to precede him through the doors. "I have a list of the stolen items, so we can move through the initial comparison to be sure everything was accounted for by your agency. Then, we can have a look at what you're doing now."

His easy assumption that he was in charge pissed her off. She felt the stirring of her former, brash self rising up to protest. As he led the way down a gorgeous wood-paneled hallway, she was devising several methods of killing him, slowly and painfully.

She hated being treated like the freshman geek.

"Mr. Bromley, I assure you, we have a complete list. And I'm not at liberty to share information with you on avenues I might currently be pursuing." Ana was pleased that she sounded professional, and firm.

"Perhaps. Perhaps not," he said, and his smile was filled with infuriating superiority.

God, how she hated smugness. She hated when someone tried to bushwhack her or the Agency, and this was shaping up to be that kind of deal.

"Let's sit here." He directed her to a table. "Coffee?"

She wanted to say no; she wanted to stalk out, head high and in full dudgeon. Instead, she repressed a sigh. Thanks to several months with the departmental shrink, she knew enough about her own patterns that she now recognized the defensiveness as her own inadequacies rearing their ugly heads. Nothing messed with her more, especially now, than someone being haughty.

"Agent?"

"Sure, why not. Black and sweet please," she said, taking very petty satisfaction that he must serve her coffee. It was small, but it was a victory in its own way.

He set down two deep china cups.

"Thank you. Now, Mr. Bromley, as I explained to you when we talked last week, I can't discuss this with you. You're not the insured, nor are yours the paintings lost."

"Actually, Agent Burton, you can." He smiled again, and it looked warmer, more . . . personal. She wondered why. "Several of the paintings on the list were owned by the corporation registered here in San Francisco. As an officer of that corporation, I'm authorized to discuss that portion of the listed pieces."

Ana wanted to seethe. She wanted to smack the warm, personal, and interested smile off his face. He could have told her he was an officer of the corporation. He could have . . .

She heard the voice of the psychologist in her head. *Is it always necessary to go on the attack, Agent Burton? Should you not consider your objective?* In the split second of silence before she spoke, she focused on the objective. She needed information.

Jeez, Ana, he's cooperating. Take it, for once. With that in mind, she drew a deep breath and pasted a smile on her face. "That does change things, Mr. Bromley. Let's look at your list."

You show me yours, she thought, smirking, *and I'll show you mine.*

He leaned forward unexpectedly, and before she could

recoil, a long finger stroked a brief caress down her cheek. "You had a piece of fluff, just there," he commented, leaning back. "It was quite distracting."

She frowned as the air backed up in her lungs, caught there by the intimate gesture. Whoa. What the heck had that been about?

The yo-yo of emotion, enhanced by his switch from superior to personal, was not helping her. Maybe she did need more sessions with the psych guy.

Shaking off the feeling that she was losing control of every part of this meeting, she managed a "Thank you" as she took the list he now offered. Scanned it.

Now her frown was for the list. "There're two paintings on this list that aren't on my list, and one that's on my list, that isn't on yours."

"Ah, very quick of you, Agent. You must have a photographic memory to have such quick recall." He looked impressed, and Ana felt an irrational surge of pleasure. "The second item, the one you noticed that's no longer on our list, is a matter you'll have to discuss with Dav . . . Mr. Gianikopolis. However, the first two, which are not on your list, were items we discovered later to be fraudulent. They were uncovered as forged long after the case went cold. In fact, neither Dav nor I are sure if they are part of this, but I wanted them included, just to check." He shrugged. "A decorator Dav was utilizing bought them on his behalf. Usually Dav buys his own stuff, but he was—" Bromley stopped, as if he'd been about to make a critical remark and thought better of it. "He was distracted."

"Distracted?" she pressed.

Bromley smiled. "Beauty can be very distracting," he commented, an even warmer smile on his face. She presumed he was talking to her now, not about his boss, but she couldn't be sure.

Weird. She was in no way beautiful.

"So you're dancing around saying that he was having," she paused, chose a less inflammatory word, "dating the decorator?"

"Precisely. It wasn't until at least a year later that we discovered those two pieces were also counterfeit. They may be connected to your case," he said, then shrugged. "Or not." He took a sip of coffee and continued. "The lady in question claimed no knowledge of the forgeries. I tend to believe her, actually. I've listed her name at the bottom of the sheet there. You can contact her." His features were poker smooth, but she could swear there was a ripe note of dark amusement in his voice as he added, "It would be nice to hear what she has to say to the Agency, rather than to us."

"Hmmm, yes," Anna murmured. She'd moved on from wondering about the decorator, and was now distracted by the data. "Red herring?" she muttered, quickly scribbling a note as her thoughts raced. "Connected? Maybe." She stopped writing, tapped the pen on the table, then realized she was talking to herself again.

Damn it. She was going to have to break the habit of talking through the data out loud. Pretzky'd warned her, and here she was doing it with a perfect stranger.

Perfect being the operative word.

She hated it when she blushed. No help for it though. "Sorry. Thinking it through."

"Good idea." This time, there was real humor in the grin he shot her, not . . . attraction.

"Do you have photographs of the paintings? Something I could take with me?"

"Of course. There's a file of materials waiting for you at your office. It has photos, copies of the original purchase agreements, authentification, and so on. I included copies of the appraisals for each of the paintings, and the secondary appraisals proving them to be counterfeit. I had it couriered over, just in case I caught you on the way and you decided not to join me this morning."

"Ah. Okay." Now what? He'd sent her all the info she needed to get started. "The other painting," she began.

"The other paintings will have to wait until we can discuss it with Dav. By your rules, Agent."

Hoist with her own petard. Now that she'd made a big deal of not discussing it with him, she couldn't ask. *Wrap it up, Burton.*

"Good, well then I appreciate your assistance, Mr. Bromley. And I'll look for the information when I get back." She rose, and he did as well, shaking her offered hand.

His hand was warm, and large. It engulfed hers, but not in a bad way, necessarily. He didn't squeeze too hard, try to overwhelm her, or anything. He just pressed her hand, and released it. Slowly.

"I'll show you out," he said.

As they walked, he let his left hand rest at the small of her back, just for a moment to direct her down the hallway to the door. Nothing overly familiar, nothing she could slap him back for, but it was a seductive touch nevertheless. Just like the caress to her cheek, it was personal. Private.

Sensual.

All without being overt. She was ready to hop out of her skin by the time they got back to her car.

"I'll look forward to meeting with you again, when Dav can be with us and we can discuss the entire matter," he said, holding her door open for her. "We want to cooperate in every way."

"Thank you, Mr. Bromley, and please thank Mr. Gianikopolis for me as well."

He looked up, and froze. This time the smile was all business, and she felt the withdrawal like a slap. "Excuse me, a moment," he murmured, easing around the open driver's side door to speak to a man who'd come up behind her vehicle. The conversation was brief, but in another language, maybe Greek. The younger man looked uncomfortable, then nodded and turned on his heel and disappeared.

"My apologies, Agent. Please call me if I can answer any questions in the meantime. This is the office number here that reaches me directly." He indicated one of the numbers printed on the card. It was all business now. The hint of warmth in his eyes was all that remained of the earlier flirtation.

"Thanks." She took the card, pocketed it, and slipped into the car. She drove away, but when she looked in the rearview mirror he was still standing there, watching her until she was out of sight.

Chapter Three

The package was waiting for her at the front desk as she came in: a copy of the list he'd given her; two eight-by-ten photos of the new paintings on the list, one a landscape, one a woman draped in a sheet looking sated and satisfied; and a copy of the appraisals and documentation on both paintings.

Circled in red at the bottom of the list were the decorator's name, address, and telephone numbers, including personal and professional e-mails and cell numbers. Ana grinned.

"So, Mr. Bromley, tell me how you really feel about this woman, eh?" She had to hand it to him; it was a good twist of the screws to have Ana call her from the Agency without any prior warning. People tended to get really wigged out when they got a call from the CIA.

Ana had no sooner dumped her loaded briefcase on her desk when her phone rang.

"Now what?" She fished it out and nearly groaned. Jen again.

"Oh. My. God. You are *not* going to believe this," Jen said by way of greeting. "Jack just called me, and he's taking me to the coolest place this Friday. We're going to an opening at the Prometheus Gallery."

"Prometheus?" That rang a faint bell in the back of her

mind. Where had she heard it? Something recent, connected to this new case.

Jen made a rude noise. "Keep up, Ana. It's only the most exclusive gallery in the Bay Area. These openings? Invitation only. Big charity deal this time too, so there'll be celebrities and power brokers and stuff."

"So who's the artist?" she asked Jen, just to keep the conversation going as she dumped the McDonald's bag on her desk. Pretzky couldn't slap at her for taking a personal call at lunch. Meanwhile, she was booting up her computers, getting into the system, opening the art fraud file.

Jen rattled out a name and then continued to gush about the high profile of the event. "And maybe meet Carrie McCray, you know, she's been nearly a recluse since her husband died. She's only like forty and she looks, like maybe, I don't know, twenty-eight or nine? I swear she's got one of those paintings in the basement, you know, the one that ages for you."

"*The Picture of Dorian Gray,*" Ana absently supplied the name of the famous book and film. "So what happened to the husband?"

"Oh, really sad, you know? Just dropped dead of a heart attack in a Peet's Coffee shop right down from the gallery. By the time the ambulance got there, he was gone."

Ana frowned, switching monitors. One of the dead guys in this cold case had died of an apparent heart attack. The only way the original team had figured the connection was that the dead man, Bob Wentz, had notes on the forgery in his safety deposit box, no history of heart disease, and a foreign substance in his tox screen.

"What did you say the husband's name was?" Ana opened the files, sifted, and waited for Jen as she muttered through names, searching for the right combo. This was probably nothing, and no connection, but she never ignored that tickle at the back of her brain that said, *Check this.*

"Oh, uh, Luke Gideon. They had different last names and all, like some people do."

Ana typed the name in and hit SEARCH.

"So, you wanna go?"

"Go? Go where?" Ana scrambled to tune in. What had she missed?

"To the gallery opening. Jack said he had several tickets and was there anyone I wanted to ask along. So I'm asking you, goofball. There will be, like, *serious* man action there. Rich man action."

Ana rolled her eyes. "Let me think about it. Hey, I gotta get back to work. I'll call you later, okay?" She was about to hang up when another thought occurred. "Wait a sec, what did you say the charity was?"

"Oh!" Jen piled pounds of enthusiasm in that one word. "It's this totally cool thing, Jack's really involved. It's called the Bootstrap Foundation. They do, like, microloans and stuff. They do some here, in South Central LA, and in Mississippi and Louisiana and Alabama and stuff. Some in Detroit, he said." Jen paused, and Ana could almost hear how hard she was thinking. "It's all about people pulling themselves up by their bootstraps or something. Do you know what that means? You know that kind of stuff. What the hell's a bootstrap anyway?"

She couldn't help it, she laughed. "It's the way you get tight boots on, with the loops at the top. Mostly it's a metaphor for helping yourself, or getting a little help and turning that into something big. I think that's probably the concept here."

"Oh, okay. So anyway, this Bootstrap thing is the charity. Jack donates to it and so does Carrie McCray, so he has like, tickets, you know?"

"Yes, I get it. Okay. I'll let you know, all right?" She was itching to dig into the file. Maybe, finally, a lead she could hook into and fly with.

Ana hung up, snatched up her burger, and began tracking down Carrie McCray, the Prometheus Gallery, and the Bootstrap Foundation. Something was there, she could feel it, and even before the burger was gone, she was beginning to see the shape of it.

"Holy shit!" Ana dropped the last French fry into the trash and let her fingers fly over the keys. The gallery's patron list read like a close duplicate of her list from the cold case. Turning to the second screen, she pulled up the information on Bootstrap. "Look at that," she crowed, noting four patrons of Prometheus listed on the platinum patrons list of Bootstrap as well, and every one of them had been scammed out of high-dollar art.

"Something new?" Pretzky demanded, rounding the corner.

Once again, Ana jumped. "Jeez, will you quit sneaking up on me?" she snapped, forgetting whom she was talking to. "You're gonna take a year off my life at this rate."

Pretzky smirked her smirk and said, "Keeps you on your toes. Told you to break the habit."

"I'll be on the damn floor needing CPR at this rate," Ana muttered, embarrassed that she'd been so immersed as to not hear Pretzky's approach.

"So? What do you have?"

"Not that much," she stalled, not wanting to reveal something she hadn't fully researched, fully documented. "Just another thread to tug, which is pretty much cause for celebration since yesterday I had diddly-squat."

"Diddly-squat? How quaint. So? What is it?"

"Just a gallery in the city. It's very prominent, and it's also connected by patronage to ninety-seven percent of the list of those with fraudulent works."

"And that? What's that?" Pretzky pointed to the second screen showing the logo of the Bootstrap Foundation and its donors.

"There's a fundraiser at the gallery tomorrow night, I decided to cross-check the art patrons list with the list of donors at the charity. Seventy-five percent duplication, and of the duplicates, all are on our fraud list."

"Coincidence?" Pretzky said facetiously. "I think not. So,

get yourself to that gallery opening, talk to some people, poke around."

"It's invitation only." Ana didn't want to involve Jen if she could help it.

"I can call Washington if you want." Pretzky's grin was feral. It was as if she could feel how much Ana now hated going out in the field for that kind of assignment. Since Rome, everything was hard. It was hard enough doing interviews, calling people cold. Once upon a time she'd enjoyed it, seen it as dress up and catch the bad guys, even though she wasn't a trained covert-ops agent.

Data was her deal. She needed to stick with it.

And Pretzky knew she didn't want to call DC for help. DC tended to jump in and take over, which every regional bureau despised. More than that, Ana didn't want anyone in DC hearing her name before her hearing with the Panel of Inquiry.

"Not yet, thanks. I think I may have an inside track. I'll let you know."

"Do that," Pretzky said as she stalked away.

Great. Now she was going to have to agree to go with Jen. Jen would take it as a sign that she was weakening on the dating thing. Ugh.

On the other hand, it wouldn't hurt to drop by a gallery opening. Check out the legendary Carrie McCray, maybe get a chance to assess Jen's millionaire, Jack D'Onofrio, in person. She might even see some nice art. However, even though she had a degree in art, what some people defined as art frequently baffled Ana.

Ana braced herself, picked up the phone, and called Jen. Before she even got more than a hello out, there was a whole new spate of Jack-this, and Jack-that. Evidently she'd just hung up with the man himself. He was out of town, on the East Coast in some kind of hush-hush meeting, so Jen hadn't expected to hear from him.

"Jen," Ana finally got a word in edgewise. "Hey, would you mind if I joined you on Friday, just for a bit?"

There was a moment of silence, then a squeal of glee. "Really? You'd go? Like dress up and everything?"

"Sure. It's business though. I need to be there. Check stuff out with the gallery owner."

"With Carrie McCray?" Jen was incredulous. "Seriously?"

"Well, I want to take a look at this guy of yours too." She was tweaking Jen now and waiting to see how she'd take it.

She could hear the pout in her friend's voice. "You're not going to weird him out with the third degree are you?"

"No, really, I won't. Besides a gun and weighted blackjack don't go with the dress I'm planning to wear," she joked, getting a reluctant laugh from Jen. "It's just that I do need to go to that gallery, for a cold case I'm checking out, and it would be great if I could do it unofficially first. You know, incognito."

"Wow, cool, like undercover?"

Ana grinned. "Sort of. I'd use another name, look a little different, but meet you there so I have an entrée. That is, if your date doesn't object."

"I'll text him and double-check, then let you know. You gonna be in your office?"

"Yeah, but text me on my phone for now rather than e-mail. I've got a go-ahead, but I'd like to keep this off the radar." Jen wouldn't question that, but Pretzky would have. Ana wasn't sure why she wanted to keep Jen's connection to her visit to Prometheus and Carrie off the official notes for now, but she did.

"Got it," Jen said, her mind obviously now on other things because she didn't have anything else to say about Mr. Millionaire. "I gotta go, I'm getting another call. Later?"

"You bet," Ana said, heading for vending to get something sweet.

Before the end of the day, Ana had a text saying there would be a pass for her at the door if she'd give Jen a name for the pass. Digging through her desk, Ana got out her folder with alternate identities and picked one of her favorites.

"Shirley Bascom. That looks good." Shirley, as her alter

ego, was about the right temperament to be going out for an evening at the gallery. A red wig and a pair of glasses would do the rest. Not that a gallery would check that closely if a millionaire gave her name as a guest. She texted the name to Jen.

She spent the rest of the week and all of Friday sorting through the data, arranging it to suit her, making sure she knew whose pieces had come from which gallery and which showing. She pulled out and sorted everything that had come from Prometheus, both before Luke Gideon's death and after it.

Only two fraudulent items were on the list after Luke's death. Interesting. She wondered what Carrie McCray had changed, if anything.

"You going tonight?" Pretzky sneaked up on her again.

Ana refused to jump, refused to give Pretzky any more satisfaction.

"Yeah. Got a pass through a connection. Using an alias, not that I really need it, but it'll keep things clear and separate."

"Good." Pretzky surprised her by approving. Ana had figured she'd bitch about it. "Keep me posted. Send an e-mail after you leave the event, fill me in."

"Will do," she said, glancing up. Pretzky was frowning at her, a strange look on her face. "Problem?"

"Of course not. See that you report in, Burton," she said curtly, stalking away.

"Have a good weekend," Ana called. She nearly winced again as the words left her mouth. She didn't want to fraternize with Pretzky. Didn't want to imply friendship. Didn't even want to hate the woman. She didn't want to feel anything for her current post other than the tedium of wading through the files.

Connecting with her peers, feeling for anyone, meant emotions. Emotions meant pain, and she wanted to avoid any more of that for a while. It had taken her a month after Rome to pick up the pieces of her heart. She'd known everyone on the team there, from their dogs' names to their birthdays, childhood hangouts, and even their favorite gelato. Knowing them that well made their loss a constant black hole, especially since she felt responsible. She'd lost her parents so young, and those memories had leapt in to compound the loss of her friends in Rome. One day they were there, the next, gone.

Talking to the agents who'd worked this case originally, she'd come perilously close to getting involved again. Emotionally invested. Dealing with an irrational attraction to Gates Bromley made it worse.

Uh-uh. No way.

Before she could dig herself a hole of despair—far too easy in her current mental state—the alarm on her PDA chimed the time.

"Shit," she cursed, cutting the thing off mid ping. "An hour to get home, damn it."

She'd waited too long to leave. She'd meant for the alarm to remind her, at home, that she had to get dressed. Shutting down her computers and flinging things into her briefcase, she hurried out.

Luckily, it took her only forty minutes to get home, a near-miracle for a Friday night. Even with that bare excess of time, Ana was still over thirty minutes late to the Prometheus Gallery to meet Jen. She hadn't finished her deep data runs on the gallery, Carrie McCray, and her late husband. She preferred to have the data at hand, but there hadn't been quite enough time to get it all done. She'd made the choice to have the info on the art be her primary focus, but she had the basics on McCray and everything else. If she had to, she could wing it.

"Good evening, ma'am." The attractive, tuxedoed man at the door greeted her with a smile. "If I could have your name?"

"Oh, certainly!" She pretended a breathy excitement she in no way felt. "It's Shirley, Shirley Bascom." She smiled in turn. "*Ms.* Shirley Bascom," she emphasized as she tossed the long strands of the red wig over her shoulder. She'd already assessed him as gay, but you never knew where a little flirting might get you. She was rusty though, and it showed.

Confirming her suspicions, he blushed a bit but suavely deflected her ersatz interest. "Yes, of course. Here you are. Please, go right in. The bar is to your left about halfway down the gallery. It's quite a crush in there," he added, his impersonal smile back in place.

"Oooh, I've so been looking forward to this," she gushed, turning toward the doors with an absent "thank you." She had to suppress a smile at his soft sigh of relief as she turned her attention elsewhere.

Once inside the doors, she moved confidently through the crowd. She'd recognize Jen, of course, but her friend was quite petite and there was, as the gatekeeper had warned, a real crush. However, she'd seen photos online of Jack D'Onofrio. It was hard to miss a six-foot bald man with a goatee.

Thought was as good as deed, and she homed in on the tall form of the supposed millionaire standing near a pillar not far from the bar. Easing through the mass of people, Ana touched Jen on the arm.

"Hey, A—"

Ana hugged her friend to cut off the use of her real name.

"Hi sweetie!" Ana gushed. "How fun is this? Ohmygosh, I told that gorgeous man at the door my name, and he let me right in." She rolled her eyes at Jen and saw her friend's expression change. "And he said, 'Here you are Ms. Shirley Bascom, go right in,'" Ana grinned at her ploy to remind Jen of the name she was using. "How about that?" She pushed the fashionable green glasses she was wearing back up on her nose. The action was always good for distracting anyone from remembering her face. The more you adjusted them, the more they focused on the glasses, the less they saw the features. Make the glasses a color and people only remembered the glasses.

"It's fun, all right," Jen agreed. "Glad you could make it. Let me introduce you to my date tonight, Shirley." Jen managed to say the name without flinching. She easily introduced Ana to Jack, and using the effusive Shirley persona, Ana took his measure. He was solid rather than fat, a good weight for his height and interesting looking rather than handsome with his shaved head, goatee, and a shadowy scruff of beard where the goatee ended.

She decided D'Onofrio seemed very self-possessed for someone who used a dating service to meet a woman. To his credit, D'Onofrio had eyes only for Jen. He did offer his services however, for drinks. "It's quite a crowd," he murmured, his New York accent making the words sharp and distinct. "What can I get you from the bar, Shirley?"

When he'd maneuvered through the crowd to get her a glass of red wine and to refill Jen's vodka tonic, Ana filled Jen in on what she was hoping to accomplish. "I want to meet Carrie McCray, if I can manage it. Other than that, I just want a look around at the facility; get a sense of the place."

"You gonna tell me about this case later?" Jen asked, handing her empty glass to a passing waiter.

"Sure. It's long cold. Probably won't amount to much." Ana shrugged.

Jen laughed. "Yeah, right. You closed that other one, didn't you?"

Pleased she remembered, Ana was forced to admit she had.

Jen grinned at her. "See? You'll do something with this one too. I know you. Why else would you be here incognito?"

"It's just procedure," Ana began when a look from Jen forestalled her.

"Here you are, ladies." D'Onofrio was back with their drinks.

Ana accepted the wineglass and gave him an absent thanks. She kept one ear half tuned to Jack and Jen—and wasn't that too cutesy for words?—as she scanned the crowd.

"So, Jack," Ana said, pretending interest. "You have that accent. Are you from New York City?"

He laughed and said, "You might say that. My business is all over. Magazines in racks, that sort of thing. I grew up near the Big Apple though, and worked there for a long time. You don't lose the accent."

Or the bluntness, Ana thought, letting his talk of his business prowess in getting West Coast contracts flow right over her. She made interested noises periodically, just to keep him talking. *I wonder if he buys art?*

She spotted someone who could only be the artist, a flamboyant young man in yellow brocade. Hideous color for his swarthy skin tone, dark hair, and dark eyes. It made his sallow tones lean toward jaundice rather than jaunty.

Had she seen this guy before? Despite the Technicolor coat, he looked familiar.

Ana felt a spurt of adrenaline. Next to the artist was Carrie McCray.

Target acquired.

"Hey guys." She turned a bright smile on her temporary cohorts and pushed up the glasses again. "I'm going to go look at the paintings, okay?"

"We'll go with you," Jack said, slipping an arm around Jen and moving them through the crowd. On one hand she was glad that he was with them, plowing a path. On the other hand, she'd hoped to slip through the crowd and make her way to Carrie McCray.

From the balcony, Gates watched as a young woman in a floral wrap and brightly colored dress made her way through the crowd with two others. Her face was lean and interesting, her full lips a splash of rich pink to contrast with her red hair.

He could see that she was animated, chattering to her companions with a great deal of verve. In the concealed earpiece, he heard Queller mention a man who was giving Dav the eye, so he shifted his vantage point. Pressing on his throat, right under the knot of his tie, he activated the walkie-talkie function.

"Keep an eye on that guy, Queller. Thompson, can you

see the woman, maybe five-foot-seven, red hair, glasses, blue flowers on her shawl or whatever they call those things? Dress is a similar color at the bottom."

"Got her." Another voice sounded in his ear. That was Pike. "Nice. That's that guy D'Onofrio, the one who's putting together that distribution deal with the Hammels for the new lux homes mag. He wanted to feature Britney Spears, but she turned him down."

"Is the target baldy's date, or is that the other woman?" Gates asked.

"Blue shawl is not his date, uh check it out." A third voice picked up the tale. That was Shuel, and she was laughing.

Gates left off watching Dav just in time to see the end of a lip-lock between the bald guy and the diminutive blonde he had tucked under his arm. Blue shawl girl looked away, a deliberate separation from the event, so she wasn't with them in any kind of threesome.

"Keep an eye on her," he ordered, pivoting slightly to check on Dav. His friend was in a quieter part of the room at the moment, although quiet was relative, chatting with the parents of the artist, Paul Winget. The whole family group was some kind of cousin to Dav, and the wife, Ehlana, didn't like Gates. She'd made her disdain painfully obvious, so he was careful to keep his distance. Evidently, she believed her older son should have gotten the job Gates held.

Gates smiled, imagining any of the young relatives trying to manage Dav. That wouldn't work. Not for one minute.

Another exchange in his earpiece let him know the lady he'd asked about was moving in on the artist and Carrie McCray.

He was puzzled by the woman. Her chattering, socialite demeanor was at odds with the watchful, appraising sweep he'd seen her give the crowd when she walked in. Even though he couldn't see her face, he'd seen that maneuver. He knew it. He'd seen it before, done it every time he walked in a door.

Since Ehlana, the cousin, wished him to hell and her son

was the center of attention, Gates had stayed out of sight, monitoring the crowd from his perch on the gallery's mezzanine level. From that vantage point, he'd seen the woman in the blue shawl walk up with a purposeful stride, a lean, elegant form outside the thick waving glass of the old building's front windows. Her long legs and flowing red hair had immediately drawn his eye, until he'd seen her simpering over the doorman. While it made him deem her an ingénue, it also had him dismissing her threat potential.

Gates had reevaluated that opinion the minute she strolled through the heavy glass doors and moved into the gallery. She'd worked hard to maintain the body language of a hesitant neophyte, but the deliberate sweep, the pauses, the back-checks, that was a professional casing. As he'd watched, she'd catalogued everything and everyone in the room. That appraisal, so at odds with her outward persona, immediately put him on alert

"She's trying to maneuver in and talk to the gallery owner, McCray." Queller spoke through the mic once more. "Any concerns, boss?"

"Not yet. She's nowhere near Dav, so whoever or whatever she is, I don't think she's hunting in our yard."

"Check," Queller said, then fell silent.

With a last look at Dav, Gates left his post and meandered down the stairs. "I'm on the move," he said, prepping to turn off his mic for now. "I'm going to check her out."

They might razz him about it later, but for now, everyone was all business as they let him know they'd heard him.

He wanted to assess this potential threat personally, face to face.

Ana continued to sip her wine as D'Onofrio moved them through the crowd. They paused here and there for Jack to introduce Jen to people, absently including Ana in the introductions as Jen's friend, Shirley. She got some appraising looks, and one definite overt flirtation, as they slipped closer to Carrie McCray.

Surreptitiously, Ana looked over her shoulder. Her back was twitching. That only happened when someone was watching her. Unfortunately, she caught the eye of the man who'd flirted with her, and he gave her a smile—more of a leer—and winked.

Ugh. Married and smarmy. She sure knew how to attract 'em.

Ana had just handed the half-empty wineglass to a waiter when she saw a familiar face out of the corner of her eye.

Had that been . . . ?

No. She was imagining it. Why would Gates be here on a Friday night? Hadn't he said his boss was out of town? Or had he?

It niggled at her, but she shook it off and focused on Jen, who'd asked her a question.

"I'm sorry." She indicated the crowd as she said, "It's so noisy. What did you say?"

"I asked if you like the display?"

"Oh, no—" She stayed in persona. "I'm more partial to uh, representational art, landscapes and stuff, you know? This," she shielded her pointing finger behind her shawl, making Jen giggle. "It's ah, kinda, too unusual for my taste."

"It's a good investment, though," Jack began. He was about to continue, his arm outstretched in an encompassing gesture, when Ana saw the accident begin.

It was as if it happened in slow motion, and there was nothing she could do to stop it. A huge man backed into the man right behind Jack. The smaller man, dressed in a natty tuxedo with a pink cummerbund, was caught by Jack's outstretched arm and went flying. Jack merely stumbled, but Pink Cummerbund was the catalyst for a chain reaction. Like the Keystone Kops, Pink Cummerbund hit a waiter with a tray of canapés, the desserts went flying, and so did the waiter. Between the tray, the canapés, and the waiter, three more guys and two women went down, their drinks flying as well.

Another woman in the chain reaction hit the floor with a shrill scream. Her glass and its contents flew toward Ana, but despite the flying liquid, she got out of the way of the tumbling bodies. From the corner of her eye she saw a tall, dark-haired man moving sideways, preventing the pin-wheeling arms and legs from hitting his older, but equally spry companion.

Problem was, his action put him right into the path of two other young men and a shrieking, high-heeled matron, all of whom went down as they tried to avoid the spills. The welter of flying shoes and tangled clothing made for a continuing trail of hazards.

To Ana's surprise, the man turned the fall into a controlled roll, which brought him right to her feet.

"Here," she said, instinctively offering a hand to help him up, as more people went down like dominoes. If he stayed on the floor, he'd be flattened. Bracing herself, she lent him balance as he rose, then yanked him toward her as she moved back, to keep them both out of the continuing fray.

His head was turned away, but she could see the surprise written on his familiar profile. Internally, Ana cursed. *Crap, crap, crap.* The fragile flower appearance of Shirley Bascom, all fluttery and female, was totally blown by the strength she'd used to help him, and if she wasn't mistaken . . .

"Why thank you, ma'am," the man drawled as he turned, his lush brown eyes going from amused to surprised to a sharp, piercing assessment. Every alarm bell and curse she'd ever learned flowed through her mind in a rush. Damn it all to hell. She'd recognize the voice anywhere, much less that smiling face.

Why, oh why, did this have to happen now?

"Thank you for the timely rescue," Gates Bromley whispered, pressed against her to allow the gallery's young helpers to start bringing order to the chaos. The crowd moved toward them, squashing Gates into her. "Hold on to me, we'll both keep our footing if you do."

Seeing no other option, she did.

How was it possible to regret such a heady rush of pleasure with all these people looking on?

Oh, Lord, he must work out every day. The irreverent thought was the first thing that leapt to mind as her hands slid around his waist to anchor them together, brace them from the ebb and flow of the mass of patrons. Now there were emergency personnel, coming in to check on the clientele who'd hit the deck.

Gates pulled her closer, murmuring, "So, what's a nice agent like you doing in a place like this?"

"Pleased to meet you too, Mr. Bromley," she managed, in spite of the fact that every blood cell in her body was doing a tango in time with her pounding heart. What was this irrational reaction to him? "I'm Shirley, Shirley Bascom. Just here with my friend and her date, you know. Nothing special." She vaguely remembered to push up the glasses, keep up the façade.

For once, without effort, she sounded just like the flighty character she was portraying in Shirley.

He eased back, slowly. An agonizing withdrawal of warmth and masculinity. "I'm pleased to meet you, Ms. Bascom." Gates's amazing voice was all she heard, even with the cacophony around them.

"Honey, are you okay?" She heard Jen's voice behind her. It was hard to switch gears, get into the mode of Agent Burton while she was still standing this close to the hottest man she'd ever met in her life, but she was desperately afraid Jen would forget and call her by the wrong name.

Pinning on a bright smile, she turned. "Oh, Jen, come meet my new friend, Gates. He's just so nice. Oh, look, they've brought in paramedics. How exciting."

She didn't have to gush anymore as a slim, elegant woman hurried up, apology written all over her face.

Target in the gun sights. Thank God. Carrie McCray's appearance helped Ana remember why she was at the gallery in the first place.

"Is everyone all right here? I'm so sorry you were inconvenienced. Oh, hello, Gates." Carrie smiled, and she took his hand, relief written all over her face. He bent in to give her an airy kiss on the cheek. "You weren't hurt, were you?"

"Oh, no. In fact, I turned the accident to my advantage and bumped into this lovely woman." He turned toward Ana and winked.

"Oh, good. Why don't you introduce me to your friends then, Gates?"

Direct hit.

Chapter Four

Gates performed the introductions, never letting on that he knew Ana at all. "Carrie, this is my newly met friend Shirley Bascom," he indicated Ana. "We stumbled into one another, but managed to stay on our feet." He turned to her with a decided twinkle in his eyes. "You're all right, aren't you, Shirley?"

"Oh, I'm fine." She pushed up the sliding glasses again. "It's just such a pleasure to meet you, Ms. McCray." She pumped the other woman's hand. "Really, a pleasure."

"Carrie, I believe you know Jack D'Onofrio, but perhaps he'll introduce us to his lovely friend," Gates offered smoothly, once again resting his hand in the small of Ana's back as he'd done right before she left the estate.

The gesture was like an arc of pure electricity, zipping from her back to her belly, to her libido. Yowza.

Ana could hardly focus on Carrie as D'Onofrio introduced her to Jen. Gates was slowly, erotically brushing his fingers back and forth over her spine. It was a light touch, barely felt were it not for the intense warmth of his hands.

She needed to cultivate the gallery owner. She needed to step away. She needed . . .

What you need, you can't have. Not that *anyway.*

She considered it a supreme act of willpower that she

edged forward to disconnect herself from the mesmerizing power of Gates's touch. It was subtle, but the movement caught Carrie McCray's attention. She homed in on Ana.

"Oh, look at your lovely wrap," she exclaimed. "I am so sorry. Oh, my goodness, is it ruined?" She reached out, a concerned look marring her beautiful features. "The wine's soaked in. Please, forward the cleaning bill to me here at the gallery and I'll be sure it's covered."

Ana demurred, but to no avail. She hadn't realized the gaudy thing was stained. Then again, calling about dry cleaning would give her a reason to talk to Carrie again. Not such a bad deal.

Carrie extended a card, swiftly pulled from a hidden pocket in her slim suit. The skirt and blazer were so well tailored, Ana didn't see how the woman could possibly have a pocket big enough to hold a business card, much less the three she handed around to Ana, Gates, and Jen, in case their clothes had been affected by the events.

Two younger staffers came to her at a gesture and one was sent to procure fresh drinks for everyone. The other she directed *sotto voce,* but Ana caught the mention of coffee for several people, and cabs for others.

In her guise as Shirley Bascom, Ana fluttered. "So much excitement! I know it wasn't supposed to happen, but it sure did get a lot of cameras flashing. That's good for the guy, isn't it? The artist?" Jen's date snickered a bit over her comment, but Carrie wasn't as insouciant.

"Of course, but it's better if the news clips focus on the art and the gallery, rather than someone getting hurt, don't you think?" The subtle reprimand was delivered so graciously that if she'd been as dim as Shirley Bascom, she'd have never caught it.

"Oh, for sure," she replied, forcing a puzzled look onto her face. "It must be interesting, though. It's an amazing gallery, Ms. McCray, and the party totally rocks. Do you just love buying art?" she gushed.

To her credit, Carrie McCray was quick on her feet. Ana had hoped to catch her off guard with the serious question slipped in with the bullshit, perhaps learn something, but Carrie was all business.

"It never ceases to be interesting, Ms. Bascom. Are you an artist?"

"Oh no," Ana-as-Shirley shook off the idea with an impatient gesture. "Just an appreciator," she said, fluttering her eyelashes at Gates, in true bimbo fashion. "Such amazing talent this young man has, the use of color, the depth of field." She dug into her art background, tossed out the terms to keep the conversation going.

"The young man has many admirers, both personally and artistically," Carrie said, smiling. Her smile warmed a fraction as the older man Ana had seen earlier came up to stand next to Gates.

Her feeble brain finally put two and two together as she recognized Davros Gianikopolis, who was obviously not out of town. She flicked a look at the artist, and at Gianikopolis, and put two and two together. Paul Winget was distantly related. The family matter that had taken Dav's time was about the gallery opening. The young man at the estate who'd pissed Gates off when he came up to the car had been Paul Winget.

Gianikopolis was thinner than in his last photo. His smile and appreciative look said he was also a very magnetic personality, and he treated Jen, Carrie, and Ana to the exact same degree of courtesy and warmth. Ana dragged out dusty flirting skills and used her Shirley persona to deliver them.

"Well, hello," she purred, holding out a hand. "I'm Shirley Bascom. This is Carrie, Carrie McCray, she owns the gallery, you know," she offered with a fluttery smile. "Oh, and this is Gates." She turned to Gates as if she didn't know him, letting a frown cross her face. "Oh, I'm sorry, here we've been chatting on and I don't know your last name."

"It's Bromley. And Shirley, this is my friend, Davros." He

stepped back, letting the billionaire move into the proverbial spotlight.

"Please, call me Dav." Gianikopolis smiled at the three women. "Good to see you again, Jack." He briefly shook Jack D'Onofrio's hand, giving him a brief nod as he shook Jen's hand as well. "How're all your business interests on the East Coast? New York, isn't it? Or is it New Jersey?"

The body language told a lot of tales in the interaction between Jack and Gianikopolis. Jack was tense, uncomfortable at the questions, but doing his damndest to mask it. He'd stiffened when Dav asked about the East Coast. Dav seemed indifferent to the reaction. If Dav was baiting him, it was working. Gates was taking it all in with a hint of cool amusement.

Maybe she needed to dig deeper into D'Onofrio after all, and not just because of Jen. No love lost between Dav and D'Onofrio, that was for sure.

Gates sent her a quick flick of a gaze, as if to say, *Break the tension.*

Following the cue Gates offered, although Shirley wouldn't have been smart enough to see the move, Ana said, "Oh, I love New York, don't you? So vibrant. Not that this isn't. The City's just such a beacon for art, you know?"

That broke the tension and redirected everyone's attention to the art. Ana flirted lightly with Dav and kept up a bright flow of chatter. What she really wanted to do was stand over to the side with Gates, watch everything the way he was doing.

Personally, she also wanted to feel his hands on her back again, which was stupid and irrational. She was unaccountably attracted to him, even without the obvious provocation he offered with his hot hands. She couldn't help being intrigued. Fascinated, in fact.

"So, Carrie," Dav shifted his attention to the gallery owner. "I believe you have a hit on your hands despite the difficulties, my dear."

Carrie's faint blush was either from heat, or a reaction to Dav, Ana couldn't be sure.

"So, do you like gallery openings?" Gates asked at her elbow. She'd been so wrapped up in observing Carrie, she hadn't seen him move to her side.

Bad sign. He hadn't set off her radar when he moved, which meant somewhere in her subconscious, she'd decided he wasn't a threat.

Jen wiggled her eyebrows suggestively at Ana as D'Onofrio excused himself and Jen, and led her away. It amused her that Jen's millionaire didn't want to compete with Dav and his entourage. "Congratulations, Carrie," D'Onofrio said in parting. "Dav, Gates, good to see you again. We're going to the next room. Shirley?"

"Oh, I think I'll hang here for a few." She simpered toward Gates and Dav. "I'll catch up."

"Or not," Gates muttered, low enough that only she heard. His fingers slipped to her back again, as he leaned in. Smooth move, she decided.

"Who's the friend?" he asked.

"Just that, a friend."

"Tell her to watch out for Jack D'Onofrio," he whispered, never faltering in the featherlight stroke, stroke, stroke on her back. She'd always griped about people getting distracted by the physical when they were on the job. If this was what they went through, she had a new sympathy.

"Danger or jerk?" she said, acting as if she were laughing at a joke.

"Mostly jerk," he said, before answering a question Dav had thrown his way. "Not sure about the danger."

With no visible effort, he eased her forward into the conversational circle. He was obviously strong, but when she'd put her hands on him, it had been like a shot to the gut. Her imagination had gone into overdrive.

Stop thinking about his abs and focus on the work.

Redirecting her thoughts, she observed just how careful he

was of his boss's safety. She pretended to natter on about the art, but kept one eye on him, as he kept both on Dav. All without ever ceasing that restless pattern on her spine.

It was driving her mad.

"It would be a privilege to discuss that with you, Dav," Carrie was saying warmly, and Ana wondered what she'd missed.

"We'll make an appointment, shall we? I'll be in touch in the next few days, and we'll set it up."

"Lovely," Carrie replied, an edge of puzzlement in her smile.

"It's always a pleasure to do business with you, and with Prometheus." It was such a hearty endorsement that Ana surreptitiously scanned the nearby faces. Dav was making a point, giving Carrie an all-out seal of approval.

The crowd shifted again, and Dav's demeanor changed from social politeness to distinct interest. There was a keen awareness in that shift, and something else, something Ana didn't quite recognize, as Dav took Carrie's hand and bowed over it in a courtly manner.

"We'll make that a date, then."

"Absolutely," she agreed, the puzzled look still a faint crease on her brow. Ana caught the masculine interest in Dav's reply, but Carrie seemed oblivious. From the corner of her eye, she saw Gates's scowl. *What, no nookie for the bossman?* she wondered irreverently. Or was it just a matter of security? Tough to date, she decided, if one was a marked man, as Davros seemed to be.

She'd pulled up more than five attempts on his life in the last couple of years, and that just here in San Fran. She wanted to dig further into that. She'd turned up business rivalries from at least one of the Central American nations, but what notes she'd scanned said one of them went back a long way and it was family oriented.

Filing that for later consideration, Ana saw with amusement that Dav had truly flustered Carrie. She withdrew her hand, but kept her businesslike smile firmly in place. "Of course, it will be a delight to do business with you again."

Ana nearly broke character and snorted over how oblivious the woman was. Ana was pretty sure Dav wanted to discuss something other than art. To cover the gap, Ana kept to her vacuous chatter as Shirley. "Oh, how fun, even if business is involved. I love dates. You should go to that new restaurant over there by the twisty street, you know, Lombard." She beamed, naming the famous San Francisco landmark. "It's been written up all over the place. You know the place, I'm sure." She acted as if she were searching for the name. "Parasol or something."

"Well, since we'll be discussing business," Carrie reiterated, a bit repressively, "we'll probably want to stick with something more staid. Thank you for the recommendation, though, Ms. Bascom. Tell me"—Carrie deftly flipped the conversation back to art—"is art a passion of yours as well?"

It took only a split second for her to make her decision on that one. She didn't want to be pegged as an art patron, not in her current guise. "Oh, I'm just Shirley, and no, I mostly love a great party. My friends"—she waved toward the now-disappeared Jen and Jack—"were meeting here and invited me along." She grinned at her hostess. "It just seemed the coolest thing to do, you know? And I was right. It's a lot of fun."

She caught the sardonic look that crossed Gates's face before he managed to recover the bland façade he'd worn since Dav's arrival.

"Interesting," Dav added, smiling her way, but with eyes only for Carrie McCray. Dav, it seemed, wasn't picking up any clues from his erstwhile security expert. He'd dismissed Ana as just what she was portraying.

Interested in Carrie, more than in having an interesting evening, I think, Ana silently decided.

"Well, thank you for coming, Shirley." Carrie was at her gracious best, but obviously ready to conclude the chat and move on to her other clients. Dav was making her nervous. "Gates, it's good to see you. Thank you for being here as well. Are you in the market for something new to grace your walls?"

"No, I'm just keeping Dav company." He waved toward his boss. "And making new friends." He nodded Ana's way, turning those gorgeous brown eyes on her. He treated her to a slow, deliberate wink the others couldn't see. It was all she could do not to give it away and react.

With what little undercover work Ana had done, she was unprepared for a real flirtation under the guise of a fake one. It was usually the other way around. That she was prepared for.

Leaning toward her, Gates brushed her cheek with a kiss, just at the same place he'd stroked it with a long, lean finger. "I slipped a card into your purse. It's between your cell phone and lipstick. Call me. Tonight."

It was all she could do to keep the shock from showing on her face.

"So. That was interesting." Davros Gianikopolis's faintly accented voice was as smooth as silk, delivering the bland statement into the quiet of the limo. One of San Francisco's frequent nightly fogs had rolled in and was curling around the hills as they made their way out to Dav's compound in the hills.

Gates laughed at the evaluation, reading all the meaning behind the words. "Interesting, yes. Informative, yes. Irritating? I'd have to say again, yes."

"Irritating? But you seemed so taken with the young woman you ran into," Dav teased, with the ease of long practice. "And she so energetically shook your hand on parting." He smirked. "Such enthusiasm."

"Yes, enthusiastic." He kept his tone bland. Dav was used to his tactics and had a sixth sense about him from long association. He wanted to see how long he could keep Dav from catching on.

"You believe her to be more than she seemed?"

About six seconds. Slanting a glance his boss's way, Gates decided to let the cat out of the bag. "Did you happen to see the fall I took?"

"I saw you roll, but it was a bit of a blur." He rubbed his arm. "The young man, Queller, was pulling me out of the way."

Gates nodded, reminding himself to thank Queller. "Then you probably didn't notice just how strong she is."

"That little thing?"

Gates laughed. Ana had played it perfectly, coming across as flighty, diminutive, and weak. "Not that little. She was strong enough to help me off the floor, pull me out of the way of those idiots who kept knocking people over like ninepins. What does that tell you?"

"Really?" Dav sat up, interest flaring in his eyes. "That slip of a girl? In heels?"

Dav held up a hand for silence, closed his eyes. Gates knew he was replaying the scene in his mind. When he looked at Gates, he was frowning. "Wait. How did she make herself seem so small? I can see her now, in my mind. She was nearly as tall as you."

"Well, she's at least five-seven," Gates temporized. "But yes, she had on heels. Think about that though. The shoes were high, which would change the leverage point when she helped me up." It was his turn to frown. "That makes her even stronger than I thought." He considered the physics of it, the feel of it. It made him intensely curious about Ana Burton, the agent. It made him even more interested in her as a woman. Long, lean, strong described the planes of her face as well as her body. Her hazel eyes, sparkling behind those ridiculous green glasses, had gleamed with humor and interest.

When she'd come to the estate earlier in the week, she'd seemed reticent, angry. Even now he wasn't sure why he'd felt the need to prick that reticence, or even why he found her decidedly attractive. It was unaccountable, since long, lean, dark-haired women weren't his type; especially if they worked for the government and carried guns.

Dav was usually the one on the prowl, but this time, with this woman, Gates was intrigued.

He hadn't let himself think that way for a very long time. Ana Burton had given him a shot in the gut he never saw coming.

Gates cut the thought short as Dav said, "I thought you went on high alert after that tumbling escapade, but I never pegged the woman. Hmmm. I must be getting slow in my old age. What a bunch of young idiots." He rubbed his forearm again. "By the way, Queller has a hell of a grip. He's left a bruise."

"Well, he got you away from the flailing bodies, that's what counts."

Dav made a noncommittal noise, and Gates laughed. "Hey, free drinks, tottery socialites in equally tottery high heels, and the addition of the artist himself being fairly inebriated and in a mood to hug everyone, and you're gonna get that," Gates commented with a straight face. "San Francisco, you know?"

As he intended, Dav laughed and stopped rubbing his arm. They exchanged some snarky comments about his artistic cousin, and the appalling paintings. They dissected the crowd at large, as well as the art. Gates knew more about art from the seven years he'd worked for Dav than he'd ever learned in school. Then again, business majors didn't take art. Nor did computer geeks, and he qualified as both.

Dav's unalloyed humor let Gates know he wasn't going to brood again about being watched so closely. The death threats he received, and the regular attempts on his life, sometimes got to him. Gates could argue till the cows came home that dealing so closely with some of the Central American factions, especially those with less savory reputations, could engender that sort of thing. Then again, in Dav's case, it hinged on his unwillingness to handle illegal shipments along with the legal ones. The other problem, the family one, was another matter.

When something happened, Dav would brood for days, never leaving his office or the house. But despite the threats, Dav managed to get out often and live a fairly normal life.

If there was such a thing when you were a billionaire.

"So, what will you do?" Dav returned to the previous discussion about Ana. "About the woman, this Shirley Bascom. She truly worried you?"

Gates yanked himself back to the conversation. "Do? Nothing. I know who she is." He grinned at Dav. "She's going to call me tonight."

Once again, Dav laughed. "Of course she is. You sly dog. And if she checks out? You could always take her to Parasol," he said, mimicking Shirley Bascom's breathy delivery.

"Oh, she'll check out." Gates laughed as he parried further comment about his social life before it could even be delivered. "Now, I'd have to say that Shirley is too . . ." He flapped his hands the way Shirley Bascom had fluttered her rose-bedecked evening wrap. "Floral."

The mimicry and the concept were again a source of amusement for Dav, but he stopped laughing at Gates's next words. "However, as Agent Burton of the Central Intelligence Agency," he shifted to face Dav so he could read his expression, "I'd certainly ask her out."

"You're shitting me." Dav's comeback was inelegant, but heartfelt. He hadn't known. "*That* was an agent?"

Gates grinned. "Yep. Met with her Monday about the art fraud case, the paintings you lost just before I came on board with you. She's the one working cold cases and checking some new leads on the case, she says."

When Dav sat silent, he continued. "Could have knocked me over when I realized who it was in that flowery getup." His grin widened, and he said, "She was dressed much more conservatively when she showed up at the estate."

The problem with reminding himself of that was he

pictured her immediately in her snug but unrevealing suit, her hair tamed into some kind of twist. He'd sat next to her at the table, watching her, seeing the temper flare in those hazel eyes when he threw a barb her way, seeing her lock it down as she did her job with a cool façade and a sharp mind. That alone had been hot, but that snap of fire in the look she'd given him was pure, flat-out sexy.

He wasn't sure he was going to do anything about it—he seldom did. He realized he was, however, looking forward to her call. It lent a certain anticipation to the last part of the night.

"But what the hell was she doing at the gallery?" Dav finally asked. "What's going on? You don't think Carrie is being watched by the CIA, do you?"

"No, not this time." Gates caught him up on the case as Ana had outlined it, letting him know that she'd caught the changes from the original list within seconds.

"She knows art, and she knows this case, so you may see some results."

"That would be—" Dav hesitated, then smiled. "A significant change. I admit it still pisses me off all these years later. I hate being suckered." The last was delivered with a bit more heat. Davros Gianikopolis was scrupulously fair, determinedly honest, but he was also sharp as hell when it came to business and he knew how and when to cut the best deal. Not much got past him. It still burned him that someone had bested him over the paintings, and that no one had ever figured out where the switch was made. That irritation was why Gates constantly swept the nets for any mention of the pieces Dav had lost through the forgery scam.

"We'll see what she comes up with," Gates said. He decided that was enough talk about Ana. He didn't want Dav clueing in to his interest, and he had the perfect redirect. "So, tell me how you know Carrie McCray."

"I don't," Dav answered with bland inattention. That was

a dead giveaway of interest if he'd ever heard one, especially for Dav.

"Hmmmm, tell me another lie, man. I've known you too long."

Dav rubbed at his arm again. Queller must really have clamped down. "Really, I don't. However," he winked at Gates, "I'm sure you could tell that I'm intrigued with her. My assistant and several of the marketing people have dealt with Prometheus on this Bootstrap organization. The main organizer is a shipping magnate named Drake Yountz. I had brushed them off, but there were a number of calls from other business leaders urging me to participate."

Dav now rubbed at his temples, then grimaced. "Several of the calls were from people I'm working deals with, so I caved, as they say. We've donated a minimal sum to it, so far. Also, we've bought many things from Prometheus, corporate purchases mostly, though not much since Luke died. I don't remember Carrie looking quite so . . ." He paused, then to Gates's surprise, moderated whatever he was about to say. "Professional. The only other time we'd met was at Luke's funeral and once at another charity event."

Gates had a sudden memory of his mother's paintings displayed at her funeral. It floated to the surface of his mind, and he let it, appreciating it before he filed it carefully, and ruthlessly away. He didn't dwell on the past, on his parents or their deaths. He couldn't. Doing so usually took him days to recover, so he avoided all but the most casual remembrances of them.

"Anything else turn up on your searches these last few days, my friend?" Dav broke through his momentary silence.

"Only that our agent's on probation."

"For what?" Dav asked in surprise.

"I don't know." At Gates's admission, Dav laughed.

"Yet," Dav added. "Your vast network never fails to intrigue and amuse me."

"Ah, the humor factor. That would be why you pay me

the big bucks," Gates quipped. "However, she's pretty well cloaked. I can get all the info I want on her current employment at the Agency, but most of her background has been shielded. I'll set off a number of inquiries if I go searching too deeply into our agent."

Once again, Dav laughed. "I don't pay you nearly enough. Are you still determined to say no to a raise?"

Gates shook his head, a definite negative, before he said, "Yes, I'm going to refuse. Your idea of a raise is equal to the GDP of a small independent country, Dav."

"How about I fire you and you finally go build that information research and security company idea you've toyed with for so long?"

"Your unemployment insurance would go through the roof. I'd just live like a bum for a few years and draw food stamps on your dime."

Dav chuckled. "Can't have that. I guess it'll have to be the raise."

"No. No budgetary increase necessary."

"It isn't like the gross domestic product, Gates," he said, impatient now. "You regularly save me more trouble than it would be to run such a country, so you deserve it," Dav reasoned slyly, hands spread to show how obvious it was that he should accept. "So, fifteen percent increase this year, I think."

Gates rolled his eyes and let his head drop onto the soft leather headrest. He hadn't realized how tired he was, how much he'd been on alert, until he was in the safety of the bulletproof limo with their usual escorts, front and back. The banter was easy and familiar. They'd had the same sort of discussion every year for the past three years, up to and including the offer to fire him so he could go start his own company.

If he ever did, Dav would be the first in line to buy his services. It was pretty much a sure thing. Every now and then, when Dav's wandering lifestyle palled, he considered it. Then they would stay put for a while and he would realize that a so-called stable life would be too painful. It would mean relationships, and connections. Those connections required emotion, and he wasn't sure he had it to spare. He had it for Dav, but so far, he'd been able to keep Dav safe. Gates's work for him was a penance for all he hadn't done for his own family.

"No," he said, realizing Dav was waiting for a reply. He kept his voice firm. He didn't let on any of the weariness. One whiff that he was capitulating would have Dav drawing up the papers for fifteen percent in a wink. "It's not about the money, Dav. You know that."

Dav hissed out a breath. "Of course I know it, Gates. However, it is in my power to give generously because I am alive to pursue my business interests. I am alive because of you, my friend," he argued. "Ergo, you have increased my business holdings geometrically. In fact, given your computer prowess, you've done more than that just with what you improve in communications savings."

"Three percent," Gates muttered, knowing he'd have to let Dav do something or the man would never drop the subject.

"Fifteen," Dav insisted. "Think of it as profit sharing."

Gates snorted out a laugh. "Profit sharing, my ass. No one else gets profit sharing."

"That's because there is no stock, no centralized holdings. Your idea," he reminded Gates, referring to the business model Gates had set up that kept the multitude of small connected businesses, each earning vast amounts of money individually, but never taxed collectively, reducing the financial burden operating under multiple international governments usually caused. "An idea for which you should be compensated."

"You paid me well for the idea when I initiated it five years ago. That money's quadrupled in the last four years. No need to pay me twice."

"Ah," Dav argued, "but it still pays *me* dividends, so why should I not pass them on?" Sighing dramatically, he added, "Thirteen percent."

"Four."

"Twelve."

"Four," Gates insisted, his voice firm.

"I'll wear you down in the end," Dav said on a laugh as they rolled through the gates of the vast estate just north of the city. They had climbed into the hills as they wrangled, neither of them paying much attention to the route, although Gates would have noticed any deviation instantly.

"No," he said firmly, "you won't."

Dav had one last comment about Carrie McCray as he got out of the car. "I know she grieved her husband deeply." He stared off into the night, turned back to Gates, and winked. "Now, however, she appears to be past it."

"Perkins, if you contact me again, without authorization, I will have you terminated."

Dead silence greeted the pronouncement, and the caller wondered if Perkins had died of fright on the spot.

"Well?" he demanded. "Obviously you thought *something* was important enough to breach the silence despite my earlier warning. What the hell is it?"

"I did a deep search on her. I wanted to figure her out. She shouldn't have been able to catch it, but she did." Perkins was almost whining in distress. "She's smarter than those others working up there on the fifth floor." He hesitated, a long moment, then blurted, "She went to Prometheus tonight. She was talking with the owner and with that Greek, Davros Gianikopolis. I don't want anything to get loose here, and I want to keep you *informed,*" Perkins stressed the word. "If you don't hear from me it's because I'm compromised, so keep that in mind. She has the resources to dig things out. She's done it before."

Perkins was an idiot. He'd let the woman know someone was worried. Stupid. To cover his irritation, he laughed. "She's in disgrace, Perkins. She doesn't know *us*, after all. We had nothing to do with those bunglers she's hunting, now did we?" he injected his tone with a false heartiness. "If she catches on to Santini, on the East Coast, more the better. He was stupid to kill those people that way. If she turns the spotlight his way, figures him out, it's actually a plus." He had, of course, been playing both sides of the deal, but Perkins didn't know that and never would. If Perkins displayed enough courage to get anywhere near that data, he would be eliminated and quickly. "Keep an eye on her, but don't get so torn out of the frame, you idiot. She's not that smart. Few are."

"But this one is," he protested, a direct contradiction. "She's good. She should be IT, she's so good."

"If you contact me again, you'd better have more information than that a lone, computer-savvy agent is following up on old leads from a long-dead case. In fact," he said, with rising irritation, "if you contact me again, you better have a reason for me to take action. Do I make myself clear?"

"No," Perkins complained.

He ground his teeth in frustration. *Idiot.* "Find out what she knows. For heaven's sake, you work in the same building, you can get into her computer. Call me if there's anything of interest, but *don't* call me, Perkins, with *trivia!*" He roared the last word and slammed the small phone down on the desk, knowing the sound would reverberate through the line. He disconnected and smashed the phone once again. In disgust, he picked up the pieces and disposed of them in trash cans throughout the now darkened freight terminal outside his offices. The cleaning crew would be through before morning, and the pieces would be on their way to the dump in separate bags. Efficient.

Picking up yet another disposable from the storage area, he placed a call.

"Ja?"

"Two jobs."

"The first?" The heavily accented voice of Jurgens, one of

his best assistants, rang sharp and clear. No hesitation, thank God. At least some people knew how to do their jobs.

"Watch Perkins."

"That one." Jurgens's voice held disdain. "Ja. And the second?"

"A woman. An agent with the CIA. Be very discreet. Observe only and don't be seen. That's Perkins's job, and if he's not doing it, I need to know. If he gets clumsy, I need to know."

"He vill. Be clumsy, that is," came Jurgens's flat reply.

He agreed but didn't say so. "Just watch them."

"Ja."

"Good," he said before clicking off.

Chapter Five

Turning his back on the front doors, Gates debriefed the staff in the two other cars, soliciting their impressions of the event at the gallery, mentally approving the mention of Shirley Bascom—only one of the men had taken note of her pulling him to his feet—and getting information from the others about the guests, the artist, and the manager of the gallery, as well as the owner. He made mental notes as each of the team spoke, organizing his thoughts about the guests and any other items of interest.

To a person, his team had disliked the art, which amused him.

"Good work tonight, ladies and gentlemen," he said by way of dismissal. "You all blended in well. I don't think anyone was aware how many of our people were present. We've got nothing off the grounds tomorrow, so have a good day. Georgiade and Thompson, you're on at eleven tomorrow in the main security room."

"Got it, boss," Georgiade answered. Most of his team dispersed into the darkness, as three of them detached from the group to take the cars to the garage.

"Queller, a word?" He singled out the one person who'd noted Shirley.

"Sir?" The young, gangly man moved forward, into the lights of the portico.

"I just wanted to say good catch on the woman, the one who helped me up. She checks out, by the way."

Queller grinned, and said, "Great work if you can get it."

"No kidding." Gates returned the grin, then turned serious. "We've not had an incident in several weeks, which is good. However, that doesn't mean we're clear. I appreciate your attention to the details," he commended. "Keep it up."

"Yes, sir. I appreciate the opportunity."

"Yep. Have a good night," he said, turning away and hearing the younger man move off toward the security quarters. Shifting into the shadows, he put his back to the pillar of the portico and watched until he could no longer see Queller in the darkness.

The night air was cool, even for San Francisco, and the chill seeped into his bones. Still, he stayed outside, watching the stars twinkling over the line of fog blanketing the city. He mulled over the images of the evening, in spite of the chill. For some reason he just didn't want to be inside.

Shirley Bascom. Ana Burton. Only one was an enigma, but Ana in a cocktail dress, even a flowered one, had been a sight to behold.

If he hadn't already known who she was, he would have been inside checking her out, despite the late hour. She was physically strong and capable, as well as smart. The close scrutiny he'd seen her give the crowd told him she was hunting for something. He wondered what she'd uncovered.

Then there was the friend, Jen-something, who was hooked up with D'Onofrio. Interesting matchup there, but obviously a hot attraction considering the lip-lock in a public venue. He'd always considered D'Onofrio a bit of a cold one, distant and polite. He'd never seen him anywhere with a woman. He'd always gone solo.

Something niggled at him, something about the East Coast

connection, but he couldn't pinpoint it. He took out his PDA, tapped in a note to check on D'Onofrio.

Inexorably his thoughts turned back to Ana. Gates huffed out a laugh when he realized he was waiting for her to call. The sound echoed faintly in the high arch of the stone entry next to him, but carried no farther. He'd have to sleep on that one, see what his subconscious made of it. He avoided women like her, serious, attractive, interesting women. Not that he didn't date, or serve as an escort to some incredibly attractive women, thanks to his association with Dav. He didn't get intrigued though. Interested. That was too complicated.

Either she wasn't going to call, or she thought it was too late. How funny to be on the other end of the "waiting by the phone" joke.

"Yeah, brilliant," he half-whispered to himself. "Dav's going to howl with laughter." Not that he was going to tell Dav anything about it. It was hard enough to keep his professional and personal lives separate as it was. He was far too close to Dav, far too enmeshed in his life. "Not like it's going to change, either, Bromley, so get over it."

For all Dav's talk of pay, they were more like partners or brothers than employee and employer. The thought of losing another person in his life made Gates obsessive about Dav's safety, and Dav never made a business decision without running it by Gates.

Gates cared too much, and he knew it. He didn't sleep much, even now. It had taken him years after the accident that killed his parents to actually go to sleep without drugs. He managed five or six hours now, which was better than the two or three that had been the norm even with medication.

"And bed is where you should be, you idiot," he muttered, pushing off the wall. He'd taken one step when his phone rang.

He didn't try to stop the grin that blossomed. There was no one to see it anyway.

"So is this Shirley or Ana?" he asked.

"Hmmmm," she purred. "Who do you want it to be?"

The flirtatious chuckle was nearly as hot as her long legs and her looks. "Well, I like Shirley's slinky heels, but Ana's mind and smile. What about a combo?"

"The heels?" He heard her surprise. She wasn't as used to flirting as she was trying to let on. "Now there's an image. A smile and high heels."

"Hotter than hell," he said, seeing it in his mind. He needed to coast back to cooler territory for now. "So Agent Sexy, what did you find out with your little undercover adventure?"

"Now I'm Agent Sexy? I think not." Her verbal dismissal of the moniker puzzled him. "I'm just praying I wasn't Agent Oh-So Obvious."

That made him laugh. "No, I'm not sure anyone caught on, not even your friend's date. How's she know D'Onofrio?"

"Long story." He heard the rustle of clothing and immediately pictured her undressing.

Biting back a groan at the thought, he said, "I've got time." He'd listen to the sexy purr of her voice for hours.

"I don't," she laughed. "Saturday or not, I've got work. Tonight gave me about four more reports to write."

"Sounds . . . dull."

He liked her laugh, low, feminine, and husky. "Pretty much. So why did you want me to call, other than to tell me you liked my shoes?"

That snapped the picture of her in nothing but the strappy black shoes, stockings, and a smile back into his mind. Oh, yeah. This one got him in the gut. Not what he needed, or wanted, but sometimes, life threw you an interesting curve.

"Well," he drawled. "I was hoping for a bedtime story, but you won't give. What about a tale of undercover work, instead? What's the lead?"

"Not at liberty to say, Mr. Bromley." She made his name sound like a caress, and it was killing him. One minute she was being an agent, flirting a bit awkwardly; then she turned that hot voice on and said his name *that* way. Two parts of one woman, like she was out of practice, or trying not to be interested. Either possibility was a puzzle. He loved puzzles.

"So, Anastasia . . ." He treated her to some of her own medicine, letting her full name roll off his tongue like a caress. "What do you want from me? Intel? More lists?"

"How did you know my name's Anastasia?" More rustling of fabric, then he could hear her sit up and her voice changed.

"It's on your card," he answered truthfully, frowning. What made her suddenly wary? "Problem?"

"No, no, it's just—" She hesitated.

"Just?"

"Did you do a run on me, Gates?" The words came out in a rush. "A deep search?"

He frowned. "I did a standard run, got your general information. You know most of your data's blocked, thanks to your job. Deep search past those blocks is illegal." He waited for her to agree, which she did. "I read the article you wrote on data mining. Excellent information there, by the way," he added. "Made sure you worked for who you said you worked for. That's about it. Why? Is someone running deeps on you?"

"Someone did. The night after I set up our meet." She muttered something else he couldn't catch, so he asked her to repeat it. She sighed, but did so. "I said, I don't know why I'm telling you that. Or why I believe you when you say it wasn't you."

"Hard to say." He smiled into the darkness, relaxing a bit. "But I'm an honest guy. I only lie to the people I don't like."

"Hmmmm." She was back to flirt mode. "So, you like me?"

He laughed when she squeaked a bit. She must have realized how it sounded. "I do, I really do," he mocked the infamous Sally Field acceptance speech line. "Seriously. I do like you. I'd—" He hesitated, unsure. It had been so long since he'd even considered dating.

"I'd?"

In for a penny, he thought, bracing himself to do something he hadn't done in a long time. An eternity. He couldn't even explain to himself what motivated him, but he said, "I'd like to ask you out." When she didn't speak for a moment, his gut clenched. To break the tension, he added, "Ana, not Shirley."

She laughed, and he knew she'd agree. He grinned. Now for the interesting part. "So, can you do that, working on a case, or do I have to get a writ or a special exception or something from a judge?"

They bantered back and forth for a bit, even talked about the art case, but eventually agreed on dinner the following Friday. That would give him long enough to work it out with Dav's schedule. There was nothing on the schedule next Friday, but if he didn't put a word in, he'd be on duty.

"Get some sleep, Agent Anastasia," he said, wishing he could think of a reason to keep her on the phone that didn't involve art, or the case or anything remotely akin to work.

"Thanks, I will. You too." Damn, she sounded as reluctant as he was to hang up. He checked his watch. Two-thirty. He needed to be up by seven-thirty. That was short, even for him. "Sleep tight, Ana. And call me if you need more intel."

She laughed as she hung up, and he enjoyed the sound as he continued to stand in the darkness. A date.

Something caught his eye, and he forgot about the date, and Ana. The watchfulness that had saved his ass in Iraq alerted him now. A trickle of unease had him tensing, scanning the darkness.

A movement to the left. He eased down, dropping to one knee to crouch in the shadow of the pillars. Silhouetted for the briefest moment, a slight figure scurried along the top of the rough security wall. There were sensors on the ground on either side of the wall, but no one had wanted to damage the decorative stone and brick structure of the original fencing.

Last time I let historic preservation prevail.

Gates eased his PDA from his pocket and texted by feel.

Sighted 1 intruder. Top of SE wall. Disabled sensors? Going 2 alert Dav. Send squad, recon & do 911.

The phone vibrated briefly, letting him know the on-duty crew had gotten the message. Gates slipped around the portico. If he was quick he'd only be visible in the porch lights for a second.

Two of the windows next to his head exploded in a shower of glass the minute he stepped into the light. He hit the deck, rolling to the far side of the inset door, and yanked the phone from his pocket.

Switching to walkie-talkie, he growled, "Shots fired, hit the windows in the front door. Missed me. Gotta have night vision. Let the cops know."

The sudden whoop of a siren split the air. Lights sprang up all over the compound as the intruder hit one of the full-alert tripwires. It was possible the team had done it, but he doubted it. The wall wasn't predictable in its width, and pivoting to fire a weapon from the top of it wasn't the smartest thing.

Gates's smile was grim. It was a twenty-foot drop along most of the backside of the seven-foot fence, and the contractor he'd hired had planted thorn bushes along the miles it took to circle the estate. Most likely, the intruder had left him a nice blood sample if nothing else.

"Boss? You okay, boss?" Declan's voice rang out, and the kid appeared at a run, weaving to avoid fire if there was any, putting his back to a column.

"I'm fine. Single shooter, so I think we can stand down on the evasive maneuvers," Gates stood and moved away from the wall. Another of his security team tapped on the interior glass. They signaled thumbs-up. Dav was safe, and within minutes he got word that his employer was going on to bed.

"No rest for the wicked," he said, trudging toward the cart Georgiade had brought around. The other team had already headed out along the exterior of the wall. He and Declan would take the interior.

At four-forty-five, they found the spot where the gunman had fallen. The sensors had pinpointed it within twenty feet, but it took them a while to check the ground and begin the search along the proper stretch of wall. Sure enough a welter of broken branches, some bloody thorns, and several hanks of black fabric lay strewn around the area they illuminated with heavy-duty flashlights.

"Thompson," he radioed back to the team at the driveway. "We're ten feet past marker fifty-two. Bring Detective Baxter along to collect evidence," Gates snapped. He was tired and angry. The sensual buzz he'd had from talking to Ana had evaporated, and he was well on to full-out pissed.

How had the shooter known they were back?

The serious possibility of an inside leak reared its ugly head. And why had he been targeted, not Dav? They were built so differently, it made no sense. Perhaps it was a warning. Either way, there was another organization in play. They'd managed to mollify the last two Central American groups who'd sent hits on Dav, turning the contact to advantage rather than death. It had been exhausting and dangerous, but in the end, profitable.

More flashlights winked on and moved toward him. He wondered if any of the company phones would show an outgoing call at the time the limo left the gallery. He'd check that himself. People could—and frequently were—stupid enough to use a traceable phone for such things.

The necessity of that unpleasant task left him feeling hollow, momentarily defeated. He could guard against intruders, help redirect business issues that devolved into personal attacks, but traitors and crazy people never followed a *type* of any kind. They killed for reasons other than greed, and seldom for glory. Whatever cause they espoused was usually so personal, so unpredictable, they couldn't be traced. Or prevented.

He was deathly afraid that this was a vendetta, one that couldn't be solved with money or jail time. If the old family discord was rearing its ugly head again, he would insist on calling in some additional help. His security measures were comprehensive, but they'd need a special team if it turned out the Gianikopolis feud was heating up again.

"Bromley?" a voice called from beyond the bobbing flashlights coming toward him.

"Here!" He flipped the light he held from side to side.

The detective the county had assigned to Dav's various cases hiked into view, along with a slender crime scene officer. For once Baxter had on jeans, boots, and a heavy canvas coat to keep out the chill, far more practical for this night's work than his usual dark suit.

"Damn mess, this," Baxter drawled as he shined his Maglite around the smashed landscaping. Baxter's Texas burr made the words softer than the sentiment. He was a solid cop, but his finite county resources didn't stretch to chasing international-level assassins.

"Got some blood, some cloth." Gates directed the CSI officer with his light. Two of his team came up with a portable floodlight and got it working. The tech nodded her thanks but didn't say anything, so Gates turned back to Baxter. "Not much else to go with. Tracks go nowhere. Can't find a vehicle trace either," Gates said, with a grimace and a flick of a hand toward the tracking dog his team had hurried out to the scene.

The dog was tugging at the end of the lead now that he'd come back from a run halfway down the scrubby hillside without alerting. The would-be assassin had evidently had a car waiting, and had disappeared fast. "One of these days I hope we actually catch one of these sons-of-bitches."

"Tell me about it." Baxter added his own testy note to the night's lament. "Mr. G okay?"

"He was on the back side of the house. Didn't even know there was an issue till the alarms went off."

"So, who's pissed at him this month?" Baxter grunted as he moved carefully through the thorns to the wall itself.

"The usual. Central American cartels. United Arab Emirates. Hong Kong conglomerates. Fellow Greek shippers who didn't get business. Half of America's corporate movers and shakers. Most of them don't go in for shooting first, however. They'd rather kill him financially."

"Yep, the usual," Baxter muttered, peering at the wall. "Kelsey," he called to the tech, waiting for her to finish bagging something before he pointed at the wall. "Got some marks here, maybe climbing pitons, but there's some trace. Want me to get it?"

She shook her head. "Nah, I'll do it." She shot a look at Gates, but continued to silently collect samples where the bushes were flattened before rising and making her own careful way to the wall, bags and envelopes in hand.

He watched for a moment or two as she dug minute metal fragments from the stucco and brick, but turned back to Baxter when the man cleared his throat.

"So, off the record, you got any idea what this is about?"

Gates shook his head. "Not this one. On or off the record, I have no idea. We've been clear for months on the thing with Hong Kong, and the other one from Honduras. Nothing brewing to warrant a threat." He frowned, his tired brain working slowly. "I don't know, Bax. Seems more old-fashioned Ninja-style. Most hits these days are pretty straightforward, on the street, in the car, sorts of things. This?" He gestured at the wall and the bushes. "This is both professional and amateurish since they shot at me. I don't know what to make of it. Besides, I'm better at the business security part of things than I am at this."

Baxter nodded, and checked the tech's progress. "I don't think there's much you need me for yet. Or that you need to be here for," he added. "You look like hell. Go get some sleep."

"Yeah." Gates managed a smile. "That'll happen."

"So, what did you think?" Jen said as she lounged on the couch in her condo as she and Ana shared a pizza on Sunday night.

"Of the guy?" Ana pretended to be confused to buy time.

"Uh, yeah." Jen's sarcastic response was immediate. "I give you chapter and verse on the date, the Prometheus thing, the private jet to Vegas on Saturday, the whole deal, and you've barely batted an eye. You've got something smoking in that mad mind of yours. You've hardly heard a word I've said."

"Oh, I heard it," Ana stalled. She didn't want to admit she'd been thinking about Gates. Or that she'd been running scenarios about the art fraud case. Or that she'd been wondering again about Dav and Carrie.

"So?"

"So what?" She wasn't going to get away with that one, but how did she tell her best, most supportive friend that the millionaire she was dating was tweaking Ana's suspicion radar? She didn't want Jen hanging out with the guy, possibly getting into something she couldn't get out of, but she hadn't found anything to hang her hunch on, nothing solid. There were some peculiar things in the files, some weird codes that might even be Agency codes, some stuff about him from New Jersey, but she hadn't had time to dig them out.

Jen sighed and set her plate aside. "I know you ran him, Ana. I could tell it at the gallery. So let's get that out of the way. I forgive you, all right?"

Ana was shocked that Jen wasn't going to ream her. Relief followed hot on the heels of shock. "So when I tell you he gives me the willies, you'll know why you shouldn't see him again, right?"

"Nonsense," Jen parried. "Everybody gives you the

willies. Stupid, if you ask me." Jen made a tsking sound as she recovered her plate. "Look, honey," she said, a look of sympathy suffusing her features. "You've had a crappy run of it. First that married guy in Rome, then the whole work deal and all that crazy scary stuff with your job. You're gun-shy, I know it and you know it. I'm just sayin' it's time you got over it. You've never let fear get you, all these years we've known each other. I mean, when I met you, after your parents died, you were shy and hurt. You climbed out of that when we were in college, really played the field. Hell," Jen laughed, shaking her head over the next words. "You blew the field wide open, girl. You went to work for the CIA."

"I know, I know. But they recruited me," Ana reminded her. "And I do have skills they need, right? But this guy, D'Onofrio. There's something about him I don't like."

Jen rolled her eyes and continued eating pizza. "I appreciate you trying to save me from myself, honey. Here's the thing: I like taking the risk, you know? And you used to take 'em right along with me. Don't you think it's about time you found that part of you again?"

"Yeah, but Karma's a bitch, Jen," Ana managed, feeling old and sad all of a sudden. "I screwed up. Maybe if the married guy hadn't made me so crazy, I'd have been sharper at my job. Maybe I would have seen things differently."

"Bullshit," Jen answered. "Doesn't apply. You got screwed with that guy, sure, but I know what you give to your work. You were on the straight there, girl. Whatever was going on with him was over anyway, the minute you found out he was hitched."

"I know," Ana said, still fretting. "But Jen, this guy, he's dating through an agency—don't you think that's weird?"

Once again, Jen rolled her eyes. "A lot of people do. He's not perfect, right? Anyway, I'm going to see how it goes. He's fun, you know? And what's not to love about being whisked off to Vegas, and wined and dined?"

Nothing she could say to Jen would dissuade her from her choice. To her surprise, Jen changed tactics on her.

"Enough about me. I saw you being all up close and personal with that sexy stumbler. What was up with that? He was touching you, had his hand on your back and stuff. What's going down? Did he ask for your number?"

Ana nodded, uncomfortable with the spotlight being turned her way. "I gave it to him."

Jen sat up, her meal and the brief argument over Jack forgotten. "Really? You did? Oh, my gosh. Seriously?"

"Yeah, but it's the number for the diner down the street," Ana said without cracking a smile.

"Aaaaannnna!" Jen's disappointment was palpable. "You didn't."

Ana laughed. "Of course not. I wouldn't do that to Paolo," she said, naming the diner's owner. "I like his food way too much. I had a non-working number to give to anyone who asked, if that came up. They'd get the I'm-sorry-it's-temporarily-out-of-service message and give up."

"Why? He was prime," Jen said, theatrically smacking her lips. "And you could tell he was interested. C'mon, what's to lose?"

"Who said I lost anything?" she dodged. "I talked to him. As a matter of fact he gave me *his* number."

"Really? Oh, man. Tell, tell," she urged, leaning forward in anticipation.

Ana laughed over Jen's enthusiasm. "It was talk. He knows who I am, that I'm Agency. I met him last Monday on the job. He wants to go out, but I don't know."

"Did you say you would?"

"Well, yes, but I'm going to back out. I'm getting some leads on this case, and I'm not dating. I was using an alias to check out an art gallery. Maybe he finds that exciting or something. I don't know, but I'm not going."

"Ye-ha!" Jen exulted, shocking Ana into dropping her pizza. "She's baaaaaaack," she singsonged the word. "If you're finally taking risks again, even eeny-teeny ones like taking his number, then you're getting a bit of Ana back. What a relief."

"Stop," Ana protested. "It's not that bad." She didn't know why she was protesting. It *was* that bad, and she knew it. Hell, everyone knew it. Even the cat.

"Really? You've been moping around like you just watched *Old Yeller* and someone shot your dog too. You won't go out, you won't date, you won't even go out to dinner with me and a group of people that might include men. If we have one more pizza night in, I think I'll turn into a pepperoni." She saluted Ana with the slice before taking a neat bite. "And then where would we be?"

"I'm not, I didn't—" Ana began her protest, but Jen cut her off.

"No, don't spoil it. Just hush and let me savor the idea that you might be back to normal." She snickered as she took another bite. "Or at least heading toward what resembles normal for you."

They continued to joke around, and Jen left still insisting that normal for Ana was way off the charts toward sick-o. Nothing else was said about her concerns about D'Onofrio.

As she locked up, she wondered how Gates would react, seeing her on Tuesday. She'd made another appointment to meet with Dav, this time through the secretary she'd first spoken to. The woman knew her name and said she'd been expecting the call.

Gates had paved the way for that, she'd lay money on it. He'd missed nothing about her, from her heels to her evening wrap. She'd be willing to bet money that he could describe what color nail polish she'd had on. Jen was right, she realized. Her confidence when it came to him was more like the "old" Ana. Was that a good thing or a bad one? She just didn't know.

Thinking about the high heels sent her in another direction. What was it about men and high heels? Then again, the idea of being with him, wearing nothing but heels, did have its appeal.

Damn.

She paced her bedroom, trying to walk off the intense memory of his hard body, of the sound of his voice teasing her about the shoes. She tried to picture him rolling on the floor at the gallery, tried to use that silly picture to disperse the aura of power and sensuality he'd bewitched her with.

It didn't work. All she remembered was the power in his grip, the feel of the muscles hot under her hands. She could describe him too, right down to the size of the silver buckle on his belt, which had pressed firmly into her belly, and to the make and model of the weapon he'd worn holstered under his suit coat. She'd been pressed into his side when the crowd shifted toward them, imprinting the grip on her chest. No other weapon had a grip like a Sig.

Somehow, she doubted he'd be surprised that she'd already run the gun for permits. Legal, of course. He was also permitted for a variety of other weapons, many of which the estate owned. She'd lay odds that he had plenty that weren't legal too, given how difficult gun permitting was in California.

"Wonder if I should call him about Tuesday?" she asked the cat. "Probably piss him off if I don't, even though I'm sure he's already seen me on the schedule. Another budding relationship cut down before it's even started."

More weary than truly tired, Agent TJ Michaels leaned back in the hard chair he'd been using to keep him awake as he listened in on his quarry. Several more phrases for Ana to translate. Both his Italian and Greek were passable for someone who'd learned it from a textbook and from living in each country for a bit. It did not, however, cover the idiom and slang in use by the people he was watching.

Standing to stretch, he moved to his laptop and linked up with the Internet. There were no new e-mails from Ana to enlighten him about the abstract phrases his quarry had used. Too bad.

Noting down another set of phrases, words he understood but which made absolutely no sense in literal translation, he readied another e-mail to his long-time compatriot. A vision of her lean strength and the long, attractive planes of her face reminded him that he missed her.

They were good together, in so many ways. Too bad he'd nearly gotten her killed with his own stupidity. Too bad she was bearing the consequences for something to which he dared not admit.

"What a tangled web we weave," he quoted softly, "when first we practice to deceive."

Shakespeare knew about deceit. And pain.

Smart man, Shakespeare. TJ sat back down and tuned back into the tapes from the micro bug. He had a lot more deceit to go before he could clear his own name, and by doing that, clear Ana's as well.

Chapter Six

Tuesday morning, Ana drove into the hills to Dav's estate. She'd been in to the office, collected her notes and the photos of the fakes and the real paintings, as well as photos of the fakes substituted for the items he'd sold via another gallery in Milan. She'd also dug around for information on the two additional paintings Gates had mentioned.

"And wasn't the decorator surprised to get a call out of the blue." She laughed aloud at the thought. From the woman's surprise and annoyance, Ana guessed the decorator had wanted far more than Dav was willing to give. "Yep, push the billionaire too far and he'll drop you like forged art," she mocked, thinking of the woman's outrage at being called over the purchased paintings.

Even when pushed, the decorator denied all association with the gallery in SoHo that had sold the forgeries to her for Dav. Then she'd gotten off the phone as quickly as she could.

"She'da hung up on me sooner, if she hadn't been worried about me being CIA. I love the power of the badge," Ana said, as she laughed like a theater villain, amusing herself.

It was bugging her that Dav had purchased only two items from Prometheus since Luke Gideon's death. Something about that was off. Why change after so many years of doing business?

"Am I the only one who notices these things?" she asked the rearview mirror, shaking her head. "Then again, once burned, twice shy. And Dav got burned to the tune of over five million dollars."

As Ana pulled through the gates, she could see people working in the distance, apparently digging in some new plants at the wall. The tall form of Gates Bromley, waiting under a portico, was her compass point for where to park. There was another vehicle there already, a stretch limo with dark windows.

The sight of more workmen, this time replacing the glass by the front door, distracted her as she stepped from the car.

"Wow, rowdy after-the-Gallery party?" she quipped, finally looking at the man she'd been thinking about all weekend. God help her, he was just as gorgeous, just as magnetic as she remembered.

"More like a bad penny," Gates said solemnly, moving forward to hold the car door for her.

Uh-oh. What had she said? Did she always have to start on the wrong foot? She sighed inwardly. "I'm sorry. Is that a reference to my turning up without letting you know?"

"No, it's a reference to trouble turning up after a very nice evening. You're more of a gem than a penny," he murmured as she picked up her briefcase. They stood with the car door separating them, but the heat between them was palpable. The sizzle was back in his eyes as he said, "A ruby, I think. Fiery, but warm."

"A ruby?" she whispered, nearly mesmerized by his voice. Lord, she could listen to him read the phone book. The meaning sank in, and she frowned. "Me? More like a bit of costume jewelry, I think. All flash and no substance."

He looked shocked, and she realized with that one statement, she'd said more about how she was feeling about herself than she had in session after session with the department counselor. Before he could respond, Dav and a group of suits skirted around the workmen. She was just far enough away that she couldn't make out the discussion, but there was a bit of bowing and handshaking and everyone smiled as they departed in the limo.

"Delegation?" She broke the silence, hoping to get back to an even keel.

Gates smiled and the warmth in his eyes returned, but there was sorrow there too. Damn. She'd blown it again. Typical. Italy had been a sinker for her, both personally and professionally. She used to be good at the man-woman game.

He took her hand, eased her out from behind the car door. "Kobe government leaders working on a banking deal to revive a manufacturing plant. They're trying to get Dav to buy in and bankroll the project."

"Is he going to bite?"

"Probably. He could use it to his advantage even if the plant loses money. It won't," he assured her. "Dav's very, very good at making money. But the real value is in doing a favor for the Kobe prefecture."

"Hmm, I can see that." She might feel that she'd sanded her candy with Gates, but he was evidently still in the game because his hand was at the small of her back again, doing that little flutter with his fingers that made her want to melt into a puddle of goo.

"Good morning, my dear Agent Burton." Dav grinned, cocking his head to one side as he gave her a long, searching look. "Or should I call you Shirley?"

"Surely, you can call me Ana, Dav," she said with a matching grin. "Or if we're to be formal, I'll say, Agent Ana Burton, arriving as scheduled for my meeting with Mr. Gianikopolis."

"Well and good," Dav said. "Gates, would you show Ana to the office? I need to make some notes about our Kobe friends while they're fresh in my mind. I hope you'll excuse the slight delay, Ana."

"Surely."

Gates's mouth twitched at her pert rejoinder. "Well, Ana, if you'll follow me?"

Dav broke away and went in a different direction. She and Gates followed the path to the office where they'd met before.

"So, I only get to call you Shirley on Friday nights in an art gallery, right?"

"Exactly. It's my code name."

"Like *Raising Arizona*?"

The laugh slipped out before she could censor it. Damn, he was quick. "Yeah, we're usin' code names," she said, mimicking the character from the movie. "So, does that mean I get to call you Grace for your dancing act, or Nimble for your balance?"

"Done," he proclaimed, his demeanor relaxed and easy as he poured her a cup of coffee.

She watched him move, appreciated his body while he wasn't looking. His looks would age well, she decided, then chewed on her lip as she continued her appraisal. The only problem with that magnificent face was that he looked exhausted. That would age anyone prematurely.

Hadn't she seen the crow's feet in her own mirror? She chalked them up to no sleep and lots of stress.

"So what's going on out front?" she asked, then took her cup.

"An interesting event," he said, sitting at the small conference table as he had before, in the chair at her side rather than across from her.

"Looks like you had some damage. I would think you'd have to get specialists to replace that glass."

Gates stirred his coffee, looked up and into her eyes. "Yes, we do. Someone shot up the doors on Friday night." He lowered his voice to an intimate level. "Right after we hung up. Of course, he might have been aiming for me," he mused with a wry look. "He missed, barely. The doors took the brunt of the damage."

"That would be Saturday morning," she said absently, calculating the time. The rest sank in, and she dropped the cup into its saucer with a clatter. "Wait. Shot at you?"

He nodded. "Not the first time. We had police up here

within minutes, and the Bureau has been apprised of the situation, as always."

Now she knew why he looked so tired. He must have stayed up to direct the investigation.

"Dav gets this sort of issue from time to time. We thought we'd headed off any new threats a couple of months ago, but evidently not."

"You're not hurt?" She leaned forward, put her hand over his. "Tell me the truth."

Gates grimaced. "Flying glass got me in a couple of places, nothing serious."

She tightened her hand on his, forcing him to look at her. "You're telling me the truth?"

"Of course," he said, sounding faintly offended. He was looking at her hand where it gripped his wrist. When he smiled this time, it was smoldering with meaning. "Are you worried about me, Agent?" he asked, his voice a caress. "Would you like to see my wounds? I assure you, they aren't life-threatening."

"Gates." How she managed to speak, she had no idea. Her mouth was dry; her knees were quivering. Now, as he leaned forward with a wolfish, hungry look on his face, she wanted to moan in anticipation. Where in the hell was this reaction coming from?

"What, Ana? What do you want to do?"

She couldn't answer in words. *Everything. I don't know. Something. You. I don't know.*

He was close enough now to brush a kiss on her cheek, whisper in her ear. "I thought about you. Even with all that was happening, I thought about you."

He nibbled a hot path along her jaw, and she tilted her head to give him access. She was on duty, she shouldn't let him do anything like this.

"Ohhhhhh," she whispered back, nearly dying with need as he moved inexorably toward her mouth. He was working too. They had a meeting. She tried to refocus on her priorities, but she wanted to kiss him so badly, to taste the dark heat of his mouth, to feel—

The snap of dress shoes on the polished wooden floors had them leaping apart like teenagers caught necking in the library. Ana looked at him and saw the quirk of his mouth, the laugh that was struggling to break free, and she giggled.

Oh, God, how unprofessional. But she couldn't help it, she laughed. "Oh my God," she whispered. "He nearly—"

"Caught us, yes." Gates laughed as well, but as the footsteps drew closer, he growled, "But don't think I won't finish what I started. Later."

Ana closed her eyes at that thought, forcing herself to breathe. Dav was about to walk in the door, and she was quivering with need for his bodyguard, who'd nearly destroyed her ability to talk at all, much less speak coherently.

"Ah, there you are, Dav," Gates said, and his voice was easy, inviting Dav to join them. "I was just telling Ana that the door was a casualty of Friday, ah, Saturday morning's events. We were discussing the specialty glass industry."

Like hell. Of course, she wasn't about to disagree. "We got a bit off track," she said, and she saw Gates grin. "As glass has little to do with your losses in the art world."

Dav hadn't gotten to the pinnacle of business by being unaware of the undercurrents in a room, but Ana could tell he wasn't sure if they were joking together or if the joke was somehow on him. With an aplomb she envied, he jumped right in. "Then since you've both been skiving away the time, you'll have to stay for a working lunch, Ana. You'll also have to tell me why you were being so brightly inventive at Prometheus."

Before she could speak, he held up a long, thick finger to forestall any imagined refusal, and used the other hand to push a button on his desk.

"Sir?" A voice answered his summons, probably the chef since she could hear pots clanging in the background.

"Can lunch be pushed up to eleven-thirty?"

"Of course, sir," the man replied. A spate of Italian, a heavy dialect she didn't recognize followed. She caught about every third word, but guessed at the rest. He'd cursed and ordered the staff to get moving. Evidently, Dav didn't speak Italian. "We will be sure to bring it in the right time. *Perfetto.*"

"Thank you." Dav turned back to her. "Now, that's all arranged. More coffee?" He brought the carafe to the solid but elegant meeting table.

She accepted, and he warmed hers up before pouring a cup for himself. "You like my cups, Ana?" Dav asked, gesturing to the outsized china. "I love the elegance of china, but most of it is too delicate, too diminutive for me." He wiggled his fingers, which would never have managed a lady's teacup. The obvious humor in his eyes won her over. Thank goodness neither he nor Gates were suspects.

"I do like them. I never understood why china cups were so tiny, even for women. I use a mug most of the time," she answered his grin.

Much as she was enjoying herself, she decided she'd better set the tone for the meeting. "So, we should get to business. First, thanks for agreeing to meet with me. I had already told Gates that we are going over old case files, trying to determine if newer technologies can help us solve them. Now," she said, pulling files from her bag, "there wasn't any DNA or trace evidence in this case, however, I've begun to piece together some information that may turn into a lead."

"Excellent." Dav betrayed no hint of concern.

That was good. This had been an inside job, she had no doubt, but she was nearly certain that none of the collectors were in on it. Most had lost significant money, and none had shown any increase in holdings or any shift in their wealth that would indicate a trade or an added bolus of viable art.

"So, first things first. Have you had any further contact about any of these paintings since they were stolen nine years ago?" She laid out the glossy photos of the real art he'd put up for sale and been duped out of, through Prometheus and the gallery in New York, Moroni.

Dav leaned back, steepled his fingers. "And if I have?"

Ana felt the twitch in her shoulders that meant she was on to something. "I'd like to know what it is. It might lead me to finding the original thieves, and assist me in solving the murders of Colleen St. John, Nathan Rikes, Keith Griffin, Kelly Dodd, and Rod Atwell." She named the victims, hoping that the emphasis on them as real people would encourage even more cooperation.

"Interesting. And how much of my information would be entered into the record, and how much would be kept confidential?" Dav inquired. The twitch of Ana's instincts grew stronger.

"Dav . . ." Gates injected a world of caution into the use of his boss's name.

"I know, Gates. This has been a thorn for me though, you know it," Dav said. Was the statement an oblique apology to Gates? Or a cue to her?

She opted for cue. "I like pulling thorns."

Dav laughed, a rich, rolling sound. "Good. Good for you. Off the record, however," he cautioned with a nod to Gates. "No notes about this. Nor do I wish to be quoted or called to testify. Are we clear?" The calm but flat surety in his voice let her know he wouldn't be moved from his position. His body language was pretty clear on that point as well, so she agreed.

"Excellent. So, let us speak plainly." He leaned in and tapped one of the pictures. "One of the paintings was recovered. I made sure it was given to the collector who purchased the fraud. Neither of us had deceived the other; both of us lost our money. I felt it unfair to leave this individual . . . hanging, shall we say." His smile was catlike in its satisfaction and faintly predatory in the same catlike way.

"So Fraulein Messer has the real painting, even though the world believes it a fraud, correct?"

Once again, Dav laughed, and Gates grinned. "Very quick,

this one." Dav directed the comment to Gates. "You said it, you told me. You should hire *her* when you start that security company of yours, one day. Obviously, she is good at it." He turned back to Ana. "Yes, Liza has the painting, the original work. However, neither she nor I wish to advertise the fact since our insurances paid in full, and the work was returned to me through less than legal channels, you might say." He closed his eyes briefly. "It is safer for all concerned that everyone believes this painting lost. If you dig into this case and find these items, I would consider it a favor if you would alert me. I would be sure to alert Liza, and we would deal with the situation from there."

"Considering that five people are dead, Dav, I agree with your desire to keep the details quiet. Was the painting recovered in the United States or somewhere else?" She wasn't going to mention her suspicion that Luke Gideon might be a sixth victim.

"Elsewhere," Gates interjected, directing her attention his way. "Since Dav is determined to cooperate," he shot Dav a resigned look. "and we're off the record, I'll tell you I recovered it in Russia."

"Russia?" That was a surprise. Nothing else had pointed to . . . wait . . . the torture.

"See, Gates?" Dav leaped in, gleefully watching her. "The wheels are turning. I like this one. So, Ana, we have been forthcoming. You would like to return the favor, I think?" It was a strong encouragement to share. Ana resisted the temptation and shook her head.

"No, not yet." She stayed firm, ignoring his smile. "Anything I have is supposition, Dav."

Gates snagged her attention again. She was already hyper-aware of him, feeling warm and tingly on the side nearest him, as if she'd brushed against a warm stove.

"Do you have any information on the other items, Ana?"

"Of course, but most of it isn't ready for prime time. Gates," she rolled his sexy name off her tongue with ease, "was kind enough to give me the data you had put together on the other two paintings. I checked with the people who did initial investigations, faxed them the certification on the fraudulent paintings. They are a match, these two," she pointed to the pictures he'd added to the discussion, "to the forged paperwork for a number of the others, so I'd say they're included."

She looked from Gates to Dav. "I'm grateful that both of you are willing to cooperate with me. I've interviewed a number of the other collectors. Some would like the matter forgotten. Some had honestly forgotten all about it." She fought to keep the wry disbelief from showing on her face or in her voice, but evidently she missed.

"Hard to believe on either count," Gates replied.

Ana shrugged. "Some trade art like kids trade baseball cards, I'm guessing. They forget which card wasn't *really* the Babe's rookie card, and which was."

"The Babe?" Dav inquired.

"Babe Ruth," both Ana and Gates chorused, then looked at one another.

True to form, Dav laughed. "Baseball fans, unite. I have heard of Herman Ruth and know of his record, but growing up in Greece doesn't inform you of the nicknames, I guess."

Since she'd had this conversation with a friend not long before, she smiled. "No, it doesn't. As a kid, I lived all over the world, but my father loved baseball. When I got to a new place, knowing baseball helped me fit in."

"Interesting. I knew how to make money. I found friends that way, no matter where I was," Dav commented.

"A useful skill. I wish I'd known it," Ana replied, not sure what else to say. "Still do, I guess. Anyway," she said, shifting back to the matter at hand, "most of the other collectors and patrons who were victimized cut their losses and have no interest in the case. Their insurance paid, or didn't, and they've moved on. Or closed down."

"The Moroni Gallery," Gates growled.

Ana nodded. Three of Dav's losses had come through Moroni's New York gallery. The owners had closed up shop and disappeared. "For one. Three other galleries connected to the thefts either shut down because of the losses or, in the case of Pratch, the gallery in Berlin, were closed due to misadventure."

"Pratch, the owner, was never found, correct?"

Ana nodded, turning her reply to Gates's question as well as his unspoken words. "And yes, he's presumed dead. I count him as the sixth murder associated with this case, although my case files list only five." She wasn't willing to mention Luke Gideon just yet, but he would make the seventh murder.

"Is it possible he was involved?"

"Possible," Ana agreed. She had instantly thought the same thing, but the Berlin police and the agents who'd handled the case initially thought not. Gates didn't need to know about any internal disagreements, however. "According to Berlin though, no probable cause, so they've listed it probable death by misadventure and moved on."

"Hmmm, so what is stirring now, Ana?" Dav asked.

"I'm working these cold cases, as I told Gates, utilizing technologies not available nine years ago. In some instances, we've been able to resolve cases thanks to advances in DNA processing, fingerprint databasing, and so on."

"Yet you said there was no evidence left at any crime scene." Gates made it a statement.

"True, but the advances in computer searches, like crime management and tracing papers and documentation, have been monumental. These forged papers could lead us to something, although I'd prefer you keep that to yourselves," she requested. "Online major theft catalogues are growing. They're still difficult to access, but I'm working through the data."

"You've searched the TrustGuild list?" he asked, throwing out the name of a private data pool for missing items. "And the Pullein?"

"The Pullein, yes. I don't have authorization to pay the fee for the TrustGuild." She leafed through her notes to see what else she'd already searched, since he was obviously going to ask.

Gates made a note, smiling. Suddenly Dav's booming laugh startled them both, and she looked up to see him pointing at Gates. "You should see yourselves, the two of you. Jockeying for position, trying to determine what *you* know." He pointed to Ana. "And what *you* know." Now he pointed at Gates. "You're well matched, you two."

Ana didn't know whether to be pleased or offended.

Gates evidently had no trouble being offended. "For heaven's sake, Dav. I'm not jockeying for anything."

Dav didn't take umbrage at his friend's tone, or his words. "I'm not saying you mean to, you're just competitive. I believe Miss Ana is as well."

Knowing it was true, even if that competitive streak had been flattened a lot by all that had happened, she grinned. "Either way, Dav, there are things I can't say about the old case, or anything I'm finding now. However, I will keep your information in confidence since you told me off the record. And," she turned to Gates, "I'll be sure to look at Russia without giving any clue how I knew to do so." It would open new avenues, that was for sure. "I appreciate the leads."

"Gates, you will help her with this," Dav said, gesturing toward Ana. "These are difficult people, you understand," he told her. "Touchy. Gates knows how to get around that without getting into trouble. Also, he can search several of the databases you might not have access to on your budget."

Gates looked troubled, but didn't deny either the willingness to help or that the Russian mob could be "touchy." She wondered if he was concerned about working with her. Either way, she itched to get to her computer and track the Russian lead.

"Do you have any news on any of the other pieces?" she questioned, watching Gates this time.

The faintest frown told her he knew something. "Nothing solid," he began.

"Anything would—"

"Ah, here is lunch," Dav said, to warn them both that there were others in the room and the discussion would have to wait. "Let us table this for now and enjoy our meal. Ana will tell us what she thought of the . . . art at the gallery on Friday." Dav changed gears smoothly, evidently noting that Ana had scooped up the photos and stored them away when the staff came in.

"There was art at the gallery?" she said sweetly, looking at the two men with her vacuous Shirley Bascom smile.

It was becoming lovely to hear Dav laugh, but to get both men laughing was even better. Gates's rich baritone was wonderful when he laughed. She had a sudden memory of him whispering in her ear at the gallery, the banter on the phone that night.

Suddenly, it felt very warm in the room. She slipped her jacket off, draped it over the chair. The men followed suit.

"Ana? Wine?" Dav's eyes twinkled as he indicated the server who stood at her elbow.

"No thank you, I'm on duty."

"Too bad." He gave his orders in Greek, and the servers shifted like pieces in a shell game, taking the wine away. "You'll have to come for dinner sometime, without your credentials pinned to your suit. My cook sets a good table." He paused for a moment, then turned away to mask a furious sneeze.

Without thinking, because Dav had been speaking Greek, she gave the usual Greek response to a sneeze. "*Yitzes,* Dav."

Everyone turned toward her in unison.

Chapter Seven

"You're full of surprises, Ana," Gates drawled, breaking the silence at the table. The servers, sensing the tension, hurried to move away. "You don't look Greek."

"I'm not, I just lived there for a while. And we've had much more interesting things to discuss," Ana managed, frantically looking for something to change the subject. The last thing she wanted to do was talk about her time with her family in Greece. "This looks like a lovely salad. Ah, fresh feta too."

Dav recovered quickly, she'd give him that. Not as fast as Gates, but fast.

He waved a hand to the servers, "Carry on. Carry on. Yes, the feta must be fresh. Otherwise the whole salad loses flavor, don't you think?"

"True," Ana said, picking up her fork as a distraction. The men did the same, and they all began to eat. "So, Dav, overall, what did you think of the showing?"

"My young cousin has talent, I'll admit, but it isn't my sort of art."

"Cousin?" *Oh, crap, I forgot the artist was a relation. I've stepped in it now, joking about the art.* In her flirting with Gates, she'd been so quick to enjoy the repartee, she'd been incautious.

It was Gates's turn to laugh at Dav's expense. "He has cousins everywhere, Ana, so don't feel like you've been tricked. Distant relatives come out of the woodwork when they've got something to show or sell. Dav's buying power, and generosity, are legendary."

"Currying favor with a wealthy uncle?" She smiled into her salad. "Yep, that's an age-old ploy." She glanced up, hoping to regain any ground she might have lost. "Did it work?"

"Cheeky," Dav said, grinning. "I like that about you. No, it didn't induce me to purchase, but I believe my presence did assist him some with the opening."

Gates nodded. "It did. And fortunately, nothing got damaged during the tumbling session we were both involved in." He turned a look on her that was part puzzled, part amused. "Of course your arrival today did dispel several questions for me . . . Shirley."

"Perhaps you can answer another one, Ana-aki." Dav used the Greek endearment—a diminutive akin to "little one." "How do you know to respond so fluently in my own tongue?"

She shrugged, hoping to dispel the slight tension that edged in once again. "Nothing nefarious, I assure you. I spent my . . ." She had to stop and count in her mind. "Fourth, fifth, and sixth grade school years at the embassy in Athens. My best friend was the daughter of the Greek ambassador, and we both had nannies who insisted we speak proper Greek, like civilized people."

Gates grunted. Dav still looked skeptical, but said, in Greek, "And who was the ambassador at the time?"

"Georgius Deminokus." She named the man without even having to think. "His daughter DeDe and I still keep up."

"Keep up?" Dav was obviously trying to translate the term.

"We're still in contact with one another," Ana said, smiling.

"Didn't Deminokus . . ." Dav began, then stopped. A look of sad comprehension suffused his features.

Gates leaned in, his gaze switching from her face to Dav's.

Obviously he wasn't familiar with Greek politics from more than fifteen years before.

"Yes," she replied, setting her fork down. "He was killed, as were my parents, by a bomb. There are still those in Greece," she explained to Gates, "who don't like the close ties the government keeps with the United States."

"They don't like much of anything," Dav said tersely. "I am sorry for your losses. It seems that you and Gates have something in common, losing your parents so young." The assumption that she would know about Gates's parents hung out there for a moment.

"Yes, it is an unfortunate place of common ground. I'm sorry for your loss as well, Gates." She did her best to keep her voice level. "I hope you didn't suffer a similar loss, Dav."

He smiled, but this time there was no humor in it. "No. My parents lived for much longer than either of yours, but we were not close." And that, it seemed, was that, because he changed the subject immediately. She remembered nothing in the file about his parents. She'd have to check that.

"Now enough gloom," Dav said. "We've cleared up the little mystery, so I hope you'll enjoy the meal."

"It looks delicious." It did, so she picked up her fork. "Buon appetito." She added the Italian to tweak them both.

"Italian too?" Gates caught the clue first.

"*Si,* for first, second, and third grade," she said. "I kept track of everything by what grade I was in."

"And where were you born?"

"Djakarta, Indonesia," she and Gates responded at the same time.

Dav treated her to another one of his booming laughs. "There now, the agent and the security expert, both at my table. We all probably know far more about one another than we'd like to let on. Yes," he replied to her unspoken inquiry. "I knew the answer before I asked. Gates briefs me thoroughly, of course. Most of your data is blocked, thanks to your profession. What your scant data didn't tell us, however, was that you were quite so clever. Or so lovely and interesting."

Ana scoffed. "Not sure I'd describe myself as clever, but thank you."

"I understand you have worked on some high-profile cases," Gates began.

"Some. My current assignment to review these cold cases is proving very interesting," she deflected.

"How so?" Gates asked.

"I'm meeting the most interesting people," she said, poker-faced, and was treated to another laugh.

"A wit. Yes, yes indeed. So"—Dav pushed away from the table and crossed his legs, totally relaxed—"these paintings, these murders. Are they connected? Hard to believe with some of the murders here, and so clean if you will, with the single bullet. Then there, on the East Coast, so messy, so tragic. Nine years ago they didn't think so at first. Then they did, but time marches on and memory fades. Why now? And why you?"

"I have an art degree, which I'm sure you both know. I'm reviewing cold cases because I'm on leave from my post in Rome, which I'm sure Gates already determined. This one seemed interesting. It had threads to pull."

Dav frowned for a moment over the idiom. "Leads, things you can follow up on now, that they didn't nine years ago?"

"Exactly. Perhaps more perspective as well. With the tempering of time, the connections are pretty obvious." Ana ticked points off on her fingers. "The paperwork is by the same forger, even if it had multiple destinations. While some of the galleries were cleared, both Prometheus here in the City, and the Moroni Gallery in New York, were implicated. Ms. McCray was cleared, and that seems likely since her gallery took such heavy losses. Moroni, on the other hand, was apparently hip-deep in the whole matter. The disappearance of the principals and staff for Moroni is a fair admission of guilt as well."

"Would it help you," Dav said slowly, as if feeling his way, "if I made some calls to the other victims, the ones you've said have shut you out? Encouraged them to assist you?"

Although he didn't look at Gates, she did. He looked resigned, and once again, exhausted. "How does your security expert feel about that offer of help?"

Dav smiled. "As is obvious, he doesn't like it. However, he knows that this bothers me, continues to bother me. It was something I asked him to look into when he began working for me." He shrugged, a very Continental gesture. "I was never satisfied that it was over. Luke Gideon and Carrie McCray were personal friends as well. As good as it was to see them cleared, the suspicion was difficult for them, and for Carrie after Luke's death."

Gates leaned back as well, a more relaxed posture. "He's right, of course, on all counts. Another thing to consider is that these people were never caught. The more you pursue this, the more dangerous it may be. We," he indicated Dav, "feel that the group went under, quit cold until the heat died down. You're the first person in nine years to touch this. I've wondered about the lack of interest in the case. The why of it. As in why no one pursued it."

Ana did her best to match their calm demeanor. The idea that the two agents she'd talked to might have stalled the case jumped to mind, but she pushed it aside. Even so, it set her stomach churning. Seven people, five for sure, were dead, and they deserved some justice, not only for the fact of their deaths, but for how they had died.

"I'm not sure what to tell either of you about that, but I can say that I'm very good at what I do," she said, putting aside her doubts. She looked at Dav now. "And any nudging you'd care to do with your fellow victims would be helpful."

"I have no doubt of that," Gates said, a scowl twitching his features. "That's why you need to be cautious. I'm not in favor of Dav pulling any strings here, you should know that up front."

"But—" she began.

He held up a hand. "Hear me out. There are enough people targeting Dav as it is, domestically and outside of the US. The authorities," he circled a hand to indicate the US policing forces, "have a lot on their plates and can't focus the manpower to fend off nebulous threats to Dav's safety. That's not only my full-time job, but employs a lot of other people around here. Stirring this up may bring on more heat from areas we're not expecting."

"I have no doubt. Powerful, wealthy men attract enemies, whether they deserve them or not," she stated. Her parents hadn't deserved the enemies they had, nor had Gates's parents, from what she'd read. She turned to Dav. "No matter how you do business, and from reports, your business is strong and above-board, you make enemies. If nothing else because you refuse to do business under the table."

"Precisely," Dav agreed. "How do you say it? Damned if you do, damned if you do not."

"It also means," Gates interjected, "that we have a lot already going on, as I said. Putting yourself out there about a nine-year-old dead case of art fraud may bring on more heat than any of us want to deal with, Dav." He sighed. "Not that I don't want to help you, Ana. I do, but I get paid to keep Dav alive and anything that might draw more fire his way has to be carefully considered."

"I've read about some of the threats he's faced," she said. "None of it good."

"You don't know the half of it," Gates muttered.

"Gates," Dav reproved. "You must forgive him," he said mildly to Ana. "He doesn't do well on two hours of sleep, and being shot at pisses him off, all out of proportion."

"He told me about that."

Gates nodded, a sour look for his boss. "Not the first time, not the last, Dav. I'm fine."

"Hmm. So you say, every time." Dav rose and brought a cart closer to the table. Another thermal carafe of coffee along with several dessert options rested on lovely china. "Would you do us the courtesy, Ana?"

It was a poignant moment, harkening back to her days at her mother's side, hosting tea parties at the embassy. Lifting the heavy silver cake server, she turned to Dav. "For you?"

"The torte, I believe, and more coffee if you would. *Efarhisto.*" He thanked her in Greek as she slipped the plate in front of him.

"Gates?"

"The strawberry shortcake, thanks. No coffee for me. I've got more caffeine than blood in my system as it is right now."

She laughed. "Been there," she said, serving his plate and making her own selection.

"Now, let's be frank, shall we?" Dav began. He then outlined a course of action that had Ana's head spinning, and Gates's frown darkening with each word.

On her way back to the office, Ana tried to come to terms with what she'd been handed, free of charge. The keys to resources she could never command on her own. As far-reaching as the CIA's databases were, they didn't hold a candle to what the private sector could muster for some things, and she knew it. Sure, she could gather some information more effectively than Gates could, but his abilities were amazing, the truth of which had become far clearer in their discussion.

She was thinking so hard she nearly missed her turn into the garage under the building. Swiping her card, she clicked the button to raise the window. It didn't budge. The car was getting older, and some of the electrical systems were going wonky. The thought distracted her from her pondering her attraction to Gates, her gratitude that he'd help her with database searches. Evidently that type of work was a specialty they shared.

"Jeez, that's all I need," she muttered, still jiggling the

power window switch. "Another five or six hundred dollar car repair." Leaning forward to jiggle the button saved her life.

She'd let the car roll forward as she worked the button, and the bullet aimed at her head shattered the reluctant window and buried itself in the headrest.

"Holy God!" Ana screeched in terror as she stomped on the gas. Fear and adrenaline were her safety net as the car shot forward, fishtailing to slide under the security bar. She gained the relative safety of the garage, her tires squealing as she wound down the ramp. She snagged her phone, dialing the emergency code. She'd never used the emergency code while in the States, so her fingers fumbled with the unfamiliar numbers but she managed to hit SEND.

"Agent Burton, entering HQ at Gate B, I think, off Seventh Street, shots fired," she panted. "Shattered window, missed me. Kill shot though. Hit the headrest." The thought of that made her blood run cold.

"On it," a dispatcher snapped. "Are you still under fire? Do you need medical assistance? What is your location?"

"No," she said, speeding down the last of the ramp and shooting into the main part of the garage. Several people, leaving for a late lunch or early exit, spun and crouched as she roared into the clear and hit the brakes hard. Above the engine's whine and the huge noise of her heartbeat, she heard the clanking rumble of the garage lockdown doors. "I'm okay. Just the car. I'm at the elevator bank."

Two uniformed guards exploded from the door to the building, racing for her car.

"Ma'am? Are you all right?" one snapped, opening her door, reaching for her wrist. "Do you need the EMTs?"

"No, no," she said, panting in reaction. She thanked dispatch and hung up to talk to the guards. "I'm fine. Just scared shitless. Bullet's in the headrest," she squeaked, throwing open the door so she could get as far away as possible from the bullet. She stood up, then regretted it because now that the danger was passed, she felt faint.

Get it together, Burton. You have to keep it solid. Breathe, girl.

"Outside perimeter alert's found nothing, ma'am," the other guard said. "I'm going to pull in over there." He pointed to an open area, usually reserved for confidential visitor's vehicles or other uses. "We'll get the team down here and get that bullet. Should be able to get someone over here to fix the window for you too." He glanced at his watch, winced. "Shit. Oh, sorry, ma'am. Probably not today though. Too late."

"S'okay, I'm feeling pretty much like screaming that very word right now. Oh, hell," she said, leaning on the car and bending forward to counteract the faintness. "Wow, never come that close before. You know all that stuff they say about your life flashing before your eyes?"

The guard nodded.

"It may not happen right at the moment, but it sure does hit you when you're done. Whew."

The younger of the two men took her arm and helped her to the bench by the elevator. "Here, grab a seat. I'll get your things for you, okay?"

"Thanks," she managed before easing down onto the bench. The guard followed her car over to the reserved space, and retrieved her briefcase, purse, and files.

"You okay to leave the keys with us?" the younger one said, holding them out. "Or if you need the other keys, you can take the car key off."

"Oh, sure." She detached the car key and handed it to him. "Sorry, should have thought of that." More people were pouring out of the elevators now, including techs and another pair of security guys.

"Wow," the other guard said, peering at the headrest. He pointed at the passenger-side headrest, set equal with the driver's side. A large hole showed the path of the bullet from one headrest to the next.

"Long-range rifle," the older guard asserted. "You said kill shot. I think you were right." He cocked his head. "No offense, but how the hell did they miss you?"

Ana braced her knees, which had begun to knock again. "Window jammed. I leaned forward and took my foot off the brake. Car rolled forward."

The man whistled. "Better thank your guardian angel for that one," he muttered.

"Believe me, I will," she said. "Thanks for handling this." She gave him her floor, department, codes, and numbers. It took another twenty minutes for the techs to finish asking questions, but once they had her info, they passed her to go to her office. She was so grateful, she could've kissed them.

"Thanks again, guys," she said, getting her things and calling the elevator.

"Welcome," one tech said, watching her as she turned away.

She'd blanked out the mutters and discussion of the other people in the garage, as they were debriefed—a quick process since they didn't know anything—but she was glad none of them were left to ride up with her. All she wanted was to get to her desk, put her head down for a moment. Maybe let the shaking pass. If it would.

The elevator moved like molasses, as it climbed to the fifth floor.

"Please hurry," she implored, feeling the tears of reaction threatening to burst through the dam she'd built as she answered questions and given her statement. "C'mon, c'mon." Maybe she should go to the bathroom first. No way she wanted Pretzky or worse yet, that slimeball Davis, to see her crying. *"Come ON."*

Unfortunately, the doors opened on chaos.

"Burton!" Pretzky shouted her name, before Ana could take in the scene. "Get over here. You're a computer whiz, figure out what the hell's going on here, damn it."

Ana took a staggering step off the elevator, feeling like her head was going to explode. Shot at, then this, with no time to recover? What the hell had she opened up with this case?

"What's wrong with you, woman?" Pretzky demanded as she grabbed Ana's arm and dragged her to a terminal. "Look at this. What the hell?"

Data scrolled over the screen in random patterns. File boxes would appear, then blip out and reappear.

"Shit, we're being hacked. Why hasn't the IT department shut it down?" Ana cursed. Greek and Italian expletives mixed with English as she dropped everything and started pounding the keys.

"Call IT, Pretzky. Shut us down, *now.*" When the woman hesitated, she shouted, "NOW or all our data could be compromised!"

"I'm on with them," Pearson appeared at her elbow as she entered command after command, trying to block access to files as best she could. She was making some headway, but IT's own blocks were hampering her efforts. Their fixes blocked her from doing anything as well. "IT says they're shutting us down as fast as they can. They said for you to keep . . ." She stopped, listening to someone on the phone. "They're cutting it . . . now."

The screens all over the office went dark. The hot hum of conversation stopped, and the three women, Ana, Pearson, and Pretzky, stood in a ring of watching, silent agents.

"Yeah," Pearson said into the phone. "Thanks. I'll tell them. Yeah. Bye."

"Well?" Pretzky demanded.

"IT says they have it isolated and are tracing it back. No data lost, but it was a close call. It was only our files, our floor." After dropping that bomb, Pearson turned to Ana. "The guy in IT, Monroe, said to tell you thanks for the blocks you threw up."

Ana nodded, then staggered. She felt the wave of faintness slide over her, and she slid into a chair.

"Oh, God," she mumbled, dropping her head down again, between her knees. *Oh, God, please don't let me faint now. Not here. Not in front of everyone.*

"What the hell?" Pretzky was at her side in two strides. "What's wrong? Pearson?"

"No idea," Pearson murmured, bracketing Ana, resting a supportive hand on her shoulder.

"Got shot at coming into the garage." Ana managed to get the words out from between chattering teeth. "Just now, coming back from my meeting. Security's got my car." She added the inane detail for lack of anything else to say. "That's where I've been. In the garage, giving a report."

"Shot at?" Pretzky got shrill now. The computer issue was set aside. Obviously hacking was a pisser, but news of one of her agents being shot at seemed to insult her to her core. "Who? When? Where?"

The three W's. Ana realized the random amusement was a form of hysteria, and she locked it down.

"Sorry," she said, her voice still shaky as she eased up to a sitting position. Pearson kept a bracing hand on her shoulder, and Ana couldn't believe how much it helped. "It uh . . . hit me," she began, wanting desperately to weep, to scream out her fear.

"You're hit?" Pretzky crouched down. "Where?"

"No, no. I'm okay. I mean the reaction. It hit me, just as I came off the elevator. I was gonna go sit down, have a private moment to get the shakes out of my system."

Now she was the center of attention. For the first time, she saw camaraderie and concern on the faces of her colleagues. Evidently, no matter what she'd done in Rome, they would close ranks when anyone outside the organization took pot shots at one of their own.

Somehow, it was reassuring. Ana straightened her spine and managed a smile. "First time, getting shot at," she said, not meeting anyone's eyes. "Gotta say, it pretty much sucks."

That got a few laughs, and some conversations broke out. "They comin' up to debrief you?"

She nodded. "I guess someone will. Got the short version over with in the garage. Not much to debrief. I was key-coding into the garage. If my window hadn't jammed, I'd be in a body bag."

"That's enough." Pretzky cut her off. "Everyone get back to work, now." She rested a hand on Ana's other shoulder, gave the faintest squeeze. "Let her tell it to IAD first."

Internal affairs. Yep. They'd be right along. Ana sighed. Great. More questions.

About then, her mind started working again, revolving back to what she'd been wondering when the IT systems alerted. Her brain might be on slow mode, but her mind was now full of questions.

Shit, shit, shit. What had she gotten into? Was it Rome? Was it the fraud case? Was it merely visiting with Gianikopolis? SHIT.

"And like clockwork," Pearson muttered, as the elevator dinged and three agents stepped off. Two of them hesitated, scanning the room, obviously noting the dark monitors, the grouping around Ana.

"Special Agent," they both acknowledged Pretzky. "We need to talk to Agent Burton."

"Of course. You'll note, all of our computers are dark, Agents. We just had an attempt to breach our computer security, just about the time Agent Burton was shot at."

"Noted," the darker agent said. "I'm Keyes." He held his hand out, and Pretzky shook it with obvious reluctance. No one liked IAD, even though they were necessary.

"Charles," the other agent said, but didn't offer a hand. "Conference room?"

Everyone turned to the third agent, who was nervously tapping a pen on the top of a cubicle wall. "Oh," he said, when he realized everyone was waiting for him to identify himself. "I'm Perkins, from IT. I heard there was a problem, and headed up, but," he looked around. "Seems like they shut you down all the way."

"They did," Pretzky stated. "You need anything else?"

Perkins managed a nervous negative bob of his head. "Uh,

guess not. No. I'll just be going." He pointed at the elevators and, as fast as he could, got in a waiting car and left. Everyone sat in silence for a heartbeat. Ana wondered what the hell the guy had wanted, or thought he could do. She rubbed the back of her neck, wishing she had some Advil. Her head was pounding, and her muscles were as tight as a drum.

"Well, if that's all on IT," Pretzky broke the silence. "Let's get the debrief over with. This way." Pretzky pointed them all toward the small glassed-in conference room. "Agent?" she waited as Ana gathered her things, then motioned her forward as well. "I'll sit in."

"There's no need—" IAD Agent Charles began, but Pretzky cut her off.

"Yes. There is. If there's an issue here, the buck stops with me."

To her surprise, Pretzky stayed for the entire interview. Ana laid out her movements over the last seventy-two hours, going back a bit to include the trip to the gallery. She didn't mention she'd used an alias, but that would only mean a wrist slap if it came out later. Pretzky didn't mention it either, so she figured it wasn't a major problem.

"This case you're on, the cold one," IAD Agent Keyes asked, watching her closely, "do you think it's the cause of this incident?"

"As I've already said," Ana clenched her teeth, desperately holding onto a level tone, "I don't know. It could be something from the incident in Rome. It could be something from this cold case. I've been making calls and contacting victims for nearly two weeks. It could be something connected with Mr. Gianikopolis. He's known to have a number of enemies, according to his security people. I was there to interview him, and did so. It could also be from my contact with any one of these high-profile, highly sensitive individuals. Have to say, though, that I haven't had any issues on Rome and nothing like this has come up until I pulled this case."

"You're an analyst," Charles interjected. "Trained to assess these kinds of events."

She didn't look at anyone but Keyes, focused on him. "I can't speculate on which case this incident is related to without more data about the weapon, the triangulation of the shot, and anything recovered from the round. As to the forensics of the computer hacking it's remotely possible the two things are related. Then again, they may be coincidental. I'm not privy to what other people in my department are working on. Something from one of their cases may have triggered it rather than anything I'm doing."

She managed not to shudder at the thought of the bullet, but addressed that one too. "As to the shot, I may not be the target. In fact, I'm probably not. I'm not working on anything volatile, to my knowledge. Besides, five other agents drive the same make, general color, and model car I do. Two drive the same model year." She actually relaxed a bit as she said that, realizing the attempted hit could have been a mistake. A shot meant for someone else.

Of course that meant someone else was in danger, but it was a relief to think she wasn't a target.

Pretzky shifted positions so that Ana could see her without turning. The faintest of smiles twitched her lips, and one eyelid closed in a subtle wink.

She cloaked her surprise with a cough, took a sip of Mountain Dew from the cup at her elbow. Pearson had brought it in. Another surprise. Apparently, the ladies of the fifth floor were closing ranks for her.

"Thank you, Agent Burton," Agent Charles said after the silence had drawn out to irritating proportions. "We'll follow up with you when and if we need additional data, or have data to give you. Let us know if you receive any communiqués, contacts." Charles stopped, smiled briefly. "You know the drill."

"Yes, I do. And yes, I will." She stood and shook hands with both agents and remained standing until the door whispered shut behind them.

"Sit down before you fall down," Pretzky ordered. "You eat yet?"

"Yeah," Ana managed to reply before she put her head on the table. "I'm just whipped. Like I said. Never been shot at before. Pretty much sucks to be grilled on top of it too. Hate that part."

"Yeah, me too," Pretzky admitted, spinning the blinds open so the curious could see Ana was okay. Pearson was hovering at the door. "Yeah?" Pretzky opened the door enough to ask the question.

"I know it's a bitch, but IT wants to come up, when you're ready. Want to talk to both of you, and me."

Pretzky frowned. "Send 'em in. Tell Davis I said to get some drinks for everyone," Pretzky said with a malicious grin. "He can take the orders when everyone gets here."

Pearson's grin was equally feral. "Sure thing, boss."

"She'll enjoy that," Pretzky said, not looking at Ana. "I will too, come to think of it."

Ana was too tired to censor the laugh that snorted out, or the weary comment. "Davis is a pus-ball."

Pretzky snickered. There was no other way to describe the sound. "Yeah. Perfect description."

She didn't move from her spot at the conference room window, but Pretzky added, in a more serious tone, "Here they come. You up for this, Burton?"

"Yeah. I'm good." She wasn't, of course. Far from it. Her brain felt like mush. Her thoughts were running like gerbils on a wheel, and the gerbils were on crack, running like there was a world record at stake.

"Right. Suck it up. Here we go," Pretzky muttered. "Agents, you know Agent Burton. Thanks, Pearson," she said and nodded her approval to the woman who settled drinks and cups on the table. "Lay it out for us, Monroe," she snapped. "What the hell happened, and how did anyone get around our security?"

With Pretzky on the attack, Ana let the conversation—mostly deflection of responsibility and rants about budget—

flow around her. One comment finally caught her attention, and she spoke up.

"I caught five ISPs," she interjected. Monroe, the IT guy, had said he only caught three.

"Five?" Monroe leaned forward, ass-covering forgotten in his interest in a geek problem. "How'd you see five? What were they? Here." He shoved paper toward her with numbers scrawled on it. "Those were the ones I caught before they self-erased. What'd you get?"

Ana closed her eyes and pictured the screens flashing in front of her mind's eye. "This one, and this one, I saw. This one I didn't. Here's the other three I saw. She neatly printed the series of numbers on the sheet under his scratchings.

"Six then. Damn. That's a hell of a hacker. Outside the US too," he said, and Ana nodded.

"What? Where?" Pretzky demanded, yanking the page around to look at it, as if she could determine that from the numbers.

"See this?" Monroe was all eager-teacher now. "This prefix? Yeah. That's Belgium, Antwerp maybe, or close. This one's somewhere in, uh . . ." He paused thinking.

"Turkey. Probably around Izmir, on the coast," Ana said, recognizing the prefix. Monroe looked impressed.

"Cool. So, yeah, Turkey," he continued, getting more excited. "This one here is in Canada. That's probably a bounce though. Most of the Canadian signatures are bounces 'cause not a lot of bad guys in Canada. Too cold, I guess," he joked, snickering at whatever made that funny for him. He finally noticed they weren't laughing and said, "Yeah, well, here, this one, that's somewhere in the Balkans. We caught those a lot back when the US was active there, so I recognize it."

"What about the other two?" Pretzky demanded.

"Don't know," Monroe admitted immediately.

Everyone looked at Ana. "I don't recognize either of them. Monroe can track them though." She put the ball squarely back in his court.

"Oh, yeah, yeah, I can track them. But six. Wow. That's righteous."

The other IT agent, silent up to this point, finally spoke. "I think one of those is Georgia, the country, not the state."

"Russia?" Pretzky and Ana said together.

Chapter Eight

"Um, yeah, former Soviet state? Independent now," the man said.

"Agent . . ." Pretzky waited for the IT guy to fill in his name. Monroe shot an elbow into his side.

"Oh, uh, Talmadge, sir. I mean ma'am."

"Special Agent Pretzky," Monroe hissed.

Talmadge blushed. "Um, sorry. New," he muttered as if that explained everything.

"Yeah, he took Wade's place. You know, guy that went to Cisco, big bucks."

Pretzky looked irritated. "No, I hadn't heard, but it has no bearing at the moment." She paused for a moment. "Who's Perkins, by the way? He was up here before you came."

Monroe looked confused, then irritated. "Oh, him. He's a programmer. Don't know why he came up. He might have thought he could help, I guess."

"It doesn't matter, then." Pretzky focused on the other man. "Well, Agent Talmadge, why do you say it's Georgia?" Pretzky demanded, and the habitual foot-tapping began. Ana wanted to roll her eyes, but it just took too much energy. She felt like she'd been run over.

"Um, it's got this series here?" he indicated the middle set of numbers. "That's usually um, one of the groups that operates in Georgia. They don't have their own satellite? So, um, they bounce off a particular one all the time. Kinda stupid, really."

Monroe made as if to elbow him again, but Ana sat forward, because she'd decided it was better to cut these guys some slack. She needed them. "They're probably all bounces though, Special Agent Pretzky." She used Pretzky's formal title in front of the geeks. "Anyone who's competent enough to hack us, *just* us and not the whole database? They're not going to be pinpointed by their ISP or satellite. Right, gentlemen?"

She directed the question to Monroe and Talmadge, wanting everyone to stop gawking at her. She just wanted to go home. Now.

She wanted to forget that someone had tried to put a bullet in her head. A cold feeling of dread crept over her again, and she could feel panic rising up to shake her.

"Burton? You okay?" Pretzky's sharp inquiry cut into her funk.

"Yeah, sure. I'm okay," Ana said. "Just freakin' a bit over getting shot at. Sorry."

"Shot at?" Monroe squeaked. Talmadge looked appalled.

"Agent Burton was coming up to be debriefed about an incident that occurred as she pulled into the garage when she walked into this, this . . ." Pretzky stopped. Took a breath, and finally added, "SNAFU."

Talmadge looked puzzled, so Monroe whispered, "I'll explain later. But it's a mess."

Talmadge nodded, but looked at Ana with respect verging on awe. "Serious, dude. Glad you're okay."

"Thanks." Ana had to laugh at the simple sentiment. Somehow it was just the tonic to the incipient panic. "Me too."

"Wow, into the breach, right?" Monroe was more the squirrelly, tell-me-the-details type, obviously. She could tell he was busting to ask. He flicked a glance at the frowning Pretzky, and instead said, "So you have a photographic memory? You got those ISPs."

Ana nodded. "Pretty much. I've seen one of them before, the Turkish one, so I recognized the source code."

"Source code?" Pretzky looked puzzled. "Part of that's a source code?"

Monroe was back to teacher mode. "Yeah, see the middle section here? Yeah, that's kinda like a country code, like we said. Satellite code. Pretty distinct. But this hacker bounced it probably, like Agent Burton said. You set up this pattern thing, beforehand, and then it takes your real ISP—computer identity code, you know?—and hides it behind all these others. Pretty cool."

"Cool aside," Pretzky's stern look repressed even Monroe's enthusiasm. "Can you track it?"

"Probably not." Talmadge was the bucket of cold water on a growing spark. "Guy who did this? Real good. Sneaky. Trackin' it would mean lots of man-hours for probably nuthin' much. Hard to justify, right?"

Pretzky's sour grimace said it all. "Right. See if you can get anything, but don't spend more than twenty man-hours on it or the director will have my ass."

"Got it." Talmadge's reply was snappy, succinct.

"We'll patch the hole though, for sure," Monroe said, shooting a look at Talmadge. "That's first priority. Gotta get you back up, right?"

"Immediately, but safely."

"Right-o." Monroe jumped up. Ana got the impression he didn't sit still much. "Thanks for the soda," he said, grabbing two more as he scooted toward the door. Talmadge just nodded and followed.

"Mutt and Jeff?" Pretzky muttered as the two men left.

"More like Phineas and Ferb." Pearson, heretofore silent, muttered the rejoinder.

"Who?"

Pearson looked embarrassed. "Kid show on Disney. Two

brothers who build wild stuff all the time, get their sister in trouble. Uh, they're like that. Geeks. One talks, the other doesn't say much."

"Got it," Pretzky snapped. "So, ideas, next steps?"

"I'll boot up my personal, hook into the Wi-Fi. Check out the Net. Call in some favors if I need to," Ana said.

"Keep IAD in the loop, Burton. They want to be apprised of everything going down. They don't like agents getting shot at under the watchful eye of our own security cameras. And if you got dead it would really piss them off." She paced toward the wall, pivoted. "Pearson, you have your personal laptop with you too?"

Pearson nodded, crossed her arms. Ana hadn't known it was frowned upon to have your personal in the office until she'd been in two weeks and brought her computer every day. Pearson had obviously bucked the stricture too.

"Got Wi-Fi?"

"Yeah, I do, standard-issue three-G remote Wi-Fi device. What do you need?"

"Backup. Come to my office please and pull up whatever server and e-mail you use. We'll need to keep working. God," she groaned. "This is going to take hours to sort out, and I didn't have time for this shit. I've got five reports due tomorrow."

For the first time, Ana saw Pretzky as a person. A worker with a job, with reports, with someone she had to answer to. It was enlightening.

"Okay, let's move, Agents. Burton, you want to head out, or stay here?"

"Stay here, I guess. I don't have a car at the moment," she said, shrugging off the immediate offers of a cab or help. "Really, I'd rather try to work. Do like IAD said, go through my communications over the last week and see if there was any warning of this. Anything."

"You got any ideas right off the top?" Pearson asked, shooting her a speculative glance as they walked out of the conference room.

"Not a one. Wish to hell I did."

The three women moved through the office, and all conversations ceased. Agents rolled out of their cubicles, away from their desks, to look at Pretzky, judge her mood.

"Davis, thanks for getting coffee and sodas," Pretzky snapped. "Caldwell," she barked at another agent. "Order in some lunch. The office will cover it, so get a list and call it in. Everyone, list files you need so IT can focus on getting you access for anything you've got heating up. They're cleaning things, making sure they've locked whatever door that hacker came through." She took a breath, rubbed the bridge of her nose. "Also, I need all of you to go through anything you're working on. Make a list of hot spots that might have precipitated today's event. I want those lists by COB. The tech geeks need a place to start in backtracking this hacker, so if you're the key, we need to know it. All of this is gonna take time none of us has, so just suck it up and get it done."

There was some muttering, but it quieted when Pretzky continued to stand there, obviously not finished. "Last thing—" She took a breath, let it whoosh out. "When you leave today, be careful and watch your backs. Agent Burton was fired upon as she entered the garage. It may be personal, but then again it may not. There are enough crazies out there who hate our guts because we work for the Agency. Random isn't out of the question, so stay sharp."

Everyone gave assent, shooting her a respectful nod or glance. Caldwell hustled over with a pen and paper. "Stile's Deli okay with you?"

"Sure. Reuben. Chicken soup. Brownie. Pepsi." Pretzky's lunch order was as clipped as the rest of her delivery.

"Got it. Agent Burton?" Ana and Pearson gave their orders. Caldwell moved to other people, which gave them all a chance to more naturally disperse to work.

"Huh," Ana muttered, deciding Pretzky was smarter than she let on. Getting everyone involved in lunch or listing files took their minds off Ana, off the hacking. Focused them on something they could do, that they needed—lunch—and distracted the attention they'd all been focusing on Ana.

"What?" Pearson said without looking at her.

"Pretzky. Lunch was a good ploy."

Pearson laughed. "Caught that? I didn't until about the third time she'd done it. Productivity in her unit's about the highest in the building. She brings that up every time someone gets pissy about the deli. She knows how to keep the drones at work."

"I guess." Ana was trying to figure out how to say something to Pearson, but the words were difficult. "Pearson . . ."

"I know. Forget it. We gotta cover each other, you know?"

Relieved, Ana nodded. "Yeah. Thanks."

"Don't mention it." She grinned. "Seriously."

"Right. Enjoy hanging with Pretzky." Ana felt just comfortable enough to tease.

"Bite me, Burton." Pearson grinned as she said it, disappearing around the cubicle wall to retrieve her gear.

For her part, Ana dumped her bag on the desk and slumped into the chair. She hadn't even had time to unload her notes and files before her cell rang. She frowned over the number, one she didn't recognize.

"Hello?" Damn it, her voice was shaky.

"Ana? It's Gates. I wanted to—" He paused. "Are you okay?"

"Fine," she lied. "I'm fine. How'd you get this number?"

He laughed. "Do you really want to know?"

Shaking her head, since the technology to strip the number on her cell was illegal, she declined. "No, really, I don't."

"That was better. You sounded better when you laughed. Did something happen?"

"Why would you think that?"

"Agent Burton." Gates switched to the more formal. "I may not know you well, but the woman who . . . chatted . . . with me on Friday night and traded barbs with my boss this morning doesn't answer the phone the way you did just now." Someone must be listening for him to be so cagey, but it warmed her that he mentioned their call.

Ana sighed. She hated showing any weakness, but she'd already decided to call Gates, tell him about the incident in case it was connected to her meeting with Dav.

"Well, *Mister* Bromley." Ana returned the favor of formality. "My car was targeted as I returned to the building, and our computers were hit by a hacker at exactly the same time. Think it might have anything to do with my visit this morning?"

"Targeted?" Gates latched onto the word. "What do you mean?"

Ana's gut clenched at the sharp worry in his voice. "Someone took a shot at me."

"Damn it!" He cursed viciously. "Where? Any details? Wait," he snapped before she could answer the first questions. "You got hacked too? Man, what a sucky day for you."

"Yes to all of the above." Admitting it made her feel a hundred years old. She could feel tears threatening again at the warmth of his sympathy. "I barely wrapped my mind around the shot when I walked into the hacking situation. It's been a hell of an afternoon."

"Tell me about it," he said. His velvety voice was warm and reassuring, which, if she'd been sharper, would probably have set off alarm bells. Or, her reaction to it would have, at least. As hot as he was, her reaction to him was out of proportion. She wanted to worry about it, but she was too tired. Instead, just for now, she simply appreciated it. "I'm sorry, Ana. How about a meal and a glass of wine?"

That did set off alarm bells. "Beg pardon?"

He laughed in that velvet voice, and once again, she could almost feel the sensuous sweep of his hand at her back, the whisper of his breath on her skin. "Just dinner, Ana. I'd like to get the details of your misadventure. The fact that you were . . . what did you call it? Targeted. Yes. Interesting terminology. The fact that you were targeted after you left here is a huge concern for me. On the hacking, were they aiming for your files, do you know? Or was it a random attack?"

"We don't know yet." Ana let her head fall back onto the high-backed office chair. "No rhyme or reason to either. Or both. Not yet. There are enough issues that I'm embroiled in to keep IAD busy checking leads for a week."

"They're already on it?" He sounded surprised.

"Yeah, because it's me. I've been in some trouble. That's why I'm on cold cases," she admitted. "But, on the shot and the hack, it may not be me. Like I told IAD, there are a lot of people who drive a vehicle like mine. Any one of them could be the target. The hack? There are fifteen other agents working cases in this division, most of them active, unlike what I'm doing." She closed her eyes, wishing she knew more, felt less. "Any one of their cases could have triggered the hack."

"Hmmm. I'm not hearing a lot of conviction in your voice about those options." He let silence fall between them for a moment. Then he used his sexy voice at its most persuasive. "I think it sounds like dinner's just the thing you need. Want me to pick you up at the building, or at home?"

"I'm sorry, what?" Had she agreed to dinner? She didn't remember agreeing.

"Dinner. A meal. A discussion. You did your homework, Ana," he said. "You know what my specialty is. If you have any more info on the hack, I may be able to help. We can also run some probabilities between us, as to whether the *targeting* is related to Dav."

"I'm not sure it's a good idea, Gates," she prevaricated. Part of her really wanted someone—no, scratch that; not just anyone, Gates—to take her to dinner, make sure she got home. She wasn't sure she could trust herself to drive anyway.

Her car. Crap, she wasn't going home in her own car tonight. They wouldn't be done with it yet. Plus, she'd have to get the window fixed, report it to insurance.

"Ana? If you don't want to run probabilities, that's okay. In fact, we probably shouldn't. We can pretend it's Friday," he said, referencing the date they'd already made. "Just let me take you to dinner, make something in your day go right."

How could she refuse? "A lot went right today. The meeting with you and Dav. That was good. I enjoyed it." She had to admit that. It was true.

"Did you, now?" He sounded pleased, a bit smug. "Just because of all that lovely data, right? You can tell me, I know about this data stuff."

"Oh, you do, do you?" She nearly giggled at his teasing. Of course, that was probably incipient hysteria. "Like I'd share my secrets with you."

"Afraid I'm better than you? I can take you, Agent. Bet ya'."

"No, I'm not afraid," she said, just a little stung. She was afraid. A bit. Not so much of his computer prowess, but he was a magnetic, powerful personality. He affected her in equally powerful ways.

Not what she needed right now.

Maybe never. She wasn't sure she'd ever be able to handle that kind of intensity turned her way. It was business now, even with the teasing. What if it turned personal? Hell, it was already personal; he'd nearly kissed her. She got the shivers, the so-bad-it's-good kind, every time she heard his voice. She had to keep her cool, her distance from Gates. He was trouble in all kinds of ways.

"Then it's settled. I'll pick you up in three hours, there at the building. We'll go someplace for a nice quiet meal, and then I'll get you home. I'm sure they've arranged for protection for you, yes?" His cadence was enough like his boss's that it surprised her, coming as it did in his crisp New England accent.

"I'm sure they have or will, yes. Which means they'll know you and I had dinner."

"I'm not worried, are you? It's a working dinner, Agent Burton." His voice was a low rumble of humor. "I have some additional information for you, of course. So, since I'm going to be in the city, and you are in the city, we'll have a dinner meeting." He laid out the logical explanation without batting an eye.

"Practice that line much?" she drawled, finding a bit of her old spark. It helped that she enjoyed the sarcasm as a change from the edgy panic that was a constant companion.

"Absolutely every chance I get," he popped back, and she laughed.

"In that case, Mr. Bromley, I accept. I'll bring my case notes, and we'll compare . . . techniques."

"We'll see to that, Agent," came the brisk reply. "Excuse me a moment." He moved the phone away so that she couldn't catch what he said to whoever had interrupted. She wouldn't want the tone she could hear used on her, however. Remembering his discussion with Dav's nephew when she visited the estate, she decided it didn't take much to push his bullshit meter into the red zone. After a brief pause where she could hear nothing, no voices, he came back to the phone. "So, Agent," he said, in that melted-chocolate tone, "I'll look forward to seeing you in three hours."

"Gates," she began, suddenly unsure.

"Yes, Ana, I know. See you in a bit."

And he was gone. Just like that. Revved her up and left her hanging.

Wait. What did he know? Had he realized she was wavering, thinking of backing out?

"Damn it," she cursed softly, not wanting anyone to hear her frustration. Then again, most of them were still placing their lunch orders.

No sooner had the thought formed than Caldwell popped into view. "Hey, Burton. Since lunch is on the boss, you gonna eat something besides a salad for once?"

"I don't always eat salads," she protested, surprised he'd noticed.

"Sure you do. Nearly every day. Hey, I'm an operative, I notice these things." He lowered his voice in mock severity. "I notice everything." He wiggled his eyebrows in a comic parody of a leer. “So, now, I’ve got your order, we’ll get some good fattening grub into you so you can work.”

“Uh, about that. Change it to just fries and a drink, will you? In all the craziness, I forgot I’d had lunch. Now I’ve got a dinner meeting,” she said, absently. What did Gates know about her?

“Ooooh, dinner meeting,” he teased. Someone called his name, and he shifted into a more serious mode. “Coke and fries, got it,” he scribbled the order down. “Hey, you should let the boss know you’re going walkabout, though. With a mark out,” he used the shorthand for marksman, “you need eyes on you.”

“I was just going to tell her. Thanks though,” she said, smiling at him.

“Sure. No worries. Hey, fries in and dinner out. We’ll get some meat on those skinny bones yet.”

“Yeah, yeah, yeah,” she pretended to grouse at him. “Get out of here.”

He scooted away, laughing. Reluctantly, Ana picked up the desk phone and buzzed Pretzky.

“Yes. I will check in with the security detail,” Ana assured her. “Yes, I’m sure San Francisco’s finest will be up to the task. Dinner. Yes. A meeting. Well, he’s outside the city. Yes. Coming in for another meeting, wanted to follow up . . .” Ana sighed and decided to see if playing a trump card would help. “I’m going for one reason, Special Agent. Mr. Bromley mentioned a Russian connection related to the old art-fraud case. I want to interview him about that without being too obvious. If there’s a connection between my visit to Mr. Gianikopolis and our computer security breach this morning, especially a Russian connection—yes, Georgian—I want to root it out.”

By the time Pretzky was done with her, the Coke was on her desk along with the steaming fries. Caldwell had dropped them off with an amused expression for her trials with the boss.

Fitting into the office had only taken the expedient of getting shot at. Evidently, for this crew, it made you one of the team.

It took her most of the Coke and another promise to check back with the office when she got home before she got off the phone.

When she pivoted to her left, she saw that Pearson was standing at her cubicle entrance.

"Computers are back up on safe mode," Pearson began without preamble. "Also, wanted to say thanks. Your bomb about dinner got me out of Pretzky's office. I had shit to do, so . . . appreciate it," she said with a grin. "Hot date."

"Hope you make it," Ana said, checking her watch.

"Nah, no worries. My kid's with his grandma for a few more days. She took him to Disney. Even if I'd had to put the date off till tomorrow, I'd be okay."

"How old's your kid?"

"Seven. He's great." Pearson was about to say more when Ana's phone rang. "Go on and get that. See ya tomorrow."

"Yeah, thanks," Ana said, picking up the phone. She'd been in the office almost four months, and this was the first she'd heard about Pearson having a kid. It explained the Disney comment though. "This is Burton."

"Back off."

Two words and the line went dead.

Jurgens called him at eight on the office line in his home office. Jurgens was the only one who had it.

"Problem?"

"Ja. Perkins fucked up. The computers were compromised. He threatened her, called from a pay phone." Annoyance surged in Jurgens's voice, an unusual occurrence. "That phone is compromised. It's outside the Agency. They monitor it. They will be talking to him shortly."

Closing his eyes, he sighed. What the hell had made him

pick Perkins? What an idiot. Well, flawed tools pretty much guaranteed a flawed job. "Repercussions?"

"Ja. Issues. We will need to monitor them. A messenger will drop something later."

"Good. That job we discussed, let's see to that. I'll call Perkins."

"Now? He's alone, at home."

He sighed. He needed to finish a proposal for the county. It was due at noon the next day. Well, sometimes you just had to make time for these things. "Yes. Give me a moment to get a disposable. I'll call him. You can act then."

"Ja."

They clicked off, and he opened the bottom drawer to get a GoPhone from the desk drawer. He needed to procure some untraceables soon. He hated to be that obvious; it was much safer to skirt the law than break it outright.

He pocketed the unit and strode into the kitchen. His wife was clearing away the dishes and making a snack for their son's preschool the next day.

He kissed her cheek. "I'm going to run over to Staples real quick. I don't want to run out of ink for the printer at two a.m. if it takes me that long to finish this bloody proposal."

She frowned for a moment. "But I thought—" she began, and he remembered that she'd bought ink cartridges at Costco. Ever thrifty, his Caroline.

"Color. You got the black and white, so that's good. I've got charts and graphs. You know."

Her face cleared, and she smiled. "You worry too much, honey. But okay. Take it easy out there, it's raining."

"Will do," he said, closing the door behind him.

He dialed as he drove to the Staples. It wouldn't do to come home without the ink now.

"What?" Perkins answered the phone, his voice shaking. "I didn't call you."

"Idiot," he stated calmly. "In this case, you should have. What the hell happened?"

"Nothing happened," Perkins lied. "Nothing."

"Perkins, don't be an ass. Would I be calling if nothing happened?"

"It was a fluke," he began, protesting his competence. "The computer virus should have just corrupted her files. I didn't know she'd been shot at, I didn't know anyone had a hit on her. How could I know? That wasn't me, the shot. I just diddled the files, trying to get her off the scent."

There was a small popping sound through the phone, and he heard the thump of the other man's body collapsing onto some hard surface. He quickly held the phone away from his ear as Perkins's phone clattered to the floor.

He smiled, relieved. At least Jurgens could be counted on.

Right.

Now to find someone competent to monitor the situation. Perkins was a terrible liar, but he had truly been concerned enough about the new searches to act rashly. The idiot. Now what might have passed off as a cursory review would be amped up to a full-scale check. Perkins's death might or might not be a factor, but either way, Perkins had put the operation in jeopardy and he never allowed that.

Problem number two, though, was the shot. Had his rival on the East Coast gotten wind of the investigation as well? If he'd stepped back into this to muddle the works again . . .

There was a faint rattle of sound from the phone, and he put his ear back to the receiver.

"Well?" he demanded.

"Done and done," Jurgens said with satisfaction. "Last deposit?"

"In thirty-five minutes, same Swiss account. You'll transfer the money out by morning this time, understood? And dispose of the phone."

"Ja."

"One more thing." There was a waiting silence, so he continued. "Perkins mentioned a shot at the woman. Were you aware of it? Oh, and any suggestions on a new monitor for the situation?"

"It is possible." Another silence. "A second messenger will come."

"Good."

The line went dead, and he walked into Staples to get ink.

Chapter Nine

"We'll trace the call, but it probably won't register." The internal security geek qualified his answer. "Too short."

"Thanks." Ana hung up, and went to report the latest to the boss. She had to call McGuire and Hines before she headed out as well. If she'd stirred this much insanity up by making phone calls, she needed to warn them as well.

She didn't want to tell her boss about the call, but if she let it wait till tomorrow, Pretzky would fry her ass.

"Back off what?" Pretzky mulled. Ana was pretty sure it was a rhetorical question, so she kept quiet. "I'm thinking this isn't about Rome, Burton. How 'bout you?"

Reluctantly, Ana agreed. "There are ways it might be, but they're a stretch," she finally said. "And the first closed case I finished here is just that, closed."

"Yeah, with that perp dead, that isn't a bone to pick." Pretzky paced back and forth in the small office. "Your dinner date cancel?" she said, turning suddenly to face Ana.

"Uh, no." Ana checked her watch. "He'll be here in about twenty minutes. He'll pick me up downstairs. On the call though, I wanted to be sure and follow procedure, let you know."

"Good, good," Pretzky muttered. She shot Ana a sharp

look. "You've had a shitty ride, haven't you, Burton? Pretty shitty day too."

Ana wanted to cry. Instead, she managed a laugh. It was watery, and weak, but it was a laugh. "Yeah, that's an understatement though."

Pretzky nodded. "When one of us screws up, it's bad. May seem like a little thing, but you and I both know those little things have a way of turning into one damn all mess. Been there, done that. Go finish up, and get out of here. Ring me here when you get in tonight." She handed Ana a card. Neatly printed on the back was a telephone number. Ana looked up at her.

"That's my personal cell. I want to know you're in and okay."

"Thanks. Will do." Ana kept her voice clear and sharp, even though the gesture made her want to crumble into a heap of quivering goo. Personal gestures, closeness, had that effect these days, no matter how hard she worked to shut them out, keep them at bay.

Or maybe it was just this day.

"Don't mention it."

"I—" Ana began. Pretzky forestalled her.

"Seriously. Don't mention it. I got a hard rep to maintain." She kept her expression bland, but her eyes twinkled.

"Got it. Good night."

"Uh-huh." Pretzky was already on the other side of the desk, reaching for a folder.

At her desk, Ana looked at the card. It was the number, nothing more, but somehow it was like a mini-lifeline. A connection.

That alone made her want to weep again, a luxury she wouldn't—couldn't—allow. If she started, she might never stop. Straightening her spine, she cleared her throat and dialed McGuire first. He'd been the friendlier of the two agents who had originally worked on the case.

"That sucks," McGuire said bluntly, when she filled in the

details of her day. "Related to the case, you think?" Before she could agree or disagree, he was moving on. "You're gonna let Hines know too, right?"

"Yes, he's my next call. Or did you want to call him?" Ana asked, thinking the former partners might want to talk.

"Nah, you go ahead. Me'n Hines weren't close. Fact is, that case is the last one I worked before I retired. My partner got out couple of months before I did so I got paired with Hines. Still, he should know." Ana got the impression that McGuire didn't think much of his former partner even now. Then again, if they'd only worked the one case, and not solved that one, it probably grated on the retired agent.

"I'll let him know. Thanks again, McGuire."

"Good to be in the loop," he said, a dark tone infusing his voice. Ana wondered if that was a reference to Hines and if the other man had been one to keep the details to himself. They hung up, and Ana dialed the Oregon number for Hines.

"He's out of town," Hines's secretary told Ana when she asked for the Senior Special Agent. "He had business in Washington State today, he said." The woman offered to give Hines a message, or give her Hines's cell number. Ana took the number, and left a message for Hines to call. She wanted anyone connected with the old case to have a fair warning.

Her due diligence done, all Ana wanted to do was put her head on her desk and cry.

As predicted, Gates was waiting for her in the traffic circle in front of the building. When the guard called to let her know he was there, Ana struggled to pull herself together. Now, she wasn't sure why she'd agreed to meet him. She was playing with fire, and she'd sworn to give that up when she got burned in Rome.

She heaved a sigh, irritated with her own melodrama. It

was just dinner, and God knew, she could use the distraction from the trouble of the day. If she went straight home, which was her impulse, she'd just brood. Or cry. Or scream. None of that was productive, and dinner with Gates might be, so she went.

She kept her pace brisk and level as she came across the lobby, but it took every ounce of willpower she still possessed not to duck and cover on the way to the car. There was a misty rain falling as she came out the doors, and Gates's driver held an umbrella up to shelter her. With that kind of service, she was glad she'd approved him to come through security rather than meeting him on the street.

It was only five steps, and she was nearly a jelly-kneed weakling by the time she slid in beside Gates in the back of the town car and the driver closed the door behind her.

"Hello, Ana," he murmured, handing her a wineglass. As she took it, he leaned in and kissed her cheek, taking her completely by surprise.

"It is," he said, smiling.

"What?"

"Your cheek. It's as smooth as I remember it to be. Now, have some wine, relax, and tell me about your day." He paused for effect before adding, "Dear."

Surprised at his quick switch from sensuous to banter, she blinked. "O-o-okay." She caught up a split-second later and grinned. "Dear. Brought home the bacon. Fried it up in a pan. Got shot at, wigged out on the boss. You know, the usual."

"Nearly got fried, then got hacked." Still playing, he made a mock-derisive sound. "So little happening in your narrow world, Agent. You really should broaden your horizons."

"To international commerce, like you and Dav? No thank you," she joked. "It's just too dull. Although, you had shots fired too, so perhaps it isn't as mundane as everyone says."

He laughed. "There, you have the right of it. See, we have so much in common. Computers, getting shot at, mayhem, a love of good wine. So, let's relax and enjoy this lovely vintage on our way downtown. We'll get back to pandemonium and computer hacking over dinner, of course."

"You know, you really need to get more action if this is your idea of a date," she flipped back without thinking. Just banter, right?

Evidently not.

His fingers curled around hers, where they lay on the bowl of the wineglass. "Oh, I'm sure we could come up with some diversions if we put our minds to it," he said, leaning in to brush her cheek with another kiss. Using a fingertip, he turned her head. She let him. He brushed a feathery touch of his lips over that cheek as well. "This, for instance," he whispered as he took her mouth in a soft, probing kiss.

When she would have leaned in, taken more, he eased back. "But we wouldn't want to spill this excellent wine, would we? Especially since you were so adamant that this was just business."

She almost heard the sound of her jaw dropping at his dangerous, sexy play. She wasn't ready for it. She didn't know if she could handle it, not now, not tonight. Once upon a time, she would have been able to toss off the lines, make the right moves. Now, she was mired in emotion, jumbled by the whole day as well as her incipient reactions to Gates.

Since she couldn't manage a coherent thought in the face of such a blatant assault on her senses, she resorted to an age-old ploy. She drank the wine.

He smiled and drank as well, once he'd touched his glass to hers.

Still feeling half a beat behind, she registered the full-bodied taste of the wine, the rich pear and fruit scent of it. It was like drinking sunshine.

"Wow," she verbalized her surprise, staring at the wine-glass like she'd never seen it before. "That's fabulous."

"Thank you." His smile was smug now. "It is good, isn't it?"

She knew she was still being incredibly slow on the uptake, and replied, "It is. And so are you. I'm presuming you had something to do with this," she wiggled the glass, "since you look so pleased at my appreciation."

"Oh, yes, I did," he said, taking another sip, but giving nothing away.

"Hmmm. Smooth is a word that comes to mind." She sent him a challenging look.

"Ah, a good word. Another word I like is creamy, like your skin."

"Hmmm. Yes, but strong also applies, don't you think?" Surprising herself, she slipped into the groove of the banter. Oddly enough, it helped her feel more like herself, the real Ana.

"Oh, yes. This sort of thing, it's strong enough to go to your head if you're not prepared for it." He seemed to be talking about more than the wine as he let a fingertip caress her hand where it lay on the wineglass.

For some reason, the words and the touch hit a nerve. Memories and sorrows flooded into her heart. "Are you ever prepared?" she managed to say as her ghosts grabbed her by the throat. She'd held them at bay all day, but his kindness, his interest and banter, and his touch were her undoing.

He must have seen something of her devastation on her face, because he slipped the wineglass out of her hand and slipped it into a clip in the small table. "Ah, Ana, I'm sorry," he whispered. "Here, come here."

She couldn't move, couldn't close the distance between them. If she did . . . if she did, she might never recover. She had to maintain. Had to.

He gave her no choice. He came to her. His warmth enfolded her, his voice murmuring soft words she couldn't understand for the roaring of emotion in her mind. Everything crashed in.

Everything.

Rome. Her friends on their biers in the morgue, their bodies burned beyond recognition because they'd followed her directions, gone after the bomb. Her parents. Never seeing them again after the attack. Their funeral, the devastated hold her aunt had kept on Ana's shoulders. All the images and feelings tore through Ana like a scream, adding to her fear and panic over the afternoon's events.

Ana struggled to keep up the façade, to regain control. Then streetlights lit the car, outlined the driver and the headrests behind the smoky glass between the front and back of the car.

A bullet in the headrest; a threat by phone. It was too much. Ana lost it.

Vaguely through her shaking and the moan of pain that rolled out of her, she heard him instruct the driver to give them ten minutes' delay.

Ten minutes. How could she ever recover? Much less in ten minutes.

"There, now. Ana." When he called her name, it was a caress of a longtime lover, rather than a new flirtation. "Anastasia," he murmured. "Look at me."

She raised dry eyes to his with soul-deep reluctance. She expected pity. Maybe superiority. Instead she found an echo of her own pain.

"Let go," he said with soft insistence. "Feel it and let it go."

The command, the darkness of the car, like a cocoon where no one else could reach her, did what no amount of debriefing and counseling had been able to do.

She wept.

As the tears flowed, it was as if she thawed her soul. Everything within her seemed to take on new life, to stretch and open up to life like a napping child who's waking to a new afternoon.

The car continued to circle the neighborhoods as Ana brought herself under control. It hadn't been a long, drawn-out session, but the short burst of emotion, held in someone's sheltering arms was deeper and more meaningful than it ever would have been alone.

Gates presented her with a handkerchief, and she accepted

it gratefully, easing out of his embrace, trying unsuccessfully to regain her social distance. Lord, she knew she looked a mess. She didn't cry well. It was vain, but for the first time she regretted not carrying a makeup kit with her.

"I'm sorry," she said, her head bowed over the soft cloth as she wiped her eyes. Streaks of mascara made dark smudges on the snowy fabric. "I don't usually cry all over . . ." What the hell was he?

"Colleagues? Friends?" he suggested some terms. "Dates?"

"None of the above. Ever," she confessed, finally looking up. "I've never cried on anyone like that. I'm sorry. How do I look? Like a weeping, idiot female?"

"No, you look vulnerable," he said, his expression sympathetic. When he saw her reaction, he winced. "Ouch. That pissed you off, I see. Sorry, didn't mean to."

She shook her head. "No, don't worry, that's just one of those trigger words for me, like weak, or silly. I don't think of myself as any of those things and resent it if anyone else sees me that way."

"The key to pissing you off, now in my hot little hands." He grinned, encouraging her to laugh with him.

"Right," she drawled. "But I have your handkerchief, and I'm holding it for ransom until you agree never to call me vulnerable. Ever."

"Oh, man. Tough terms." He pretended to consider the ransom terms as he unclipped their wineglasses and handed hers over. "I'll have to think about it. I can't do that on an empty stomach." He stroked a finger on her cheek again. "I seem to be unable to keep my hands off you, and that's dangerous."

"Dangerous?" she stuttered, unsure what he meant. Was he still teasing, or was he serious?

"Very dangerous. A simple touch had you weeping in my arms," he made the blatantly false statement with a poker face. "Can't have that."

"Right," she managed to laugh. Somehow, his dry humor was

helping her recover her equilibrium. "You're a real button-pusher there, Gates Bromley. We women should beware."

"Exactly," he said, then asked, more seriously, "Do you think you could eat?"

"Yes." Her stomach protested the long wait with an audible growl. "Obviously."

"Good, me too." He tapped on the smoked-glass panel, and the driver smoothly changed lanes and made a turn. Before she could finish her wine, they were there.

"Wow, I'm feeling the impact of the day," she said, clipping the glass into its holder. "Between the crying jag and the wine, I'm not sure how steady I'm going to be." Much as she hated to admit it, she figured it was better to forewarn him rather than drop like a rock at his feet if she was overextended.

"Food then, first thing."

"Good." She glanced out the window, trying to figure out where they were. Nothing looked familiar, which bothered her.

She hated feeling out of control. Being vulnerable with Gates had given him too much insight into her. She needed to find her footing, be sure she was on solid ground before they got back into this dark, cozy town car and he took her home. She'd made too many mistakes with suave, handsome men. She didn't want to repeat them.

When she'd refused Jen's attempts to get her to go out, this was what she'd been avoiding. Intimacy. The powerful draw of the sensual.

No one's ever done this to you, made you feel this way. The little voice in her head, referring to Gates and her reaction to him, was almost as frightening as losing control.

Whether it was the effect of the wine or the adrenaline, Gates was even more attractive, more sensual than he'd seemed before. Considering she'd had erotic dreams about him based just on his voice, that was saying something.

I gotta get some food before I do something stupid.

That was the first sensible thought she'd had in an hour, so she repeated a version of it out loud. "Seriously, you're right. I think I'd better get something to eat, and soon."

"That's the plan," Gates said as they pulled into an alleyway. "Here we are."

Startled, Ana balked at getting out. "Why are we in the alley?"

Gates's smile was charming and totally calm. "The front entrance is too exposed. Given that someone took a shot at me yesterday and you today, I'm feeling vulnerable." He grimaced. "Yeah, I guess that's a trigger word for me too. Anyway, we'll be going in the side door. We can pretend we're rock stars."

Nonplussed, Ana looked at him. "Side door it is. Now, let's go before I do something stupid like hug you and start crying again."

"Wait? There's hugging?" he said as they slid out into the dark. The driver held an umbrella over their heads. "Nobody told me there was going to be hugging," he protested, laughing.

"It's barely raining now," she murmured, trying to ignore his teasing.

"Can't shoot what you can't see," he whispered in her ear, his words as serious now as he'd been playful before. The driver opened the side door to the restaurant and ushered them in. A maitre d' was waiting, all beaming smiles.

"Welcome, welcome, Mr. Bromley. And your lovely guest. Yes, yes, come this way," he enthused. "I have your table all ready. Certainly," he answered some unasked question. "Yes, and a nice bottle of white chilling. So, lovely lady, is there anything you don't like to eat? Anything you cannot eat?"

The man paused with considerable drama at the end of the corridor, his hand on the door that presumably led to the restaurant itself. Distracted by thoughts of Gates, the ride to the restaurant, everything, including the maitre d' took her off guard. He was obviously waiting for her to answer, but she didn't remember the question.

"Yes?"

"Food allergies? Anything you detest? Are you vegetarian, vegan?"

Whoa. Now that *is service.*

"I hate Brussels sprouts and pretty much any kind of beans," she said, feeling slightly defensive about food issues when put on the spot. "I don't eat veal."

"Yes, yes, good. None of that tonight, so good. Anything else?"

"Not that I know of."

The words were barely out of her mouth when he whisked through the door with a further wave of his hand. "This way, this way. Yes, yes, yes, it's all ready. Very good. Welcome and all that. Now, here you are, sir," he directed Gates to slide in one side of a booth in a darkened corner. There were other diners, but they were separated by high banquettes. Several other isolated tables like theirs were minimally visible through screening plants. Some were occupied; some were not. "And you on this side, Madame," he directed, holding out an imperious hand for her briefcase. "Settle in now, be comfortable. I'll put this right here."

The maitre d' bustled around, fluffing their napkins and dropping them artistically on each of their laps. "Your usual vintage, Mr. Bromley?"

"Please," Gates said, and Ana could tell he was suppressing a smile. "My companion found it to be enjoyable, so we'll continue with that."

"Water too, please," Ana added.

"But of course, Madame. Sparkling?"

"That's fine, Mr. Prinz." Gates was polite, but Prinz easily read the dismissal and with a brilliant smile, he trotted off to do their bidding. Gates turned to her. "So, no Brussels sprouts for you either?"

She made a face. "Nasty things. Bitter. Bleeech."

"I know people who love them, but I agree with you. Bleeech." He tapped the menu in front of her. "Nothing in here warrants that face or reaction, I can assure you. I've never had a bad meal here, and most of the ones I've had have been," he paused, which made her look his way, "exquisite."

Somehow, he was making that all about her and not about the food. That *look* was back, and the hand he'd casually slipped behind her in the booth now toyed with the loose tendrils of hair at the back of her neck. The roller-coaster ride of her emotions took another startling dip and rise. He was putting on the serious flirt again, but it was far more than a surface thing. This was real, important, and that scared her to death.

"That's quite the uh, recommendation." She was having a hard time concentrating on the slim folder. His touch was so sure, so sensuous; she wanted to arch into his hand, purr like her cat, Lancelot. Where was her control? Where was the reserve, the shell that had served her so well since Rome?

Gone. Gone like the block that had kept her tears from flowing. Washed away by the spate of weeping.

She was still staring blindly at the menu when Prinz bustled back to the table.

"Here we are, wine and water. Essential to life, both of them, of course." He beamed, pouring a taste for Gates.

"No need for formality, Mr. Prinz. I know it's wonderful, so pour out."

"Of course, sir." He poured out and bustled off again.

Gates let the menu fall so he could pick up his wine without stopping his assault on her senses, as he continued to stroke her neck under the fall of her heavy hair. He was a dangerous, dangerous man.

"I think we should get our orders settled, discuss some business, and then I can have dinner to just enjoy your company. Does that work for you?" Gates said, watching her with just the hint of a smile.

"Of course." She returned to the consideration of her own menu as if he'd said nothing out of the ordinary. The list of luscious dishes blurred before her tired eyes, and all she could focus on was the feel of his stroking fingers.

"That would be fine," Ana said, trying once more to resurrect her equilibrium.

She felt idiotic. Then again, the last time she'd been on a date, it had been with an all-hands octopus of an Italian in Rome, just before the bombing. She'd been trying to get back on the proverbial dating horse. It hadn't worked. Certainly, the sensation of Gates's featherlight touch on her neck was nothing like the ham-handed grabbiness of the Italian guy.

"Ana?"

"Sorry," she said, distracting his all-too-sharp gaze by tapping the menu. Trying for normal conversation, she asked, "What do you think is involved in bourgeois steak with potato frites and greens? How does one make a steak bourgeois?"

She fell back on the agent's rule of thumb: When in doubt, ask questions.

"Ah, bourgeois? I have no idea, but this chef is legendary for unusual dishes. If it sounds intriguing, it probably is."

"Intriguing. Do I want to eat intriguing food? It's been a rough enough day already," Ana said, feeling every bit of that statement in her bones. Rough didn't even begin to describe how she was feeling.

"You'll enjoy it, trust me. It will be great. Here, have a glass of wine and get out your notes. Let's dig into this so you'll have something solid to occupy your mind before you wig out."

"Wig out? Nice. Thanks." Ana accepted a filled glass and reached into her briefcase for a writing pad and one of the files. How could he know that the work would steady her? For now, she didn't question it. However it worked, it would help her, so she went with it.

Gates topped off his own glass and took a set of folded papers from the breast pocket of his coat. Scrawled writing filled the pages, with a variety of boxed comments and underlined sentences with question marks.

"Interesting notes," Ana said as she opened her own folder.

"Ideas. Searches I've pulled recently on the art," he

dismissed the notes. "Nothing turned up on the two databases we discussed. So," he leaned into the banquette, wine in hand. "Talk to me."

"It started with this," Ana began, pointing to the original search she'd done when she reviewed the case for the first time. By the time they came to the dessert course, Ana had to admit that the chef was a total genius with food. Between the food, the wine, and the stimulating company, Ana felt more alive, more in the groove than she had for over a year.

"See here?" She pointed out the terms of the latest search she'd run. "This is where things began to happen."

Gates looked at the page where Ana was pointing. As much as her presence was distracting, it was also invigorating. Conversation with her sharpened his mind as well as his senses. He'd decided after she left the estate earlier in the day that he was going to pursue her. He hadn't done that in years, much to Dav's irritation. With Ana, he'd decided to make an exception. Something about her tugged at him, pulled at his intellect as well as his libido.

She said something else that caught his attention, tapping a search parameter. He frowned over her notes, over the ideas.

"Wait," he interrupted her. "That doesn't make sense." He flipped open the leather notepad he kept in his pocket, began a timeline. "If your runs on the data started here," he began drawing out the line, marking delineations of things as they occurred. "Why did you get a reaction now?"

"Hmmm, not sure," she murmured, leaning close to him so she could see what he had written. She took his pen, made another mark. "I ran a basic three-prong query on Moroni here, just to see what popped in Google and Mackie," she said.

He knew she wasn't doing it deliberately, but the warmth of her body distracted him. He thought of Ana's soft body against his, their heated exchange of kisses.

God, he hadn't felt that hot for a woman in, well, ever. He

watched her. Her brow furrowed as she scanned through the annotations in her file. She wouldn't let him read any of it—that would give him too much power, be too intrusive, which he understood—but she was sharing, matching her skills with his. It felt good. Too good in some ways. The power of it was seductive. He'd already decided he was going to pursue her. He had to be careful though, to keep his own heart intact. The combination of intellect and sensuality, even her tears, had drawn him, inexorably, to her.

"What about this?" he rattled off a series of search options, and had the interesting experience of seeing her eyes light up, feeling her body quiver with repressed excitement over the concept. He let his eyes drift shut, imagining her next to him, under him, quivering in the same way, but for different reasons.

The intensity was almost shocking. He forced himself to pull back from it, make sure he gave it plenty of thought before he leapt in. She'd been hurt, but his own pain was still fresh, despite the years since his parents' deaths. He never forgot that relationships, obsessions, had led to that loss. The woman responsible had vowed to finish the job, eradicate everything his father had loved, including Gates and his sister.

Passion took many dangerous turns, and turning toward Ana would never be simple.

"If we did *this,* it might get us something," Ana said, bringing him abruptly back to the discussion. She pointed to a series of obscure search terms she'd scribbled on a blank sheet. They surprised him. Her mind was fast and flexible. Again, he felt the undeniable surge of deep attraction to her.

Fortunately for him, she was oblivious to his wandering thoughts, as she continued. "We might trace calls from the various galleries. I'd have to get a lot of permissions," she mused. He could all but see the wheels turning in her mind. "If we took the search terms, though, and factored in each of the victim's numbers, provided they'd let us use them," she grinned wryly, and he answered it with his own smile. "We could do a multi-factor overlayment process, with multiple keywords." She was getting enthusiastic, now. "If we did that," she scribbled down a list of terms and rates, processes and multitasking data runs. "Then this," she jotted two more items. "There. That would do it, don't you think?"

Focusing on the pages, he tracked her logic.

She was brilliant. No doubt in his mind, seeing what she'd written. And damn him if that wasn't as sexy, as attractive, as her long, lean body, dark hair, and hazel eyes. As she talked, he saw the sheer creativity with which her mind worked.

"That's way out of the box," he said, continuing to read. He could feel the excitement buzzing in his blood. This was the kind of thing he loved as well, and it was revving him up that she shared it.

"You think it won't work?"

"I didn't say that, but here," he flipped her pad around, drew five lines, and intersected two of the data runs she'd outlined. "If we have these two searches in parallel, with cross-checks, we could eliminate, what?" He looked at her, calculating the ratios in his mind. "Another thirty percent of the hits?"

The look of sheer delight she gave him was sizzling. "If we did that, then we could do this too." She whipped the pad back around and added another layer at the bottom, which would knock down another eight to ten percent of the million or more calls they would be having the system sort through.

The proposed number was actually manageable, which was the whole point. He had a sudden vision of the two of them, delving into problems like this, creating solutions, working through complex problems. Together.

The idea of it was sexy as hell. Not to mention scary beyond belief. He was content to stay in Dav's shadow, doing his thing, making his way. This kind of thing, this type of partnering, could blow everything out of the water.

Startled, he shifted in the seat. The idea was so radical, so out of the realm of things he usually thought of, that he had to set it aside. Why would he see her as a business partner?

They both had jobs, jobs they loved, he forcibly reminded himself. They were just beginning to know one another, so it was far too soon to think about things like that. Futures.

"Gates?" Ana was looking at him, a quizzical, questioning gaze. He must have been staring off into space for a few minutes, if her expression was any gauge.

"Sorry, thinking about how this all ties together. There are too many loose ends at this point, of course. Too many odd angles." They wore matching frowns over the observations they'd drawn on the pad of paper between them. Her writing meshed with his, she'd crossed his t's and added a few more of her own flourishes.

Before he could think about it further, Ana flipped the pad and began listing the warrants and permissions they'd have to wangle for the search they were proposing. Gates could do it, privately, but then it wouldn't be admissible so he didn't mention it.

"Hang on," he said, reaching for the pad. She relinquished it, and he turned back to the search terms. "What about this?" He proposed another tweak that would cut the five most peripheral victims out of the search, dropping the number of warrants down to sixteen.

They kept that up for another ten minutes, back and forth. Their plates were pushed back, and the waiter came by and whisked them away, refilling water glasses. Neither of them looked up.

"Okay, okay." Ana was jazzed now. She'd moved even closer to him so they could both see the paper, scribble notes. "See this? We could eliminate one warrant for calls if we took this out of the equation."

A low, feminine rumble of a voice came out of the shadows, jerking both of them out of their contemplations of the patterns they'd listed. "My food doesn't please you and your companion tonight, Gates?"

"Of course it pleases me, Melanie," Gates managed, shifting his brain from mathematical tracking vectors and search terms, to the real world. He turned toward the voice, smiling at Melanie. "Please, come meet my friend, Ana Burton. Your wonderful food was an antidote to a bad day, and a perfect stimulus to some deep thinking."

"Absolutely," Ana supported him, also facing the shadowed voice. Gates felt the tension in her arm where it rested on the table next to his. He slid a hand over her taut fingers, giving them a subtle squeeze of reassurance.

"Well then, I'm happy to have helped." The voice moved closer, and a statuesque woman limped into the soft light at the table. She would have been beautiful, if not for the vivid scar running diagonally across her face. The cane she was using tonight was elegant and feminine, with a highly polished silver cap. She leaned on it easily, but obviously with a great deal of pressure. Her leg must really be hurting; he remembered that it frequently did hurt on rainy nights.

Gates hoped she would smile, because her smile drove the specter of the scar away and let her grace shine through. Once upon a time, they'd been lovers, then gone their separate ways when the passion cooled and Dav's business intervened, taking him around the world once more.

"It was fabulous," Ana complimented, never betraying for a moment that the scar or cane bothered her. "How do you get the meat . . ." she trailed off, waving a hand. "Never mind. It's not like I could or would duplicate it. Suffice to say," she grinned at the chef. "It was great."

"I have dessert for you, if you've room to enjoy it," Melanie said. "It's something I only made a small quantity of, but I found some beautiful blueberries in the market. Do you both like blueberries?"

"Oh, yeah," Ana enthused. "When I was a kid, there was this blueberry thing, with ouzo and pine nuts . . . oh my gosh." He enjoyed the catlike look of pleasure on her face. "Ever since, I adore blueberries."

Melanie's face took on a sharper, more keen look. "Blueberries? Pine nuts? Really?"

"Yes, it was just . . ." Ana seemed at a loss for words. She made a very Italianate gesture with her hands. It intrigued him, to think she'd grown up in Italy, and Greece. He'd traveled around the world, with Dav and escaping his own demons, but not the way she had. "Simple. Marvelous. Really magnificent. Of course," she laughed ruefully, "it might be far better in memory than reality, but at the time . . ."

"You grew up here? Where?"

"I'd bet that was in your Italian phase," Gates answered the question, letting Ana off the hook from explaining her traveling childhood. "Ana's well travelled," he explained to the chef.

Melanie grinned, a fierce-looking thing rather than the gentle smile she usually brought out for customers. "That could be quite a winner around here if I could duplicate it. I know you have business tonight, but I'd be appreciative if you might be willing to stop by for lunch one day, on me of course, and tell me more about that dish."

"Really?" Ana accepted the card Melanie held out. "Sure. I mean, I'm no cook so I don't know how . . ." She trailed off because Melanie was shaking her head, still grinning.

"Doesn't matter. If you can give me the gist, I can play with it until I get something good."

"Okay, sure."

"Wonderful. I'll let you get back to your discussions," she said, then pointed at the notes. "But next time, Gates, bring the lady here for fun, not business. You don't enjoy my food as much when you're working, and hey," she finished with a whimsical note, "it's *alllllll* about the food."

They laughed together, and Melanie moved to another shadowed table. They heard her pleasant inquiry about the meal, but the answers were lost in the general rattle and clank of the waitstaff and the effective barrier of the plants and banquettes. Gates found it reassuring. No one could have heard their discussions either.

"Did we get anywhere?" he asked, flipping through the

pages he'd written. "I think we've got more questions than answers here."

"That's always the way it is." Ana's voice held a note of enthusiasm and energy he'd not heard before. This was the Ana he'd sensed lurking under the surface. It was . . . arousing. "Look here." She pointed to a series of questions they'd written down. "I can take this and do a Boolean search on the keywords. May turn up something useful. I can drill down on this one." She pointed at another name, another gallery Dav had used for purchasing art. "Of all the galleries your Dav used, this one wasn't hit. Sometimes it's the blanks that mean more than the bumps, you know?"

It was interesting to hear his own thoughts echoed in her words. He often thought the negative spaces spoke louder than the chatter. He was already intrigued by her. Hearing her enthusiasm, he wanted her even more.

How odd to become so entranced with a woman because of her mind. Not that the body wasn't prime, he decided, leaning back once more to study her, because it was. She wore another of the conservative suits. He'd admired it that very morning as she sat with them at their early lunch. Now, hours and a dreadful day later, she still looked good, well put together.

"What? Did I spill something on my shirt?" Ana said, distracted by his scrutiny.

"Not at all. I was just thinking. I agree with Melanie. I need to bring you back here without files. Perhaps we'll come back on Friday night."

"I'm never without files," she said, putting up a small defensive wall around the idea of the date. Perversely, it made him want to jump the wall, get to the heart of her.

"Never?" he teased. "That's interesting." He laughed as she considered the words. Obviously it was more natural for her to quip—a quick sharp response—than to ponder before speaking. Something had changed her, he decided. The Rome incident she'd referred to. He hadn't been able to break through the clearances about that, but he'd pulled news reports and other data. There'd been a bombing, an attempt on the parliament about the time she'd come back to the States. He'd lay odds that was part of what had put the hesitation in her step, in her decision making.

Dessert arrived with coffee, and it looked, smelled, and tasted like heaven. He'd never considered blueberries an aphrodisiac, but apparently, where Ana was concerned, he was going to be discovering all kinds of new things.

"Oh, my God, this is fabulous," she murmured, slipping the fork out of her mouth and licking the back of it. The sweep of her tongue over the tines had him reacting, and he felt the beat of excitement in his blood. She portioned off another bite, but before she lifted the fork, he intercepted it.

"Here, let me." Dipping the bit in the whipped cream, he conveyed it to her mouth, waited for her to open, and slid the fork in. The simple dance of it, the connection, was sensual and powerfully arousing.

"Mmmmmm," she murmured, holding his gaze. There was a flicker of excitement in her eyes, and a feminine smile curved her lips; lips he wanted to capture, lips he wanted to take. With studied care, he brought the fork to his own mouth, licked the tines as she had done.

"Delicious," he murmured, never breaking eye contact.

A presence at the edge of the table distracted them both.

"I'm sorry, sir," the driver apologized, his nervousness shouting from every twist of his hands around his hatband. "Mr. Gianikopolis needs you right away. He said to tell you there's been another incident."

Chapter Ten

Ana was as fast to gather her things as he was. The bill was settled without incident, and the mood turned dark as the driver led them to the car.

"You can drop me at the Rialto, I'll catch a cab there."

"No," Gates's answer was unequivocal. "We'll take you home. It's on the way." He nodded to the driver as they slid into the back, and within seconds they were easing into traffic.

"You should call," Ana said. "Please, go ahead."

"Okay." Gates had the phone in his hand before he finished the word. Dav had been in all evening, working on a major restructuring of a small Algerian shipping company he'd acquired a year ago. He'd let it run with minor changes for the last ten months, waiting to see if it had been the owner's personality driving the business into the ground, or the internal accounting. With a year's worth of accounting to reflect on, Dav was now making drastic changes. Dav hadn't, however, planned to leave the estate, which was why Gates had felt he could be absent.

"Dav?" Gates put all his questions into his boss's name.

"I'm fine. The incident was outside the gates. Two of your guys were coming back from a quick trip for coffee. There was a bang-strip at the bottom of the driveway, and someone shot up the car. Neither of them are hurt, thanks to the bulletproofing, but it's outrageous." Dav was worked up, and pissed. "It wasn't even dark," he snarled. "It is too easy to access us here in the United States. I think it's time to head to the house in France."

"I don't think so," Gates disagreed. "We'll talk when I get there. The team called Detective Baxter, I presume?"

"Of course," Dav dismissed that. "They picked up shell casings and hauled the car away. The usual."

Gates hated that it had become SOP—standard operating procedure—to have things happen at the estate, to get shot at. He'd left his PDA in the limo, locked in his briefcase. As he retrieved it, he heard the soft chime that meant he had voice mails, texts, and other contacts.

"We'll talk about it when I get there," he said to Dav, absently scrolling through the e-mail on the PDA, all while making sure Ana was settled and they were going the correct way to drop her off. "I'm sorry I wasn't available."

"Don't be ridiculous. Did you find out anything useful?"

"Still working on it. I'll be back shortly," Gates said by way of good-bye and disconnected. He shifted to look at his lovely companion. He hated that their ongoing difficulties were ending the evening. He'd been dramatically attracted to Ana from their first meeting at the estate. Having dinner with her tonight had only heightened the sense that he wanted to know her better, get to her intense core of brilliance both mentally and physically.

"What's up?" she demanded, her mobile face alert, her eyes scanning his face for telltale signs.

"Another attempt on the compound. Dav's getting pissed, so I'm going to have to set something up with the local police to catch some of these irritating idiots."

"Any way I can help?"

He gave it a moment's thought. They'd waded through the case file, discussed her current searches and others she might try. He'd offered his expertise on the search, but he now realized that despite his searches he hadn't uncovered exactly what she did for the CIA, nor what the difficulty in Rome had been.

His own life was one thing, he realized with a pang. Before he let her into the inner circle in Dav's life, he had to know more.

"There probably is," he prevaricated. "I'll know more once I've gotten the details. Any chance we could meet up again tomorrow? Cover some more of this ground?"

To his surprise, Ana pulled out a slim leather-bound date book. He figured her for an electronic gadget type. Then he remembered she had that too. Dual systems, built-in redundancy.

"Good with me, although I don't know what's going on with my car. Can I call you in the morning?"

"Call me tonight if you know more, or tomorrow. You can e-mail me or text me here." Gates offered a card, on which he'd written both his private e-mail and cell numbers. The one he'd given her before was a company phone.

He couldn't say why he already trusted her. Probably, it was because his gut told him she was straight-up loyal and driven by justice more than anything else. He ignored the little voice that questioned whether or not he just wanted her, and any reason to be with her.

Ana betrayed her surprise with a quick glance and an odd look, but made no comment as she tucked the card into her date book and put both into her briefcase. "Thanks," she murmured, then pulled out a card of her own and scribbled on the back. "Here, you obviously have the office number and my cell, but this is my home number, and private e-mail."

They'd crossed some vast emotional line in the course of the evening, between her tearful release and his own internal revelations about his attraction to her. The car slowed to a halt by a neatly maintained bank of condo apartments, brightly lit and surrounded by a genteel neighborhood and boutique-like shops.

"Just pull in there," Ana directed the driver, and he followed her lead. Gates walked her to her door.

The apartments were older, and well maintained, with full plantings and flowerbeds just showing spring's arrival. They were far enough away from the car, which the driver had turned around, so he didn't feel watched as they said good night.

"Thank you," Ana began, holding out her hand as if to keep it all business.

"You don't really think I'm going to shake your hand, do you, Ana?" he said, bending down to close the distance in their heights. He let his lips caress her cheek, feel the soft texture of her skin. She didn't wear heavy cosmetics, and most of what she did wear had been washed away in the crying jag. He could still smell the faint echo of her perfume when she swayed toward him.

"Gates," she said, hands rising to his chest. "I know I was upset earlier."

"You're not upset now, are you?" He looked into her eyes, making sure she was with him. He saw no trace of fear or hesitation, so he dove in. When he kissed her, his hands resting lightly on her hips, it was Ana who leaned in, deepened the connection. To his delight, she gripped the lapels of his coat, tugging him closer. Taking it as permission, he wrapped her in his arms, letting one hand twist in her gorgeous fall of black hair.

He could have stayed there forever, tasting her, discovering what made her sigh and what, like the kisses along her jawline, made her moan. The bark of a neighbor's dog and the porch lights coming on reminded him that they were out in the open, exposed to not only the prying eyes of her neighbors, but anyone who wanted to target either of them.

"We need to stop," she whispered, and he reluctantly agreed. "You need to go, and I need to go in." She tried to pull away, but he kept her close, kissed the end of her nose, which seemed to surprise her more than the passionate kisses had.

"I know," he murmured, kissing her nose again, just to see the surprise flare, keep her guessing. "I'm looking forward to another dinner. What about tomorrow night? Your car won't be ready for a couple of days, if I know the dealerships. I'll pick you up again after work. You can let me know how the warrants are progressing."

"Oh, but," she began to demur, bring up her defenses. He could almost see the wariness edge back into her eyes as the heat between them naturally cooled. He knew it was manipulative, but he did it anyway, he claimed her mouth in another searing kiss.

"Just say yes, Ana."

"Yes." Having answered, she kissed him back, rocking him to his toes with implied promises and sensual heat.

"Tomorrow then," he rasped, releasing her, stepping away so he wouldn't be tempted by the lush curves on that long frame. The need to touch her, everywhere, was nearly irresistible.

With one last kiss, he tore himself away. All throughout the long drive into the hills, he thought about her, wondered if tomorrow night he'd be driving home or if she'd let him stay.

In a daze, Ana stumbled into the apartment. She was so exhausted, mentally, physically, and emotionally, that it was all she could do to feed the cat and fall into bed. She woke at two in the morning when her phone rang.

"Burton, you okay?" Pretzky demanded. "I told you to call when you got in."

Ana switched on the light, trying to wake up. "Sorry. It's been a pretty overwhelming day," she admitted, yawning enough to make her jaw crack. "I've been home since nearly twelve. My apologies, Special Agent. I did say I'd call, and I didn't."

"Don't beat yourself up about it. Thing is, with all that's gone on today, I wanted to be sure," Pretzky said, and her voice held no rancor. "Get some sleep. See you tomorrow."

"Good night," Ana replied, but Pretzky had already hung up.

The blink of a waiting text message caught her eye, and she opened her phone back up, retrieving it.

Sleep tight. See you tomorrow, and no, I won't let you renege on dinner.

Ana had to laugh at that, since she probably would have tried to call it off. Now, she couldn't since he'd never believe any excuse she gave.

Despite your sucky day, I had a good time tonight matching wits and programming skills with you. I look forward to more. Gates.

"More what?" Ana wondered in the darkness, cocooned in her bed. She wanted to stay awake, ponder everything. Something teased at her brain, some errant fact that she knew must be important. For the first time in months, with no drugs in her system to help her sleep, Ana dropped with no hesitation back into a deep, healing slumber.

When her alarm went off, Ana leaped out of bed. It was so shocking not to already be awake, already pondering the day's schedule, that she was shocked into wakefulness.

"Jeeeez," she complained, rubbing a hand on her chest to still her pounding heart. "I'd forgotten how loud that stupid thing is."

As she showered and dressed, she went, step by painful step, through the previous day's events. What had she missed? Or, conversely, what had she found that someone else was afraid for her to find?

Opening her daybook, she found the day's blank page and listed names.

Carrie McCray/Prometheus. Moroni Gallery? Pratch/Berlin? Artful Walls/Miami.

She'd contacted each of the galleries that still existed, but the biggest losses had come through those four. In lieu of talking it out, writing it out helped her think. Even though she was alone, she decided Pretzky was right: walking through the data out loud could be dangerous.

She made a list of all the victims she'd contacted, but underlined the five who had lost the most. Dav, a German businessman, and a New Jersey socialite had lost the most, both in money and number of paintings.

"That's close," she murmured, noting that the German businessman was in Berlin. Pratch, then, for that one. The Jersey socialite would have been Moroni. "And Dav's Prometheus."

A random fact was still pestering her, though. The killings were so different, East Coast to West Coast. "Who knew something?" she questioned, as she underlined Moroni, remembering that one of the women tortured had been a gallery clerk. "And what did they know?"

Knowing she couldn't do more from home, Ana replaced her daybook in her briefcase and got her phone, so she could call a cab. Before she could open it, it rang.

"Good morning." Gates's luscious baritone rolled through the phone to shiver her bones. Without even meaning to be, the man was sexy. How was she supposed to cope with that?

"Good morning. Is everything okay with Dav?" she asked, not knowing what else to say. Why was he calling this early? She hadn't even gotten to the office.

"Dav's fine, nothing to worry about," he said, dismissing that issue. "When you step outside, there'll be a car waiting. I couldn't come in myself this morning, but Damon, the driver from last night, will be there to get you to the office."

"Gates, that wasn't necessary," she protested. She refused to admit what a thrill it gave her that he would think of it. "I was about to call a cab."

"Which would be why I called so early. Have a good day, Agent Ana." He all but crooned her name, and the intense tug of sexuality that his touch engendered flared in her belly. Without another word, he was gone.

Ana peeked out the window. Sure enough, the black town car sat waiting in the space marked for her car.

"Which reminds me to call about my car," she muttered, as she got her keys and gave Lancie a last pat. "Go do your cat chores," she ordered, and headed out.

Nothing prepared her for the luxury of riding to work, rather than driving. People touted the BART—the Bay Area Rapid Transit—for giving them time to read, or study, or just relax before work. The BART had nothing on a chauffeured car. The driver stopped for Starbucks, when she said she preferred it to Peet's. There were Danishes waiting for her, and the day's paper neatly folded on the seat.

When she got out at her building, after clearing through the security at the bottom of the driveway, she was pinching herself to be sure it was real.

"Thanks, Damon," she said, getting out before he could come around. That would have been too much, way too much luxury to start an ordinary work day.

"You're welcome, Agent Burton. Have a nice day," the man said, and drove away. Ana walked into the building, still a bit dazed over the whole incident.

"Wow. If that's what you get when you investigate a billionaire," Pearson said, jumping on the elevator with her, "I'm going to see if I can find a few cases like yours."

Ana had to laugh. "It's crazy, isn't it?"

"Hey," Pearson said, patting her shoulder. "You had a crappy day yesterday and he knew you'd lost your car, right? Pretty cool, I'd say."

"Yeah, pretty cool," Ana agreed. The difference in her relationship with Pearson, evidenced by the friendly words and familiar gesture of a pat on the back, was indicative of the change in her office status. Everyone, barring the pus-ball, Davis, had suddenly changed to treating her as one of the team.

When she met with Pretzky behind closed doors, she mentioned it.

"Sure, they warmed up some, but you changed too,

Burton," Pretzky reasoned. "They just met you halfway." The older woman paced back behind her desk and sat. "Tell me about this case. Start at the beginning and don't leave anything out."

"I ran through the listing of cold cases," Ana began. "This one had an art connection, and some interesting angles, so I pulled it next." Step by step, she went through her process, detailing everything from the calls with the former lead agents, to her calls with the victims.

"Any word from the other agent, the one you didn't talk to?" Pretzky said, as they broke for lunch.

"No, and I need to follow up there. His secretary said he was out of state yesterday, so I'd better try again. I have a different pattern to try, as well," Ana admitted. "A different set of searches. I'm going to need your help, though."

Pretzky gave her an odd look. "That's good to hear. Put it together, bring it in after you've had some lunch, and we'll discuss it."

"Will do."

At her desk, a stack of pink message notes lay propped on the keyboard. It amused her that with all the computer gadgetry and instant message capability, most people still preferred handwriting reminders.

Ignoring them for now, she turned on her laptop, and while it was booting, she called the number the secretary had given her for Hines.

"I'm sorry," a mechanical voice stated. *"This number is currently unavailable. The subscriber you are trying to reach may be out of the area or have the phone turned off. Please leave a message . . ."*

She frowned. They were in the same time zone, so Hines would be up and about. "Probably in a meeting," she muttered, then left another message for Hines to call her. Opening e-mail reminded her to send the one she'd cued up for TJ.

She was really curious about what her old friend was stirring up. It was really peculiar.

She had an e-mail from McGuire.

> **Sending the grandkids and daughter away for a bit. Just a bad feeling, but I trust those. Keep me posted, girl. McG.**

"Paranoid agents live to retire," she quoted one of her academy instructors. Obviously McGuire had retired, so his paranoia was bone deep. She e-mailed him back, answered the calls that were about the case, and spoke with the dealership about her car.

"Two days," she told Pretzky when they reconvened so Ana could tell her about the proposed search and the warrants she needed. "What's so hard about replacing a window and the headrests?"

Pretzky shrugged. "No idea. I gave up on trying to figure out car dealers a long time ago. Let's hear this plan." They ran over the policies, the warrants, and the issues that would be covered or come up based on the parameters Ana laid out. That took them right up till the end of the day. When she was packing up, Ana realized she had no idea if she needed to call a cab or if Gates was picking her up again.

Right on cue, her phone rang. "Hey," he said, his deep voice making one word a caress. "I'm nearly to the building. You ready to head out, or do you need more time?"

"I'm ready. How did you know?"

"Magic," he intoned, then laughed. "I'll see you downstairs."

The evening was nearly a repeat of the previous night, in all the good ways and without the emotional upheavals.

"Hello, dear," he said, when she slid into the car. He kissed her, long and deep, then handed her a glass of wine. "How was your day?"

Shaking her head, she laughed. "It was boring. Agent stuff. Databases, searches, calls—the usual."

"Sounds exciting to me. Say *databases* again. You know how it turns me on," he joked, chiming their glasses together in a brief salute.

Though they discussed the case, and more about their respective businesses, the meal was lighter, and briefer than the previous evening. Throughout it, however, Gates kept up the same torturous, drugging massage of her neck; drove the same tingling awareness throughout her body.

"Shall we go?" he finally asked, when they'd eaten dessert. She barely knew what she'd eaten, or how long they'd been sitting there. Every point on her body, every nerve, seemed to be rooted to the spot where his hands caressed her, warm and promising.

She knew this dance. It was leading to bed, to sex, to them being together. Ana knew it was crazy. It was nuts, in fact, but she was heedless to stop it. She didn't want to stop it.

They were silent in the car, riding back to her place. He held her hand, his thumb making restless circles on her palm. Her imagination was in overdrive, thinking of having his hands on her body.

"Ana, you are going to invite me in, aren't you?" he asked, his voice sure.

Part of her, the part that was so afraid of screwing up again, wanted to say no. That part wanted to scoot away to the other side of the seat; deny, deny, deny.

The rest of her, the part that was more truly Ana, agreed. "Yes," she said, forcing herself to meet his dark gaze. "I am. I'm not sure it's smart, but I'm going to do it anyway."

Gates watched her for a moment, assessing her decision. He felt the smile blossoming on his face, saw the answer on hers. "Smart?" Gates asked, knowing it was a rhetorical question. "Hmmm. I'm not sure I'd call it that, either. Ana—" He started to tell her that this wasn't something he did on a whim. He didn't get to finish.

The window next to her crackled, and there was a sharp snapping sound as the bulletproof glass buckled, but held.

"Get down!" he shouted. "Damon, get us out of here!"

They both ducked below window level, and the driver, caught off guard, swerved out of the parking place he'd been aiming for and peeled out of the parking lot. Gates and Ana were both already both on their respective phones.

"Yes," Gates answered the dispatcher, rattling off Ana's address, all thoughts of passion dismissed, transmuted into adrenaline. "Shots fired, that address. No, we're not there. No, we'd be sitting ducks. Contact Detective Baxter, with the county, he'll know what to do. Yes, I know." He answered the woman's question about making a statement, being available. "You can send someone here." He rattled off the address of the estate.

Meanwhile, Ana had Pretzky on the phone. "We've got another incident. Shots fired, my address."

"What's the situation? Report, Agent."

Ana laid it out. Pretzky snapped orders for her to come in, but Ana cut her off. "Bromley's driver is taking us to Mr. Gianikopolis's estate. Locals are meeting us there, since there was an incident at the estate last night as well."

"Incident? What incident?" When Ana laid it out, Pretzky demanded the address and said she would meet them there. She hung up before Ana could deter her.

"My boss is meeting us at the estate," Ana said, rising from her crouch as they got farther away from the city. They wound into the hills and pulled up to the hyper-lit front of the estate. There was a police cruiser under the portico when they pulled up.

"Good, Bax is here. We'll talk it through."

Alexia, Gates's ultra-perky assistant, led them to a cozy living room. A fire burned in the fireplace where Dav and a detective waited for them.

"Hey Baxter," Gates called, his tone weary. "We've got another one for you."

The detective gave him a sharp look, then took in Ana's appearance. His eyes narrowed, and she wondered if she had some kind of I'M A LAW ENFORCEMENT GEEK sign over her head.

"This is Agent Burton with the CIA." Gates seemed to relish the look of shock on the detective's face, but Detective Baxter masked it quickly and shook Ana's extended hand. "We've been working together on another matter, and she was with me tonight when we were fired on. I was just getting ready to drop her off." He gave the address. "We called City dispatch, but I gave them your name. If they send CSI over there, they'll find at least one casing since the shot impacted on the bulletproof glass."

"You think it's related?" The detective was writing things down, and didn't even look up as he asked the question.

"Don't know," Gates said, without leaving Ana's side. "Agent Burton was targeted yesterday on her own. Could be separate. Her SA's coming up to the house."

"We're going to need to step up our patrols here, while Dav's in town this time," Bax said, still writing. "Someone's going to get hurt with this going on, even if it's not Dav."

"I agree."

"Ana," Dav finally spoke. "It's good to see you again. I'm sorry it had to be under these circumstances."

"And you, Dav," Ana replied. "I'm sorry you had trouble as well."

He made a dismissive gesture. "It comes and goes. However, I'm thinking that you aren't usually one to be fired upon. This is not good. Either you are being targeted for being here, or something in your case is the reason," he said, tucking his hands behind his back and rocking from his heels to his toes, and back.

"Special Agent Pretzky, my superior, is on the way," Ana offered. "She tends to agree and would like us to work together on this if you have no objections. If checking these old leads gets this kind of response, it's likely that there's a whole heck of a lot more to this case than meets the eye."

"We thought that at the time," Dav replied, shooting Gates

a glance. "It was prior to Gates coming to work for me, as you know, but he reviewed everything. It was agreed that something about the entire affair was skewed. We were not sure if, at the heart of it, it was about the art or not."

"Really?" Ana was surprised. Neither of the agents she'd talked to had commented on that; they had obviously still considered it to be mainly an art-fraud case, even with the violence of the deaths. Then again, McGuire and Hines were not in total accord on that, a point that was becoming more obvious each time she talked with McGuire. "Why would you think that?"

"It was too random," Gates interjected, pouring himself a cup of coffee from what she now presumed to be ever-ready carafes. "The way two of the dealer's employees were killed was way over the top." Ana watched him closely. He'd made the statement with calm detachment, but there was something in his posture, his demeanor that clued her in to his anger. He was offended by those deaths; incensed. Then again, she reflected, so was she. The details were messy, the torture overkill if they were simple revenge or cover-your-tracks killings.

"The money was never recovered." Ana offered another point. "Nor were there any other art thefts of this nature, or none connected to subsequent fraud."

"That we know of," Dav smiled grimly.

"True, but it would have been dangerous to do any other similar crimes with the investigation under way."

"Ah, but variations on the theme," Dav offered, with a wink at Gates for some reason, "slip under the radar. This is how we recovered the piece I mentioned. We won't discuss that with your Special Agent, I think, but it is, nevertheless, true."

So they wanted to play it that way? It was odd that they'd been open with her so far, despite her deception at the gallery, and yet they didn't want to deal openly with Pretzky.

Baxter stepped out to take a call as they moved to the office they'd met in the previous morning. It seemed like a hundred years ago. The conference table they'd used had been expanded, with several leaves added, and additional chairs were now posted around its expanse. "We will meet here, utilizing the knowledge of your SA and Detective Baxter, who has been our liaison with the local police. He is quite good, but as with all departments these days, especially in California, his options are limited."

"I understand that." Ana felt she had to make some kind of response. "We've all felt the pinch of budget cuts."

Obviously Dav's organization hadn't, since both men made noncommittal noises. When you've got billions, what's a drop of a few million on the market? Or on a painting or five, for that matter?

"Got a team over at your place, Agent," Baxter said to Ana, as he came back in. "Found the bullet, where it bounced off the car. Your man's taken the car back to your garage, now that we have pictures."

He sat down on a heavy sigh. "So, what the hell's this all about? And you got shot at too, Agent, yesterday I hear?"

"Yes," Ana confirmed. "Missed me, but it was a near thing."

"You think it's connected?"

"No idea," she replied instantly. "I have to consider, though." She shrugged. "It doesn't make any immediate sense. You have anything on all this that might tie into a nine-year-old art fraud case? 'Cause that's my only connection to Mr. Gianikopolis and Mr. Bromley."

"So the shot at you might be something else?"

"Maybe, but then the shot at Mr. Bromley might be something else too," she said.

"Doubtful." Another voice joined the conversation as Pretzky came in. The men stood, and she nodded to each of them, shook hands, and sat down, pulling out a file as she did. It was a neat maneuver, and Ana admired the smoothness of it. "Agent Burton hasn't been on this case long, but we've had two incidents since she began making her calls and nothing prior to that on other cases she worked on. I'm thinking it's related to this case." She turned to the detective. "If your people could send me the data on the bullet you found, that would be helpful."

"Done," he stated, with seemingly no rancor. "I already cleared it with the city police. You have any leads on this, Agent Burton?"

"Nothing solid that would lead me to believe I'd hit a nerve with anyone. You know what I mean."

Gates scowled at them, then said, "Your computers got hit, then you got shot at, then we got shot at when we were together. It's all connected somehow. We didn't know you till you reopened the case. I think you've turned up something someone doesn't want unearthed."

Pretzky looked a bit uncomfortable, but laid it out on the table. "We need to work together on this. I'd like to keep everyone alive. I have to tell you gentlemen, my agent was very lucky yesterday. No bulletproof glass in her car." She leaned back, looking everywhere but at Ana. "One second later or earlier, a different angle, and we'd be having this discussion without Agent Burton."

Gates cut his eyes sharply to Ana. "It was that close?"

Pretzky nodded, saving Ana from answering. It gave her the willies to think about the bullet in the headrest, without discussing just how close it had been. She still hadn't processed the whole incident, and obviously, based on her breakdown yesterday with Gates, she wasn't going to deal with it well.

"Bullet lodged in the headrest, but only because Agent Burton inadvertently rolled forward." The image of that obviously shocked everyone, since the silence was profound.

"Well, I made it through," Ana said, breaking the tense moment.

"Holy crap," the detective said. "And you're here? Hell, I'd still be out getting drunk to celebrate being alive."

She had to grin at that. "Considered it, but got busy when someone hit our computers with a bug before I could even process the whole shots-fired thing. I got through today okay, then . . ." She paused, processing it as she said it. "Round two."

"Very dedicated, our Agent Burton." Pretzky smiled tightly.

"None of us realized she'd nearly been hit until after she'd jumped in and helped shut down the virus. We have a very talented resource in Agent Burton, and I, for one, want to make sure we figure this out so we don't lose her to someone else's stupidity."

You could have knocked Ana over with a feather at the words, and it was a struggle not to let her mouth drop open in surprise. Pretzky'd been better, more friendly in the last two days, but that kind of approbation wasn't what Ana expected.

"Thank you, Special Agent," she finally managed.

"Very commendable," Dav interjected, and Ana could have kissed him, she was so grateful for the diversion. "I have to confess, I would like to quit getting shot at as well."

"Third incident this month," the detective growled, shifting restlessly in his seat. "Gettin' annoying."

"Tell me about it." Gates's reply was just as much a growl. "Not to mention how irritating it is to get the glass out of your shirt."

"Don't be such a fashion priss, Bromley," the detective complained. "You're gonna give us a bad rap."

The exchange broke the tension. By the time they were done hashing things through, it was after ten.

Pretzky stepped out to make calls and came back to the room to say, "Agent Burton, your apartment's been checked and cleared. A security detail's on standby over there."

Great. More people to feel responsible for. "Thanks. That's good." It wasn't, but she had to express some gratitude.

"Agents." Baxter shook hands all around. "I'll forward you my files on these incidents. We'll compare notes." He headed out, and Pretzky left as well. The three of them, Gates, Dav, and Ana, stood looking at one another for a heartbeat.

"This has gotten a great deal more complicated than we could have thought when we chatted about this yesterday," Dav said on a sigh. "Gates, you'll see Ana home?"

"Of course," Gates replied, and Dav smiled. He kissed

Ana good night, an airy touch on both cheeks. "Take care, Ana-aki."

They rode in silence through the dark miles back to the city. As they pulled into the entrance to her complex, they saw a marked police car sitting near her building.

"I should go speak to them," she said, turning to thank Gates. "I want to—" she began

Before she could get the words out, he'd drawn her close, kissing her with a pent-up passion that rocked her to the depths of her body, to the very center of her soul.

Holy cow.

Holy cow.

Then she had no thoughts as her mind spun and she responded to his kisses, to the power of his embrace. She never wanted to stop kissing him. She wanted to drag him into her apartment and have him. All of him. Now.

"Ana," he said, smoothing the damp hair curling around her face. She was overheated, ready for more. "You make me crazy." He kissed her as he said the words. "But I don't want to take advantage. It's been another roller coaster of a day," he said, pressing kisses to her cheeks now, easing away, letting the cool night air slide between them.

"You're right, you're right," she agreed, hating every bit of it, from her own conscience, and ethical issues because he was part of a case, to the irritating, wonderful, crazy buzz of sexual frustration that jangled her nerves. "I'm going to get out, go say hello to the officers before I go in." She didn't look at him as she added, "Before we go in."

She opened the door, stood for a moment so the uniforms could see her. She recognized the instant they noticed her standing by a stationary vehicle and went on alert.

Still, Ana didn't move. She didn't look back at Gates, sitting behind her on the seat, waiting. She hesitated, then said, "Gates? Is it just because . . ." She waved her hand, used it to encompass the whole crappy couple of days.

"No," he said, simply. "It's you."

Chapter Eleven

"You missed, Jurgens," he said, still in a state of disbelief.

"Ja." Jurgens's anger was burning through the phone line, cold and dangerous. "Luck only, for her. I will not be missing again."

"No, don't kill her. I think we were about to make a strategic error there. Maybe this will work in our favor. She's involved with Gianikopolis now, and his security expert, Bromley. Did you know someone took a shot at him the other night? After your miss this evening, and the attempt on him, they are quite distracted. I hear as well that there's been gunfire up at Mr. G's estate. With all these attempts, anything we do will be washed away in the larger effect. Also, I believe our former rivals weighed in yesterday."

The surprised silence on the other end of the phone made him chuckle. Jurgens was far more manageable when he wasn't furious. It was always a balancing act utilizing something like family history and college bonds to keep his hired killer leashed.

"Yes, yes, someone else took a shot at our girl." He laughed when Jurgens responded with only a growl. "Now, now. We may have competed for the lovely works that we craved nine years ago, and we obviously had different methods of disposing of loose ends, but when it came down to the finale, our

New York rival worked with us to avoid detection. Since Perkins hacked into Agent Burton's files—" he began.

"Foolish," Jurgens interrupted.

"Yes, it was, wasn't it? However, stupid as it was, I'm grateful. It's going to be useful when it comes to covering our tracks. So, as I said, it's a nice cover that our rival shot at the lovely agent."

"Hmmmmm." The hum of interest and, perhaps, satisfaction erased the last of the fury he'd heard in Jurgens's voice. "Possibly."

"So, what we must do now is discover who is targeting Mr. G. Only by understanding that can we use it. I do believe we're going to have to more carefully monitor our rival as well. Do you have someone who can take that task on? I'm not having much luck in that department, you know." He grimaced in annoyance. "My last attempt in that area obviously was a serious fail."

"Perkins."

"Exactly," he said on a sigh. "He wasn't any use unraveling our New York rival's new name or status. So, thoughts?"

"I have a man for one job. I'll find another."

"Excellent. Good work. I've put half the deposit in the account."

"*Neh,* job isn't done."

"But it's started. Consider it a good faith advance. I know you'll find me what I need, so," he shrugged, even though Jurgens couldn't see it. "It'll be there."

"Ja, *gut.* Same number?"

"Sure. We don't have to dispose of these phones quite yet. Tomorrow?"

"Next day."

"That works. I don't want too much time to pass before we finish this up; however, we do need to work our efforts into the overall scheme. It is nice of them to be so conveniently shooting at all our targets," he said facetiously. "So thoughtful."

Jurgens gave a short barking laugh and hung up.

* * *

Where was she?

Agent TJ Michaels paced the room. This wasn't working the way he'd planned it. Nothing had. He'd really screwed up in Rome, and both Miller and Stanley had paid for it with their lives. Had he gotten what he wanted? Sure. He never expected the cost to be that high, though.

He was trying to make it right, wasn't he? Trying to be sure that no one else took a dive for his stupidity. At the same time, he had to be sure that Ana continued to help him. She was his only hope of getting out of this tangle alive. She'd known something was wrong in Rome, but the data had said otherwise. She'd gone with the data, just like he knew she would. She trusted it more than her gut. It was her one flaw.

"Facts don't lie, right, Ana?" he asked the computer screen, wishing he had an e-mail from her. "Where are you, gorgeous? Don't let me down."

He paced some more. It wasn't like her not to return his e-mails promptly. He had to know what was going on, and these phrases were key to it. He had a hunch that there was more to the scenario than met the eye, but all this stuff, stuff that didn't translate word for word, was making him crazy.

His inbox pinged, and he clicked it open immediately, sagging with relief when he saw that it was her.

Hey dude! she'd written. He could almost hear her saying it out loud, so he smiled.

> **You've got some doozies here. Context would be helpful, but here goes:**
>
> ***Hai unpo di pasta da un'altraparte*** **is literally, you have pasta elsewhere. It means you're getting some on the side, or you have a piece—woman—on the side.**
>
> ***Riprendi la buona strada*** **is literally, "Walk the straight road," but what it really means is, in essence, "Mend your ways," or as**

we would say, "straighten up and fly right." Somebody's warning his pal here to be really, really careful about his flirtations.

Non ti lascieremo smerdare la nostra famiglia is literally "Don't cover people with shit" but means that your words embarrass the family. This usage is a definite warning. It's about the family, so about the good name or reputation and this person is in danger of sullying that.

Non la smettiti faemo fuori is literally "We'll put you outside," but it's a serious threat. It's a death threat. "We'll put you outside," is essentially, "We'll kill you." Same idea.

And the last one, *Falla finite con quella putana* is literally "Get rid of the female dog," but it means stop whoring around.

The other one, *Avrai a che fare con noi,* is literally "You'll have business with us" but is another threat, and is only used as a threat. They're telling whoever this is that they WILL take care of business. They'll kill him, if he doesn't stop embarrassing the family and/or whoring around.

What's this all about?

God, if he could only tell her. Maybe, if he could . . .

He thought about it for a moment. No. He'd already put her head on the block with his fuck-up in Rome.

He hit REPLY and typed back.

Hey babe! You're a lifesaver. I'll fill you in over drinks in a few weeks when I'm back on the left coast. Heatin' up the town in Ottawa right now on a low key op.

He was actually in White Plains, New York, but neither she, nor anyone else needed to know that.

Back to ya' shortly. Appreciate the help.

He sat back, comparing the two sets of translations. Both of them were warnings to stay away from other women or the wife would exact revenge.

Wives. Families. Warnings to stay on the straight and narrow. What the hell did it mean?

"Warnings. Warnings. Warnings," he muttered. He got up to pace again. Wives. Mistresses. Two wives. A mistress.

"Oh no, you didn't," he said, as an idea, a crazy idea, shot into his mind. Racing back to the keyboard, rearranging data, moving the translations around in his timeline, he ignored the rumble in his stomach, the sweat plastering his shirt to his back. He powered through the info, shifting things, and in the repositioning, a new pattern emerged.

"Shit, shit, shit," he cursed, knowing the issue had now escalated beyond all reason.

"You stupid, crazy son of a bitch." He leaned back in the chair, seeing the full pattern for the first time. The idiot target was a bigamist. Each of his wives had become aware of another woman in his life. Both fathers-in-law were issuing warnings. Added to that, the idiot was seeing a third woman in California as well.

He got back up to pace. "How the hell does he have the stamina? Not to mention the time."

Obviously, his target liked strong women, and couldn't stay away from either the two wives, or the other woman he'd met. He'd been so hooked, he'd married both the Greek in New York and the Italian in New Jersey. Idiot.

"Neither family is going to let him get away with cheating on the only daughter," he muttered, sitting back down to make more notes. The two wives seemed tolerant to a degree—he thought of them as pragmatic. However, after a year of this, both women were becoming suspicious and territorial. Both had powerful families who were pressuring the target to stay home more. Both families were exerting pressure on the target in their own way.

Slimy bastard spoke both Greek and Italian, ran with both major families as if he were the prodigal son, and juggled the wives and the families so carefully, so easily and cheerfully that you had to admire the sheer brass *cojones* of the guy.

"This one is so gonna get dead," he said as he made notes. "He's gonna get so dead, one way or the other. Either one of these women is gonna shoot the hell out of him, or one of their brothers or dads." He sighed and mocked, "Nobody treats daddy's little girl that way, *capiche?*"

He wasn't sure what the Greek equivalent was, but he was pretty sure the Greek father-in-law felt the same way. Soon his freight-flying target was going to get himself dead. Problem was, this guy was the keystone to what had gone down in Rome, so TJ needed him alive, and talking.

"You can't get dead, dude," he said, returning to the keyboard. "Not yet."

It was time to do some serious work. He snagged a cold piece of pizza and popped open a warm soda, cracked his knuckles, and got down to the business of hacking.

Ana strode purposefully toward the patrol car, stopping about ten feet away. Both officers were rigidly attentive, watching her every move.

"Officers, I'm Agent Ana Burton, CIA," she stated, keeping her hands clear of her raincoat, well away from her body. "I just wanted to let you know I was in for the night. And to thank you for your service."

"You're welcome, Agent, now get back in the car. You're a target," the driver replied.

She nodded her thanks, pivoted, and got back in the car. Damon took the vehicle smoothly up the drive and parked outside her building. He made no move to open her door, so she turned to Gates.

"Come in," she said, making it a request, not a question. "I don't think Dav expects you back tonight." She opened the door herself, drew him out. "Come in."

With a smile, he tapped the driver's side glass. "Thanks, Damon. I'll see you in the morning."

"Very good, sir," he replied, never taking his eyes off the steering wheel. "I'll wait till you get in."

Ana skirted the back of the car and went up the steps, feeling Gates right behind her. It was like he was a furnace at her back, heat radiating out of him, warming her, making her feel safe. She fumbled with the keys, but only for a moment.

"Ana?"

"It's okay." She opened the door, took his hand to draw him in. "I want this. I want you."

"I can just be here," he said, pulling her close, leaning them both against the closed door. Keeping it light. "If that's what you need," he murmured into her hair, kissing her forehead like he would a child's.

"Gates," she whispered, feeling powerful, feeling as if nothing could touch her here, in his arms. "What I need is you, touching me, making me feel alive and whole. You touch me." She laid a hand on his cheek. "You touch me, and it's like I want to explode right there."

He cupped her face in his hands, tilting her chin slightly so he could see her eyes in the dim light. "You're sure?"

To answer him, she dropped her things to the floor, unfastened her coat, and let it slide away. Pressing him into the door with her body, she rose on tiptoe to kiss his cheek, just as he had kissed hers earlier, a whisper of a touch.

"I'm sure."

He groaned and dragged her mouth to his, plundering and taking all she would give.

Just as eager, she fumbled with his belt, jerked the tail of his smooth dress shirt from his pants so she could run her hands up the heated skin of his back. He groaned into her mouth and pressed her into his body, imprinting the feel of his erection on the softness of her belly.

"Here," she muttered, pulling off his suit jacket, tossing it toward her dining room chair as they moved backward together in a blistering sexual tango. Her own blazer followed, and he somehow managed not to pop the buttons on her shirt as he wrenched it open to feast on the curve of her neck, slide lower to press feathery kisses to the high mounds of her breasts that showed over her conservative bra.

"Your bed," he demanded, picking her up, urging her to wrap her legs around his waist.

"There, down the hall to the right," she gasped, bending now, from her higher vantage point, to kiss his neck, push his shirt as far off his shoulders as she could in order to taste him, scent him, feel the pulse hammer in his throat. That rapid-fire beat only fueled her desire for him.

His need, his almost frenetic pace was a balm to her soul; it filled some empty place inside her she hadn't known existed. Feeling it, she could slow down, savor, touch.

"Shhhhh," she soothed as he turned to lay her gently on the bed. God, he was strong, to lift her so easily, set her down with no strain or stress. "Come here, come to me," she murmured drawing him with her.

They knelt, face to face in the center of the bed, stopping to caress and appreciate as they stripped one another, peeling away the layers of the everyday that stood between them and the primal urges that drove them both. "You're so beautiful." He pulled her close, matching them perfectly from knee to breast. "So soft." He caressed her cheek again, leaving a trail of warmth and comfort that made her want him more than ever.

"You're beautiful too," she said, locking her gaze to his, feeling the passion rising faster between them, faster than she could—or wanted to—tame. She laid a hand on his heart, let the pulse of it excite her. "Oh, God, you are so sexy," she said, sliding her hands up to fist in his hair, bring their mouths together, lock them irrevocably into this passionate spiral. "Touch me, touch me everywhere."

"I want to see you," he declared, between kisses, pulling her toward him so he could take charge, lifting her as he laid them down together, still face to face, but now in a tangle of arms and legs.

He moved back, just a little, letting his hands and eyes speak for him, murmuring appreciatively as he spread his long fingers around her breasts, to massage and tease. "Beautiful," he repeated, gliding his hands to her back now, shaping them around her backside, letting her set the pace.

She followed his lead, but instead of pulling back, she moved in, rolling him to his back and rising above him, straddling his hips. Unpinning her hair, she let it fall free, and brushed the tips of her hardened nipples over every inch of his chest. Slowly, with agonizing lightness, she skimmed her body over his, as she dropped the pins on the bedside table.

"Temptress," he murmured, locking her in place with the strong band of his arms. Taking advantage of the position, he laved her breasts, tugged the nipples into his mouth to suckle them one after the other. "Such a magnificent temptation," he said, just before he reversed their positions, trapping her under his superior weight, but without any effort at all.

"Now," he said, a gleam in his eyes, "I'll look my fill." He leaned on one elbow and proceeded to kiss his way down her body.

"This is lovely, this right here," he declared, running the point of his tongue over the curve of her taut belly. "Exquisite."

The slow, delicious torture of his exploration had her so hot, so ready to explode that when he eased his hand between her legs, still kissing his way down her belly, she gasped and cried out, letting the blinding orgasm blast through her.

"Yes, Ana. Oh, yes," he murmured, sliding up to capture her mouth, kiss her deeply, share the ride as she pressed into his hand, gripping his wrist so he wouldn't move, couldn't move until she'd milked every last erg of energy from the explosion.

"Oh, my God," she moaned. "That was . . . that was . . ." She stuttered to a stop. What the hell did she say? What was it?

"Amazing, gorgeous," he groaned right along with her. "God, woman, you are magnificent."

Everything within her lit up with his praise, the scent of him, of her own passion, of them together made her want to leap and dance. She hadn't felt this free since before her failed affair in Italy, maybe since college.

She wanted more. She wanted him.

"I need you, Gates, inside me. I need to feel you, please." She tugged at him, trying to bring them together more quickly.

"Wait, honey, just a minute, okay?" He fumbled in his pants, protected them both.

"Now-now-now," she demanded, pulling him back to her, lifting her hips to give him access. When he hesitated, about to speak, she denied that. "Now. I won't change my mind."

"Now," he agreed, easing into her slowly, inch by agonizingly luscious inch.

"Ahhhhhhhhh!" The cry was drawn out to a crescendo as he locked them together, fully engaged in her body, throbbing to the racing beat of both their hearts.

"Ana," he growled. "Ana, open your eyes."

Through the haze of pleasure she heard him and obeyed, reveling in the sight of him above her, the inferno of their mutual desire sparking in his gaze. "Watch me, Ana. See me as I move in you, make you wetter and wetter." The words were hot, demanding, and they fueled her need, her hunger for him.

"Yes," she rasped the words. "I see you, Gates. I see you. I see what it does to you when I move with you." She timed her rhythm with her own thrusts, nearly faint with pleasure at the heat they were creating, the power, the rising blast of another mind-blowing release.

"You're beautiful, Ana." He quickened the pace, then slowed it, then drew out only to come back to her in a rush. "You make me crazy with wanting you."

"Gates." She found his name, but could say little else as her body responded to his thrusts, to his words, to the intensity that built between them. "Give me . . ."

"What? What do you want, Ana?" he demanded, one hand braced on the headboard, the other lifting her to give her even more pleasure, letting her feel even more of him filling her, firing every nerve.

"You, I want you, now," she moaned, writhing in her need to bring him closer, extend the feelings that swamped her, cresting higher and higher. "Gates!" she shouted as she exploded around him, driving him even deeper into her body as she rose to meet him, her hands on his hard, muscled ass.

"Ana!" he echoed her cry, finding his own release in the blazing glory of hers. "Ana," he gasped, still driving forward, extending her pleasure as well as his as he rocked them together, continuing to murmur her name until they were both panting and spent.

He began to move away, but she stopped him. "No, stay." She reinforced the words, wrapping her legs over his hips to keep him still.

"I'll crush you," he said, resting his weight on his elbows, his head bowed nearly to her breast, his hot mouth teasing her skin as he tried to slow his breathing.

"No, you won't." She ran her fingers through his hair and down the expanse of his back. Damn, he felt so good in her, and around her. Nothing had ever felt this good. Nothing.

They lay together, letting their pounding hearts slow to a normal beat, silent in the dark room, enjoying the feel of one another's bodies with tender caresses and long, slow kisses.

He brushed the hair from her face and smiled, rubbing his thumb over her lip. "I think I bit you," he said, obviously unrepentant. "Sorry about that."

"Uh-huh. Sure you are." She let her hands roam where they would, loving the long strength of him, the warmth that seemed to blanket her. "Somehow, Mr. Bromley, your body language tells me otherwise. You know, they teach us how to read body language in agent school."

"Agent school, eh?" He laughed, bending to dance kisses

up the left side of her jaw. "So what is my body telling you now, Agent?"

"That you want me," she murmured with delight. "Again."

"Ah, you are a marvel, Agent," he said, his voice muffled in the skin of her shoulder as he skimmed more kisses down her collarbone. "You have the most delicate bone structure here." He traced a finger up her sternum, between her breasts, and down the opposite line of her collarbone. "Deceptive, that delicacy." He nipped her chin, then kissed her mouth.

She got lost in the drug of his mouth for several minutes then, and only when they broke apart, panting, did she question him. "Deceptive? How? What do you mean?"

"Relax, Agent." Amused now, he lifted away, and she was instantly chilled. "I'm not impugning your strength, body, or character. It's a compliment."

"Well then, I guess I can take that," she said, leaning onto his chest. "You're pretty strong yourself there, Mr. Bromley." She wanted to stretch and purr in sensual pleasure at the memory of him lifting her up, bringing her to orgasm with just his hands.

"Hmmm," he murmured, and she could sense how relaxed he was, how near sleep. He was still aroused and so was she, but when he yawned, she followed suit and every bit of the day's trauma's came down on her like a wall. All she wanted to do was sleep.

She needed to get up, wash her face, check on Lancelot. The cat didn't like strangers, so she knew he was hiding somewhere.

"We should move," he said, yawning again. "Get cleaned up."

"Mmmm-hmmm," she agreed.

He pulled her closer, then flipped the covers over them, tugging them from one side so they cocooned them both in warmth. "So sweet," he murmured, nuzzling her hair. "So beautiful. Ana."

"Mmmm." She let herself drift in the motion of his fingers

on her back, loving the hypnotic sensation of the sweeping motion.

It was nearly dawn when she woke. Lancelot had jumped onto the bed and curled himself into a furry ball behind her knees. He looked at her for a moment, then purred loudly as he put his head down on his paws and closed his eyes. Sandwiched between Gates and the cat, she decided to just close her eyes for another minute. Just another minute, then she'd get up.

"Ana?" Gates murmured her name into her hair. His arms were banded around her, his body a furnace of warmth that made her want to stretch like Lancelot and luxuriate in the feeling of being held so tight.

"Mmmm? Hey," she replied, eyes still closed, just enjoying being able to run her hands over his chest, feel the springy hair tickle her fingers, trace the muscles that excited her so much.

"We have to get moving. It's nearly eight."

His words hit her brain like a bucket of cold water and she sat up. "What? What? How can that be?" She pushed her hair out of her eyes, staring at the clock. Sure enough, it read seven forty-two. "Oh, my God, I have to get to work."

"Whoa, whoa!" He stopped her frantic attempt to unwrap the mummifying blankets and leap up. "Both of our bosses practically ordered us to sleep in. We've followed orders very nicely, I think."

"Yes, but—"

"No. No buts. We both needed the sleep, and now," he grinned wolfishly, "we need a wake-up call."

She shoved at her hair again, sure that it was a rat's nest and that she must look like something the proverbial cat dragged in. "I look like hell," she said, trying to get loose. She wanted to be sexy for him, as beautiful as she could be, since he seemed to think she was attractive.

I should brush my teeth, at least.

"No," he growled, hovering over her, the blankets making

a cape on his back. "You're gorgeous, sexy, and rumpled, with your sleepy eyes and your hyper-responsibility. I'm going to make us both late," he said, swooping in to kiss her. "Very late."

"Gates!" she protested, but it was half-hearted, because his mouth was working magic on her neck, the curve of her ear, and her mouth. *Oh my God, it's even better in the morning.*

She met him kiss for kiss, caress for heated caress. "Here, touch me here," she moaned.

"Yes, like that," he directed as she shifted her hips to meet him, making them both groan with ecstasy as the maneuver brought a fresh wave of sensation to taunt them, bring them higher.

"Ohhh, yes," she said, pulling him into her, deeper and faster. "More. I want more of you."

"Look at me, Ana."

She did, and what she saw in his face, in his eyes, made her heart race even faster. The wild passion was there, but so was something else. A tenderness, a desire that transcended the physical.

It made her want to weep. It made her want to dance. Instead, she arched up to claim his mouth, to fuse them together.

They broke the kiss only to gasp out their completion as they soared together over the edge into orgasm.

In the aftermath, he flipped them, holding her steady where she lay limp and spent on his sweaty chest. Her hair draped in damp ropes over his arm, and her head rose and fell with the powerful depth of his breathing.

He smoothed a possessive hand down her back, resting it for a moment in the spot he seemed to like at the small of her back. His fingers drew patterns there, lulling her mind, derailing all thought.

"Good morning, Anastasia," he finally murmured as his restless fingers continued their lines and curves.

"Good morning, Gates," she said, the words muffled by his chest and the fall of her heavy hair. With effort, she swished it to the side, freeing the dark strands from her mouth and using her fingers to untangle it from the chain she wore around her neck. The simple cross had twisted to the back and lay warm and heavy on her spine.

"This is a superior way to wake up," he said. She could feel the chuckle that accompanied the words, heard it echo in his chest.

"I think I have the superior position, but yes, it has a lot to recommend it."

He sighed, and she decided it sounded regretful. "Much as I don't want to move, I guess we should."

She propped herself up, sweeping more hair out of the way to look at him. "You stopped me from rushing out of here, so I guess we'll just take our time. You want the first shower?"

His grin was wicked. "How about we share? I'll wash your back."

The mental image of that was divine. "Okay. Race you," she said, flinging the covers away and dashing for the bathroom.

"Unfair, wench!" he called, caught in the welter of blankets she'd tossed aside.

They played in the shower like slippery children, making love again as the warm rain of water flowed over them both.

She found them towels, offered him a toothbrush, shared her hairbrush. It was a surreal bubble of delight. No one had been there in the morning with her, like this. She'd never lived with a man, never shared a sink or a razor. She'd always been the one to slip away in the morning. Even when she'd dated her long-term boyfriend in college, she'd never let him stay at her apartment, she realized as she dried her heavy hair. Always cautious, she'd kept people slightly at arm's length since her parent's death.

"You have beautiful hair, Ana," Gates said, standing behind her wearing only his trousers. They were only slightly wrinkled from their night draped over the foot of the bed. Hers were crumpled on the floor in the hallway, she realized, blushing. "Ah, now, that's nothing to blush over, it is beautiful."

"Thank you. I was—" She hesitated, then realized it was ridiculous to be embarrassed at this point. "I was thinking that my suit was going to have to go to the cleaners. I didn't give two hoots about it last night, so I'm not sure where my jacket ended up."

"It's on the coffee table with your shirt."

"Ah, okay." She couldn't help the continued color in her cheeks. "Your shirt?"

"I won't be buttoning the top two buttons this morning." He grinned at their joined reflection in the mirror as he slid his arms around her waist, hugging her from behind. Seeing them together that way, reflected in her small bathroom, she felt a change, a shift in her heart that nothing could stop. What had he done to her? "What?" he questioned. "Ana, what is it?"

Not ready to define her feelings, she smiled. "Nothing, I just like the look of you, of us together."

He grinned at her and bent down to nibble on her ear, still watching her in the mirror. "I like the way your eyes go dark and heavy when I do this," he whispered, easing a hand under the crisscross of her robe. "Or this." He tugged her nipple gently until it peaked into a nub under his searching fingers.

"Hmmmm." She couldn't help the sigh of enjoyment as she leaned into the caress. "That feels . . . divine."

She dropped the hair dryer on the counter with a clatter, bracing her hands on the granite as he bent to run a hand up her thigh, under the robe to caress her hip, sliding both hands under the cloth as he pressed into the curve of her backside. She could feel the power of him, the throb of his erection on her flesh, separated only by the cloth but obviously ready to spring forth.

"Gates," she stuttered as he found her wet heat, stroked the inner folds of her body, heating her up and making the slick wetness of desire leap forth to lubricate the way for him.

"I can't get enough of you, Ana," he rasped, lifting her hair to one side as he kissed the sensitive flesh on the back of her neck. "I want you again, like this, where I can see us both, see us in the mirror as I slide into you."

He let go of her long enough to undo his trousers, let them drop, before he pulled her back to him.

"Aaaaahhhhhhh." She couldn't stop the delicious near-whimper of pleasure as he slid into her.

They'd just found a rhythm when their phones rang.

Chapter Twelve

"No," he said firmly, feeling her falter in the pace they were building. "This is for us. Anyone else can wait."

"Gaaattteeesssss!" She drew out his name, half in protest at his decision, half from powerful enjoyment of what he was doing to and with her body. Seeing them move together, feeling it and watching it as he touched her, caressed her breasts, rocked into her from behind was as arousing and erotic as the way he made her feel.

Her orgasm built to a crescendo, and she urged him to come with her, both with the rotation of her hips and her voice. "You see me, Gates, feel me coming for you? Do you feel it? You make me feel so good," she rasped, never stopping her pace, never looking away. "You fill me up and make me soooo hot, so ahhhhhhh!" She couldn't keep it up. She couldn't keep thinking. Nothing existed but her completion, his gorgeous face behind her, his hands on her hips, gripping her, holding her to him as he shouted his release.

"Ana! Ah!" He twitched and pressed deeper, pulsing within her as they both dived into delight yet again. No one, ever, had made her feel this way, brought her to such easy passion, delivered so much pleasure, so many times.

He banded an arm around her waist, holding her still. "You're bewitching," he stated, keeping them connected for another minute as he kissed her behind the ear. "I think I'm going to need another shower."

"Mmmm, yes," she agreed. "But we have to check our phones."

He sighed, loosing her with obvious reluctance. "Yes, I know. Duty calls, but Ana?"

She turned in his embrace, facing him. "Yes?"

"Nothing changes how special this is, was. Nothing."

Joy welled up within her, knowing he felt the same way she did. "Yes."

"A woman of few words," he said, resting his forehead against hers. "Thank you for the best night's sleep I've had in . . . years."

He rested his big hands on her shoulders, kissed her. "We'll check the phones, and I'll wash off. We'll go from there, okay?"

"Okay."

He stripped, then walked into the living room to retrieve his BlackBerry. "Hmmmm," he muttered, scrolling through e-mail and scanning the entries. Back in her robe, she did the same, trying not to stare at the sheer masculine beauty of his body. There were scars on his back, one that tracked down the back side of one bicep, but they didn't change the overall vision of incredible manhood. To say he was a prime specimen seemed too pale a term.

"What?" he said, catching her looking.

"You're gorgeous," she said honestly.

It was his turn to blush. "I'm not. Men aren't gorgeous."

"Hey, I'm the one looking," she teased. Delighted that she could shake his constant, even façade.

"We're never going to get to work if you keep looking at me that way."

"I know," she mumbled, ducking her head to look at her own messages. Now she wanted him again, not even for sex, but just to hold her, anchor her in the moment. The list of e-mail and calls blurred before her eyes.

"Hey," he said softly, coming to her and doing exactly what she'd just been hoping for. He wound his arms around her,

tucked her head under his chin, and held on. Tears sprang to her eyes, and she returned the favor, drying her eyes on his shirt, which still hung open, pressing her face into the cloth and inhaling the scent of him as if she'd never smell it again.
"Don't worry. We've got a lot to do, but I'll be back. Tonight if you'll let me." He pulled back, tried to see her face, but she ducked her head to erase the last of the tears.

She'd cried more in his arms, in two days, than she had in fifteen years.

"It's not that," she managed. "It's everything." He stiffened a little bit, and she squeezed his ribs. "Stop that. I want you to come back. I do," she insisted, looking up now to let him see the truth of her words. "I'm just a little overwhelmed."

She was holding him closely enough that she felt him relax, felt his relief. "That's understandable. I've sent for the car; it should be here in about forty minutes. Where do you want me to drop you?" He said it as if there were no question that he would be doing it, no argument.

Well, she wasn't in a mood to argue anyway, she decided, letting it go. By the time the car arrived, she'd managed to make them coffee, and a bagel. Other than an intimate smile, and a thank you, he'd been immersed in his work, as had she. She quickly answered a text from Jen that said she was meeting Jack D'Onofrio in Vegas again. Frowning, she wondered if Jen was getting in too deep with this guy before she really knew him. Realizing the irony of the thought, since she'd just slept with Gates, she answered with a positive spin.

Other than the click of texts and an occasional comment about work, they rode in relative silence to her office, each engrossed in the details of their business. The caresses and absent touches were a conversation of a whole different kind.

"Do you have anything on The Bootstrap Foundation?" she asked, flipping through her daybook, noting the list of names she still had to check and how many times she'd been turned down for an interview, or just how often its founder and major backer,

Drake Yountz, had been unavailable. The man was a shipping magnate, but Bootstrap seemed to be his big charity cause.

He looked over, a quizzical smile hovering around his mouth. "There's a joint fundraiser for them tonight, shared with San Francisco TeenCare, the organization that works to get teens off the street, get them involved in the community," he told her. "Silent auction at the Opera House down on Van Ness."

"Busy, busy, busy, aren't they?" she said, wondering how she could get an invitation to the event without having to cough up from the departmental budget.

"Would you like to go? Dav will be going, since he's a very involved sponsor for San Fran TeenCare and a number of people with whom he deals are large donors to both organizations. He's not very fond of Drake Yountz, but he does admire the concept he's developed in Bootstrap."

"Dav's a sponsor? That's wonderful." She wondered how a man like Dav had time to see to those details. "It's a great organization."

"Very close to Dav's heart, since he claims to have been a hoodlum with no place to hang out. He thinks his early life would have been more pleasant if he'd had a TeenCare type of club to go to." Gates's look was grim. "The darker side of Athens is a tough place to be running loose when you're a teenager."

"I'd guess. I need to get to Drake Yountz. He won't return my calls. As to the gala, I'd have to clear going to the event with Pretzky," she began, but he cut her off.

"Why? I'd like you to come as my date." He smiled. "Nothing to check. I hadn't planned to go to this one. Dav had already arranged to escort Sophia Kontos to the event, so I would have been at loose ends anyway. If I go, I wouldn't be working, per se. Either way, we anticipate no trouble."

"You don't?" Ana thought it would be a prime location to go for a hit, then stuttered over the thought of the glamorous Sophia Kontos as Dav's date. She was one of the hottest actresses in Hollywood, blasting onto the American scene after starring in a blockbuster thriller with the legendary Carl Appleton.

"The governor will be there too." Gates grinned, dropping his voice to a guttural imitation of the former actor turned politician. "He'll be back."

"Ha, well, I see what you mean. There'll be security out the wazoo for that." She nodded, running probabilities in her mind. The probability that Pretzky would balk, the probability that she had anything to wear that was suitable. The probability that she could get something before the event tonight.

He took her hand, gave it a squeeze. "Say you'll come."

How could she refuse when he asked her like that, all intent and focused on her alone? "Okay," she whispered, hardly aware that she'd answered him as she lost herself in looking at him. He leaned forward and kissed her lightly on the mouth.

"Good. And now . . ." he said as the car slowed and turned into the driveway of her building, stopping at the guard gate to check in. They were waved through and cruised to the door before he finished. "I'll let you off, but not without this." He pulled her into his arms for a searing kiss that rocked her to her toes.

They broke apart, breathing like they'd run a race.

"I'm supposed to work after that?" she groused, knowing it would be hard to focus on anything after his sensual assault.

"Hmmm, have a nice day dear," he said with bland humor. "I'll think about you," he admitted, his eyes still dark with desire.

"I'll call you about tonight."

He nodded and tapped the glass. The driver strode round to her side and opened the door.

"Tonight, then," he said, running a finger down her cheek as a last farewell.

With that delicious parting, she got out of the car.

Chaos once again prevailed as she walked through the door, but at least this time it was controlled madness of an office working on problem solving. Everyone was still sifting files, pulling notes, and trading information to see if they could pinpoint the target of the computer hack. She got some absent hellos and a couple of questions on how her car was, but other than that, they kept working.

"Get shot at," she marveled again, "and you're just one of the guys."

"Burton, my office," Pretzky called, before Ana could even set her things down. She double-timed it, and walked in just as Pearson, Davis-the-pus-ball, and Caldwell showed up. "Davis, I need you to check with Montrose over in Clandestine Services about the bounce from Turkey. Get me the latest intel on what's brewing there. Caldwell, you call Sci-Tech and see if anything new is on the market that might simulate the bounces. Pearson, follow up with the two IT guys, give them the latest intel from our crew," she snapped, passing over a file. "See if that makes sense. Burton, we may have a lead on the hack, tied to something Caldwell was working on. However, I still want you lying low. You got your car handled?"

"I think so. I have to go over there in an hour, check everything with the adjuster. Then they'll issue me a loaner."

"Good. IAD goons want you again for some additional info." She rolled her eyes and grimaced. "Four o'clock. In the meantime, get me your lists and keep working on the case." She eyed all of them for a moment. "Well? What are all of you waiting for? Get busy."

The other agents filed out, but Ana waited behind.

Pretzky looked up. "Something you need, Burton?"

"Yes. Those additional searches, the data mining project." She began laying out the path of the project, but Pretzky stopped her. "You mentioned this yesterday. Cut to the chase, Burton. In regular English."

"Like I said yesterday, if we can get warrants for phone records on these businesses," she handed Pretzky the list of five of the galleries. "And these individuals, we can coordinate a data run that will essentially sift the data down to common denominators, things like calls on the day the fraud was discovered, calls from the gallery to the victims, calls from the gallery right after those calls."

"Wasn't that accessed at the time?" Pretzky demanded. "Pretty shoddy work if it wasn't."

"It was, but the records aren't digitized in the file. Also, they don't look at all the individuals I believe are involved. The old warrants are beyond statute by at least three years."

"Shit. You were right then, new warrants." Pretzky frowned, tapping her foot in the familiar irritated tattoo. "Give me the list. I'll see what I can do."

"Thanks," Ana said with relief. If they could just find a lead, something, anything, to go on, maybe she could solve this one too. The need to prove herself, using her skills, was a hot burn in her gut. She'd been condemned for failing with those skills; she felt it would take the same skills, well used, to redeem herself. Pretzky waved off the thanks, dismissed her.

She had her hand on the doorknob when Pretzky called her name. "Burton?"

"Yes?" Ana turned back.

"He stay for breakfast?"

It took every ounce of control not to let her shock flood her face. "Yes."

Pretzky waited a heartbeat, a tactic to trip up a suspect, make them reveal more than they'd intended. Ana kept her mouth shut.

"Get to work," Pretzky said, when she finally spoke. "And Burton? Be careful."

That was all she said, but the way she said it, the tilt of her head and her posture, told Ana that she meant Gates, and that Pretzky knew a whole lot more than she was letting on.

"I will. It's complicated, but I'm checking all the angles."

Pretzky nodded, sure now that she'd gotten her point across. "See that you do. Four o'clock, my office."

"You bet." Ana made her way back to her desk and unpacked her things. The three boxes pertaining to the art fraud case were still sitting on her desk, just as she'd left them.

Frowning, she scanned her workspace. Something was off. Something was different.

Her eyes widened as she realized that the other cold-case boxes had been moved, just half a foot down the table, but moved nonetheless. She hadn't done it, which meant that someone had been in her space, looking for something.

Damn it. She made a decision and headed back to Pretzky's office. In Rome, she'd been too much of a lone ranger, sure her analysis was dead on, certain of her skills, confident in her read of the situation. If she'd done there what she was doing now, asking for help, two people might be alive. She'd never know, but she knew she couldn't live with more souls on her conscience.

She tapped on the door frame, and Pretzky looked up, the phone to her ear. She motioned Ana in, holding up one finger in a "wait a minute" gesture, directing her to a chair with the same motion.

Ana perched on the edge of the seat, still at war with herself about what she'd seen. Had she moved them yesterday and just forgotten in the turmoil?

No. She knew she hadn't. Gut-level knew it.

"So, what do you need?" Pretzky slapped the phone down and growled the words in Ana's direction.

"All right if I shut the door?" That got an instant reaction. Pretzky paused in the act of pouring herself coffee, pinning Ana with a gimlet stare.

"Problem?"

"Possibly."

"Shut the door and spit it out," she ordered, muttering, "Like we need anything else."

"I agree, for what it's worth. Look," she said, deciding that she had to lay her cards on the table with Pretzky, make an ally if she could. "I know you may not believe me, but I did everything I could in Rome to be sure, *absolutely sure,* I was right. Two people are dead because I didn't run it by someone, double-check my data. I won't make that mistake again."

Pretzky's grim look shifted to a more thoughtful, appraising glance. "And?"

"Someone moved the files on my desk," Ana began.

The other woman shot forward, leaning on the desk. "You're sure?"

Rubbing at her tired eyes, Ana nodded. "I've been second-guessing myself with everything, Special Agent. And I do mean everything. I've crossed my t's and dotted my i's so many times, I'm practically blind with it. You'd think I was OCD the way I've checked and double-checked things since Rome."

"Obsessive-compulsive disorder notwithstanding, I'd expect nothing less. You have to be sure."

"I've gone beyond the usual 'sure,' Special Agent. Trust me. The point is, because I've been so—" She hesitated, then just used the word that popped into her mind. "Paranoid, I know where everything is in and on my desk down to the last paper-clip. I'm not going to miss something through carelessness. I know it's been moved," she finished with firm conviction.

"The cleaning crew is cleared, but they know not to touch anything."

"I know." Ana brooded as she sat, wondering who would have been in her files.

"What was moved?"

"The other paper files. There are five boxes; I've gone through three. The last two are paper copies of the old phone records, interview duplicates, jurisdictional cross-checks. The last box, the one with the phone records, was moved just enough to set the lid down in the blank space. Someone shifted them down so they could open the one box I've not finished going through."

"You're sure?"

Ana nodded, feeling the twinge of doubt in her gut. She shut it down.

"That changes things," Pretzky said with dark anger. "What else?"

"I—" Ana started, then stopped. Oh, hell. In for a penny, in for a pound. "I've been invited to attend a gala this evening. I wouldn't do it, given the situation and your, uh, warning. However, a person of interest whose donor list very nearly matches the loss list is going to be there. I'm not sure I could get to him any other way." That was her story, and she was sticking to it. "I wanted to make you aware of it."

Pretzky relaxed into the chair's embrace. "I see. Are you prepared for that kind of evening?"

"Prepared?"

The other woman rolled her eyes again, something Ana hadn't realized she did with such regularity. "Do you have a dress, Burton? Are you prepped for that level of contact?"

"Shit," Ana blurted out, mentally skimming through her closet. "No. Nothing."

"Get out of here, go get something. But," she cautioned, "be back by four."

"Or I turn into a pumpkin?"

Pretzky laughed. "Something like that. Let me think about the other situation before you mention it to IAD, okay? I'd like to shake it off as nothing, but I'm taking no chances with this. Too much has happened too fast for this to be coincidence."

Ana nodded, not trusting herself to comment. "I'll be back by four."

Ana didn't even consider trying to bargain hunt. She took a cab straight to Maiden Lane, near Union Square. Bypassing Chanel and Prada as beyond her price range, she walked into Misioia Couture. An attractive young woman, painfully thin, glided her way.

"Good afternoon," she said melodically. "I am Su. May I help you find something?"

"I need an evening dress for a gala." She waited a heartbeat and dropped the bomb. "It's tonight."

Horror leaped into the girl's eyes, and she scanned Ana's muscular form and height. "Oh. My." To her credit she recovered quickly. "If you would have a seat? I'll be a moment."

I'll bet. "Thanks." Ana sat in one of the plush-looking but very hard chairs. Jen had raved about this designer's stuff, and she'd been featured in *San Francisco* magazine in the winter, just before all the holiday events. Ana was praying that because she wasn't as much a "name" that Su might have something affordable that would keep her from looking like an off-the-rack vagabond.

"Ma'am?" A soft voice broke through her thoughts, and another woman stopped by her side. "If you would come with me?"

This woman was older, serene in a way Ana equated with people who did yoga and tai chi. Ana shrugged and followed her.

"I am Cara Misioia. May I ask which gala you will be attending?"

Oh, man, the designer herself. She was either going to get what she came for, or she was going to get a hell of an embarrassment. "The TeenCare–Bootstrap Foundation gala at the Opera House."

"Ah, a worthy pair of causes. I am fond of the TeenCare people. Many of them will be wearing my designs tonight," she said with a smile. "And are you interested in teens, Miss . . . ?"

"Burton. Ana Burton." Ana decided to leave the whole agent thing out. She also decided it might be time to do a little name dropping. "I've been invited by Mr. Gianikopolis and his—" She didn't get any further. The woman gasped and stopped in her tracks.

"You will be with Mr. G?" She fluttered her long-fingered hands as if she were having a panic attack. "*THE* Mr. G?"

Taken aback, Ana said, "The only one I know. He's partnered with Sophia Kontos, but I'll be—"

"Ohhhhhh." Cara fluttered some more, her face alternately flushing and going pale. "La Kontos is one of the most elegant . . . if I ever got . . . oh, my. I must sit. Please, please. Be comfortable." Cara opened a lovely armoire decorated with Asian scenes, and opened a thoroughly modern refrigerator concealed inside. “Water? A soft drink? Wine?”

“Water’s fine, thanks.” Ana waited as Cara took out glasses, filled them with ice, and poured sparkling water into two glasses. Ana surreptitiously looked at her watch.

“Miss Burton, I think I have something that would suit you. It is very expensive, I’ll tell you that up front. However,” she preempted Ana’s objection, “if you are to be in Mr. G’s party this evening, wearing my design, I will benefit greatly. There will be pictures, you see, national press, and he is so prominent that the pictures of him will be included.”

Ana was following the discussion, but not sure how it related to a really expensive dress. “Okay, so there will be pictures.” She put that together with her being with Gates and froze. “Oh, Lord, there will be pictures.” What the hell was she going to do about that?

“Yes, yes, you see then. You will wear the dress. I will only charge you a rental fee.” Cara clapped her hands together once, sharply to finalize the point. She smiled at Ana, and there was a manic look to it. “Sophia Kontos will also be wearing a rented gown, so do not look so stricken, young lady. If it is good enough for her, it is good enough for you, yes?”

“No, I mean yes. But that’s not what I’m worried about. The pictures. Crap. Maybe I should call this off.” She pulled out her PDA, ready to call Gates, when Cara put her hand over the keypad.

“Miss Burton, I would take it as a great favor if you would do this. I have been working for fifteen years to build my business. This, this is the sort of thing that can take a designer over the top.”

“I’m no model, Ms. Misioia.”

“No, no, and you don’t need to be. This is the point of my designs. I design brilliant gowns for the woman who has shape, form. For a woman, Miss Burton, not a stick.”

“But your assistant,” Ana blurted before she could censor the remark. Jeez, fashion must be rattling her brain.

Cara laughed, a light, tinkling bell sound. "Yes, odd, isn't it? But certain women buy better from an assistant like Su." She shrugged. "It is a mystery. Now, let us begin. Please, here is the dressing area. If you would go down to your underwear, please, yes?"

If Cara was disturbed by the sight of Ana's weapon lying on top of her suit pants, she didn't show it. She measured and muttered, twisting Ana this way and that before finally handing her a robe. "Put this on. Stay here. Don't sweat."

Unsure how she would manage the latter, Ana slid her arms into the silk robe. It smelled of lavender and sunshine. Before she could tie it, Cara was back, with Su in tow. Together, they carried a dress the color of midnight. A deep rich blue that shimmered as it moved.

"The robe," Cara demanded, and Ana took it off. "Su," she said imperiously, directing the assistant with some unseen command. Su took the robe, turned Ana to face the wall.

The fabric swooshed around her and after what seemed an eternity of pinning, clucking, and one oddly New York–sounding curse, Cara clapped her hands again.

"Perfect. Turn and see."

Ana did and nearly dropped her jaw with shock. The dress fit as if it were made for her. It showed off the line of her collar bone, and the strength of her shoulders. Her neck looked long, graceful. Enhanced by the neckline, her breasts looked full and lush. "Oh, my God."

"Yes, yes," Cara beamed. "Perfect. Now, walk."

"Walk?"

Cara made an impatient noise. "Walk to the mirror, I must see if there is need to adjust the hem." Ana moved forward, and the dress flowed with her, the fabric whispering as it surged with her. "No. Perfect. You will wear shoes with no more than a two-inch heel. They will be black or silver. You will wear nothing at the neck, do you hear? Nothing."

Since Ana was pretty sure she didn't have anything that would do the dress justice, she stayed quiet. "Earrings, silver, long and sweeping your shoulders, a bracelet, maybe two, also silver. Nothing more, you understand? The dress must shine."

"It already does," Ana murmured.

"And you in it. Here, let me help you. You must go, get your jewelry, your shoes, and come back. We will work out the fee then, I will make it so that you can do this. In return, you will look beautiful in this gown and be in pictures. Do we have a deal?"

Ana looked at the dress, at the way it looked on her, and imagined what Gates would say when he saw her. She smiled. Oh, yeah.

"How should I wear my hair?"

Ana was back at the office by four, but just barely. She was actively praying that the IAD team wouldn't keep her long. She had to get to the bank and retrieve two of her mother's jewelry boxes, run by her apartment for the shoes, and get back to Misioia before six. At least going in to town on a weeknight would be easier than getting out. She'd already texted Gates to pick her up at the Sir Francis Drake, which would give her time to finish up at Misioia and do her makeup and hair.

"Agent Burton." The two IAD agents were waiting, along with Pretzky, in the conference room. Pretzky seemed relieved that she wasn't dressed in anything different.

"How was your meeting, Burton?" Pretzky inquired.

"Successful, thank you," she said, letting Pretzky know she wasn't going to let the Agency down by looking like an idiot.

By the time they were done, Ana decided the IAD were jerks. They covered the exact same ground they had before, only minimally bringing up Gates and Dav, before they gathered their things and left.

"What the hell was that?" Pretzky wondered, shooting Ana a look before watching the agents board the elevator to leave.

"No idea. Seemed pointless."

"Get a dress?"

"Oh, my God," she said, thinking of the blue confection. "You wouldn't believe it," she began, then remembered that it was Pretzky she was talking to. She cut it short. "Yeah, I got a dress."

Pretzky didn't turn, but Ana could tell she was laughing. "That good?"

"The best. It rocks."

"Good. I started the process on the warrants," the older woman stated it as if it were the least of Ana's worries.

"Really? When do you think—" she began, eager to know when she could get started on the search with Gates.

"Burton?"

"Yes?"

"The gala?"

Ana looked at the clock. "Shit, it's almost five."

"Then get going. IAD idiots," she muttered, throwing Ana a brief smile. "Well? Go on."

Ana went.

"You look . . ." Gates seemed to be at a loss for words. "Wow." The look he gave her was pure passion, and promised dark, sensual things when this night was done. She managed not to shiver in response, but felt her body tighten and her breasts grow heavy with the thought of his hands on her. "Magnificent," he murmured, bending to touch his lips to hers in a brief, electric kiss.

The contact stole her breath, and she felt as she had moments before, dashing through the hotel. Cara Misioia had pronounced her fit, and she'd run for a cab to get to the Sir Francis Drake in time to meet Dav and Gates. Thank God Sophia Kontos was staying at the hotel as well, which made it seem perfectly natural for the men to meet them there.

"Beautiful, my dear," Dav added, an appreciative gleam in his eyes. He'd missed nothing about the exchange between the two of them. "Ah, and here is the lovely Sophia. What a pleasant surprise that she's on time."

Ana didn't even want to know about the look that passed between Gates and Dav over that remark.

The gorgeous actress swept across the lobby with the ease of someone used to cameras and staging. She was dramatic, with flowing black hair and snapping blue eyes.

"Davros!" she exclaimed in breathy delight, taking his hands and kissing him on both cheeks.

"Sophia, *kouritsaki-mou,* I am so glad to see you. Come, come, meet my friends." Dav introduced them all and nudged everyone to the limo. To Ana's amusement, Dav was treating Sophia like a young cousin come to town; by using the affectionate Greek designation of her as "littlest one," he let her know it wasn't a date. For all she knew, Sophia *was* another cousin; however, the actress was visibly unhappy at being treated with such avuncular regard.

"We are lucky men, are we not, Gates? Ana, may I say that I have never seen you look so lovely. You do us an honor to be with us tonight." He turned to Gates and grinned. "Well done, Gates."

Gates just slipped Ana's hand into the crook of his arm, despite the fact that they were in the limo and there was no need for it. "Thank you, Dav." Dav didn't miss the significance of the gesture, but Sophia evidently did. Then again, the younger woman was still processing the shift in dynamics with Dav.

"And to have you with us, Sophia-aki." Dav patted her hand where it lay on the seat beside him. "It will be quite the coup for me to be seen with such a beautiful woman."

"My goodness, there're a lot of limos ahead of us," Ana said as they pulled up at the Opera House.

"Yes, the governor's here tonight. TeenCare is one of his particular favorites, and he touts it as an example of public-private partnerships truly working." Dav leaned forward to peer through the darkened glass. "There is Tom Hanks, and his lovely wife. I believe that's their son with them as well."

From disgrace to the Opera House, what a week. The irreverent thought followed her from the limo, down the red carpet as they paused for photographs, both as couples and as a foursome, and into the bustling event inside.

"Davros, my friend," a hearty voice called as they entered, and Ana felt Gates stiffen beside her. The leering man from the gallery opening was bearing down upon them, hand outstretched.

Ana searched for a name, but came up blank.

"Drake Yountz," Gates murmured, his voice carrying no farther than Ana's ears. "Founder of Bootstrap."

New target acquired.

Chapter Thirteen

"Mr. Gianikopolis," Drake began. "Dav," he corrected himself, using the familiar address. His eyes widened at the sight of Sophia, but Ana would have bet money that he'd known she was going to be there. "And what a coup for us, to have you here, Ms. Kontos," he said, oozing charm and kissing the hand she offered rather than taking it in the traditional handshake.

Sophia recovered quickly. "Thank you, for the warm welcome."

"No, no, it is we who are privileged to have you with us. Dav, will you introduce me to the rest of your party?"

Dav was quick on the uptake, Ana would give him that. "Drake Yountz, founder of Bootstrap Foundation, let me introduce you to my associate, Gates Bromley, and his lovely guest this evening, Ana Burton."

Yountz shook hands with Gates and did as he had done with Sophia, kissing her hand with what he must have thought was Continental flair. Ana was unimpressed and wished she could wipe her hand on something. She wasn't about to wipe it on the dress, but she wondered if Gates had another of those soft handkerchiefs handy.

It annoyed the shit out of her that the one target she'd been trying to pin down was this slimy piece of work. He'd refused to talk to her about the case, refused to answer her calls, had his secretary call her and tell him he was unavailable. She hadn't recognized Yountz's name at the party at Prometheus, but she knew it now.

"Do come and let me introduce you to some people, Dav, Gates, ladies. It's a wonderful turnout tonight." Drake started them all down the stairs into the main gallery where all the bars were set up, directing them easily through the crowd.

Gates's hand was on her back again, and he whispered in her ear as they paused in their progress through the throng. "He's an annoyance, isn't he?"

She gave a slight nod, careful to keep the pleasant smile on her face.

"I want to take your dress off and make love to you, right now," he continued in the same whisper, never letting on that he was seducing her in the middle of the crowded room. The heat of his hand, the sweep of his fingers in that hypnotic rhythm were a poignant reminder of how they'd been together, and she could feel the blush rising from her cleavage up her neck and into her cheeks. "You're beautiful when you blush." His parting shot left her hotter than ever, but thankfully the jam-up of people shifted and they moved forward once more. If he continued to tease her, stroke her all night, she was going to explode.

The mental image of the two of them tangled together in bed made her wet with anticipation.

Forcing herself to focus, she pasted on a social smile and shook hands with the governor and his gracious wife, several congressmen and a congresswoman, along with a welter of social lions from the San Francisco community. At every turn, the cameras flashed, and she fielded numerous questions about her dress, the designer, and her jewelry.

They were alone with Dav for a few moments, which gave her a chance to speak to him. "Thanks for bringing Sophia. It takes the spotlight off me," she said, watching the paparazzi maneuver in the crowd to get a shot of the gorgeous woman, now talking with a director who lived in the Bay Area.

"My pleasure," he drawled. "She is a distant relative, and it did us both good to be seen here tonight." He smiled at her, a twinkle in his eye. "I did not, however, want her to get the wrong impression." Something over her shoulder caught his eye, and she saw his gaze sharpen and his body language change. For a moment, she saw something in his face that could have been hunger, something so deep and personal, that she caught her breath. Then he pulled down his social mask once more.

"Dav?" Gates must have seen it too, because there was more than a question in his voice.

Without answering the question, Dav smiled at Ana, but his attention was still across the room. "If you'll excuse me?"

"Of course." Standing together, Gates and Ana watched him move through the crowd, stopping only briefly when someone detained him for a handshake or introduction. Looking ahead, she saw what Dav had seen, the goal he was aiming for. "Interesting," she breathed, remembering the gallery opening, and Dav's interest in Carrie McCray.

"What?"

"Carrie McCray," she murmured, directing his attention. As they watched, Dav reached her and even from where they stood they could see the pleased smile that suffused her face, the slight flush in her cheeks as Dav steered her toward the bar.

"So that's who it is." Gates's murmur carried no farther than her ears. "I've been wondering."

"Wondering?" Gates and Dav were close, she knew it, but their relationship was still opaque to her in so many ways. Gates was far more than the security droid he made himself out to be. While he was less than a full partner in all of Dav's businesses, she believed he was as close to that as Dav might ever allow.

"He's been distracted in the last week, and not just with the incidents. At first, he mentioned relocating to Europe." Gates let his hand resume its restless movement at the small of her back. "I wasn't in favor of that," he said, his voice warm and caressing as he added, "for a variety of reasons." After a moment, he continued. "Usually, he just makes a decision and goes, but this time, although he talked about it, he didn't pack, didn't change anything. That frequently means there's a woman in the picture. He's always had a soft spot for Carrie, but I wasn't sure it went any deeper than that. In fact, I thought it might be Sophia."

"She's too young for him." Ana kept her voice low as well, unwilling to provide fodder for the gossip columns by speaking too freely or too loudly.

"Yes, but young women are often attracted to men like Dav," he said, cynicism ripe in his voice. "Trust me, I usually bear the brunt of their disappointment."

Ana smirked. "Bet that's tough duty."

His breath tickled her ear as he said, "You have no idea." He paused. "Want to find a dark corner?"

"Gates," she hissed as Drake Yountz approached them again, frowning and obviously looking for Dav.

"Hello again, I was looking for Dav, I wanted to introduce him to Mr. Chang." He indicated the man and his petite wife, tagging along behind Drake like ducklings. "Zhenji-san, I've lost him again. I'm so sorry. We'll be sure that you get to meet him before the evening is out." Another couple moved over to intercept Yountz and the Changs, and Yountz neatly stepped between Gates and Ana. When Gates asked her if she'd like another drink, Yountz beamed. "Oh, Gates, since you're going to get a drink for Ana, here, could I impose on you to get the Changs something as well?"

Trapped by good manners and a ring of watching faces, Gates acquiesced with good grace. Ana, however, saw the flash of fury in his eyes.

She regretted his departure immediately as Drake fixed his eyes on her cleavage and asked, "Did I hear you say that was a Misioia? I told Mrs. Chang," he nodded to the woman, "that one of our most prominent San Francisco designers has relatives in her province."

Mrs. Chang beamed, and Ana got an idea of how Drake Yountz had built his shipping business as well as the Bootstrap Foundation. He worked connections and knowledge with eel-like fluidity.

"Your dress is lovely." The woman's accented English made the comment musical.

Drake used the compliment as an excuse to slip his arm around her, pull her close. "Wonderful to see beautiful women like yourself supporting up-and-coming designers." He turned and kissed her cheek, and she gritted her teeth. A camera flashed, and Drake beamed, giving her waist an extra tug. "And they got us together—how wonderful is that?"

Resisting the urge to break his fingers, Ana pulled out of his hold. "Unpleasant, but a necessary evil, I guess," she said sweetly. The Changs looked confused because her words didn't match her tone.

Drake's laugh was hearty and loud, "Of course, of course. Some people don't like photographers," he agreed jovially, although the tight look around his eyes betrayed his anger. "But some don't photograph as well as others either," he said, slipping in a verbal jab.

Gates returned at that moment, to Ana's relief. She felt more than heard Gates's chuckle.

"I would say that Ana has no problem there, Yountz." He let the heat of his voice wash over her, and the way he moved in close was enough of a nonverbal clue that Yountz backed off another step.

"Ah, of course." Drake still looked angry, despite the smile he was showing.

Gates motioned a young server forward, and the woman offered a tray bearing drinks. Ana took her wine and sipped it, reining in her seething temper. The Changs were distracted enough that they missed the byplay of emotion.

"Ana, I see someone I want you to meet. Would you excuse us?" Gates's exit from the group was smooth as silk, so was the brush of his hand over the bare skin at the top of her dress in back. Once again he leaned in to whisper. "I want to put my mouth right here." He trailed a long finger along the top of the dress. "And make you quiver."

Anger dissipated by the frisson of desire, Ana moved closer to him, felt him laugh. "Like that, do you?"

"Yes, I do. The party's wonderful, isn't it?" She answered the question and managed to keep up the social façade at the same time.

"Of course. Why don't we go up there?" Gates indicated the upper gallery. "I'd love to see the artwork."

Unsure if it was another personal ploy or a reference to the case, she agreed. From the higher elevation, they could see the interplay of people on the floor below.

"Look, Yountz has Sophia cornered now," she muttered, watching as the young woman deftly deflected the grab and squeeze. Evidently she'd had more experience with the maneuver.

"He's an ass. A rich one, mind you," Gates drawled, his hand at her back again. "Has a gorgeous wife, Caroline, but she hasn't come to any of these things for a while now. Certainly since we've been back in the States. Last year when we were here, she was out to here." He held out a hand, indicating pregnancy. "Yountz spent the next few months cornering people to show off baby pictures instead of being a sleaze."

"But he's returned to previous form?" Ana disliked him even more now, knowing that. Some men were pigs, and Yountz was evidently an oinker of the highest order.

"Seems like. You looked ready to string him up when I got back." Gates sounded amused rather than irritated now. "It was tempting to just let you have a go at him, I confess."

"I have to watch my temper with that sort," she admitted, leaning into him when he warmed her bare shoulder with his hand. "I was contemplating dismemberment."

"Vicious thought."

"Hmmmm." She scanned the crowd, found Dav. He was standing with a group, Carrie McCray at his side. His date, Sophia, had flicked Yountz off and was surrounded by adoring men, young and old. "Do you think Sophia will be riding home with us?" She directed Gates's attention to the crowd.

"Probably. That was one of Dav's stipulations when he offered to chaperone her."

"Oh, really?" Chaperone. Didn't sound like something Sophia would ask for, so Ana presumed there was some family maneuvering afoot.

"Yeah. Hang on a sec." Gates gripped his throat, activating his walkie-talkie. In a low voice, he ordered, "Declan, close up the back. You're too far away from Dav."

"I thought you weren't on duty," Ana said, as she watched a young man with dark red hair shift in the crowd, ambling toward Dav's position. If she hadn't heard the order and connected the red hair with the name, she'd never have noticed. Looking again, she noted faces she'd seen at the estate, including the driver, Damon. He looked as dashing in a tuxedo as he had in a chauffer's uniform, and the slim, beautiful woman on his arm was quite a bit more attractive than she'd looked at the guard station.

"Full complement tonight, Gates?"

"Big crowd. I don't care how much security the governor has, it isn't looking out for Dav. That's my job. Or it is when I'm on the job."

"Aren't we always on the job? I may be your date tonight, for fun, but I'm working too." As much as she'd rather be here to just be with Gates, she said it out loud as a reminder to herself, as well as to Gates. "Dav's on the move," she said, grinning as she saw Dav take Carrie's hand and tuck it in his elbow. "They're going to look at the auction items."

She shifted toward the stairs, but Gates stopped her. "Where are you going?"

Puzzled, she looked at him, noting the mischief in his eyes. "Don't we need to . . ." She trailed off as he crooked a finger.

"Come with me," he said softly, his hand at her back once more. "I've something I want to show you. It won't take long."

"Oh, really?" Ana was intrigued, sure that she should be down on the floor, mingling, taking note of who was there, managing data about those who had lost paintings and those who wanted nothing to do with resurrecting the case. At least seven of her targets were present tonight, including two actors she'd been unable to speak with.

Instead, despite her better judgment, she followed Gates as he sauntered through the looser grouping on this mezzanine level. He came to a door and opened it, gesturing for her to go through before him.

"What's this?"

"Security area," he said, walking through the dimly lit room. "There's something I want to show you."

"What?"

"This," he said, opening the door to a small, neatly appointed room, then closing and locking the door behind them. "Come here."

All the fantasies that had flitted through her mind earlier slammed into her head as he kissed her long and deep. "Ohhhhhh," she moaned as he slipped a finger into her bodice to tease her nipple.

"We won't take much time," he whispered. "We'll go back, but I had to touch you. Kiss you. My God you're beautiful." He said it over and over as he rained kisses on her lips, her neck, the vee of her breasts where it was exposed by the fabulous dress. "You make me crazy."

It was the desk that gave her the idea. This time, she would take the lead. She edged away, to arm's length. He looked surprised. "Problem?"

"No," she smiled. "No problem." She glanced over her shoulder. The sturdy, built-in desk would do nicely. "Sit here," she said, drawing him forward to the comfortable office chair. It was padded and had an angled back. Perfect.

"Sit?"

"Yes, sit," she said, pushing on his shoulders until he complied. "So I can do this," she said, bending into him, kissing him deeply, a war of tongues and passion. "And this," she said, swishing the dress apart at the dramatic front split so she could kneel between his knees. "We have to go back out, be presentable, but I think that this would work, don't you?"

Without any other preamble, she freed him from his tuxedo pants, letting her hands and mouth bring him to near orgasm within minutes.

He groaned his pleasure as she laved his cock, sucking it gently until he was on the brink, then backing off to blow cool air on the length of him, teasing and tasting to her heart's delight. When they'd been together the previous night, they'd been so tired, so eager, they hadn't had time to play, or tease.

They didn't have time now, not really. They both felt the weight of responsibility, of the need to be working. Somehow that made the interlude feel that much more illicit, that much sexier.

"Ana, we should," he began, eyes nearly crossed in delight. "Ahhhhhh."

"We'll go back in a minute. I know. We shouldn't be . . ."

"What? We're off duty, remember?"

"Yeah," she growled. "That's why you've got your mic and your weapon. That's why I've got my credentials in my bag. We're off duty."

"Ana," he moaned, "I . . ."

"You what?" she teased, rising over him, spreading the dress farther so she could straddle him, kiss him again with passion and verve. "You want me, Gates? Do you?"

"All of you. Sit on the counter so I can taste you, do to you what you did to me," he muttered between kisses.

"No," she said, still in charge. "Not now, not enough time," she explained, knowing that if he started on her that way, they could never avoid the total disruption of their clothes. It would be too obvious.

Instead, she moved away, which made him protest, but just for a second. Aroused beyond belief, she smiled. It only took her a moment to step out of the flimsy lace thong and scoot up on the solidly built desk. "Now you," she said with deliberate intent, "Come to me."

She'd never been so wanton, so free of inhibition. It couldn't be the wine, she'd had very little. It was Gates, gorgeous, intoxicating Gates Bromley. She twitched the silk and lace of the bottom of the dress to her sides, leaning back, exposing the creamy flesh of her thighs, with their silky stockings and lace garters, to his gaze.

"Oh, God," he said, moving up and to her, his hot hands spreading over her hips, lifting her slightly so he could touch her, slide into her with the deepest growl of delight she'd ever heard. He'd protected them both, but that hadn't slowed him down at all.

She was so wet, so ready for him, that they joined easily, almost effortlessly. She could see his arousal in his face, feel him everywhere. The sight of their joining was titillating, tantalizing, and driving her higher.

Just as revved, Gates murmured words of passion, moving with strength and power, but with the utmost control as they rose together. "That's it," he crooned, when she licked her lips, her mouth dry from panting her excitement. "Let it go for me. You're so excited," he murmured. "I can feel you, so tight, so hot." He leaned in, reaching down to tickle her innermost folds with his finger until he found the sensitive nub buried in curls. One flick was all it took. The sensory overload of seeing him in passion, knowing they weren't alone, weren't entirely safe from being disturbed all came together for her in a sensual haze, and she vaulted over the edge into freefall, her body clenching and throbbing.

Through her release, she heard him cry out as well, muffled as he bit down on his lip to stifle the noise. More, she felt him, felt the powerful thrust of him inside her and the heated grip of his hands on her hips, drawing him as close as possible, locking them in love's embrace.

"Oh, my God," he managed to say, the words ringing softly in the cool room. Still pulsing together, they rocked, unwilling for a moment to move apart, to let the moment pass. "You are"—he shook his head, a bemused smile lighting his features—"incredible. I can't believe you."

He grinned, and she felt relief steal over her. He wasn't upset about her taking it farther than a mere kiss. "I couldn't resist you," she murmured, inordinately pleased with herself.

"You make me crazy, woman," he muttered. "I don't usually do this sort of thing, you know that." He made it a statement. Watching her. He was still panting from their exertions, but he was telling her something important, and she realized it immediately.

"I know. I don't either," she said, her own breath catching a bit, realizing that they were both implying a deeper connection, an intimacy beyond the physical.

"I'm glad you see it," he said, tracing a finger down her cheek. "Know it. Whatever this is," he murmured, indicating the passion between them. "It's more."

"More?"

"Just more. More than I was looking for. More than I expected."

She nodded and sat up farther to embrace him. They stayed like that for a long minute as their breathing leveled out. Finally, they cleaned up and helped one another set their clothes to rights. She made a move to straighten his tie, but he deflected it. "I don't want to risk activating the mic," he explained, a boyish grin slipping over his face. "No need to advertise our indiscretions, even if I'm not here in my official capacity."

"No." She grinned back, smoothing his lapels and refastening one of the studs that had slipped out of place. "That's the last thing we'd want."

She checked her makeup, noting that she looked flushed,

and satisfied, but that nothing had run or smeared. Thank goodness for waterproof mascara and good cosmetics. Taking a small compact from her evening bag, she swiped a light dusting of powder over her nose.

"You look beautiful," he said, running a light touch down her neck as she refastened one of the jeweled clips that held her hair.

"Just as long as I don't look like I just had mind-blowing sex in a . . ." She looked around the small room. "Security waiting room," she concluded. "Then we're okay."

"No, but you do look—" He cocked his head, considered.

A bit panicked, she looked at her mirror. She couldn't see anything wrong. "What?"

"Delicious."

She snorted out a laugh, "Stop. We have to get out of here before someone misses us."

"I doubt we'll be missed, seeing as how we're not bigwigs." He sighed dramatically. "But, I guess we must."

They checked one another a last time, which was occasion for a bit more kissing and play, but eventually they slipped out the door and into the corridor, melding into the crowd without anyone being the wiser.

They were nearly to the mezzanine railing when a huge surge of noise and applause rang out. Shrill voices called out for silence, and to Ana's surprise, the noise died down. Gates shot her a questioning look, but she had no idea what was going on.

Together they hurried to the upper mezzanine rail.

The phone rang, and Drake Yountz recognized the number. Jurgens. The party was in full swing so no one would miss him if he stepped out to take a call.

"Yes?"

"The job we discussed. I have someone. An insider." Jurgens's message was clipped, precise. "Already he has given me product." Jurgens's use of the term meant that the insider had been able to give him something or do something that would throw off the search, or deflect it away from any connection to him.

"Good. What else?"

"Your rival, he is under scrutiny, but I do not think it is sanctioned. He has—" Jurgens paused. Drake sensed strong disapproval when Jurgens spoke again. "He is in trouble with many people, some of them family."

"Fascinating." Drake let the word stretch out, pleased to know that Santini, his East Coast rival, was snared in something nasty. "Did you get his name? And the trouble, can we use it?"

"Ja."

"Good. Start that going. Do you need resources?"

"No. I will work first."

"Excellent," Drake said. "The original party we were discussing?" He paused, waiting for Jurgens to figure it out.

Jurgens filled in the blank. "The woman?"

"Yes," Drake agreed. "A guest this evening at my event. Quite lovely, really."

"Huh. With the Greek?"

"His assistant."

"Bromley," Jurgens snarled. He didn't like Bromley on principle, it seemed.

"Exactly. On the resources, let me know." Drake nodded to a couple strolling down the terrace, turned his back, and murmured, "Is that all?"

"Ja. I'll call."

The line went dead, and he stood, contemplating the new turn of events. If his New York rival could be neutralized, or better yet, if he could be opened up to take the fall for all of the art-fraud cases, Drake could step away and no one would be the wiser. None of his collection would ever be questioned, since he already claimed them to be no more than excellent copies.

It was his own delightful joke to show off his paintings all while discounting people's praise with the comment, "Oh, I never buy the real thing. Too much money for too little return. I like art, but it isn't my kind of investment."

His friends would nod and smile and move on, never knowing they'd just seen millions of dollars of real art, casually hanging on his walls.

Chapter Fourteen

"Where's Dav?" Gates questioned, scanning the seething crowd below. "Ana?"

She was looking as well, but saw no sign of Dav. "I don't know. We need to get down there."

Moving to the left to find another gilded, but blocked door, Gates ignored the sign directing him to go another way and pushed through to a smaller anteroom. They crossed it at a near run and hit the door to the stairs as one.

With the elegant dress streaming behind her, Ana managed the stairs easily. She prayed that the lace wouldn't snag on anything because if Dav was down, or hurt, she would rip the dress if she had to, to get where they needed to be.

At the bottom, Gates stopped. "Hang on," he said. He yanked up the back of his coat and turned his back to her. "Hook me back up. The wire's come undone from the battery."

She plugged the wire back into its socket, and he was immediately online. "Thompson, report," he snapped, opening the door and moving into the crowd, Ana at his back.

He gave her a terse, but very quiet rundown as he got the live feed. "Dav's still in the auction room. The newcomers are members of the Opera, in costume. Evidently Dav's still with Carrie—they're avoiding the crowds out front."

"Thank God," she sighed, wanting to sag with relief. Since

no chairs were in sight, she sucked it up and kept moving in Gates's wake. They were both feeling guilty about sneaking off for a moment to themselves.

"Dav's at twelve o'clock," Gates murmured, bringing her along. "It's stupid, I know, but I'd like to get over there. Make sure."

She understood, and let him get ahead of her just a bit so he could see what he needed to see. The rush of adrenaline was fading, and she was feeling the pang of regret. What if Dav had been in danger while she and Gates were fooling around? Neither she nor Gates would ever forgive themselves if something happened to Dav while they were supposed to be on watch.

"Not on duty," she reminded herself, but it didn't really matter. They'd been there. Duty was implied, for both of them.

She nearly bumped into Gates's broad back as he stopped abruptly. With a hopefully inaudible "Oof," she sidestepped, merely grazing his arm instead of plowing through him.

Recovering her aplomb as quickly as she could, and ignoring the looks of disapproval tossed her way by matrons and youngsters alike, she searched for Dav.

There. Safe. He and Carrie were standing to one side, his arm at her back. They were obviously engaged in a lively conversation.

"Make way!" a loud voice called from behind Dav and Carrie's position. "Make way for the players!"

Pushing through the throng came a number of vividly dressed performers. They were laughing and shaking hands with people, bussing cheeks, and making their way through the crowd.

"Hang on," Gates said, moving into the open space the caller had created, slipping them both closer to Dav.

Ana saw him activate his mic. Before she caught up with him, a lovely woman stopped him. "Gates, so good to see you."

"Miriam." Gates bent and kissed her cheek. "How lovely to see you."

"And you," the woman replied. "Are you here alone?" She looked around, spotted Dav. Then said something Ana couldn't hear.

Gates laughed and pointed her way. The woman looked at Ana, did a double take, then looked back at Gates. "Okay. Wow."

Puzzled, Ana hoped Gates was going to explain the comment, but before she could give it any more thought, Drake Yountz appeared at her side.

"You seem to have been abandoned, Ms. Burton," he drawled, again slipping his hand around her waist. "Can I get you a . . . drink?" His insinuation was obvious, as was the groping rise of his fingers.

"If you don't remove your hand in one second," Ana said, as pleasantly as she could, "I will break all your fingers."

"What?" Drake recoiled, his hand dropping away.

"That's better." Ana smiled but not with amusement. "Don't touch me again, Mr. Yountz. My . . . friends," she almost said contacts, which would betray something of her place in the order of Gates and Dav's lives. "May be donors, and may hold your Foundation in some regard. I, however, am not interested. Are we clear?"

"Of course, of course." Drake oozed charm, as if she'd not just threatened to break his hand. "I totally understand. Just making sure you were all right. I noticed you disappeared." He smirked, lowering his voice on the last phrase. "Trouble with that gorgeous dress?" Now his features shifted into a mask, which was probably the true Drake Yountz, she decided. Plain and nasty.

To quash his egotistic jab, she just smiled. "Of course not. Madame Misioia would never let that happen."

The mask hardened, but dissipated the moment someone called his name. Like a chameleon, he smiled and answered the hail. The only sign that he wasn't exactly what he seemed was the look he shot her, as he turned away.

"If looks could kill," she murmured, "I'd be headed for the morgue."

It wasn't long before Gates returned to her side. "You okay?" He touched her arm, then without hesitation, linked their fingers together. "I saw Yountz. What did he want?"

"Down boy," she said, appreciating his willingness to protect her. "No problem. I just threatened to break all his fingers if he touched me again."

She said it with such nonchalance that it obviously took him a minute to process her statement. When he did, he began to chuckle. In full view of God and everyone, he bent and kissed her. "Oh, my God, that's perfect."

She laughed, embarrassed to be the focus of so many eyes, thanks to his public display of affection. The noise level rose back to normal as the performers rolled through the crowd and out into the spacious outer hall.

"Miriam's the artistic director for the Opera. She's got something prepared to keep the crowd busy between the end of the auction and the announcement of the winning bids."

"That's good. Lots of high spirits in here. I'm surprised at how many people are bidding. I know the economy's tough, but it hasn't stopped this crowd," she said with amusement, watching two elegantly coiffed matrons argue over a lovely framed print. She caught snatches of, "Beautiful in my bedroom," and "Perfect for the foyer." Apparently, they were trying to dissuade one another from bidding on the piece they both coveted.

"We should look around, since we're here," he said, glancing at her, then looking away. She could tell he was upset.

"Gates?"

"I nearly panicked when I couldn't find Dav," he admitted.

She nodded. "Me too. If anything had happened . . ." She let the "might have been" trail away. Thank God, it hadn't. "Gates," she began.

"Shhhh, let's just get through the rest of the evening, okay? There's still the performances, and then the auction. We'll talk about it then."

"Oh, is that all?" she said sarcastically. "So, you think we should act like we're looking at auction items?"

"No, I think we should actually look at the auction items," he said, laughing. "I'm a fan of the organization too, so I'll put in at least a few bids." With his hand at her back again, directing them forward, they made their way toward the show tables. She could get used to that warmth, that amazing sensuality.

The thought stopped her dead in her tracks.

"Ana?" Gates looked at her, concern written on his handsome features.

"It's okay. It's nothing," she lied. "I just slipped out of my shoe a bit."

"Oh." His features cleared, and he gave her a sly, knowing look. "Nice shoes, by the way."

Heat suffused her face again. *Damn that blush!* God, what he could do to her with just that kind of comment. It was insane. It was delicious, and scary, and no . . . not scary; terrifying. She wanted him, but not what he represented. She wanted the feelings, the passion, but not the fear and the depth of emotion he brought out in her. She'd cut herself off from that in order to survive.

Part of her, a little whispering part of her mind, said, *Isn't it time to start living again, instead of just surviving?*

The thought followed her as they wandered along the tables. Ana saw very little of the magnificent prizes everyone was bidding on. Instead, she was focused on the feelings that were pouring through her. How could she be falling for Gates? Was it just the mind-blowing sex?

No, she shook off that thought. She'd had good sex before, although not quite *that* good. It wasn't sex, or at least not entirely. That she, that both of them, had been willing to set duty aside, even briefly, was a testament to the power of what pulsed between them.

"What do you think of this?" Gates asked with a poker face, pointing to a garish, glossy painting of a nude woman, her face pink, her body a screaming electric-blue blob with enormous, pointy breasts. "For the foyer, perhaps?"

A laugh snickered out, and she bumped him with her hip. "Stop that." She glanced behind them. "The artist could be nearby."

"Oh, of course. What about that for the bedroom?" he said, his hand at her back directing her farther down the line to an amazing bronze sculpture of amorphous human shapes, one obviously female, the other blatantly male, but joined together so that the obvious wasn't so obvious. It was erotic, but somehow not overt. It spoke of heat and joining, reminded her of their midnight rendezvous at her apartment.

"Remind you of anything?" he murmured.

"Hmmmm."

"Lovely, isn't it?" Dav joined them, Sophia on his arm. Carrie was nowhere to be seen, and Dav's face was a study in deliberate nonchalance.

"It is, yes," Ana responded, smiling at the other woman, trying not to be obvious in her scanning of the crowd. Sophia looked spooked, uneasy, and tension radiated from her in waves.

"Problem?" Ana asked.

"She thought she saw someone she knew," Dav said obliquely, locking eyes with Gates. "Someone from another time, another land."

"Do we need to go?" Ana read the signs of imminent threat on both their faces.

"No." Dav's voice was flat, sure. "I confronted the individual." He smiled at Gates now, a look of dark amusement and self-deprecation. "You'd be pleased to know that every one of our men was at my side within three seconds."

"I'd be royally pissed if it had been otherwise," Gates said, his voice even and calm. Ana could feel the quiver of his muscles under her arm though, and realized how tightly he was leashing his emotions.

"It wasn't him, Gates," Dav said, his mood changing with mercurial speed. He looked off into the distance. "I frightened a total stranger half to death," he said, turning back. "For nothing."

"It wasn't nothing," Sophia said, her teeth chattering slightly. "It looked so much like him, the build, the hair. Everything."

Dav stroked her hand. "Sophia-aki," he soothed. "We were both fooled. We must maintain our dignity now. We must be strong." He seemed to be trying to convince himself as well as Sophia.

Ana was lost at sea, unsure who or what had caused the uproar. What she did know was that somewhere back in Dav's past, his family's past, someone had put together one hell of a threat. A threat so widespread that even a distant relative like Sophia was aware of it and alarmed by the thought of it.

Ana tapped Gates, whispered, "Is this something I can help with?"

He shook his head, but smiled. "I'll tell you later," he said quietly. "It was before my time, but deadly serious."

"Now," Dav said with forced joviality. "Let's examine the rest of these treasures, see what we can see. We will not let this ruin our evening, eh?"

By the time they reached the end of the rows of tables, Dav had revived, joking with Sophia about the befrilled dressing table that was up for auction, and the huge gilded parrot in an equally huge gilded cage.

They passed the rest of the evening in relative ease, with Dav, Sophia, and Gates bidding on several things. Gates and Sophia were making a game out of trying to read one another's bids, with much peering and guessing going on. They each made a great show of protectively writing their bids and sealing the envelopes.

"Is there anything you'd like to bid on?" Gates asked her, noticing that she wasn't joining in.

"As well as I get paid," she remarked facetiously, nodding at the frilly dressing table they'd returned to, "that is out of my league. It's also out of my," she searched for a delicate way to say the thing was hideous, "um, design strategy." She reminded herself once more, the artist could be anywhere, and being offensive wasn't on the evening's agenda.

"Yeah, I'll say," he teased. "But desks," he said, pointing out an ornate ormolu writing table with a spindly, elegant chair, "are your style." He gave her a sly wink, hinting at their tryst. Evidently his unease at not being able to find Dav was passing. Or he was tabling the discussion of it, for now.

Before she could reply to his saucy jab, there was a ring of brassy music and a rumble of kettledrums. The sound reverberated in the foyer and in the room they were in.

"Time for the entertainment," he said, bending low so he could be heard over the cacophony.

The crowd pressed forward, packing into the huge grand entrance. Above them on the mezzanine where she and Gates had watched the crowd, a small orchestra had been set up and several performers stood, waiting for the gathering to settle.

Drake Yountz and an attractive silver-haired woman stepped to the railing, each with a microphone in hand. They thanked everyone and indicated that the auction room's doors would now be shut for tallying, and the program would begin.

"Winners of auction items will be able to either take them home this evening or have them delivered for an extra charge," the woman said with a smile, outlining the procedures, the payment process, and all the niceties of silent auction bidding.

Yountz took up the program. "And now, as my lovely co-host indicated, five of San Francisco's finest artists are here to perform a selection from the Opera's magnificent upcoming production of Wagner's Ring Cycle."

He did the usual "please help me welcome" type of introductions, then handed over the microphone. Ana's aversion to the man grew with every sighting, and she made a mental note to do a run on him when she got back to the office.

They endured the four operatic selections, and then the announcement of the auction's highest bidders began. Gates slipped away to get something for them to eat, while she,

Dav, and Sophia chatted. Since the earlier scare, Sophia was sticking close to her cousin. Her circle of admirers ebbed and flowed, but most stopped just long enough to say hello and comment on how much they admired her work.

Ana wondered how Dav was going to explain the young woman's presence to Carrie. Then she wondered why she was wondering.

Relationships aren't your thing, Burton, Ana reminded herself. *Data is. Don't get involved. Don't begin to care.* The familiar litany she'd been reciting since Rome felt like dusty nonsense in her mind. Life was all about relationships.

"Here," Gates said, offering her a loaded plate and another glass of wine. "There's more on the way." As he spoke, several other team members stopped by, casually handing Dav and Sophia plates as well, before disappearing into the mob of patrons.

"Ah, Sophia, my dear, you've taken the field," Dav said by way of congratulations. Ana couldn't see what it was, but Sophia's bidder number appeared on the tote board over the head of the lead auctioneer, along with an enormous photo of the frilly dressing table.

Gates looked at Ana, as if to say, "See, someone liked it." It was all she could do not to burst out laughing. *Relationships add spice to life,* that other, traitorous part of her mind whispered.

It was well after two when they called for the limousines and migrated toward the doors. Each of her three companions had captured some prize or another in the auction, although Gates wouldn't tell her what his was.

"You'll just have to wait and see," he said, giving her a mysterious look. "You'll like it, though." His laughter was an intimate caress on her spirit, a buoying lift to remind her that maybe it was possible to open up again.

That warm sense faded as they waited in line for the limos in the cool dark of the early morning. Something about the scenario made Ana unaccountably nervous, and she began to scan the minimal crowd, note the security locations.

Ana and Gates were off to one side, with part of the security detail, but there was an awful lot of open space around them and overhead as well, despite the number of police and private security. Their number was called, and they and their security detail moved forward, the team waiting until Dav, Sophia, and Ana were in the limo before they took their final notes from Gates and dispersed to the cars in front and in back.

Ana was adjusting the folds of the dress on the seat, leaving room for Gates when she heard it.

The soft, wet twack might have gone unnoticed, but she recognized it. It was the sound of a bullet hitting flesh.

She looked at Gates, in time to see him gasping and gripping the glass of the window.

"GATES!" she screamed, leaping toward him from her sitting position. Just as it had in Rome, everything slowed to an infinitesimal crawl. He began to fall, his eyes showing white as he did so. The crackled, spiderwebbed glass was mute evidence of the bullet's passage through his body.

The team spun in place, drawing weapons, but no further shots were fired. The people nearest Gates saw the crackled glass, and the blood that now poured from Gates's wound.

Security surged forward, and the crowd pushed back toward the Opera House. Screams tore through the night, and people trampled one another in their haste to return to the relative safety of the building.

"Get him in the car," Dav ordered, as Ana cradled him, half in, half out of the vehicle. "Quickly!"

Hands from outside lifted and pushed, and she and Dav pulled Gates into the vehicle.

"Now, drive, Declan," Dav ordered. The limo peeled away from the curb heading for the nearest hospital. The glass whirred down, and the driver spoke. "I've got the hospital on the line. They'll be waiting for us. Police escort should be coming up now." As he said the words, a squad car bullied its way in front of them, sirens blasting, its lights a blur of blue and red.

"Keep pressure on," Sophia said, oddly businesslike and firm for someone in her profession. "Talk to him, keep him with us."

Gates lay sprawled over Ana, both of them on the floor of the limo in the space between the plush seats. Sophia's hand was on Ana's shoulder, lending strength as Ana pressed a wadded up stack of monogrammed napkins onto the wound. The thick napkins absorbed the blood, but were sturdy enough to allow her to keep pressure on the wound.

"Gates," Dav said, his voice firm, though his hand shook on top of hers as they both strove to staunch the bleeding in the front. With her other hand, she pressed more towels to the back. They had to keep the wound track sealed. At the very least, Ana knew his lung was punctured. At worst, he was bleeding internally and would die right before their eyes. "You need to stay with us. That's an order," he said. "I know, I know, I don't give them often, but you're not to disobey me on this one, do you hear me?"

"Gates," Ana said, and she thought his eyes changed, rose for just a moment to fix on her face. "I'm here too. We're getting you to the hospital, hold on. We've got you, okay? We're here, and we're not letting go."

They kept it up for the four-minute ride to the closest hospital. They squealed into the emergency entrance, and the car was quickly mobbed by medical personnel. They whisked Gates away, into the bowels of the building where none of them could follow.

Still in their bloodied finery, they found seats in the waiting room outside the operating suites. The police came, took statements, left. They raised their eyebrows over her professional status, but didn't comment, taking her statement along with the rest. The team brought coffee, drank it or didn't, but they all stayed.

Detective Baxter arrived near dawn, bringing the news

that there were additional casualties at the Opera House, thanks to the panic. With his news, Ana pulled out of her funk enough to remember to text Pretzky; her boss had known where Ana was going, what she was doing. If she saw the news before Ana contacted her, she'd fear the worst.

Pretzky arrived no more than forty-five minutes after Ana hit SEND.

"Give me a sit-rep," she snapped, ignoring the disreputable state of Ana's dress. One of Gates's team had given her his coat, and she gripped the sides of it, just to have something to hold on to. "Snap to, Agent."

Heads turned at Pretzky's tone, and several of the team, Detective Baxter included, began to protest, but Pretzky was insistent.

"Burton. Report," she said, shaking Ana's arm.

"We were waiting in line," she rasped, and someone handed her water. She thanked whoever it was with absent courtesy and drank. "It wasn't a secure area, it made me uneasy." She rolled her shoulders, remembering the feeling, wishing now that she'd said something, anything that might have prevented the night's tragedy. Things blurred before her eyes, and she thought she might pass out, but Pretzky shook her again.

"Burton, I said, report," the woman insisted, with infuriating calm.

There was a mutter among the group, but Dav silenced them all with a look. Ana envied that kind of power, she decided in a hazy sort of side track.

"Burton?"

"Yes, Special Agent, I'm getting there," she answered. Her voice sounded stronger, felt stronger, despite the bone-deep weariness in her soul. "The security detail was in lead, two up; Dav and Sophia, two middle; me and Gates, two behind." The formation was good, they'd been watchful, everything was clockwork. She said that, too.

"Everyone was in the vehicle but G . . ." She couldn't say his name. Couldn't. "Bromley." She used the impersonality of his last name to get her through. "He stopped, issued a last order, or made a comment to his team." She looked around blindly, searching for the one he'd been talking to, the one who'd spoken, scanning for anyone who might fill in the blank of what Gates had said.

The redhead, Declan, rose, came over. "He rattled off who was in which car, told us that once we'd dropped Miss Sophia off at the hotel, the Sir Francis Drake, we'd regroup, get further direction."

"We'd mentioned a late supper," Dav added wearily, not rising from his chair. "Or an early breakfast, I guess you'd say." Once he'd spoken, he let his head drop into his hands, scrubbing them over his face in a gesture of frustration and sorrow.

When no one else spoke, Pretzky turned back to Ana. "Everyone followed orders," Ana said. "Gates had one foot in the car, ready to get in," she said, staring blindly beyond Pretzky's shoulder, seeing it unfold again in her mind. "I heard that noise." Ana met Pretzky's eyes. "You know the one, where the bullet impacts—" She couldn't continue. Pretzky put a firm hand on her shoulder, squeezed.

"I know. Go on."

She finished it out. "He just dropped, half in, half out of the limo. We pulled him in," she waved toward Dav, "and tore out for the hospital. They were waiting for us. We came here. That's it, I think."

"Angle of the bullet?" Pretzky demanded, making her focus, making her think. Ana pictured the wound.

"Down, back to front."

"Sharpshooter then, from a rooftop or maybe even the Opera House itself."

"No, had to be a rooftop," Ana corrected, seeing the angles in her mind's eye. "Gates was at a right angle to the building." She demonstrated with her hands. "Couldn't have been the Opera House."

Baxter was taking notes, but Ana paid him no heed. She

continued, using her visual memory to key into the details her shock had masked. “This isn’t about me,” she stated, knowing it flat and sure in her gut. She stared Pretzky down. “And it isn’t about him.” She pointed to Dav. “Gates was the target. That shooter could have taken any of us out—Dav, Sophia or me—during the walk to the car. They didn’t. They waited until everyone else was secure in the car before they took the shot. That shot was meant for Gates Bromley, and him alone—”

“Gates was the target,” she said as she scanned the room, locking eyes with Dav. “That was never a scenario any of us ran.”

Pretzky was about to say something when the squeak of rubber-soled shoes silenced everyone. A doctor, still wiping his hands dry, paced into the waiting area. He looked around the group, noting the blood on Dav and Ana. Responding, perhaps, to whatever pleading look must be haunting her face, the doctor honed in on her, spoke.

“He came through surgery. It isn’t wonderful news. He’s got damage to his lung, of course, but not as bad as we thought. Some bruising to the spleen. The bullet nicked his kidney, and we had to really work to stop that bleeding. There was some intestinal damage, but that was fairly simple.” It was a dry recitation of what must have been hideously difficult surgery. “He’s lucky though. The bullet missed everything major. He’s alive, and he’s hanging in there. We’ll know more in a few hours.”

“Can any of us see him?” Dav asked. He’d moved to her side without her being aware of it, she was so focused on the doctor.

To her distress, the doctor shook his head, a negative. “He’s not stable enough yet. Give it a few hours, and we’ll see.”

He strode off, and Pretzky took charge. “You,” she summoned one of Dav’s men. “Can you get someone to bring them a change of clothes?” She indicated Dav and Sophia. “Unless they’d like to go home?”

Dav was a firm no, but he urged Sophia to go. "There's nothing you can do here, Sophia-aki. You have an early flight as well." When she would have protested, he overrode her, speaking in a spate of soft, hurried Greek. Ana caught only a bit of it, but the gist was that she would be safer in Los Angeles, safer away from him.

When she finally agreed, he had Declan take her to the hotel. Someone else had already been dispatched to get Dav a change of clothes. "Give me your keys," Pretzky said, holding out an imperious hand. "I know you won't leave, but you can't stay in that." She waved at the dress.

"Oh, my God." Ana looked down, clearly seeing the ruin of the elegant gown for the first time. "Misioia will be furious."

At that, she burst into tears.

"What the hell is wrong with you?" Drake demanded, pacing the parking lot of the darkened Opera House. "What were you thinking, shooting Bromley? You may have ruined everything."

"Neh." Jurgens denied everything with one cold word. "I am in Oakland, arranging the thing we discussed." Drake could hear the icy fury in Jurgens's voice at the very idea Drake would blame him. "Careful what you say."

Drake yanked his hair, the pain of it grounding him, helping him to focus. "Damn it. Sorry," he said, knowing he'd better mend fences. "The shot was so damn good." He stopped, scanned the lot, decided he'd better get into the closed confines of his BMW before he said anything else. "Hang on."

He started the car before he continued. "Really, man. I apologize. Bromley's at the hospital, not sure if it was a kill shot or not, but it was a hell of a thing," he explained. "No muzzle flash, just a snick and Bromley went down. You're so good." He let admiration fill his voice, knowing he needed to make up for his earlier accusation. "I just, well, you know. I thought it was you."

"You did not designate Bromley as a target." Drake thought he heard a little lessening of the anger. "Therefore, no action on Bromley. This is the way it works. I do not do other jobs."

Drake winced. Jurgens was well and truly pissed. It was going to take something major. Groveling might be his best bet. "I know. I know that, I do," he said, letting the weariness he actually felt suffuse his voice. "I overreacted, damn it. Stupid of me. I thought I'd gotten over that." He said it ruefully, reminding Jurgens of easier times when they'd put together deals in college, made money for tuition, cars, and women with their joint escapades. Jurgens had always twitted him for being hasty, getting ahead of himself.

Drake didn't agree, but he had moderated the tendency. Jurgens liked a long con better than he did, but they both liked the money. They paid one another, kept it straight so neither of them felt used or cheated.

The thing he always had to remember was that Jurgens was a killer; unstable, volatile, like nitroglycerin. Amazingly useful, but best handled with care.

"Seriously," he said, hoping a last bit of eating crow would even things out. "It was that good. You can't blame me for thinking it was you."

"Huh." Jurgens's grunt didn't sound convinced, but he didn't sound like he was going to leave Oakland and come hunting Drake. "Be careful. Accusations are not wise."

"Very true." Drake decided it was time to shift gears. "Oakland, eh? What's up?"

"Our discussion," Jurgens said impatiently. "More product from our new watcher."

"Ah." The light dawned. Jurgens was suborning the inside man at the CIA he'd cultivated. "Good. Listen, I'll say it once again. Sorry. I'll e-mail you a new number. These shouldn't be used again. Also, we need to step up our check on our East Coast rival. If this was him, he's gotten better. If it's something else, someone else muddling the works, we need to know that too."

"Ja," Jurgens agreed, disgust ringing in the single word. He cut the line off, and Drake was left sitting in the dark, seething.

If he'd thought it once, he'd thought it a hundred times. Jurgens was dangerous. He got out long enough to drop the phone on the ground in a puddle from the Opera House's landscape sprinklers. Starting the car, he ran over it, smashing it. He got out to retrieve the destroyed SIM chip. The pieces of the phone were indistinguishable in the dark, useless and unidentifiable without the chip.

On his way home, he got two cups of coffee, sipping one and dropping the chip in the other. At the gas station where he filled up the car, he dumped the unused cup into the trash, taking off the cardboard sleeve where he'd touched it. That, he would recycle at home.

He smiled, thinking that the lovely Ana was now without her protector. Meeting up with her again would be . . . intriguing.

Chapter Fifteen

No one left the hospital for two days. Pretzky had arranged for a change of clothes for Ana, taking the fabulous but ruined dress away. By the time Gates was able to accept visitors, Ana was running on two hours of sleep caught in a chair in the waiting room.

Dav went in first, and when he came out, he was pale. "He'd like to speak to you," he said, taking Ana's hands and bussing her on the cheek before he led her to the doors to the ICU. "Remember, he's medicated. Lucid, but medicated, all right?"

She wasn't sure what that meant, but she set it aside in her hurry to get to Gates.

Her first thought was how drained he looked. His wavy mass of brown hair was the only warm spot of color on the white sheets; his skin was barely a shade pinker than the fabric.

"Ana," he croaked. "I told Dav," he said, rasping as he looked at her. He looked angry now, irritated.

"What?" She hurried over. "What is it? What can I do?"

"You can go home, Ana. You don't need to be here."

The words were a hard slap to her face, a harder blow to her heart. "W-w-hat?"

"We've had fun, Ana, but you don't need to be hanging out here. You've got your work, it's not like we're—" He drew a deeper, harsher breath. "We're not an item here, Ana. Let's be real. I'll be leaving with Dav, you've got your job. We had a good time, but you don't need to be here, okay?"

Stricken, Ana backed away. "What the hell was this then? J-j-ust a fling?" she stuttered.

"It was a joint project, a good way for us to solve this art thing." He grimaced in pain. "Didn't work out. I'm sorry, Agent," he said, using her title rather than her name. The way he said it was slightly demeaning, the ultimate dismissal. "I wouldn't have ended it this way, you gotta know that, but we both know it would have ended. We've both got our work. We shouldn't have," he restlessly waved a hand. He stopped and took a few long breaths. "On duty, in the middle of things. No. I have to focus here. Focus on getting better, not uh . . ." he paused, perhaps searching for a less painful way to tell her to get lost.

"It's okay. I understand. Obviously, I misread the situation between us." She drew on every bit of early training she'd had as a diplomat's daughter. "However, I would have stayed for anyone. I want you to know that. Someone goes down on my watch, I stay."

He nodded, looked away. "I get that. I'd do the same."

The silence drew out, and he closed his eyes. He didn't open them again, but he did speak. "It would have ended soon anyway, Ana. I'm going to be following Dav, wherever he needs me. He'll jet off to Europe, and that would have ended it anyway. Where he goes, I go." He made it sound like Europe was the end of the world, but she got the drift. "I'm a bad bet anyway, for flings or relationships."

It was her, then.

He didn't want to care about her, or put up with some weepy, clinging female when he was trying to recover. He didn't want *her.* Obviously, nearly dying had made everything very clear for him.

"It's been real, Gates," she choked on the words but managed to keep her voice firm, level. "Someone else will be in touch if there's anything on the art case."

Now he just nodded, eyes still closed.

"Just so you know, Pretzky pushed the warrants through this morning. They've started the data run."

He nodded, but still didn't move. "That's good. Let me—" He stopped, redirected to a neutral term. "Let us know the results."

Tears closed her throat as she stood there, but she forced them away so she could speak and not sound weak. "I will. Heal quick, Gates. And be well."

As exit lines went, it was piss-poor, but heartfelt.

She passed through the halls without seeing anything. In the waiting room, she went straight to Dav, pressing a kiss to his cheek.

"Thanks for everything. Either I or one of my colleagues will be in touch, professionally, about all this." She didn't look at him. Couldn't. "We'll keep at it."

"Ana-aki," Dav murmured, but she shook her head.

"Don't," she whispered. "I can't, okay? Not here. Leave me with something."

She felt, more than saw, his nod. He squeezed her arm and let her go. Blinded by tears, but with her head held high, she made for the elevators like they were the last lifeboat leaving the Titanic.

Dav shook his head over her departure. How two people could so thoroughly screw up a budding relationship was beyond him. As much as it pained him to admit it, though, he could do nothing to help. They were stubborn people, both of them. Meddling from him would only make things worse. He'd found that out to his pain, many times. Getting in between Ana and Gates would only end in disaster.

There were at least a few things he could do, though, to ease the pain he'd seen in Ana's eyes. He had already been on the phone, insuring that the dress was paid for and that additional private security was watching over her. There wasn't much more he could do.

"So," he said as he came into Gates's private room. "You have sent her away."

"It's for her own good," Gates rasped, his throat still showing the effects of the intubation for surgery. "That shot, and the shot at the compound the other night weren't aimed at you, Dav. They were aimed at me. Drugs or not, I've been thinking, running through every incident for the last few years. I came up with at least six times that I could have been the target, when we assumed it was you."

"We were complacent, which means stupid," Dav grunted. "Obviously. I have already had calls to assure me that certain parties were not involved in this."

"The Central American group?"

"Among others, yes. They want to be sure I don't pull any funding or stop the three deals we have in the works. They don't want me to think they had anything to do with it."

"Good, I guess. More avenues to talk means fewer errors." Gates coughed a little, then lay rigidly still to absorb the pain the cough caused.

"The Saudis have also called, expressed their concerns."

"The desalinization plant."

"Precisely. Ohmad bin Serra offered to send his private physician and a bevy of nurses to see to your care." Dav smirked over that. "I declined on your behalf. I think Dr. Anderson can manage you at the house, don't you?"

Gates nodded, closing his eyes to the pain. "When can I get out of here?"

"Tomorrow, to my amazement. Modern medicine seems to believe you should arise and go, lest your insurance not pay," Dav said, letting his opinion of the health care industry show in his sarcasm. "In the meantime, you need to think. Forget the how of it, leave that to the police. Think about the why of it. This was well planned, well executed." He shifted to look out the narrow window. "It was meant to kill."

"It would have too, if I hadn't pushed off to get into the car. I was higher, maybe by three inches, just for that moment."

They sat in silence for a moment, as they both absorbed how close it had been.

"Who's with you while I'm out of it?" Gates broke the impasse.

"Queller and Jones," Dav smiled. "They're annoying."

"Overstimulated." Gates smiled. "They're still new to all this."

A nurse came in to check on Gates, gave Dav a meaningful look, and tapped her watch.

"I'll go now, let you get some rest. Think about the why." Dav collected his raincoat and headed for the door. Without turning back, he said, "And Gates?"

"Hmmm?"

"Remember that she's smart, and very good at what she does. She's going to figure out what you've done in sending her away. Whatever chance you had with her will be shot to hell if you don't acknowledge that."

Gates didn't answer, so Dav departed, off to face the maelstrom of media, business challenges, and emotional turmoil Gates's injury had stirred up.

It was never silent in a hospital room. The whirring, beeping, and crackle of the overhead speakers, with their endless announcements and calls to various people made sure that Gates couldn't be alone with his thoughts. Gifts and flowers had begun to arrive. Dav had sent Gates's assistant Alexia over to deal with them, write thank-you notes, and disperse the flowers appropriately. Gates had asked her to deliver the enormous basket of fruit, towering over her head, to the surgeons' break room.

"Sir?" Alexia knocked and came in. "There're more flowers and so on, but I'm sending them out to the house. I hope that's okay with you."

"Fine," he said, just wanting her to go away. He'd contacted his sister as soon as he was conscious, but she'd seen nothing and heard nothing that might indicate an attempt on her life. She promised to have her husband let the base commander know.

Then again, living on a military base in a foreign country tended to insulate anyone from the rest of the world. With no attempt on Patty, the shootings might not be related to his parents' deaths. He couldn't be sure though. He'd asked Baxter to check on the woman responsible for his family's murders, for the arson, see if either she or the arsonist had been paroled.

Maybe it was her, but that seemed improbable. It had been more than a decade.

"And sir, there's considerable press." Alexia broke into his circling thoughts. "Mr. G's publicists have suggested a statement. Would you like to prepare it or see something they've worked up?"

"No, just have them take care of it."

"Yes, sir. Are you comfortable enough to read through some things? We've been stalling the VanRoss paperwork, but they're getting antsy."

Gates had to smile at that. He'd written a database program and registered the copyright. VanRoss had come looking for him with a deal to license and sell it. "I'll bet they are. Sure, give it to me."

"Yes, sir. This will be easier at the house," Alexia added, in her perky way, smiling at him as she handed him a portfolio and file folders, then bustled about to get the sliding table arranged just so. "I have to leave the floor to make calls."

"I'm looking forward to sleeping all night," he said by way of agreement. "It's noisy here."

"Yes, sir," Alexia said. "I'll be back in a bit if you need anything. I've got to ride down several floors to get a signal." She waved her bright pink, bespangled phone.

He didn't answer her, since he was already opening the envelopes, diving into the work to take his mind off of Ana. Everything reminded him of her, of their time together. The nurse wore dangly silver earrings. They were nothing like the ones Ana had worn, but they made him think about the curve of Ana's neck, the shape of her ears.

Alexia had on shoes with a silver sheen, which reminded him of Ana's elegant dress shoes for the event. He had only the vaguest memory of her getting into the limo ahead of him, the flash of those silver shoes.

"I did the right thing, damn it," he muttered, forcing himself to focus on the contracts. "I can't get her killed too."

Ana buried the unimaginable hurt in sleep. Mother Nature took over and shut her down for a full fifteen hours. She woke in the dark and wept, and when that brought no solace, she went back to sleep until morning sun, streaming in the windows, woke her.

Like a robot, she dressed and went to work. The minute she stepped onto the floor, Pearson headed her way, diverting the others, many of whom had gotten up from their desks as Ana left the elevator.

"Boss wants you," she said, walking Ana all the way to the door, like a visitor. Ana squared her shoulders and knocked.

"Status, Burton?" Pretzky said when Ana came into her office. "Shut the door."

Frowning, Ana did, then took the seat Pretzky indicated. "Status is null at this point. I'm running some other leads. Suddenly all the other victims are willing to talk to me." She smiled, a wry twist of the lips. "I expect Mr. Gianikopolis had something to do with that."

"No doubt. Any trouble with the interjurisdictional pissing match you've stirred up?" she said, grimacing. "You sure know how to do it right."

"Sorry," Ana said, not knowing what else to say. The locals and the FBI had gotten involved now, and Baxter, even as county, was in the mix since he'd taken all the initial information and was the point of contact on other incidents at the estate.

Pretzky had barred Ana from doing anything on the shooting, citing orders from IAD. Knowing she'd be monitored, Ana had resisted running checks on the people from Gates's background, his business associates besides Dav. She itched to do it, but with everyone breathing down her neck, and Gates sending her away, essentially dumping her, she didn't know what to do. Any tracking she did would send up flags, mark her as disobeying orders. With her hearing pending, she dared not make waves.

Anyway, she was staying the hell out of it.

"Forget it, let them sort it out," Pretzky continued, oblivious to Ana's internal turmoil. "In the meantime, this case is firing up and breaking open. You've got your warrants, and the search is running, right?"

"Yes, it'll be a while though. The data sets are massive."

"What else is up?" Pretzky asked. "Has that idiot Davis," she paused, and a sly smile curved her lips. "What was it you called him? A pus-ball?"

Ana nodded, flushing because it sounded so terrible coming from Pretzky.

Pretzky laughed. "Perfect name for him. Anyway, has he been any help, following up on the IT stuff? He's not the sharpest knife in the drawer, but he can do that."

"Some." Ana told the exact truth. Davis might be a pus-ball, but he did know how to persuasively interview a victim. "He's got a lead that may take us to New York. One of the victims remembered," Ana put the word *remembered* in air quotes, "something about the way all the items she bought were shipped. Everything that victim lost went through a shipper in White Plains, New York. Anything she kept that didn't turn into a forgery went another way. This lady didn't think to mention it when the case was hot, nine years ago. When Davis asked two other victims about how they shipped, the same shipper's name came up."

"Shit. Trust Davis to find the one thing we can use." Pretzky shook her head in disgust. "How the hell he manages it,

I'll never know. It's that one miniscule thing here and there that repeatedly saves his ass."

"Really?" That was news to Ana, and she tried to muster some interest, but she couldn't.

"Really," Pretzky answered. "Davis has been on probation so many times, it's ridiculous. In fact, if it goes too long between complaints, I wonder why I've not had to write the paperwork."

"Yeah, I get that," Ana said, since Pretzky seemed to expect some reply. The older woman watched her for a moment before she spoke again.

"You're due in DC tomorrow, for the final stage of the inquiry." Pretzky dropped the bomb with no further preamble. "They want you there at three."

Ana sat bolt upright, her hands gripping the arms of the chair. How could it be now? It had finally come, the yes-or-no vote that would determine the fate of her career. She'd been praying for it, waiting. Now, of all times, she wished it were a few weeks down the road.

"It's shitty timing, but I have no doubt of the outcome, Agent," Pretzky said, calmly. "You do good work and I feel certain that you did good work in Rome. These last three weeks have been a crap hole of difficulty, but you've handled it. I've been impressed."

Ana's jaw dropped, she couldn't help it. "Uh, t-thank you," she said, wanting to curse the stutter. It made her sound like some green cadet, but Pretzky's words took her by complete surprise. So much so that she had to ask her to repeat the next part.

"I said, get your flight worked out. A room's been reserved for you at the St. Regis. Details are in an e-mail I forwarded to you. Take the rest of the day." Pretzky glanced at the clock on the wall behind Ana. "You'll need it to gather your notes and pack."

"Thanks." Ana started to rise, but Pretzky motioned for her to stay.

"That's not all. When you're done in DC, I want you to go

on to White Plains or New York City, wherever it is in New York, check out this lead Davis dug up on the shipper."

"White Plains. It's not too far from New York City."

"White Plains, then. If there's anything to it, we need to hit it hard and fast. Get him to forward everything to you electronically, so you can review it on the trip east. If it looks like there's enough to warrant further checks, let me know and we'll get it arranged. I've reached out to the New York office, but they've got four big cases pending. They're okay with us being on their turf, checking a cold case, but they aren't going to lend a hand, if you know what I mean." She waited for Ana's nod of understanding. New York was there, would get some credit if they closed it, but they weren't fronting any help or time for a cold case.

"If we could close this," Pretzky continued, "it would be huge."

Pretzky fell silent, but still didn't dismiss Ana. They sat, listening to the clock tick for what seemed like an eternity. Evidently, Pretzky made up her mind to speak openly.

"I didn't like you when you came here, Burton. You know that. I questioned your dedication."

"Everyone did. Hell," Ana admitted, "I did."

Pretzky nodded. "I get that. Here's the thing. You've done superb work. I'm in this job because I'm not built for the field, and I found it out the hard way." She didn't elaborate, and Ana didn't ask.

"I'm good at what I do," Pretzky continued. "I'm good at managing the rejects and the lost causes, the people who need desk duty for a while." She flicked her eyes toward Pearson, who was passing by the windows as she spoke. A sure indication that Pearson was no reject, but that she had issues no one was immediately aware of. Pretzky obviously *was* good at what she did, since Ana would never have guessed that anyone in the office—barring Davis—was considered a reject. "What I do is important to the Agency, I know that. I also know that I won't get someone with your impressive capabilities in this office anytime soon, if ever. I've pushed you hard," she continued, ignoring Ana's halfhearted protest. "It's my job. But you'll hear it at the inquiry. I would recommend you to any duty post, and have you back here in a New York minute if they'd let you come."

Once again, Ana felt her jaw loosen with shock. She didn't know what to say, where to look.

Pretzky laughed. "I know, I'm a hard-ass." She leaned forward, earnest now. "I have to be. Sometimes the people they send me just need a break, a chance to breathe before they get back to what they're really good at. You're one of those. Sometimes, this office is just the cruise to retirement, or the way to keep a half-decent resource plugging away at a menial but necessary task. We're the last stop for some."

Cold Cases certainly qualified in that respect.

"Most of this crap is either so opaque, with so few leads, that it'll never be solved, or so obviously botched that it was worthless to even review the data. But someone has to check and mine for the few, the very few, that may have a lead no one else saw. In the three, no four months on the job here, you've closed a case and you are well on your way to closing another." Pretzky sounded sure, authoritative. "Hell, I'd beg for you if I thought they'd let me have you."

"Thank you." Ana's voice was weak, so she cleared her throat and tried again. "I mean, I hadn't considered . . ." She paused, searching for courtesy. ". . . everything, but it makes sense. I've enjoyed working with you, Special Agent."

"Same goes, now get out of here. Let me know when you're headed for New York."

"Will do," Ana said, and rose since Pretzky had finally given her usual dismissive wave to speed Ana on her way.

In a daze, she got back to her cubicle, staring blindly at the files that lay on her desk. A new, hard-locked file cabinet sat under the workstation. It had been there when Ana came back in. Only she and Pretzky had keys to it.

The Inquiry. Oh, God. Why now?

Her e-mail pinged with six incoming messages. She frowned and opened the first.

> Hey gorgeous! Think you could manage one more round for me? I'm going to take that as a yes. Ha ha! Here's the latest.
>
> *Ti manderemo al Creatore*—context is still the guy who's cheating. Is this a threat?
>
> *No fare piu lo stronzo*—context is similar. I need to connect them. Does this do it?
>
> Thanks. You're a peach.
>
> TJ

Hell. Just what she needed. Ana opened the others to find they were all from TJ, with at least one more phrase per e-mail, most of these in Greek.

If it were anyone else, she'd tell them to go to hell. For TJ, she'd make the time. He'd saved her ass so many times, she had to help him when he needed her. If nothing else, their brief stint as lovers was the one bright spot in the whole debacle in Rome.

With a sigh, she hit REPLY and answered, easily translating both the Italian and the Greek. She knew that his recommendations, and continued support, might mean the difference at the Inquiry between a hammer blow to her career, and merely a black mark that continued good work could expunge.

She opened a new e-mail, entered TJ's address.

> They're all threats. I'm off to DC for the Inquiry. Thanks for everything. You know what I mean. I'll be incommunicado for a couple days. Hope these help. A.

Heart clenching, she picked up the phone, dialed the private number Dav had given her. When he answered, she simply asked, "How is he?"

"Cranky. Hold on, please." She heard the muffled hum of

voices and the rustle of fabric. "There, I've stepped outside. He's healing, but it's slower than he wants it to be."

Her heart eased, though it still ached from Gates's dismissal. She'd felt compelled to check on him. Dav had enabled that, to a degree, by giving her his private line.

"I wanted to let you know I'd be away for a few days. The case is moving," she added, wanting to have some real rationale for bothering Dav, a business excuse, since her personal ties were now severed. "I've got some leads to check out."

"You've got the Inquiry as well," he said, and she sat up, alert.

"How do you know that?"

He laughed. "My dear young woman," he continued to chuckle. "I have my sources too. Any number of my companies work with DOD, NSA, and even NASA. There's not much I can't uncover. I will wish you luck, but you won't need it. Safe travels, eh?" he continued, his voice warm and friendly. It brought tears to her eyes. She dashed them away before anyone could walk by, see her crying.

"Thanks, Dav. For everything. I owe you."

"No, dear lady, we're even, if anything. When you solve this, I'll owe *you,*" he said. "Take care."

"Will do," she said, hanging up. Shaking her head over all the strange paths her life seemed to be taking, she made her flight reservations for the red-eye, printed out the info Davis had managed to find on the shipper.

Before she could leave, the phone rang. "Miss Burton, it is Misioia."

Oh, God. The dress.

"I am so sorry," Ana began, but Misioia cut her off.

"No, no. I am calling to say that the new dress will be delivered to your home next week. Mr. G called, he told me everything. He wants you to have the dress." She paused, laughed. "Well, another like it. I do not usually repeat my garments, but for you, for *him,* I will."

When Ana tried to protest, the designer laughed again and told her she'd had twelve calls for custom gowns and an additional fifteen calls for interviews. "I am well paid, Miss Burton. I hope you will come back to me again. I will make my creations well within your range, yes?" She wouldn't hear any protest or comment from Ana; instead, she ordered Ana to return to her shop soon to be sure the replacement dress was fitted properly. "Now, have a good day, yes?" And she was gone.

Ana wanted to put her head down and cry. Instead, she packed up, got her newly returned car from the garage, and went home.

Jen was waiting when she got there. "I called your office. They grilled me about who I was before they would tell me you were on the way home. Someone named Pearson."

Ana managed a smile. "Yeah, she's a good agent. What's up?"

"Oh, just stopping by to say hi. Pearson said you were heading to DC. I know what that means," Jen said, tossing an arm around Ana's shoulders as they mounted the steps to the apartment. "Want some company while you pack?"

"Sure."

"Good, we can order Chinese and gorge ourselves while you debate which conservative black suit would work best. After all, you only have twelve."

Laughing, they went in, with Jen heading straight for the phone. "Total exaggeration," Ana called from the bedroom. "I only have four."

"Six," Jen called back. "I counted last time I was here."

"Six? Really?" She didn't remember having six, but Jen was actually far more in touch with her wardrobe than Ana was. She'd helped pick out the more conservative garb when Ana moved back to The City, understanding that Ana needed to look like she was serious, meant business. No more flamboyant Parisian and Italian fashion.

She pulled the suitcase from under the bed, and true to her word, Jen helped her focus enough to pack the right things. They had Chinese for lunch, and laughed over a stupid comedy on HBO while they ate.

"How're things with Jack?" Ana finally asked, sure she'd hear that Jen had brushed him off, kicked him to the curb.

Jen's dreamy smile disabused her of that notion right away. "He's good. Really good. He's out of town right now, back east, but he's already called me twice today."

Shocked, Ana managed only a "Wow, really?" before Jen was off on a tear about the wonders of dating the doting New Yorker, Jack D'Onofrio.

Maybe, just maybe, there was someone in the world for whom things could work out. If anyone deserved it, it was Jen.

"Hey, you're tired, I know," Jen said on a grin. "I've been running off at the mouth, but I need to get out of here and let you get going. Besides, I gotta go make kissy noises into the phone with Jack. You don't want to be there for that, right?"

"Uh, no. Thanks for asking," Ana said facetiously. "We'll just take a rain check on that."

"Hey, he wanted me to tell you he was sorry for everything that happened, you know, like empathetic and all."

"Thanks. I appreciate it. Where is he today?"

"Back in New York, I think. Maybe Boston." She waved toward the east. "Out that way. Why?"

"Just wondering." Ana strove to keep her voice level, nonchalant. A hunch, a very troubling worry about New York Millionaire Jack, was buzzing in the back of her mind. "Hey, thanks for coming over," she said, standing up as Jen did. "It really helped."

Her friend gave her a hug and a pat on the back. "What friends are for, right? I can do that, most of the time." She laughed, and gathered her things. "Call me, about everything, okay? I'm here for you."

Ana nodded. "I know. Thanks."

"Sure. Fly safe."

Locking the doors behind her friend, Ana flew to her computer to run Jack D'Onofrio again. There had to be something that linked him, and she was going to find it.

Chapter Sixteen

The private jet was well appointed, the nurses dressed in regular clothes rather than scrubs, but Gates still felt the irritating sting of being under a doctor's care. Two days out of the hospital and he was still annoyed by all the poking and prodding. He hated being hovered over.

He felt surprisingly good for someone who'd been shot. Then again, the doctor kept saying it was a miracle that the bullet had missed all the vital stuff. Essentially, he just had to heal from the surgery, the blood loss, and the shock to his body.

Piece of cake.

"So." Dav stood in the doorway to the plane's bedroom. "You're insisting on this. Why?"

"We've been over it, Dav. Until Baxter and whoever else he's working with can figure something out, it's better for me to be away from here, away from you."

"So you want me to take you to the Paris house and leave you there. It makes so much sense." Dav's dry answer said exactly the opposite.

"Dav, I work for you. I'm your security guru. It's my job to be there and make sure you're safe, not bring the target that's on me to you too. You've got enough trouble dealing with the Central American faction and whoever's lurking around, impersonating your dead brother and scaring Sophia, without my adding my crap to it."

"We still don't know that it's your crap," Dav pointed out. "Don't look so belligerent." Dav laughed. "I've no objection to a few days in Paris. However, we've got to stop in New York. That meeting with Goldman Sachs can't be postponed any longer. I have a suite set up at the Waldorf. You can recuperate from this flight and prepare for the next one, tomorrow."

"Yeah, yeah. I could just go on to Paris alone, you know." He shifted. He was getting stiff spending so much time in bed. That reminded him of Ana, so he went after Dav again. "By the way, don't think I haven't heard about Carrie."

Dav looked away, just a flicker of movement, but Gates saw it and knew he was on to something. "I don't know what you mean," Dav said, with bland unconcern.

Gates rolled his eyes. "The hell you don't. I know you've been calling her, asking her out."

Dav sighed, and Gates heard the puzzlement in it. "She won't talk anything but business. Won't meet with me. Especially after the gala."

"Really? Why?"

Dav looked at him with an "it should be obvious" expression. "Sophia."

"Oh. Got it." Gates saw the problem immediately. He wished his challenges with Ana were that simple. He missed her with a need that ached like a sore tooth. "Give it time."

Dav treated him to a long, thoughtful look. "Recent events have pointed out to me that I may not have time. Life's precious, Gates."

Gates gritted his teeth and sat up. The muscles in his gut protested, but he ignored the pain. "Look, Dav, just because I got shot doesn't mean the world's going to end tomorrow. I'm just saying that you should give it a week, try again when we go back. Maybe use a different approach."

The pilot appeared, announcing their imminent departure.

"Right. Get comfortable, Gates." Dav nodded to the nurses,

who closed ranks to pull out the pillows he'd shoved in to support himself and helped him lie back. "Get some sleep if you can."

"Think about it, man," Gates offered as a parting shot.

Dav got the last word, however. "Advice from someone who's had it work out so well. Thanks."

"Fuck," Gates muttered, allowing the nurses to fuss around him, anchor the equipment they'd insisted on bringing. As they buckled into the nearby chairs for flight, he closed his eyes, intending to ignore it all, get some thinking in.

Dav's words reverberated in his mind. *Life is short.* Every time he closed his eyes, Gates relived the bullet's impact. Behind his closed eyelids, he replayed it. The needle-sharp pain, the hot smell of singed flesh and fabric, the almost simultaneous crackling of the car door's glass. Ana's scream. Dav's shout. Being lifted; Ana's voice telling him she had him and to hang on.

It all came back to Ana. Every time.

She had him, she'd said it. She had his back. She wasn't some frail flower needing or wanting protection. Instead, she was there for him. Now, to add to his nightmares, he could see her face as he essentially told her to get lost, that it had just been a fling.

The pressure of takeoff was nothing compared to the pressure in his chest, in his heart.

Ana. She was it. She was the real deal, not some weak fool to be dismissed.

With a soft moan for the pain in both sides of his chest, he twisted on the bed, feeling in his body the pain of his sheer bullheaded stupidity. What had he done?

He sensed the nurses bustling around, but paid them no heed. What could he do? How could he fix it? He'd well and truly screwed everything to hell, and he knew it.

Her features, wracked with pain, leapt into his mind like an IMAX movie. She'd recovered quickly. She was well trained, well schooled in making her face show only what she wanted it to show. But he'd seen it. The same agony he felt now.

Somehow, he had to mend the breach. To make it right. Yes, that's what he'd do.

He was about to open his eyes and demand his laptop when he felt the cooling change in the IV line still taped to the back of his wrist. His thoughts fogged, and his mind drifted away from its sharp focus.

"Thank you for coming, Agent," the head of the Panel of Inquiry started the proceedings. They'd kept her cooling her heels for a day in DC. She'd spent most of the time in the CIA Headquarters, waiting, only to be sent back to her hotel for the night and called back the next day.

Seated next to her, Ana's advocate noted the time on his legal pad. "Yes, sir. I appreciate your time and efforts," Ana replied, taking her seat.

The four men looked slightly nonplussed by her thanks, but they opened files and began reading the pertinent details of the Inquiry into the record.

"On Monday, February fifteenth," the man on the far left read. "The following events occurred which are the subject of this Inquiry."

Reese, her advocate, wrote the names of the panel in order across the page. Ana tuned into the recitation only so much as necessary to be sure they were following her statement, which they were.

The flight had been long, and she'd slept for only a little while because she knew she had to. The data on Jack G. D'Onofrio wasn't panning out. He didn't have a shipping arm of his magazine business as far as she could tell. His main business was West Coast too, San Francisco, Oakland, Sacramento, Lake Tahoe, Las Vegas.

Nothing showed. The problem was, she knew something was there. He was too much a New Yorker to not have something on the East Coast. You didn't leave your roots behind when you were a New York City boy. Not one who'd spoken with such pride about his roots to a total stranger at the gallery showing.

On her own pad, she wrote: *D'Onofrio. New York? California. Gallery. Berlin?*

Reese tapped her toe with his, signaling for her to pay attention as the executive agent presiding over the Inquiry spoke. "Is this your statement, Agent Burton? Are there any amendments you would like to include?"

"No sir," Ana said, forcing her tone to be level, unemotional.

"So noted." To the woman at the far right, he said, "Please address your attention to the additional statements as they are read into the record." The woman selected a folder, began to read the statement Agent Beverly Stanley had made before she died.

To distract herself, Ana focused on D'Onofrio again, writing: *Prometheus equals California. Moroni equals New York. Pratch equals Berlin. Artful Walls equals Miami.*

Wait.

The shipper in White Plains had done all the work for Moroni. Moroni and another New York gallery had used the same shipper in New York for two paintings of Dav's for resale overseas.

The designer, the one who had dated Dav, had mentioned Moroni.

"Agent, do you agree with, or have any comment on the statements as they've been read?"

Shit. She'd missed it. She glanced at Reese and saw the barest shake of his head. No.

"No, I do not."

"So noted. Moving on. Please read into record the actions of Agent Thomas James Michaels with regards to this matter."

Wait a minute. What did TJ have to do with this? He'd been peripheral to the situation in Rome, essentially coming in at the end to help clean up and cover up, making sure everything got explained away. Confused, Ana forgot the data on the art case and focused on the current recitation.

"Agent TJ Michaels has been on approved leave of absence for several months in which time he has sought out leads in regard to this case. Upon his return to duty, he presented evidence of significant mitigating factors, factors which may have skewed the data and led to the conclusions drawn by Agent Burton. His dedication to uncovering leads on the matter of the events of the fifteenth of February, in Rome, has been above and beyond the call of duty," the executive agent intoned. "Whereas our Agency did not approve his actions, per se, he has provided substantial additional information that leads the Panel to believe that the data Agent Burton provided was, in fact, accurate as far as could be determined. His return to approved duty to continue tracking is part of the record, in as much as . . ."

My God, they were saying her analysis was right, that it wasn't the killing factor.

Ana redirected her thinking, refocused on the statements. "Furthermore, Agent Michaels's dedication to this pursuit has been noted and now sanctioned, facilitating the ability to investigate his leads."

Sanctioned. That meant he'd found something, something related to all that translation he'd sent her.

Another buzzing hunch flitted into her brain and immediately disappeared when the executive agent said, "Agent Burton, do you have anything you'd like to add, regarding this matter?"

She cleared her throat, took a sip of water before replying, trying to recapture the thought. The present took precedence however, with the panel members watching her, and the thought, the hunch, was gone.

"Sir, my only addition is a note of gratitude that Agent Michaels has been so dedicated to uncovering the truth, and the reasons for the events of Fifteen February."

Reese scrawled, *Good answer,* in big letters on his legal pad.

She ignored that, as well as the next reading as she made more notes.

TJ. Translations. Cheating spouses. Shipper? Freight?

Wait. Shipping. Another thought occurred. *Yountz. Freight. San Fran. Prometheus?*

Holy hell. Yountz had been at the gallery opening. D'Onofrio had been there as well. Most of the victims, all of the West Coast victims, had been at the opening.

Was Yountz connected too? Ana knew better than to discount the idea. She had a gift for data, and if her brain brought it up, there was something in all the stuff she'd read, something small and seemingly insignificant that had put the thought in her head.

Despite Rome, she never, ever forgot to check that sort of thing.

"And from your current supervisor, Special Agent Sarai Elizabeth Sinclair Pretzky," the first panelist read, drawing Ana's attention back to the proceedings. She'd never heard Pretzky's full name; she wasn't sure she'd even known her first name. "The following statement is read into record."

Ana held her breath throughout the narration, barely hearing words like "dedicated" and "perseverance," "unstinting work ethic," and "grace and aplomb." The overall sense of Pretzky's addition to the proceedings was positive and as fulsome as anyone could be.

Reese bumped her elbow and wrote on the pad again. *Good job.*

As if she'd done a good job in order to be reinstated, like kissing up. Right. Thinking in those terms made her think about Davis, the pus-ball. She wondered if everyone thought it was all about skating by these days, until you had to cover your ass.

That sparked a thought, and she wrote, *CYA? Who? Covering for whom?* next to the listing for the Moroni Gallery. They had closed down immediately after the forgeries came to light. Neither McGuire nor Hines had been able to track the owners. By the end of the time they worked on the case, filing it as cold, they'd still had no leads on the owner's whereabouts. Doing her own follow-up, she'd come up empty as well.

She scrawled the word *Disappearances* next to the Moroni owners' names. She also wrote, *HINES!!!* as a reminder to call the man again. He still had not returned her calls, and she needed to know if he'd checked the shipper in White Plains. It hadn't been in the notes, and McGuire hadn't remembered anything about the shipper, but he said Hines had been the one to talk to the Miami gallery owner, as well as Moroni in New York.

Then there was Berlin. The Moroni crew had disappeared; Pratch was gone too. Had his disappearance been about money, or ass covering?

And where was the body? Did they need to be looking for the Moroni owners' bodies, as well? She scribbled another note. *Pratch—body? Moroni—body? Jane/John Does? Check Potter's Field burials/timeline.*

"I have the fitness reports." Another panel member spoke up, this time the gentleman to the left of center. "Reading into the record," he intoned. "Review of the mental fitness of Anastasia Elena Burton, and her capacity to return to duty."

When he started reading the review from the shrinks, she shut it out. She'd read the files, knew what they had to say about her stability, the way her mind worked.

What she needed was for her mind to actually work, to make the leap from names on a page to a solid direction. It was there, she could feel it hovering in the back of her mind. She'd started to flip the pages back, review her list of names when the lead panelist cleared his throat, calling her attention to him.

"Therefore, Agent Burton," the executive agent intoned, a hint of a smile playing about his lips. Had he figured out she was working? Did he care? "In the matter of Fifteen February, we, the Panel of Inquiry, do hereby absolve you of any wrongdoing or fault. The matter, while noted in your record, will not be assigned as a reason for demotion or delay of benefit or placement."

Reese made a noise that was probably triumph, well muffled since the panel was still in session. Despite her distraction, or maybe because of it, Ana got the socked-in-the-gut feeling that goes with either great upset or great relief. Having her thoughts keyed into the art case had distracted her from being a sweaty, nervous wreck for the panel. Thank God.

"Oh, God. Thank you," she whispered, letting it sink in. She was not at fault. Not at fault. *Thank you, TJ.* She would never balk over doing a translation or favor for him, ever again. Ever.

"Is there anything you would like to say, Agent?"

She took a bracing sip of water before she spoke, knowing her voice was going to be shaky, no matter what. "Thank you to the Panel of Inquiry for your hard work, and for this verdict."

There, she'd gotten it out. The members of the panel nodded, closing folders and in all but one case, the executive agent, sitting back in their chairs.

"Agent Burton, I have been instructed to inform you that while your current assignment is ongoing, a number of urgent openings await you when you can wrap up your part of the investigation in progress." He looked down at his notes. "Five teams have requested either a person of your capabilities or you, personally." He smiled at her openly now. "These include several international postings, as well as a domestic case or two. While we, the panel, only felt it necessary to read three or four recommendations into record, I want you to know that there were at least twenty-seven letters of varying length that lent support to your skills and dedication to the Agency, and the security of the United States on a global basis."

"Yes sir, thank you, sir." Ana was stunned by the fact that so many people had taken time to post something positive. In her experience, more people were apt to focus on the negative, especially within the Agency.

"Very good. Unless my fellow panelists have anything further to add?" He looked up and down the line. "No? Very well, this Panel of Inquiry is dismissed at—" He checked his watch, stated the time, and brought down a gavel on the tabletop. "Good luck, Agent Burton."

"Thank you, sir," she said, standing in respect as the panelists filed out. The last panelist detoured to drop a fat manila envelope on the table in front of her.

"Some of those potential postings," she said, tapping the CONFIDENTIAL seal. "Handle with care." The woman nodded to Ana and to Reese, then left through the same door the others had used, leaving her alone with Reese.

"Congratulations," he said, offering a handshake. "You're cleared for return to serious duty," he nodded at the envelope. "Any idea where you want to go?"

She shook her head, which was swimming with all her ideas, hunches, and thoughts on the current case. "I haven't dared consider anything. I'll look at everything later, but my mind is pretty full of the case I'm working right now."

Reese frowned. "It's a cold case," he said dismissively. "Pass it off to someone else and get yourself out of there."

"No, I need to finish it out, wrap it up if I can."

Reese shook that off. "You heard the executive agent. He didn't say finish it; he said wrap up your part of it. Move on, Ana. The less time on your record in the dead zone, the better." He gathered his notepad, settled it in the pocket of his briefcase. "By the way, the pay-grade shift and increase that was frozen will be reinstated and paid retroactive to the freeze. Expect a nice bonus in your check this month."

He waited expectantly for her to get her own belongings, walked out to the main part of the building with her. "Good luck, Agent," he said, holding out his hand to shake hers in parting. "It's been a pleasure to assist you in clearing this matter off your record."

Ana stood a moment, watching him walk away, stroll down the sidewalk in the bright DC April sunshine. *All is forgiven, all is forgotten?* She wondered about that, wondered about the fraud case and her San Francisco colleagues all through the ride back to the hotel. The fat envelope full of options weighed heavy on her mind, but she didn't open it.

She didn't want to go there quite yet.

Kicking off her shoes, she lay on the bed, thinking. What was the connection she was missing? Where did all the pieces fit?

She was still wondering when she fell asleep.

Hours later, she woke in darkness. Her mouth was dry, her head hurt, and all she wanted to do was go back to sleep. Her dreams had been a welter of images, from Gates's face in the mirror behind her, passionate and loving, to the grisly visual of Beverly Stanley's burned and broken body on the cold steel in the morgue in Rome.

Superimposed over all the images were the photos of the tortures in New York, and the executions in San Francisco.

"Ugh," she grunted, going to the bathroom to splash water on her face. She had to book a flight to New York, follow Davis's lead to the shipper there. "What is it about that that's bothering me?" She puzzled over that as she went online, booked her flight for the next morning. "What, what, what?"

She paced the floor for a few minutes. "Only two centers of killing," she said, finally getting a handle on one thing that was bothering her. "But two different methods."

She opened her connection to her office e-mail and felt her heart rate pick up at the multiple pings of incoming e-mail.

A frisson of excitement hit her in the gut when she saw the subject line, *SEARCH RESULTS*. That was the first e-mail she opened.

> Agent Burton, re: the search you instigated on Case #5789420-A. Additional Warrants processed, search under way. Initial track is pointing to the shipping company designated in warrant #5832, issued by Judge Pierson . . .

Ana skipped through all the legalese to get to the results listed three paragraphs down and got a hard shock.

> **Case co-connection warning! This warrant intersects with warrant # 097843, Washington District, Case # 54973.**

Whose case? She scanned further down, saw TJ's name and stopped cold. What the hell? TJ?

It *was* connected.

She grabbed her phone, found TJ's number.

"Come on, answer, damn it," she muttered, opening the other e-mails one by one. The data was still incoming, but as the searches overlapped, the shipper came up sixty-one percent of the time in relation to the numbers called before and after the art fraud was discovered. Ana was not surprised when a second shipper came up in San Francisco.

"Two of them. Two shippers. Same fraud. Two different killers. Separate but equal, damn it," she said, continuing to pace as the phone rang and rang. "Answer the damn phone, TJ."

She stopped long enough to scribble her thoughts on her yellow pad. "Time for a new warrant," she muttered, sending an e-mail to Pretzky as she waited for TJ's voice mail to pick up. They needed all the data on that shipping company.

An e-mail popped up from TJ. She hung up the phone just as the message picked up.

> **Don't ring the phone. I'm in something complicated. I'll let you know. TJ**

She quickly wrote back.

> **I'm in your kind of town. Crossroads on your work.**

She paused, trying to think how to carefully let him know what was going on without saying it straight out.

All that stuff we talked about de Italia is connected. We need to talk immediately. A.

She waited for ten minutes, checking the e-mail over and over, but there was nothing from TJ.

She continued pacing. Should she call Gates, let him know what the search had turned up? Odd how quickly she'd come to think of him as a kind of partner, an equal. She'd never had—or let—anyone be in that position before.

"If I hadn't slept with him, if he hadn't treated me the way he did, would I call him?"

Before she could decide, her phone rang. She checked the number: Pretzky.

"Burton," she said by way of greeting.

"Pretzky here, how'd it go?"

Warmed by the interest, Ana smiled. "It went okay, thanks. I'm clear."

"Good. You deserved no less."

"Thank you for all you did," Ana said, wanting to say more, but unsure how to do it. Relief was coursing through her in a delayed reaction. Talking to Pretzky brought it home. She was free. She was reinstated. She had jobs waiting.

"Never mind the thanks," Pretzky replied, oblivious to Ana's relief. "I'm calling because we've had another incident." Pretzky sounded pissed, now. "We've also got another body in the building. Probably isn't related, but no one from this division's died in," she paused, to count, "the four years I've been here, except one guy who got hit by a bus. This was a hit."

"Who was it?" Ana gripped the desk, willing it to be a fluke, unrelated.

"Guy named Perkins from IT. He's been dead a few days. Probably killed soon after our computers got hit and you had that deep search. They found him with crack cocaine. He's got some tracks, but the ME's saying they're probably post mortem. Nothing about it adds up. It was an execution-style hit, rather than an OD. Bullet to the back of the head."

"Just like the others in California, in the art fraud case."

"Exactly. Ties in with another like-crime in Vegas as well."

Excitement flared in her gut. She remembered Perkins now. He'd been up on their floor, right after the hacking incident. She reminded Pretzky. "Remember? It was weird because he said he'd come up to help, but he was up on our floor, not down with Monroe and Talmadge, the IT guys that got us shut down. I think it's connected." Ana was sure, and her tone reflected it. "Besides that, we got another complication. I got three case-connection warnings via e-mail on our art-fraud case, intersecting in some searches and warrants on another case." She read the file number to Pretzky; her boss returned the favor with the case number from Vegas. Also cold, also unsolved. "I'm positive mine's a cross with a case from my colleague in Rome, TJ Michaels. Problem is, he won't answer my calls."

"I'll check from here, let you know. There's something else, though. You put all the files and notes from this case in the locked filing cabinet, right?"

"Of course. We agreed on that as a safety measure."

"They're gone."

"Wait, did you say 'gone'?" Ana's voice rose to a stressed squeak. "As in missing, totally not there?"

"Exactly. It had to be an inside job because no one can get in here without authorization, even the cleaning people. I've got Pearson reviewing the surveillance tapes and the visitor logs, but so far we've got nothing."

Ana opened the files on her laptop. "I've got a lot of the data scanned into my computer, including the old case notes from Agents McGuire and Hines. Should I contact them?"

"I think you'd better, see if they kept copies. Also, I got Agent TJ Michaels's boss on the phone—he claims Michaels is off on sabbatical, not on a case."

"The Inquiry Panel said he was pursuing leads on the

Rome case, on his own recognizance, but that he'd gotten sanction to pursue."

"Have you discussed that data from Davis, the info on your shipper, with any of the victims?" Pretzky asked now.

"Not yet. I was working on a flight to White Plains, and got the e-mails about the case crossovers. Then you called." Ana didn't say she'd been trying to decide if she could call Gates.

"I see. You hear anything from Davis?"

"Davis? No, should I have?"

She heard the worry in Pretzky's voice when her boss replied. "He was supposed to contact you, let you know that he'd found two more victims who used the shipper you're checking on. What the hell is the name of it? I hate calling it 'the shipper.'"

"Ark Shipping Inc." Ana read the data. "There's a probable sub-corp, D'Or Shipping."

"D'Or? That means gold. Gold shipping? That's original," Pretzky scoffed. "Ark? That's weird too. Not like they're moving paintings or anything else two-by-two."

Ana hadn't put it together that way, but Ark was a biblical reference. Gold. Gold Ark. It was worth a try. She pulled up her favorite search engines and entered *gold ark* in one search field, *gold ship,* and then *gold box* in the others and hit SEARCH.

"What else?" she asked Pretzky. "You don't sound like you're finished."

"I'm not," Pretzky said. "We got word from Berlin that Pratch's remains may have turned up."

"You're kidding, right? Why now, I wonder?"

She heard the phone ring on Pretzky's end, and her boss said, "Hey, gotta go. Call you later."

Pretzky hung up so fast there was no time for Ana to say good-bye.

Nothing obvious pulled up on her search, so she checked e-mail again, but there was nothing from TJ. Checking the time, she called McGuire in New Orleans. He answered on the fifth ring.

"Hello?" The gruff voice was hard, insistent. "Who is this?"

"Agent McGuire, it's Agent Burton. I'm calling about the cold case again, the art fraud—"

He cut her off. "Yeah, yeah. I know. You've hit on something, for sure, Burton. I've had visitors."

"Visitors?" She'd been afraid of something like this.

"Couple of thugs, aiming to rough me up, or worse."

"Oh, my God. Are you okay?"

"I'm good, but they're not. One's in the morgue. Gotta say my aim's not off by much, even if I am an old fart. The other's in jail, but he ain't got much to say. Got hired by phone, had my address." He gave a short barking laugh. "Guess their boss didn't tell 'em I was armed and dangerous."

"I know I told you we'd had more action on the case, Agent. This isn't acting like a cold case now. It's had me hopping, but I didn't feel like anything substantial was moving," she admitted. She hadn't either, certainly not on the case, even though everything else seemed to be shifting and going straight to hell right under her feet. "Then all hell broke loose over the weekend, but even then, it didn't seem related."

"I think you better reconsider that, missy," McGuire advised, his voice still gruff. "And be careful."

"I will, as much as I can. Have you been in touch with Agent Hines? I've been unable to reach him at his office or on his cell."

There was a short pause. "Yeah, tried to call him, got no answer. His office says he's on vacation."

"You don't think so." She knew the answer, but she wanted to hear him say it.

"No." The pause was longer. "No, I don't."

"Shit. Okay, listen, I'll keep you posted. If you get any more visitors, give me a call." She gave him her cell number. "You should know too, I just heard they found Pratch's remains."

"There's something to throw you off the scent," McGuire said, stopping Ana in her tracks. "Right on time."

"You think it's a diversion?"

"I think someone wanted him found, wants you to focus some time in Europe on that, rather than on this," McGuire snapped. "This is getting crappier and more convoluted by the minute. I think you need to send someone to find Hines, you get me?"

His implication came through loud and clear. Crap, crap, crap. This was the last thing Ana needed in an already brutally tangled case. Partner or not, McGuire was pissed and thought Hines was involved.

"I'm gonna say this once, missy," McGuire said slowly, reluctance plain in every word he spoke. "I'm going to tell you that Hines is a top marksman. Sniper, if you get me. You watch out, you hear me?"

"Got it," she said, feeling the curl of fear in her belly. A sniper. A perfectly placed shot at the Agency garage. A shot in the dark at her apartment. A shot in the dark at the Opera? That one still didn't make sense, not in terms of the case. Why would Hines target Gates? She'd figure it out later; for now she needed to get off the phone, get busy. "Thanks, McGuire."

"Call me if there's a change, will ya? I'm staying locked and loaded until I hear from you." He paused a minute, and he said, "Thank God I sent my grandkids away for a week or so."

"Yeah, I'm glad of that." Ana's imagination was too vivid to contemplate what might have happened if the thugs aiming for McGuire had found his grandchildren instead. "I'll call. The minute I hear anything," she reassured him, and they hung up.

Ana set her phone down, so that she could use both hands to rub away the goose bumps that rose on her arms. She left the phone and the bed, intending to get water from the mini-bar. She'd taken two steps away from the bed when her phone rang.

Expecting Pretzky, or TJ, she checked the number.

It was Gates.

Chapter Seventeen

"Hey." Gates's voice was still raspy, not quite back to the liquid velvet she'd grown to love.

"Hey." She forced her voice to be clipped, flat. She wasn't giving anything away. It hurt too much. "I was just going to call you."

"Really?" he said, softly. "How can I help you?"

She bit her lip, wishing she could hate him. Wishing that she didn't still want him. "The search we developed turned up some things."

"What?" He was alert now, all business. "What did you get?"

"A shipper in White Plains, New York. Moroni used them, so did the Miami gallery, to ship to Pratch in Berlin." She'd recognized the international number as Berlin, made the connection. "I'm flying in there in the morning."

"Fly into LaGuardia. We'll meet up."

"I don't think that's wise," Ana said, her heart clenching at the thought of seeing him again.

"Ana." He just said her name, nothing more.

"No, Gates," she said, working hard to keep her voice even. "You shut me out, shut me down. That's somehow going to be okay now? Now that I've got a lead?"

"No, no, I understand," he said, his husky voice soft. "It's just that I found something too." He was silent for a long minute.

"Gates?" Her heart clenched. He didn't sound like himself. He'd sounded sharp for a minute there, but now he sounded tired, almost sleepy.

"Yeah, yeah," he said, still talking softly. "I'm here. It's another connection."

"What?" she demanded. "You want me to give? You give."

"Yeah, okay," he chuckled, and she heard him yawn. "It's probably not much, but did I tell you I found your hacker, the deep-search one?" he said, taking her back a step. She'd forgotten all about the search, forgotten to follow up on her tracking of it. Everything else had taken precedence.

"Who? Where?"

"Fly to LaGuardia. We'll pick you up."

"You can't keep this hostage, Gates," she argued. "Talk to me. Wait. *We?*"

"Dav's here on business," he drawled. "He humored the invalid, let me tag along."

"Are you on meds, Gates?" she asked.

"Mmmmm. Just took another dose. I hate the stuff, it makes my head swim. Stops my guts from hurting though. Except for one part."

"Really?" Now Ana was concerned. "If you still have pain, you should talk to your doctor, or the nurses." She heard him chuckle softly. "Seriously, Gates."

"It's not medical, Ana." There was a long moment where all she could hear was his breathing.

"Gates?" she called. "Gates?"

"Hmm? I hate to say it, but I'm sleepy now, Ana," he murmured. "I think I'm supposed to go to sleep, okay?" He laughed, like a pleased but sleepy child would. "I have these really great dreams about you, you know."

She realized the meds had taken effect. "No, I didn't know. Gates," she said, hearing the pleading in her own voice, but unable to stop herself. As much as she wanted to know about his dreams, she needed the data he had. "Gates? I need to know about the search."

"In your own building," he said softly. "Really weird. Sleep tight, beautiful Ana. I miss you," he whispered, and the phone went dead.

What the hell was she supposed to do now? What did he mean, *in her own building?*

Ana dropped into the chair by the desk, confused and tired. Nothing occurred to her, no matter how much her thoughts raced. Tears filled her eyes. He dreamed about her, but he'd sent her away. He could care enough to keep hunting, finding out who'd been searching her, and yet be so cruel.

Now he could turn her inside out with the knowledge that he knew data, and he knew who was stalking her, then hang up because he was too loopy to stay awake. God, she was so confused.

"I guess I'm going to LaGuardia," she finally said, moving to the computer to change her ticket.

Despite her fears, she started to smile, thinking about Gates's call. What an idiot to phone when he'd taken medication. "I'd better call Dav, though."

Picking up her phone, she sent a text to Dav's phone. He'd asked her to keep him posted anyway.

> Dav, just got a "drunk" call from Gates. He says he has a trace on the deep search on me. Says it's connected. He wants me to come to LaGuardia—I'm in DC headed to NYC anyway. You okay with that? A.

She waited for a call or text for twenty minutes. When none came, and there was still no word from TJ, she shut down and went to bed. There was nothing she could do until morning anyway.

When she arrived in LaGuardia the next day, she went through security and descended to baggage claim. Among the line of chauffeurs and waiting families, a man held a sign with her name on it. She stopped in her tracks, wondering if it were a trick until the man tipped down his sunglasses and she saw Damon, the chauffeur who'd driven them to the restaurant. He smiled briefly, then flipped the shades back up.

He turned the sign briefly over, and it said, "Walk by."

Creepy. Why did he want her to walk by?

She acted as if she were scanning the overhead signs for the directions to baggage claim, just like half a dozen other incoming passengers. As she walked toward him, he looked at his watch, scanned the paper he was holding, and folded the sign with her name on it.

He took out his cell phone, just as she walked by him, and he fell into step half a pace behind her.

"Yeah," he said, as if talking to someone. "I'm here, but she's a no show. Yeah, parked outside Gate Seven. No. No, the flight was on time. Yeah. Okay. The short sedan, yeah, the black 'Cedes."

He hung up, passed by her, and walked out into the gray New York day at the exit for Gate Five.

Turning down the concourse, she made her way to Gate Seven and stopped, scanning the crossings, noting the busses and the yellow cabs that were parked or slowly moving through the terminal for pickup. Beyond the first lanes, reserved for cabs and official vehicles, were the lanes for personal pickup. She could see the black Mercedes sedan, with Damon standing by the front bumper, phone to his ear.

Her phone rang, and she tapped the small earpiece tucked behind her loose hair.

"See me?"

"Yeah."

"Come straight out and get in. Leave your bag at the curb, I'll get it. Mr. G's in the back."

"Yes."

"Welcome back, ma'am," he added, and hung up.

It couldn't have gone smoother if they'd rehearsed it.

When the door closed, a breath of relief whooshed out, and Dav smiled.

"Cloak and dagger, I believe you call it, eh, Ana?" He smiled and handed her a glass of sparkling water.

"Yeah, not really my thing, despite the showing at the gallery."

"Hmmm. That was quite the show, in itself." He chuckled.

"How is he?" The question slipped out before she could stop it.

Dav didn't look at all surprised. "Still cranky. He doesn't remember calling you, or he says he doesn't."

Ana had already braced herself for that. It was enough though, to know that in his uninhibited moments, he thought of her. It might not get her anywhere, or take them anywhere, but she hadn't been a fling. With all that had happened, both in Rome and with Gates, she wasn't sure she could stand it if everything they'd done and felt had been meaningless.

"Detective Baxter," Dav said, looking straight ahead, "believes that he has identified the sniper." Dav finally looked at her and she could see the worry, the anxiety that shone in his eyes.

"Really? Gates was the target, then."

"Oh, yes." Dav's chuckle was forced, and she knew it cost him not to show just how worried he was about his friend. Ana swiveled to face him.

"You don't need to put on a show for me, Dav. I know how much you two mean to one another," she said quietly.

He nodded, reaching out to clasp her hand tightly, then release it. He patted it now, a brief acknowledgement of the worry that connected them.

"You of all people will appreciate how many calls I received," he said as he tipped his cup of coffee, using it as a prop to keep his hands busy. She wished she had a cup of coffee too, not just as a prop, but because she needed the caffeine.

"Calls?"

"Oh, yes." He smiled at her. "Various factions from all over the world making sure I understood that *they* had not targeted my second in command."

Ana sorted the sentence for a minute then began to smile. "Ah, the rats will run, I guess."

"It made for some instant negotiating opportunities," he said coolly, smiling as he took another sip. "I took full advantage of the situation."

She laughed. "Good for you. Some good should come of it."

"It is good to hear you laugh, Ana-aki," he said.

"It's good to laugh, Dav-aki," she said, returning the favor.

The car made a turn onto the Triborough/RFK Bridge, heading into the heart of the city. "Would you like us to stop for some coffee, or can we get you some at the Waldorf?"

"Is there a Starbucks near the Waldorf?" she asked, unsurprised that he'd noted her interest in his coffee.

"In the lobby. Damon?"

"Yes, sir?"

"Would you mind getting Agent Burton a—" He turned to her, inviting her to give her order, which she did. "A venti mocha, when we get to the hotel and bring it up to the suite?"

"With or without whipped cream, Agent?" Damon asked, smiling as he glanced in the rearview mirror.

"With," she said.

They talked of pleasantries until they got to the hotel, turning off Forty-Ninth onto Park and easing up to the front of the hotel. The car glided beyond the main entrance to an unobtrusive, private canopy. In seconds, she'd spotted Queller and one of the women who'd been at the gallery opening. The redhead, Declan, was there too, but he was wearing a ball cap and coming in from a run, passing them to go in the main doors. The bellman stopped him and pointed to the cap, which Declan removed before going through the revolving door into the lobby.

"No ball caps in the public areas," Dav said with a smirk,

sliding out on the same side as Ana so they could easily and quickly move through the private entrance. "I've wanted to buy a Red Sox hat," he said, crossing the elegant boutique-style lobby to where a uniformed doorman had an elevator car waiting. "And wear it as I go through the main areas."

She snorted, suppressing the guffaw that wanted to jump out. It was over-hearty, and she knew it, but she was nervous about seeing Gates again. "Think they'd dare say anything?"

"I heard they made A-Rod, the star Yankee player, take off his Yankees cap, just days after the last time the Yankees won the pennant," he said, grinning. "Relax, Ana-aki. This will sort itself out."

"God, I hope so," she muttered as they reached the top of the Waldorf Towers, stepping onto the plush carpet and through the doors that another member of Dav's staff held open.

"Agent Burton," Gates's assistant murmured, her infectious smile blossoming. "I hope your flight was uneventful."

"It was, thank you," she said, trying to remember the perky assistant's name. She recognized the young woman from Dav's house. Alice? No, Alexia.

"Mr. G, Agent, we've set up in the conference room. Mr. B had everything up and running, but they made him go rest."

"Thank you, Alexia. Damon's bringing a coffee up for Agent Burton. I trust that you and Theresa were able to get everything we needed."

The woman looked affronted, but simply said, "Of course, sir."

"Thank you," he said, striding through a set of double doors to the left. Ana gave the woman a reassuring smile and followed.

"What have we got?" she heard Dav ask and had to stifle a gasp when she cleared the doors and saw the setup. Four computers hummed on the table, a world map hung on the wall with photos of the artwork tagged to their cities of origin and a secondary line running to the terminus city where the fraud was discovered. On a parallel board, there were pages taped together listing artwork sold at the same time that was authentic, untainted.

"Gates didn't have much else to do, these last two days while I was in meetings," Dav said at her elbow, as Alexia appeared as well, handing her the distinctive sleeved cup from Starbucks.

"Thanks. Yeah, I'll say."

"Pick a seat," Dav said. "Alexia will order us some lunch, yes?"

Ana sat down. She chose a position at the nearest terminal, watching the data that was scrolling there. On the next laptop over, an algorithm sped equations across the screen. She recognized it as a variation of the search parameters she and Gates had worked out, but couldn't decipher what data sets it was comparing.

She couldn't see the third, but when she turned, she saw *him.* Gates stood in the doorway that led to the back of the suite. He hadn't shaved this morning, she decided, but otherwise, he looked dramatically better than the last time she'd seen him. He was moving carefully, one hand trailing on the wall.

"Hello, Gates," she said, staying in her seat for fear that her legs wouldn't hold her if she tried to stand.

"Don't spill that coffee on my keyboard," he said, moving forward to grip the back of the chair nearest the door, four down from where she was sitting. "I hate it when that happens."

Dav was right, he was cranky. At least he was trying for a smile.

"Thank you, everyone," Dav said, motioning the others to leave. Once again, Ana envied his ability to command the room. "Get some sleep, Gates?" Dav continued, speaking to Gates now.

"Yeah, no thanks to you," he growled.

"Sit down before you fall down, idiot," Dav snapped, sitting down on the opposite side of the table from both Ana and Gates. "Enough of this posturing."

Gates bared his teeth, looking for all the world like a wounded lion, but he complied, sinking into the chair he'd been holding. The three chairs separating them along the side of the table could have been an inch apart or a mile. Gates wasn't giving anything away.

Dav muttered under his breath, something about fools and small children. She remembered her Greek nanny saying the same thing when she'd done something particularly dangerous or foolhardy.

"Gates." She brought his full attention her way, though he was still shooting irritated looks at Dav. "You said you knew who instigated the deep search. Who did it?"

"I don't know who, precisely, but I dug out the origin. Your building, then bounced to Oregon as a final destination."

"Perkins," she said, immediately. "And Hines. That bastard."

"Agency?" Dav said, reading her fury right. It was bad enough to have to fight the bad guys, but to have to fight your own was torture.

"Yeah. I have to call this in, let my Special Agent know."

"Pretzky? Isn't she a little low-rank for that kind of intel?" Gates sniped.

Ana didn't go for the bait. He was taunting her, trying to piss her off so she'd treat him like dirt. It would be his way of keeping her away from him.

Some time in the night, or on her trip from DC to New York, she'd figured it out. He'd sent her away. He'd decided it was too dangerous to have her with him.

Two could play that game.

"She ranks me," Ana said, her phone already in hand. "Which is where I have to start. I overstepped my wingman once, and two people died for it. I won't do it again."

That shut him up. He and Dav exchanged troubled looks, but she ignored them both.

"Burton? What's the sit-rep?" Pretzky asked.

"I'm with Mr. G and Gates Bromley. Did you get my text?"

"Got it. You need to check your e-mail. You've had incomings popping up every minute for the last twenty."

Why had Pretzky been in her cubicle, or monitoring her e-mail?

"No time for that," she said, yanking her yellow pad out of her briefcase, fumbling for a pen. Dav leaned across the table and handed her a gold fountain pen. *"Efharisto,"* she said. *Thank you.*

He nodded in answer, then braced his elbows on the table to try to follow her conversation.

She took notes as she talked, following her own steps on paper as she spoke. "Hines is a mole."

"Hines?" Pretzky repeated.

"One of the original agents on the case. You got the copy of my notes? Yeah. First page. The two original agents were McGuire and Hines, out of DC. You can call McGuire in New Orleans; he's retired. He's the righteously pissed member of the team, and he's already had an attempted hit." Ana waited out the storm of protest that came from Pretzky, noted the grim look Gates and Dav exchanged.

"Yes," she continued. "Hines is the mole. McGuire'll fill you in. Yes. I talked to him last night. That's when he told me some bully-boys showed up to go for him." She waited out Pretzky's exclamation and complaint that Ana hadn't put that in her e-mail. "The guy's a tough nut. Took one out with a head shot. The other's in the hospital, but not talking. McGuire wouldn't rat his former partner, but when I told him I couldn't get a hold of Hines, he indicated that I'd better find him. So, Hines is Oregon. Mr. Bromley tells me the data search origin is from our building with a bounce to Oregon. We're running with the theory that Hines is the one who yanked my data chain, possibly using that dead guy from IT, Perkins."

It was starting to come together.

Pretzky asked several questions, but the one Ana answered was about whether she'd begun hunting Hines's sorry ass to prep it for a good whipping. "I figured I'd start that this morning, with gusto, but when I got to my meeting with Mr. G and Bromley, their data added fuel to the fire."

"Wait, wait," Pretzky said, and Ana heard her flipping notes. "Did you report that, the deep search?"

Crap. Had she? "I believe it's in my notes, Special Agent, but I'm not sure how extensive my profile was. At the time, I never considered that it might be one of ours. Or how it might tie into the case. I considered it peripheral."

Gates chuckled, and she glared at him. Dav was smiling as well. They knew she'd suspected Gates had done the search.

"Hell, I don't think there are any coincidences at this point, Agent. We've got news on this end too."

Ana waited for the other shoe to drop, and it did.

"Davis is compromised."

"The files. My notes," Ana snapped, now understanding the extent of the problem, why she'd been unable to get ahead of things.

"Exactly," Pretzky replied, and her voice told Ana how pissed she was.

TJ typed as fast as he could, sending e-mail after e-mail. He wasn't sure how much time he had left before D'Onofrio found him. He knew now that the man was hiding his identity in the families TJ had been watching. He'd been watching Ana on the West Coast, stalking her.

"I didn't make the connection, damn it," he cursed, wondering why. Someone on the inside, someone in the Agency had blocked information. He was afraid he'd missed something and knew now how Ana had felt in Rome. He realized how badly he'd fucked everything up. If he got out of this alive, he'd do time, but that was a small matter now.

"Doesn't matter now," he muttered, typing as fast as he could. If he could get everything out, everything on paper, so to speak, maybe Ana could sort it out. Using linked computers, he sent both Wi-Fi and hardwire in case anyone was smart enough to jam the wireless. He sent copies to every e-mail he had, every one he'd registered with the Agency, every one of Ana's that he knew, both Agency and private. He hard-saved everything on the computer to a thumb drive with every stroke of the keys.

> A, this is the last thing. You were right about Colvos in Rome. He was getting inside data. It was from me. I didn't know I was giving it to him. I thought I was giving it to Interpol Italia. He had IEC credentials, he checked out with our local contacts. When everything went down, he disappeared. It was as if he never existed.
>
> I tracked him to the US, to White Plains, New York. He skirted around, but he's here, pretending to be a family man, pretending to—

He heard them coming and hit SEND, jerking the small portable drive out of the machine as the door to the low-rent hotel burst inward. His laptop exploded in the hail of bullets, and his heart did too.

Dropping the miniscule USB device into his pants as he went down, he felt the cold hand of death sweep over him.

His last thought was of Ana.

Chapter Eighteen

"Pretzky's on her way," Ana said as she hung up. "They're sending two additional agents up from DC as well."

"What, none in the Big Apple, twiddling their collective thumbs just waiting to help out?" Gates's comment was snarky and mean. He seemed to regret it, adding, "Then again, nothing in this whole affair has been easy. Why would there be extra manpower here in the city where it's needed?"

As peace offerings went, it sucked, but she'd take it. "Tell me about it," she muttered and saw Gates smile. "NYC detail has their hands full with a bunch of other operations." She waited a heartbeat for any further comments. When none came, she decided she should be asking some questions. "So what is all this?" She waved toward the walls.

"You mean my brainstorming?" Gates said with self-deprecating humor.

"Yeah," Ana said, pivoting in her chair to look around the walls. "There's a lot of it."

"Start at the beginning, Gates," Dav said, and it sounded more like an order than a request. A flush darkened Gates's face, but he complied.

"The map was Dav's idea. A graphic representation of all the pieces we knew about, as well as the two extras."

"You're missing the five from Florida," she said, moving

around the table to put markers on Miami, using the bright pink Post-it markers to point northward to New York. "They all came here, to Moroni."

"Where'd they go from there?" Gates asked, hands poised over the keyboard in front of his chair.

"Berlin."

"Pratch." Gates and Dav said the name together. Gates entered the data in the first computer and scooted the chair down to add the list to the running program on the computer next to her. She was dying to know what that one was doing.

"Exactly," Ana said, watching closely to see if she could decipher his program by his entry vectors. "Here's the other bit of data you probably don't have. They found Pratch's remains."

Dav made a low sound, and she saw his lips move, perhaps in prayer. She knew he was Greek Orthodox, when he practiced. "Rest his soul. I didn't like him," Dav added. "But the woman I mentioned—"

"Fraulein Messer." Ana supplied the name of the woman he'd told her about early on, the one he'd returned one painting to.

"Liza," Dav agreed. "She knew Pratch well. He was related by marriage, which was why she did business with him. Does she know?"

"I'm not sure, but in this case, I'd ask that you don't contact her just yet. Obviously someone's still monitoring a lot of the pieces of this puzzle, or people wouldn't be shooting at us," she said smiling, actually feeling the humor of the whole crazy situation. "One of the things Pretzky said," she held up her phone, indicating her boss. "Was that an agent in the cold case office is compromised as well."

"Wonder when you'll find *his* body," Gates muttered. He saw her quick frown, and realized how that might have sounded. "Sorry," he apologized. "But this is getting ugly. There are already what, four bodies on this deal?"

"Officially, five. However, I think it's at least seven."

"Seven?" Gates paused, then tapped the keys on the third computer. "Let's have it," he said, his mouth set in a grim line.

"Put them up on the map," Dav suggested. "Here—" He handed over more Post-its in a different color.

Using Dav's elegant pen she wrote down the names. "There were two victims in New York. One was associated with the Moroni Gallery. A clerk, for all anyone could figure out. No one that important, in the scheme of things." She wrote down the woman's name, Colleen St. John, and posted it by the city. "She was tortured."

She printed the second name. "The second body was Nathan Rikes, small-time thief, bag man, and general petty criminal. There was nothing to tie him to the crimes, nothing to tie him to Colleen, but he was found with her, dead the same way. Also tortured."

She stuck the second name up and moved to the left side of the map. "The two here, in San Francisco, were killed execution style. Clean and simple. No torture."

Posting the names of Keith Griffin and Rod Atwell, she continued near the Bay Area. Next, she wrote down both Kelly Dodd and Luke Gideon's names, but didn't put them up. She looked at Dav, trying to decide how to phrase her request.

"What?" Dav said, noticing her obvious pause.

"I need to ask you not to say anything about one of the next names I'm putting up. I have no proof that this is connected. Just a . . . hunch, a feeling."

"Data's data," Gates said, looking puzzled. "Put it up, we'll sort out whether it belongs."

"Why do you hesitate, Ana-aki?" Dav asked. His tone was all business, but she saw that his hands were clenched on the arms of the chair.

"It's Luke Gideon," Ana said, slowly. Watching Dav. "Carrie McCray's husband."

"You think he was involved?" Gates stopped keyboarding and looked over.

"I don't know, but there were only two fraudulent deliveries from Prometheus after his death. Six prior to that, two of which were to you," she reminded Dav.

"Poor Carrie," Dav said, showing where his allegiance lay. "Do you think she knew?"

Ana wanted to say no, but at this point, no avenue was closed and she said so. "I hope not, but," she shrugged. "It's not off the table."

"It is, for me." Dav was firm on that point, but he looked her way, managed a less belligerent demeanor. "I understand why you need to keep it in mind, however."

Gates said nothing, but he looked thoughtful. When he wasn't snarking, or asking questions, he was watching her with an intensity that was beginning to make her twitchy.

"The seventh?" Dav asked, obviously wanting to move on.

"Pratch, of course," Ana said, sticking up another Post-it. "When he went missing, and was presumed dead, his connection to most of the paintings was thrust into the forefront. While he's a prime suspect in the whole thing, I think someone went to a lot of trouble to make Pratch look more guilty, more involved than he was. I'll know more when we can get the report from our German counterparts, find out if they can tell how he died, when, and more importantly where he was found and how."

"What about the Moroni people?" Gates asked.

"I don't know, Gates," she admitted. "Part of me thinks I should add Nils Lundgren, one of the Moroni buyers, to the list of possible bodies; part of me wonders if he's the mastermind.

"Add him for now to the body count," Gates said, decisively. "Let's see what falls out. He's missing, so that's a data point."

"True. He didn't go missing till weeks later, though," she pointed out, sticking Lundgren's name on the wall. "Neither did Shelby Waters, his gallery manager."

"Did they disappear at the same time?"

Ana didn't remember and said so. "Hang on, I'll look it

up." She unpacked her laptop, booted it up. When the data came up, she read off the info. "Nils was reported missing by his landlord six weeks after the gallery closed, which was two weeks after the investigation turned up their involvement. He hadn't paid his rent."

"Date?" Gates demanded.

She rattled it off and continued. "Shelby Waters was reported missing sooner, only three weeks after the investigation, one week after the gallery closed."

"Six confirmed, two more suspected," Gates said. "Whoever this is, they're not afraid to get their hands dirty. Hang on a sec," he said, and his fingers flew over the keys. "There's a gap in the pattern on the dates," he declared. Gates plugged the laptop he was using into a projector, displaying the data on the cream-colored wall. "See? The dates for the two torture murders in New York are the first, then the Moroni people disappear. If Luke Gideon's a factor, he's next, see?" He pointed toward the screen, where the dates now appeared on a calendar page, the graphic lending credence to his theory. "The other California killings don't take place for at least a month after the New York murders, and there isn't any torture."

"Different killer? Different hire?" she offered. "I've been wondering that for a while. Such different styles."

"Maybe. Or maybe they got the information they needed from the tortures. They just needed to get rid of the other people who knew about the con."

An idea occurred to her, and she rounded the table to her laptop to do some key-punching of her own. Icons at the bottom of her screen flashed a fast green. She had incoming e-mail on four different addresses. Probably Jen, she decided, setting it aside for a minute as she brought up more info. She needed to look at those. If what she suspected about D'Onofrio was correct, he might be involved in all this mess. She hated to burst Jen's bubble about Millionaire Jack, but she was afraid he wasn't really named Jack, or a magazine mogul.

The thought that it might be TJ, finally answering her

e-mails, also crossed her mind, but Gates was asking a question and it distracted her.

"Got another idea?" he asked. "What are we factoring in?"

"Yeah, I do," she said. "Let's factor in when Hines, the bad-apple member of the original investigatory team, transferred to Oregon." She added the dates to the mix, posted Hines's name, and put arrow markers to what she thought of as the wilds of the Oregon territory.

"Dates aren't too long after the last murder. Anybody check his financials?"

"Nothing to see," Ana said. "We have full financial disclosure every year. We have to account for every penny that comes in."

Both men gave her disappointed looks. "Hey, I know he'd hide it. I'm just saying the average search wouldn't pull it and nothing chimed for the auditors, okay?"

"Right, so Hines hares off to Oregon," Gates said, summing things up. "The Moronis disappear, Pratch disappears, Luke Gideon dies, and four other people associated with the situation get dead. What brought you to New York?"

"New information from Pretzky." Ana stopped, suppressing the urge to curse. "I'm not sure if it plays in. This guy, Davis, worked with me the last few days calling other victims. By the way," she smiled at Dav. "Thanks for paving the way there." The pressure Dav had applied had definitely greased the wheels.

"Another side benefit of Gates getting shot, I'm afraid," Dav said. "Thank him." Gates threw a wadded-up piece of paper at him, but Dav only laughed.

"However it happened, it uncovered the fact that both Moroni and the Miami gallery, Artful Walls, shipped to Pratch in Berlin through this warehousing and shipping company in White Plains."

Cocking her head to one side, she asked a question that had been niggling at her. "What happened with the shooter? Did Detective Baxter turn anything up?"

Dav's frown went dark, and Gates scowled as well. It was

he who answered. "Turns out the woman who was hired to kill my family is free."

"Free?" Outraged, Ana half-rose. "How did that happen?"

Gates grimaced, shifting in his seat as if uncomfortable with her ire, and his own situation. "Routine transfer from prison to a prison-run farm. According to their guards, one minute she was there, the next, two guards were dead and she was gone. That was two years ago."

"They didn't see fit to tell you?"

"We were in India, I believe," Dav said, sounding apologetic. "Overseeing some holdings. Apparently the word never reached us."

She was about to delve into that when Alexia knocked and made her perky way into the room.

"Excuse me," Alexia said. "But you ordered lunch, sir? It's here."

The server and serving cart with lunch, followed by Callahan, one of Gates's team, came into the room. Ana caught Dav's inquiring look and Callahan's nod. Apparently the food had been checked out. Callahan was followed by a nurse who bustled over to take a blood pressure reading on Gates. Behind his back, she shook her head in answer to Dav's questioning look.

"We'll eat, then take an hour's break," Dav stated, glaring at Gates when he protested. "Don't give me that look, and don't torment the nurses, they're just doing their job."

Gates muttered all through lunch, but acquiesced when Ana said she was going to go lie down as well. "I've not gotten much sleep the last few days."

"How did the Inquiry go?" Dav asked.

Gates stopped at the door, obviously listening, but he didn't turn around.

"I'm cleared," she said.

"Congratulations, my dear." Dav beamed at the news. "Does that mean you'll be leaving the United States again?"

Gates waited, his back stiff with tension.

"I don't know," she said, unsure what his tension meant, or

where Dav's questions were going. "I won't know until this case is wrapped. I won't leave without seeing it through."

"Exotic locales," Gates said sardonically. "Isn't that what the recruiters always tell you?" He never turned to look at her. Something was bothering him; it was obvious from the set of his shoulders, the tense line of his back. "You'll enjoy getting back to that, I guess." He moved carefully away, through the doors to the bedrooms without another word.

"Don't let him get to you, Ana-aki," Dav soothed, as he stepped to her side. "He's angry at himself for pushing you away, and angry that he does not want to keep doing that. And furious that he doesn't know how to bring you back."

It took Ana a moment to find words to meet that unlikely statement. "It's probably not smart anyway, Dav," she said, looking anywhere but at this unlikely Cupid. "He's got his life, working with you. I've got my work, which takes me"—she swallowed her tears—"as he said, to such exotic locales."

Dav just watched her for a moment. It was unnerving. "We'll see," he said finally. "Get some rest."

Ana hadn't intended to sleep, but she did. The palatial Waldorf room was dark and cool, the bed turned down and the blinds drawn. A knock on the door woke her, and she called out, "Hang on, be right there."

Alexia was there, with a clipped set of papers and a tray of coffee. "Mr. G said to bring this in. I'm sorry to disturb you, but he didn't think you wanted to sleep for very long."

"What time is it?"

"It's around four. You've slept for about two hours or so," Alexia chirped. "Would you like me to open the blinds? It's still pretty rainy and gray, but the sun's been out a little bit."

Two hours? It felt like only five minutes had passed. "Sure, go ahead." She regretted the invitation to draw the blinds when a shaft of sunlight burst through the window. She felt like a vampire.

"Wow, that's bright. So, what are the papers?" She pointed to the stack that Alexia had set on the bed to open the drapes.

"Fax that came in for you," Alexia said. "It's from your San Francisco office, I think. We have a fax here in the suite, so it's been kept confidential."

"That's good. I'll be out in a few minutes."

"Take your time. Mr. B isn't awake yet. Mr. G's waiting another half an hour before he wakes him up." The young woman bounced out of the suite, and Ana decided she'd have to kill her if she worked with her too much. Perky just pissed her off.

It made her wonder how she and Jen had become best friends. Jen was terminally perky. "Probably a good thing we don't live together or anything," she muttered, as she pulled fresh clothes out of the suitcase. She took them to the bathroom, along with her makeup kit, to freshen up.

A quick wash and change gave her time to think things through, and thinking of Jen reminded her that she needed to check her e-mail.

"Fax first, e-mail second, new round of data crunching last," she said as she picked up the neatly printed sheets from the fax. The fax was from Pretzky.

"Couldn't get your cell. Senior Special Agent Hines, McGuire's former partner, is in the wind, his house and all financial accounts cleared," she read. "Like we didn't expect that," Ana said sarcastically. She continued to read the niggling little details of the search and was about to move on when the last note popped out at her: *Second attempt on McGuire.*

"Shit, shit, shit," she cursed, hurrying back to the conference room, to pull up the e-mails on her computer. She'd lay money that one of the e-mails was from the retired agent.

The first one was from Jen, hoping she'd passed the review. The second was from the retired agent.

> Tried your number. Second attempt down here. Locals are beginning to think I got a curse laid on me. My neighbor offered me a live chicken, if you know what I mean. It is New Orleans.

Got two more cold, but I'm getting tired of cleaning up. What's going on?

Ana went immediately to her purse and retrieved her phone. "Damn, the battery's totally dead." She untangled the charger cords, and plugged it in.

She quickly used her laptop to answer Jen and McGuire and decided she'd better give McGuire a call as well.

She left the conference room to find Alexia or Dav and get access to a phone. The first person she found was Alexia.

"Oh, yes, there's actually one in the conference room," Alexia said, directing her back the way she'd come. "Dav's on a call right now and asked not to be disturbed. Here—" The young woman opened a panel in the wall, took out a business desk phone, and set it on the table. When she finished, the phone was plugged in and ready to use. "Dav's on line one so use line three, please."

There was no answer at McGuire's, so she left a message.

"Back to the drawing board," Ana muttered and settled in with the e-mail. She waded through the rest of the spam and offers for health products in her e-mail in-box to open another e-mail from Jen. D'Onofrio had broken it off with Jen. By text message.

"Slime," Ana muttered, slamming her fist on the table. "Men are slime." Her hands were poised over the keyboard to respond when Gates came in.

"Slime, are we?" Gates said from the doorway. With careful steps, he made his way to the same chair he'd used earlier. So close, with just three chairs between them, and yet, like before, it seemed they were miles apart.

"Some of you," she said. "Some are pretty decent, I guess."

"So do I fall in the slime category or the decent category?" he asked, shifting to find a comfortable position in the seat. He looked both guarded and determined, an unusual combination.

She ignored the winking e-mails and swiveled to face him.

Oh, God, they were going to have to have one of *those* talks. *Why now?* She wished like anything that they could put it off.

Luck had never been her strong suit. "I guess that means we're going to talk about this."

"I know I'm not a good bet, Ana." Gates went on the offensive before she could even take a breath. "I'm dedicated to my job. I love what I do. So do you. I was harsh when you came to the hospital." He looked away as he said it. The investigator in her recognized it as a sure sign of remorse, or a lie. Either one said he felt he'd screwed up. She wasn't buying it.

"Harsh? You call that harsh?" She had to get up, get out of the chair and move away from the power he exuded over her senses. Even banged up and pale, he drew a response from her body, her mind; she still wanted him. "Pretty mild word for what you said, don't you think?"

"What do you expect, Ana?" he flared, and she heard the guilt ringing in his voice. "I'd been shot. An inch higher or lower and they'd be putting me in the ground. How I managed to get out alive, much less with as little damage as I had, is a fucking miracle."

"You think I don't know that?" she fired back, moving in on him now. "I was *there,* Gates. I held you in my arms all the way to the damn hospital. Your blood was on my hands"—she held them up, then pointed to her chest—"on *my* heart, on *my* watch. I thought you were going to *die,* Gates, right there. Another death on my conscience." She was close to him now, breathing hard with the sheer weight of the words she'd been carrying.

The look in his eyes was powerful, magnetic. It wasn't soft though, it wasn't acquiescence. It didn't seem to be understanding.

She threw up her hands in defeat. She refused to do this again. Refused. "Stop baiting me," she said. "You've made your decision, Gates. I don't have to like it, but I'm a big girl. If you don't want me in your life, if all the—"

She stopped. How did you condense their brief time of

deep, powerful passion into a trite phrase? "If the time we had together was your idea of a fling, so be it. I'm not built that way. My bad. Done. Move on, okay? But if you regret it, if you're trying to make up, you're doing a pretty sucky job."

She stared at him, breath coming in harsh waves as she stood over his chair.

"Is that what you really want? For me to leave you alone?" He said it mildly, but the waves of tension rolling off him said the answer mattered. Deeply.

"Arrrrrrrgh!" she half-screamed, smacking the wall next to where she stood. "What the hell are you getting at, Gates? You push me away like some cheap whore, like a fling that you were done with." She mimicked his cold tone as she said, "So long, Agent Burton, thanks for letting me bleed on you." She paced away, then back. "And you want to dig it up so you can throw that dirt at me again? What do *you* want?" she demanded. Before he could answer, she had to add, "And whatever it is, well, fuck you."

With deliberate care, he pushed himself to a standing position.

"I had a lot of time to think about it," he said, never raising his voice, which was nearly as infuriating as having to wait while he dismissed her yet again. "When I was awake, and able to think."

"What's to think about? You've already made it clear you're done with me." She turned, but he moved to her, faster than she thought possible in his condition. Bracing himself on the wall she'd smacked, he grabbed her hand in a firm, unbreakable grip. She wouldn't give him the satisfaction of struggling to break free. She stood there, furious and hurt, with her heart cracking all over again. "What?"

"I said, I had to think."

"Yeah, and?"

"All I could think about was you." His verbal bombshell had her gaping. "I told myself we were wrong for each other, that we had different needs, different lives. We're both stubborn."

"There's news," she snapped. "Get on with this, will you? I've got work. I get it, okay? We're ships in the night, peas and carrots, not going to work. All the clichés. Whatever." She tugged at her hand, trying to gesture, but he still held her fast. "We had fun, it was real, blah, blah, blah. Let go of me." She yanked at her hand, fighting the terrible urge to cry, but he refused to release her.

"No. I've done too much letting go," he said, never taking his eyes off her face. "On the other hand, I've held too tightly to the past, living in Dav's shadow, surviving, but not really living. This—" He slid his free hand around her neck, the heat of it firing her skin, sending a flush of desire straight to her innermost self, despite the way he'd treated her. "This. You. What we have together is something I want to hang on to."

She couldn't speak. Couldn't believe what she was hearing.

"I screwed up, Ana," he said.

She wanted to pull away. Where was the Ana who would stand up for herself, not be walked on this way?

The door opened behind them, and Ana caught a quick glimpse of Dav in the mirror before he retreated and the door clicked softly closed. Smart man.

That glimpse of Dav, of a man who'd faced adversity, who'd made money as a way to make friends in a new town; it gave her courage.

"Yeah, you did," she said, meeting his gaze squarely. If he wanted her back, he was going to have to grovel. "You fucked up big time. And I don't know if I can forget. I can forgive you," she said, but stopped him from speaking or moving when he would have drawn her in closer, tried to use the attraction between them to persuade her. "I don't know if I can forget though," she finished, stepping back. She didn't pull loose from his confining hand, but she did give herself distance. Her heart felt like it was in a vise. She wanted him, but would that ever be enough? Wanting wasn't loving. Wanting wasn't trust.

Gates looked both devastated and determined. "I get that. I know I have to earn your trust back," he said, hitting the issue dead on. "Ana." His voice was caressing now. "I don't know how we'll work this out. I don't know if we can, but I want to try. All that thinking time?"

"Yes?" she managed to say, her gut quivering with need, with anger and fear, with everything that welled up to choke and confuse her.

"I realized that I've been looking for you all along." He lowered his head to plant a kiss on her cheek, a tentative brush, as he had the first time they met. "If I beg," he whispered, as he kissed her cheek again. "Plead, maybe." Another kiss, a mere whisper of lips and tongues. "Get down and grovel, even."

He was seducing her with his mouth, his words. Her hands were gripping his arms now, hanging on instead of bracing to push him away. "If I do all that, do you think you can forgive me?"

If only it were that easy. She wanted to, God knew, she wanted to, but she had the feeling that her life was finally her own again, and that if she gave in now, if she let him off the hook, she'd be right back in the dungeon again.

"Gates," she said, pulling back, desperately seeking some solid emotional footing. "I don't know. I just, I just . . ." She couldn't voice the turmoil in her mind. She was an agent. Career wise, literally a hundred options lay before her. None of them would be easy, nor would any be a stable, nine-to-five sort of existence. Not one of the options in the envelope she'd been given had room for a personal relationship.

Not one.

"I understand," he murmured, resting his forehead on hers. "I'm not good at this, Ana. I suck at talking, at relationships." He shook his head. "I've had more practice shutting people out than letting them in." With that admission, he shuddered, closed his eyes. "Even if I try, I don't know if I'll be able to get past that."

"I don't know if I'll even be here, Gates. Not with my job."

He nodded. "I know. We've got a lot of stuff to figure out and this isn't the time. But I'd like to ask a favor. Please."

She was watching him when he opened his eyes. They were full of reflected pain and the strain of his injuries. How could she deny him a favor? How? She sighed. "What's the favor?"

"I want you to play pretend with me," he said, and his smile momentarily blocked out the pain etched on his face.

"Pretend?" she managed to say. Her voice was choked with the emotion she was struggling not to feel, or show, so she took refuge in sarcasm. "What is this, second grade?"

"Might be better if it were," he quipped. "Second graders are supposed to be kind, to share and to kiss and make up. Grown men aren't."

She sighed, knowing she couldn't deny him. "What's the pretend scenario?"

"I want to pretend that I never said what I said in the hospital. I want to pretend that it was the drugs talking and I was so doped up I didn't know what I was saying."

"You want to pretend it never happened?" She was incredulous. "Even if we did," she said, trying to pull away, "we still have too much between us. Your job, my job. Dav. No, you were right, Gates. We don't belong together." Her heart was breaking as she said it, but he'd been right too. It was for the best.

He sighed and pulled her tight for a moment, then let her go so he could sit back down in the chair. His care, his deliberate bracing on the arms of the chair so he could lower his body down, was a reminder of his wounds.

"I'm sorry," she whispered.

"It's okay. I can't argue too much." He pointed at his side where the bandages made a lump under his casual shirt. "But I'd like to pretend I wasn't the biggest ass this side of Texas."

They stared at one another, and thoughts, scenarios, plans, and jumbles of ideas crowded together in Ana's mind. It was so mixed up and chaotic that she could hardly think.

"Will you promise me one thing?" he asked, reaching for her hand again, taking it.

"Maybe," she said, feeling the fine quiver of tension through his fingers where they gripped her.

"If you won't pretend it never happened, will you at least pretend it wasn't as bad?" He sighed. Smiling, he finally let go of her hand. "That's better than your throwing something at my head. Or shooting me."

"Either of those options can still be arranged," she muttered, torn between laughing at his pathetic attempt to make peace, and her own desperate desire to throw herself into his arms. God, she was such an idiot to fall for someone like him, someone unattainable, someone out of her league.

"I'll bet," he murmured. He took her hand again, rubbed it with his thumb. "I'm not saying it will work, Ana. I'm not saying we're right for each other, but I'm saying we're good for each other."

"Gates," she protested softly, wanting to plead with him not to torture her, not to make her think she could be with him, when she knew it was impossible.

"Gates, Ana," Dav said, urgency ringing in his voice as he strode through the double doors. They sprang apart like guilty children, both turning to see him. His face was grim.

"Pretzky just called—she and the other two agents are diverting to White Plains. She said to get up there ASAP."

He turned to Gates. "You're not up for this, Gates. Don't argue with me. Keep working on what we've got here. There's something that ties it all together. We'll stay in touch by phone."

"But—" Gates tried to rise, but the pain and the confrontation with Ana had taken too much out of him, and he sank back into the chair.

"Stay," Ana agreed with Dav. "I'll take this with me," she pointed at her laptop, "and send back all the data I have. I think my cell's charged enough for now—we'll stay in constant touch. We need you here. You can make this work." She pointed at the computers, nodded toward the walls.

How strange that after all these years of being the one left behind, she was going and doing it to someone else.

"Ana," Gates said, but then he seemed to make a decision. "You're right. Both of you."

"Thank you, Gates," she said, giving him a hard, fast kiss on the mouth. "Dav, you ready to go?"

"The car's waiting," he answered, giving Gates an approving look before he pivoted on his heel and was out the door.

"Good," she said, gathering her purse, briefcase, phone, and laptop. "I'll patch in once I get to the car."

"I'll be here," Gates said, resigned as possible to being left behind.

Ana headed for the door at a run. She'd nearly reached it when Gates called her name. Dav went on as she turned, walking backward into the foyer. She could see Dav was already in the elevator, the doors held open for her.

"What?" she said.

"I love you."

Chapter Nineteen

Ana let the doors close behind them. The elevator began its descent.

He'd said it first. No one had ever said it first. What the hell did that mean? Did it matter? What was she supposed to *do* with I love you?

"Ana?" Dav touched her arm. "We know it's White Plains, which is north of here, north of the main part of New York City, but we're going to need a more specific direction than that."

"We'll get it. Once we get in the car, I'll call Pretzky, and we'll triangulate."

"Good."

Pretzky was in highly pissed mode when Ana connected with her. The car was headed north, weaving in and through traffic with professional skill, but Ana was getting her ears pinned back.

"What the hell are you doing, Burton? You've been incommunicado for five hours. I need a report, Agent."

"Sorry. Here's the situation," Ana said, focusing on the information rather than the apology as she booted up her laptop, shoving the Wi-Fi data card into place and watching as it searched for a signal. "McGuire got hit again, but he said he was okay. I can't reach him though. I've had e-mails out the wazoo, but I haven't gotten to go through them yet. My cell's been offline. The battery died."

Dav motioned to get her attention, holding up a cell. "You're on speaker with Gates," he mouthed.

She nodded, but kept talking. "McGuire is the only one who can connect Hines with the whole deal. From what I have, there's no connection. Far as we know, Hines is just off the grid, on vacation."

"After emptying his house and cleaning out his financial accounts," Pretzky said sarcastically. "Right."

"Yeah, but it's McGuire's word against Hines at this point. All the other evidence that he might have some tie to the case is circumstantial." A thought occurred to her, and she flipped pages on her yellow pad.

"Hence the hit on McGuire," Pretzky said, oblivious to Ana's mental change of direction.

"Wait, there might be something," Ana said as she opened files and switched programs. "My guess is that the galleries, especially Prometheus, Moroni, and Artful Walls, all shipped through this New York shipping house at one point or another." She kept searching for the info she needed.

"Let me guess," Pretzky snarked. "It's in White Plains. Why am I not surprised? This guy your TJ's been after, according to the case numbers, corresponds to your shipper in White Plains. I guess this whole case has ties to Rome, after all."

"Right in one, Special Agent," Ana grated, irked to hear it said aloud. "Hang on." She entered her passcodes and watched the e-mail open up. "I got a ton of e-mails here."

"Personal time later, Agent."

Stung, Ana said, "They're from TJ, Pretzky."

Silence hummed for a moment. "Read 'em and call me back."

The cell's speakerphone crackled, and Gates's voice broke the thick silence. "Did Prometheus ship through this company? What's the company name?"

"Gold Ark, or D'Or Shipping." She spelled the latter for him. "I think Jack D'Onofrio might be connected as well."

"D'Onofrio? From San Francisco?"

"Yeah, call it coincidence, but he was at the gallery. He's a New Yorker but doesn't operate in New York. He bought a lot of art at the same time as the frauds, but he's not on my list for any frauds."

"Got it. I'll cross-reference it. What kind of data did you dig out of that search we put together?" he asked.

"The shipper's name, the connection with Miami, some additional phone numbers that we've got someone else running."

"Your mole get his hands on that data?"

"No, but he's compromised all the original paperwork. It's going to be tough to pin anything on Hines unless we can connect him with the attempts on McGuire."

Her phone rang. It was McGuire. "Hang on," she said, and picked up the call.

"You catch that bastard yet, Burton?" McGuire growled. "I'm good, but even I got to sleep."

"Not yet, McGuire, but we're headed to shut down the shipper. We're thinking that's the source."

"What? Burrows?" McGuire said. "You got my e-mail?"

"Who's Burrows?" she said, scanning through her e-mail for one from McGuire.

"Guy who owned the shipping company back in the day. I dug out my private notes, the ones I didn't give Hines. Burrows was a young guy. Ambitious, slick. We couldn't connect him though. He was small-time in New York. You got something?"

She wasn't going to go into the methodology of the search she and Gates had devised, so she gave him the shorthand. "Computer search turned up a connection to the shipper from every gallery. It was buried, but it was there."

"There was a shipper in Cali that was a person of interest too, at the time. It's in the notes."

"Saw that." She switched from e-mail to the files she'd

scanned in. "You found less there, right? Our search didn't point that way."

"Point, no point," McGuire groused. "I'm telling you that guy was up to his fancy ass in it, but we couldn't make the connection. He was smug as shit, but we had nuthin'."

She scanned the file for a name. Too much stuff. "What's the name in Cali?"

"Sam Drake, Drake Shipping," McGuire fired back. "He's an asshole, but cool and cocky."

"Drake. Drake Shipping. Drake Yountz. I *knew* he was connected. Hang on, McGuire. Gates—" She picked up the other phone, waited for him to answer. "Run Drake Yountz and Sam Drake into your program. Reference this address—" She read the old Drake Shipping address out of the file. "And Yountz's new business too."

"Got it."

She opened her connection to the secure Agency search engine and ran *Yountz, Drake; Yountz, Sam;* and *Drake, Samuel.*

"Thanks, McGuire," Ana said. "I'll be in touch."

"Yeah, yeah, you keep sayin' that. Do it for once," the older man groused.

Ana was about to hang up when another thought occurred. "Wait, McGuire?" When he came back on, she asked, "What did Hines use when he was targeting, for sharpshooting?"

"A Tikka T3 Tactical, but he could use a Remington. He liked a Mossberg for close-in work. Why?"

"I'm thinking he's the one who took a shot at me," she said.

"Well, hell," McGuire said.

"Yeah, that's what I think," she said, still scrolling through data. "I'll catch ya later."

"You bet," McGuire tersely agreed.

"Okay," she began, then realized she was talking to dead air. "Sorry," she muttered, apologizing to the retired agent, even though he'd already hung up.

"Got something," Gates's voice called from the other

phone. Dav stopped what he was doing on his computer to listen as well. "I heard you say Burrows. Connection between Burrows Shipping and D'Or Shipping. Seems D'Or and Gold Ark bought all the Burrows warehouses about five years ago, lock, stock, and contents. The owner is listed as Jack Santini, married to Rita Gandolpho Santini."

"Holy shit," Ana cursed, hearing the Gandolpho name. She might be focused on international work, but no one in law enforcement was ignorant of the Gandolpho name. "He's mixed up with some bad people."

"Yeah, I know that feeling," Gates said. "Small world, since I know a couple of the Gandolpho grandsons. I served with Max Hopespring in Iraq. Get this," Gates continued, skimming past the comment he'd made. Ana wanted to stop him, ask about the Gandolpho connection, but he was plowing on with more important data. "Seems Mr. Santini has a partner, the owner of Gold Ark, one Jack Bates."

"Wait," Dav said, tapping his computer, opening a file. "Carrie mentioned that she shipped with someone named Bates. Said he was supposed to be at the gallery opening. She said he was vetted by . . ." He looked at Ana. "By the CIA. She said she knew her paintings were safe going through Bates because he'd been cleared by the CIA."

"Hang on." Ana entered Jack Bates in the secure search field, hit SEND. Data scrolled up.

"Hines?" Gates asked, and she heard keys clicking.

"Yeah. Jack Bates, aka Jack Burrows, cleared by one Agent David Wayne Hines."

"Bates is Burrows?" Gates clarified, and more keys tapped.

"Yes. And Burrows sold out to Santini."

"What pops on Bates now?" he asked, and she could still hear keys flicking. "Anything on your database?"

"Bates is listed for some petty stuff, an alias of Jack Burrows. Let me search that," she said, entering it and hitting SEARCH. "Dav, call Carrie. Ask her about Bates, get everything she knows. See if she's ever heard of Jack Burrows or Jack D'Or," she added, seeing another alias pop up. "Or if she remembers Jack D'Onofrio handling shipping instead of magazines."

"Ana? I've got a wedding announcement from last year," Gates said. "Jack Bates marries Gillian Keriasus, in Powhatan, New Jersey."

"Jeez, could this get any more complicated?" she complained. "What's it say about him?"

"Owner of Gold Ark Shipping, Bates is a graduate of . . ." He read the whole announcement, but she heard more clicking as he turned up more data.

"You realize you met this guy, right?" she asked Gates. "This is Jen's date, Millionaire Jack. Jack D'Onofrio."

"He's got two wives already and he's dating your friend? What is this guy doing?"

"Being slime," she said, reminding him of their earlier conversation.

"Yeah, I get that. What I meant was, what the hell is he doing messin' around with one of the Gandolphos? If they find out he's screwing around on his wife—" he started.

"Which one?" Ana asked sourly.

"I'm betting the Keriasus family would feel the same way, over in Jersey," Gates answered. "But I was talking about the Gandolpho family. They are not known for their collective sense of humor on this sort of thing."

She heard Dav saying, "Carrie, it's Dav," as he made his call. His tone of voice was like a billboard saying I WANT CARRIE.

A beep from her computer signaled her search had info.

"Oh, man. It just got even more complicated," she muttered.

"Dav, Agent," Damon called from the front. "We're on the outskirts of town. I need to know where we're going."

"Hang on, Damon," she called, ignoring the urgent e-mails, the pinging searches, and the notice of text and voice mail messages. Lord, could anything else beep? "Cancel, cancel," she muttered, dialing Pretzky.

"What?" Pretzky answered.

"We're at White Plains. Where do we meet you?"

"Rodehouse Inn, north and west of town. Get off at Highway One-Twenty north," she said, taking them up the split toward the University. "It's the exit three miles beyond the city limits, near the airport. I've told the locals to expect you."

"Got it. Damon, you get that?"

"On our way, Agent," he called back.

"TJ . . ." Ana tuned into the conversation on the phone. "Is he OK?"

"I'm sorry, Burton. Michaels is dead. His computers are in tiny pieces. I've called in some of our people to sweep the room too, follow up with the New York State Crime Scene people. It's a mess."

"No!" Ana shook her head, eyes filling with tears. "God, no."

When she could see again, the winking notice of e-mail waiting caught her eye.

E-mail. TJ.

A Greek family and an Italian family.

Bates and Burrows. Keriasus wedding.

Santini and Bates. The Gandolpho family.

"Oh. My. God." She dropped the phone, disconnecting Pretzky, and opened her e-mail. Scrolling down, she found them. Seven e-mails from TJ, seven e-mails she'd ignored.

"Carrie says—" Dav began, but she held up her hand, intent on reading.

She was so focused, so silent, he prodded her again.

"Ana, what is it?" Dav asked, more insistently.

"Oh, my God. It's all here. All of it. TJ. He spelled it all out . . ." Her voice broke. She couldn't go on. TJ had spelled it all out in his e-mails, firing off one after another in hopes they'd get through, get her the data.

"Ana?" Gates called out. "Ana I have something on

D'Onofrio, alias Burrows, alias Bates. Property in White Plains at—" He rattled off an address. She saw Dav write it down. "Ana?"

"Hang on, Gates, she's got something big," Dav murmured. Turning into his own phone, he spoke. "Thanks, Carrie. Yes. I think it is. I'll let you know."

Dav hung up, and shifted over to rest a hand on Ana's shoulder. "Ana-aki, what is it?"

She turned to look at him, saw her own stricken face reflected in the window beyond him. "It's TJ. My friend. He'd been sending me these translations, something he was working on. I thought it was just another favor for a friend, you know?" She shook her head, dazed. "Instead, he's been trying to make sure I didn't take the fall for Rome."

"This would be what prompted the Inquiry?" Dav said. "It was Rome?" he urged when she sat silent.

"Yeah," she said wearily. "I had this data, I checked it, I dug out more. I found the chinks in this group that was planning to bomb the Italian court, the *Corte Costituzionale,*" she said, remembering the thrill of finding the keys to the conspiracy hidden in the data. "I sent the team out with that data, but it was wrong."

"Wrong?" Dav questioned. She heard Gates draw in a breath to speak so she hurried on.

"It was wrong. One part of the data had been altered, just one. But that put the team I was working with in jeopardy. TJ was one of the agents who survived, but two others were killed apprehending the bombers."

"That's why you were on cold cases, why you were on suspension." Gates made it a statement, not a question.

"Yeah. I was cleared yesterday, in DC. Thanks to TJ's efforts to prove the data had been altered, to find out who changed it."

Dav squeezed her shoulder. "I know this is tough, Ana-aki. You must be strong, for your friend. This is TJ, this is the one who is dead in White Plains, yes?"

She nodded mutely, afraid that if she spoke, she'd never be able to hold back the tears. When had she turned into such a watering pot? The night with Gates sprang instantly to mind, and she ducked her head so Dav wouldn't see the blush.

"Pretzky's with him," she finally managed to say. "I need to read the rest of his e-mails, and call her back."

"Ana." Gates's voice echoed in the car. "Pick up the phone, take it off speaker."

When she did, he spoke to her, just to her. "Ana-love, this isn't on you. Your friend proved it. We're right there, nearly finished with this, and I'm with you, okay? Dav's with you. We're going to see this through together."

"Okay," Ana managed, clenching her teeth on the tears, on the scream of frustration and emotional pain.

"I've got to make some calls," Gates said. "I need to check on a couple of things, but I'll call you back, okay?"

She nodded, then remembered she was on the phone and added, "Okay. We'll wait for your call."

"I love you, Ana," he said as his parting shot. "I'll make this up to you."

What the hell was she supposed to do with that? And why now, when she was already in complete turmoil?

She was silent for a minute, and he laughed. "I'm trying to get used to saying it. Just hang on to it for me. I need to call in a couple of favors."

"Okay, I will," she promised, and wondered what she'd just agreed to do, and what favors he needed.

She set the phone aside and read the rest of TJ's e-mails. The search had led him to someone connected with the Gandolpho family. The Gandolphos hadn't sanctioned anything, would never do damage to their "mother country," according to TJ, which had stymied him for months. He'd run into the Burrows/D'Onofrio/Santini situation by accident.

"Coincidence," she said, turning a tear-streaked face to Dav. "He figured out this business about the shipping company by accident, tried to use it to get Santini to roll on someone in Gandolpho's organization, get them to admit they'd been part of the situation in Rome."

Before Dav could answer, his phone rang. "Carrie," he told her, and picked it up.

Ana knew she had to pull it together. She had put the call from Gates aside, not think about his words or his love. She had to focus on the job. If she couldn't do the job, she was nothing, and she couldn't free herself to love anyone, if she couldn't do the job.

Knowing that, Ana drew in a deep breath, let her mind clear. Things were falling into place; the obscure pieces were coming together. Everything was converging on her, all the data sweeping into place; everything lining up. She could see the end of the story as a vague, foggy resolution, even though some of the chessmen were disguised by fake names and identities.

She yanked out the yellow pad, whipped it to a clean page.

Rome was the real red herring here. TJ's information had saved her job, but it wasn't what was going to solve this case. Somehow she had to separate the data, fit the puzzle pieces together, so she started writing.

Paintings.
Galleries—San Fran, Miami, Chicago, New York

She didn't list the European ones; they'd gone through Pratch, not the New York shipper. That was peripheral, and another red herring so she left it out, drilling into the heart of the path.

Galleries to Shipper – Burrows/Bates/Santini/D'Or/ D'Onofrio – East Coast – torture killings
Galleries to Shipper – Yountz/Drake – West Coast – executions
Shipper to Berlin/Pratch

She drew a line to one side.

Pratch dead

She drew a line to the other side.

Luke Gideon, dead

She stopped, pen poised over the page as her brain connected the dots. She scrambled through her pages of data, found the information on Jack. There it was.

She'd forgotten his middle name was Gideon. Ana hadn't known, hadn't thought to check, what connection D'Onofrio had to Carrie's husband, but it was all there in black and white in TJ's notes, the proof that Jack Gideon D'Onofrio, real name Jackson Gideon Burrows, was Luke Gideon's cousin. Now she was as sure as Dav that Carrie was in the clear. She'd used D'Or because of the family connection.

Just as obvious, the East Coast shipper had been dealing with Carrie and Prometheus, cutting into the West Coast's business. Two shippers all along, two with the same modus operandi, the same connections. Was all this a double-cross?

She grabbed her computer, hit SEARCH, but nothing came up. No signal for the wireless card. "Gates, I need Gates," she said, snagging her phone and calling Gates back. "Where is he?"

"Who?" Dav said, pressing the phone into his shoulder.

"Gates. I can't get him on the phone. He said he had to check something, do a run." She looked at Dav, her heart stopping. "Oh, my God." She made the intuitive leap that brought the points of the data together.

Gates knew the Gandolpho family. They knew where D'Onofrio was. There were favors owed. If they were right and D'Onofrio was Santini *and* Bates, then it made perfect sense with TJ's notes. One guy, playing two women and two families off against one another. The translations; the warnings from both families for D'Onofrio to stop fooling around.

TJ had tried to pressure D'Onofrio to roll on the Gandolpho family, using the aliases and the bigamy as leverage. D'Onofrio had far more to hide than just women, however, which TJ hadn't known.

Hines and D'Onofrio. Working together. Hines certifying D'Onofrio's shipping company to Carrie and Luke, Luke certifying D'Onofrio as trustworthy. TJ was dead, blown to pieces. Hines liked a Mossberg for close-in work. Ana being shot at, sniper style. Hines liked a Tikka sharpshooting rifle. Hines was unavailable the day she'd been shot at.

Hines and D'Onofrio were still out there, and so was Drake Yountz.

Gates was in love with her. He'd read the data too. He knew Hines wasn't going to go down without trying to kill Ana again.

"Oh, my God." Ana nearly moaned the words aloud as it all fell into place. Gates knew the Gandolpho family. The family knew D'Onofrio and where he would hide. D'Onofrio and Hines would be together.

Gates had gone to call in some favors that might save Ana's life and solve her case. Or, might get him killed.

"Oh, God, I didn't tell him I loved him," Ana whispered, listening to the endless ring of Gates's phone.

Chapter Twenty

When they arrived at the seedy White Plains Rodehouse Inn, the scene was chaos. Pretzky was already there, state troopers' cars circled the building, their lights flashing silently off the white cinderblock walls, turning the alley to a wash of red and blue. Crime scene techs took pictures and laid down markers, or, alternately, picked them up and put them away as they finished with a section of the parking lot.

Pretzky was there, directing the two DC agents to gather data from cops and civilians alike. She seemed to be in her element.

"Burton, fill me in," she demanded when Ana hurried up.

"It's a mess," Ana stated. "It's so frickin' convoluted I can hardly stand it. Look." Holding out the legal pad, she walked Pretzky through the steps.

"How does Hines fit in?"

"He and another guy are the money, and info. Kickbacks too, I think," she said. "I can't find Hines though."

"Yeah, last word I had is he's still off the grid," Pretzky said. "What else?"

"I think he's here. He's the shooter, both at me and here, killing TJ. McGuire said he liked a Mossberg for close-in work."

Pretzky rubbed at her eyes. "That would do the job," she said, looking bleak.

"I think Hines set Perkins on me, on our computers. I think he's who compromised Davis, too." Ana showed her the data on how Hines had certified D'Onofrio. "I think he may have been playing a West Coast shipper too, Drake Yountz—that's the money guy, I think."

"Isn't that the Bootstrap guy?" Pretzky said, surprised.

"Yeah," Ana said, with some satisfaction. She hoped to see slimy-hands Yountz in custody.

"How's he connect to D'Onofrio? And TJ?"

"D'Onofrio, Bates, and Santini are the same person. I think that's what TJ found. He figured out that Santini was married to one woman and Bates to another, but he connected Bates and Santini, posited that they were the same person, that he was married under each name."

"Bigamy? This just keeps getting better and better."

"He was asking me to do these translations," Ana said. Seeing Pretzky's frown, she said, "I know, I know. I never in a million years thought they'd be connected. Believe me, I'd have come to you if I had."

Pretzky stared at her for a moment, then looked away. Nodded. "I believe you. Now we just have to figure out how to get all the data TJ had."

"He sent most of it to me," Ana said. "I had fifteen e-mails from him, a sequence of steps. They stop, though, before he can wrap it all up."

Pretzky sighed. "Which is, of course, what we need."

There was motion at the door to the second-floor hotel room: a gurney rolled out under the tape and the two Coroner's assistants lifted it down the stairs. Ana watched it roll to a stop behind the dark van, and saw one of the assistants drop a set of keys. When he bent down, she could see his boxer shorts. When he stood back up, he hitched up his pants, a natural gesture that froze her in place. Boxers. A random visual that kicked the last bit of information loose in her mind.

His pants. "That's it," she murmured. "That's it. Come on,"

she ordered Pretzky, running to where the Coroner's team was preparing to load the body.

"Wait," she called to the men as Pretzky ran up. "Hang on a sec," she said. Turning to Pretzky, she gasped out the words, winded from her run and her emotions, "We have to check his pants."

"What?" Pretzky demanded.

"Ma'am, we checked his pockets. There wasn't anything—" one of the guys began.

"No, not his pockets, his boxers." Everyone looked at her as if she was insane.

"You're kidding, right, Burton?" Pretzky was dumbfounded.

"No. TJ always used to say that the bad guys would check your pockets, your mouth, your ass, and even your ears, but never your shorts." Ana said it as fact. "When we worked together in Rome, he used to say that all the time. He sewed a pocket in all his boxers. We have to check."

The techs looked at one another, and the taller one shrugged. "Won't be the first weird thing we've had to do," he said, unzipping the body bag.

TJ had been shot in the chest at close range. The blast had taken off part of his right arm as well. He'd have never survived his wounds. She prayed that it had been quick.

Her heart clenched at the sight of his face, calm now in death. Tears rolled unheeded down her face as she remembered her friend. So many people dead.

"Pull it together, Burton," Pretzky murmured for her ears alone. The older woman gripped her arm, but it was more of a reassurance than a warning.

The tech unbuckled TJ's belt, reached into the pants, and felt around. Surprise lit his features. It snapped Ana back to the moment, kept her from drowning in the grief of yet one more friend gone.

"Hey, I got something," he said, and they heard a ripping noise. There, in the man's gloved hand was a scrap of fabric and a small data stick. Specially manufactured for the

Agency, the tiny data sticks held an inordinate amount of data in a small package.

"Holy crap," Pretzky said, stunned. "You were right."

Wiping at her face, Ana gave a watery laugh. "Yeah, that's TJ, always a surprise at the end. And smart. They don't check your shorts," she said, and her voice broke.

"Hold on," Pretzky said, recovering faster than Ana. When Ana would have taken the chip, Pretzky blocked her hand. "Hey, hey you!" Pretzky summoned one of the crime scene techs, got photos. "If there's anyone to take to court, we have to document this."

Ana nodded, trying in vain to set aside the image of TJ's damaged body and still features. He'd had such a mobile face, always with a laugh or frown pulling at his mouth. He was always restless, hyperactive. To see him like this was alien, as if who he was, what he was, had been extinguished, and this was some wax doll made up to look like her friend.

"Okay," Pretzky said, taking the chip. "Let's go see what we got."

Ana waited long enough to press a hand on the body bag, say a silent farewell, before she rushed after Pretzky. The only way to help TJ now was to finish what he'd started.

She climbed into the limo with Pretzky, Dav, and one of the NY state cops to get the file, see where D'Onofrio and Hines might go next. They were in the limo, reviewing the data when the phone rang once more.

"Gates," Dav said, and Ana snatched the phone from his hands.

"Where are you?" she demanded.

"A warehouse," he whispered. "Halfway between your location in White Plains and New York City, in Port Chester." He rattled off the address.

"Jesus, Gates, what are you doing?" she hissed, terrified that with his wounds, with his stubborn need to fix things, he would die too before she had a chance to talk to him, tell him she forgave him—loved him.

"He's here, Ana," he whispered. "Get your team down here, before Gandolpho's men find him."

He hung up.

"Damon!" Ana shouted. Everyone froze as she shouted orders to the driver. Even Pretzky jumped as she fired out directions to send them speeding down the highway. "Here's the address," she read it out to Damon. "How far?"

"Ten minutes." The answer came from the NY state trooper. "I know that section. I'll direct him."

He opened his own phone, relayed the destination to the state troopers following them. One peeled off, took a ramp, and disappeared.

A few minutes later, they also took a curved ramp at speed, and all the blue-lights went dark, the sirens silent. How Pretzky had managed this much cooperation in this short a time, Ana couldn't imagine. As she hung on to the car's handholds, she decided instead just to be grateful.

Cars lined the entrance to the industrial park. A variety of men stood by or leaned on the cars. None of them looked happy, and none of them looked innocent.

"Gandolpho Family," the trooper in the car with them murmured, puzzled. "But they're just waiting."

"Gates," Dav said, understanding dawning on his face. He turned to Ana. "You said he called in a favor."

The trooper looked at him warily. "What favor? With the Gandolphos?"

"Long story," Ana said. "Here, we're at the warehouse. What now?"

"Sir, you stay here," Pretzky told Dav. "Looks like the locals have SWAT in place. Agent Burton and I will move closer. We'll keep you posted."

"Gates is down there," Dav whispered to Ana. "He's close, watching this guy. He'd feel like he needed to do this, be part of it, to make it up to you."

She nodded, understanding what he was saying. Gates was

his priority, not D'Onofrio or the art case. Dav was willing to let anything else go to keep Gates safe.

"I understand," Ana said, knowing she felt the same way. Her loyalties were split now, between the job and Gates. Her heart might be torn up and scarred by the events of the day, but it knew what it wanted in the end: Gates.

"Be careful. He needs you," Dav murmured, his voice layered with worry, pride, fear, and frustration. Ana knew how he felt, but could do nothing to help. Dav wasn't trained for this and had to rely on her, on others, to protect his friend.

With a last squeeze of her hand, Dav released her, and closed the limo door quietly behind her. Within minutes Damon had eased the big car back, not quite joining the Gandolpho lineup, but away from the potential firefight.

The warehouse sat in a tree-lined dip, hidden from view of the main road, and the highway to the right. A phalanx of police cars blocked the drive and, Ana presumed, any other entrances and exits.

Their trooper took up a position with the SWAT team, talking in a low, hurried shorthand to fill the SWAT commander in as Ana and Pretzky joined them at the blockade of two unmarked cars. Beyond them, the wide concrete driveway to the warehouse lay empty. FOR LEASE signs blocked part of the view of the building, but the trucks were silent, the lights dark. The building was almost eerily quiet.

"I've got two men moving up on the near side," the commander filled them in after they'd shaken hands, introduced themselves. "Three going round the back." He looked over to where another heavily armed, dark-clad woman stood. "Elsa," he called. The woman nodded, banged on her black helmet, adjusted her mic, and gave a thumbs-up. "Take the roof." He pointed up, pantomiming the climb and perch of a sniper, just in case her mic wasn't working. She nodded, banged on the side of the helmet a couple more times as she trotted off. Within minutes, Ana could see her climbing the fire stair to the roof, a dark spot on the gray-white stone of the warehouse.

"So, we've got everyone in position. What's the word? We after this guy alive at all costs, or what?"

Pretzky shrugged. "It's gonna be a pissin' match to see who gets him. Our case is nine years old, but he's been running two different businesses with two different names, maybe three out of this warehouse, so the locals and state are going to want a shot too. Probably good for at least three murders with our case."

At least four, Ana thought, her mind running scenarios, thinking of Luke Gideon.

"What's the Gandolpho connection?" the commander asked without taking his eyes off his men.

"Perp's married to one of the daughters."

"Uh-oh." The heartfelt rejoinder was heavy with meaning. No one wanted to get involved with a crime family vendetta. Especially not one with a son-in-law.

"Exactly." Ana spoke for the first time. "He's got four aliases, is also married to a Greek woman in Jersey, and has his fingers in some international crap too."

"Handle with extreme care, then," the commander grunted. "Let me put that through."

"Hey." Gates had slipped up from behind without anyone being the wiser, despite his injuries and how carefully he was moving. "Thanks for coming," he said, grinning at how simple that made it sound.

"Gates!" Ana gasped, throwing caution to the winds and hugging him. She was so relieved to see him, so glad he was unhurt. He woofed out a breath.

"Obviously," Pretzky drawled, when the SWAT commander and the trooper reacted, "he's with us." At her words, the rest of the SWAT members backed down, returning to their watch on the building.

"Easy babe," Gates murmured as Ana continued to hug him, but he returned the pressure with interest, before he spoke. "There're at least two men in there with him, Commander," he informed the SWAT team leader, his arm snuggled tightly around Ana's shoulders, as if he wouldn't ever let go. "I've been watching. Four in, one left in a panel truck, but it wasn't our guy. That leaves three in."

"Got it." The commander relayed the data, gave orders to move in. "Look sharp, people."

As delighted as she was to see Gates, to feel him living and breathing, Ana tuned in to that. She frowned.

"We need to stay down," Gates whispered, "shots may still fly. They'll go for the kill if anyone pulls a weapon."

"Crap, you're right," she said, remembering the protocols. Everyone would be twitchy knowing the Gandolpho family was involved. They both tensed as the first of the team ducked inside the open roll-up door. The second set of three followed.

The end was anticlimactic. Within minutes they'd sounded the all clear, and all five SWAT members came walking up the drive, three men in handcuffs between them.

"Call the all-in, Williams," the commander said, and his second opened a channel to do so. From the tree line, she saw two dark-clad men rise and move toward their position. Another two emerged from the parking lot to their left. Another rolled out from under a truck opposite the roll-up doors and followed the prisoners up the drive. "Where's Elsa?" the commander muttered.

"Hey, Williams," he said. "Get the bullhorn. Elsa's gear was shorting. I don't want her up on that roof all day."

Williams frowned but ran back to the command truck as they all stood, watching the man she knew as Jack D'Onofrio make his way up the tarmac, along with two men wearing work gear bearing the Gold Ark logo.

Just as D'Onofrio came into view, Williams ran back, bullhorn in hand, and a worried look on his face.

"Boss," he said. "Elsa's off today. She's in Queens with her mother."

"Then who—"

"GUN!" one of the trailing SWAT team hollered, dropping as she watched, and rolling under a car.

They all ducked down, the other SWAT covering the prisoners as four shots buried themselves in the commander's vehicle.

The sniper rose, firing again, and the windshield shattered. "Patterson!" the commander yelled. "Take her out!"

"But, Deke!" the man shouted, in protest, obviously unwilling to fire on one of their own.

"It's not Elsa!" the commander roared back. Four rounds buried themselves in the warehouse wall around the sniper. Another two fired, and they saw the woman stagger. She lifted her weapon a final time, and the shot she got off whistled between Ana and Gates where they crouched behind the quarter panel.

There was another spate of gunfire and a scream. A distant, muffled crash could be heard, then silence.

Looking into her eyes, Gates said, "I think, my love, that it's finally over."

Ignoring everyone else, ignoring Pretzky's hissed call for a report, and the crackle of radios and the commander's orders, Ana kissed him.

"I thought I'd lost you," she said, her heart filling and healing with his embrace. Knowing they still had to talk didn't stop her from feeling the fullness of his embrace, the delight of his body pressed to hers.

He kissed her back, covering her face with kisses before claiming her mouth in a long, soulful connection. "Oh, Ana," he murmured. She heard love and relief in his voice, and pain.

"Let's get you checked out, Gates," she said, helping him to rise.

From the scene to the hospital, to the police barracks, they didn't let go of one another.

"We need to talk about this," he said, leaning heavily on her as they got into Dav's limo.

"Yeah," she said, pressing a kiss to his face and easing in beside him. "We do."

"Are you two going to neck or are you going to go explain all this to your colleagues?" Dav said with an indulgent smile.

The conference room at the White Plains police department looked like a roundtable for all the law enforcement branches in the US. Four CIA agents; two FBI, who'd joined in because they'd had eyes on D'Onofrio as Bates, but hadn't figured out that he was also Santini; and the SWAT team and the troopers.

Evidently TJ was the only one who had put it all together.

Then there were the local police, augmented by the state troopers, the local SWAT commander and several other interested parties including the New York attorney general. Pretzky started off by detailing the department's involvement, who she was, and what was going on.

"I'll turn the floor over to Agent Burton, since she, of all of us, has the most complete picture of what's been happening over the last few days."

So Ana walked them through it, starting with Rome, although she didn't describe any of the situation there; she merely used it as a point of reference to explain how she knew TJ.

"I transferred to the California division for a short sabbatical." She nearly laughed at Pretzky's smirk over her terminology. "And to make some decisions about my career." She ignored the huge smile that crept over Gates's face as she said that. She couldn't imagine why he found it so amusing. "I was assigned a nine-year-old case of art fraud." She outlined the same map that she, Gates, and Dav had created in the penthouse. "These clues tracked in parallel with the information my colleague, Agent Michaels, had provided me."

She went on to detail how they had uncovered the information on the paintings, traced the calls through the complex program, and all the steps that had led to their being in New

York. "Another shipper was involved, one in California we believe, but whether that individual knew, or was duped, we are still investigating."

Pretzky had assured her that California police had headed out to pick up Drake Yountz and ascertain his involvement in the entire affair.

"And I believe I can fill in the final blanks." Gates moved into the center of the room. "The woman who stole your gear and impersonated your team member is a paid assassin. My family was murdered fourteen years ago. This woman was hired to kill them. She didn't finish the job, leaving my sister and me alive. Since I served in the US Armed Forces, she was unable to get to me until I went to work in the private sector. My sister married and lives on a military base in Germany. Another difficult target."

He leaned on the wall, never letting on that he was tiring. "My current position has kept me travelling all over the world, and the authorities believe this particular assassin is either unwilling or unable to operate outside of the United States. We know that two shootings in San Francisco can be attributed to her. I believe she followed us to New York, but was stymied by the Waldorf security. They are used to high-profile clients, and the ways in which people try to sneak into their hotel to bother the rich and famous." He studiously didn't look at Dav, but the smile playing around his lips and his ironic tone said he was thinking about his boss.

"We'll be looking into that for you, Mr. Bromley. We'll backtrack and make sure we've helped you clean that up." The Bureau official gave him a look, and Ana saw him touch two fingers to his brow in salute.

Gates returned it. "Thank you, sir. This sniper managed a hit in San Francisco. However, her infrequent attempts, going back a number of years, had all of the teams believing that the attempts were connected either to my colleague, Mr. Gianikopolis, or to this most recent development in the art fraud matter." He took a bracing breath and pushed off the wall.

"We think now that she was watching me in New York and when I left the hotel to come here, she followed. I'm glad to know that your teammate," he referred to the missing Elsa, safe with her family in Queens, "isn't another victim of her vendetta. Now, since I'm still recovering, I'm going to save my energy and sit down. Agent Burton?"

The debriefing took another hour, and the call Ana made to McGuire took longer, since he had clearance and was able to ask questions and get answers the civilians weren't privy to.

"Well," he growled. "I guess I can quit shooting at anyone walking on my porch then. Let the grandkids come back from Florida. If they want to, that is."

"I wouldn't be so sure, Agent," Ana replied, wishing more than anything that she could lie down and sleep. She had to get through it, so she could go to Gates. She brought her wandering mind back to the moment. "Hines is still out there. He's a person of interest in his own right, but without you to testify against him, he'd be better off. I'd stay wary if I were you."

"Great," McGuire snapped out at her in his irritation. He relented though, a moment later. "No matter what's still out there, we'll deal with that. Gotta say, young lady, I never expected anyone to close this. Congratulations."

"Thanks, but it's serendipity, Agent McGuire," Ana said. "I was in the right place at the right time, with the right knowledge at my disposal to make it all work."

"That, Agent Burton, is called promotion material," he said, laughing. "Don't knock it. Thanks for the follow-up."

They hung up, and Ana decided she'd rather be flogged than go through another case like this. Pretzky was talking shop with the DC agents and the SWAT commander, but stopped long enough to give Ana an update.

"Just got a call from Pearson," Pretzky said. "Yountz is in the wind. The wife reported him missing early this morning."

"Thanks," Ana said, and when Pretzky turned back to her discussion, Ana headed into the corridor. Other members of the team were still chatting, hashing out points of the case.

"Excuse me," she asked the young trooper who'd taken the wild ride from White Plains to Port Chester with them. "Have you seen Mr. Bromley?"

The trooper's eyes shone. If she wasn't mistaken, he had developed a serious case of hero worship for Gates. "Yes, Agent Burton, ma'am. He's outside. He was seeing Mr. Gianikopolis off, then one of the Gand . . . uh . . . civilians involved asked to speak with him."

"Ah, thanks." So, one of the Gandolpho family was in the parking lot and the score was about to be evened up.

As she got to the doors, she saw Gates and Dav shaking hands. Dav's smile looked like it would split his face, and he pumped Gates's hand like a politician. What was that all about?

Dav got in his limo and drove away. Gates watched the car for a moment, then turned to a younger man who was waiting for him. Several other cars lined the exit driveway, close enough to see everything, but not interfering with traffic or with Gates and his friend. They too shook hands and embraced. She let them have a moment before she walked over.

"Gentlemen?"

"Ana, I'd like you to meet Max Hopespring. He's the grandson of Tomas Gandolpho. We served together in the Army." She held out a hand, received a firm, no-nonsense shake.

"Mr. Hopespring," she said, "I'm pleased to meet you."

Max smiled at her and gently punched Gates on the shoulder. "So this is her? I'm impressed. Good job, dude. Remember, send me an invite." He turned to Ana, took her shoulders in a light grip, and gave her a kiss on both cheeks. "Good to meet you, Ana. Take care of him, will ya?"

The man turned and strolled away, across the grass to a waiting Hummer. She stood with Gates watching the entourage drive away.

"So, debt paid?"

"On my end. I never looked for a debt or payback in the first place, but Max, he says he'll never stop owing me."

Gates was still watching the cars as they turned onto the main drag and disappeared. "He's a loyal guy."

"Hmmm. I've heard that."

Gates shrugged. "It's not really about Iraq," he said. "It's about family. I understand that. I've got a sister too."

Ana nodded. Although she didn't have sisters or brothers, she had come to realize she had friends. Loyal ones. Ones who would do what needed to be done, and die doing it, if need be. As TJ had.

"So, Anastasia Burton," he drawled, still not looking at her. "What about us?"

"What about us, Gates?" She leaned on the squad car behind her, closed her eyes. "You made your feelings clear about that," Ana said, then added, "Then you asked me to pretend your outburst never happened."

She felt the heat of him and opened her eyes. His arms bracketed her body, trapping her where she was.

"Yeah. Like I said, I was an idiot," he said, smiling that sexy smile, despite how tired he must be. "I thought I made that perfectly clear as well."

"You acted like an idiot, yeah," she agreed, crossing her arms over her chest so he wouldn't see how much she still reacted to him, how her body responded to his warmth, his presence. "I don't see how that's changed."

He threw back his head and laughed. He laughed so hard, she got annoyed and poked a finger into his chest to get him to stop.

"Ouch!" he protested, rubbing the spot. "Don't make me suffer," he said, but he meant far more than his tender chest.

"Besides," she said, tapping on his chest this time, instead of poking him. "You are the one who said we weren't suited. You're the one who pointed out that our lives are too divergent, too dissimilar for us even to date, much less anything else."

He grabbed her finger before she could drill it into his chest again. "I said ouch. I just got shot the other day, you know." He lifted her hand to his lips, kissed her fingers. "I don't know how many ways I can say I'm sorry, but I'm willing to say it all, in every language you know and I know, and any I need to learn."

"I forgive you," she whispered, kissing his cheek.

"Thank you," he said, his voice reasonable and even. "But is that enough? Can you forget that I was cruel, in a stupid, misguided attempt to keep you safe?"

"Gates," she protested, feeling her knees weaken as he gently kissed her palm, nibbled along the edge of her thumb. "Stop that."

"What? This?" He continued to watch her as he kissed her hand. "Or loving you beyond reason? Will loving you more than I can imagine help you forget that I was an ass? Or do I need to tell you that I'll follow you anywhere, be there for you?"

"Wha-what?" Ana said, hearing his words but not getting what he was saying. "What do you mean?"

Gates smiled. "I've handed in my resignation."

"You did *what?*" Shocked to her toes, she stood up, yanked her hand free to grab the front of his shirt. "But Dav was happy," she protested. "He was smiling."

"He's been trying to get me to do it for years." Gates untangled her fingers, brought them to his mouth to kiss them some more.

"He's been trying to get you to *resign?*" Ana's emotions were in such a welter, she couldn't make that sentence compute. She couldn't figure out the whys or hows, especially with Gates torturing her sense with his mouth.

Gates was laughing now at her shock. "Yeah, I've got four or five patents going for search products; I'm a partner in four of his many businesses. I have this idea," he said, boxing her in again, "for a security company. Complex stuff." He kissed the side of her neck, then her cheek. "Really intricate. Really detailed." He kissed the other side of her neck, her other cheek. "I'm not sure I can manage it all, but I'm going to try." He kissed her forehead, the tip of her nose, then set his hot mouth to hers.

For a moment all she could do was feel. She wanted to absorb the sheer deliciousness of his taste, the luxurious play of their lips fused together, the dance of tongues and the feel of his arms holding her tight. He loved her. He wanted to be with her. He was willing to do whatever it took.

"So," he said between kisses, "I was thinking I would talk to you about it. See what country you were heading for. Maybe tag along."

"Tag?" she repeated, through a haze of sensation. "Tag?" She didn't understand, so she forced herself to stop, using both hands to push him back. "What do you mean, tag along?"

He smiled. "Look, Anastasia," he said, all persuasion and passion. "I'll say it straight out. I love you. I want to be with you and do whatever I can to convince you that I'm going to be there for you. I'll follow you wherever you want to go. I'll set my business headquarters up wherever you are." He swooped in for a brief kiss, then leaned back. "I'm used to travel."

"You'd go?" she spluttered, thinking of the stack of requests in that fat folder. "You'd really do that?"

"For you? Yes. I would." He ran a finger down her cheek, just as he had done in Dav's office, weeks—it seemed like years—ago. "Bromley men don't marry early. It takes us a long time to settle down, find the right one. It's my time, Ana. It's you. You're the right one."

"Gates," she said, feeling her heart melt within her, and joy begin to burst through. He was the one for her, too. Finally, she could let go the chains of the past, the agonies she'd kept in her heart since Rome, and since her parents had been killed. "What are you asking?"

"I'm asking if you'll marry me, darling Ana. Make a life with me. Maybe . . ." he said with a twinkle in his eye. "Maybe even be my business partner."

The idea of that took a few minutes to sink in. The whole of it.

"Marry?" Ana eased him back to look at him, look in his

eyes, see if he was serious. What she saw there was love. Pure and simple. Respect. Trust. Everything she could have ever wanted.

"Yes," he answered. "Marry me."

"You?" She stuttered the word, trying to make her brain work, follow the patterns, and assemble the data.

He looked pained. "You make it sound so horrible. Yes, me." Now he looked worried. "What do you say?"

All the data snapped into line. She loved him, he loved her. They were good together in every way. She knew the answer.

Careful of his healing side, she hugged him, stood on tiptoe to whisper one word into his ear.

"Yes."

Epilogue

Gates strolled into the office where Dav sat, waiting till he got off the phone before moving forward to grip his hand, accept his brotherly embrace.

"You're back!" Dav crowed, holding Gates at arm's length for a moment before pulling him close for another hug. "I'm thrilled to see you. You enjoyed yourselves?"

Before Gates could answer, Dav laughed. "Wait, forget I asked that. Honeymoons are for enjoyment, and nothing else, so I'm sure that you made the most of it. Was the plane comfortable? The house in order? You found everything to your liking?"

"Dav," Gates chided warmly. "The house could have been a wreck, for all we cared, you know that. That said, it was great." He punched Dav's arm with manly affection. "I don't have to tell you that you didn't have to kit it out with a year's worth of gourmet food, but we appreciated it. Have to say though, I'd forgotten how beautiful the sea is off Mykonos." He grinned and added with sly humor, "Not that I saw much of the sea or the pool or anything else."

"If the wicked look you're wearing is any indication, I'm betting you didn't get much sun, eh?"

"Oh, I wouldn't say that," Gates answered, still grinning.

"That roof deck has a marvelous view. It's very private too, but I'm sure you knew that."

Dav laughed uproariously. "Good, good. Yes, I did know, but wonderful to hear that it was satisfactory for you and Anaaki as well. Now, come sit down and tell me everything." He motioned Gates to a seat at the table. "Well, perhaps not everything. Coffee?"

"Of course, and you can pour a cup for Ana, she'll be along in moment. Her friend Jen called just as we pulled up." Gates grinned again. Jen had been a hit at their wedding, dancing with everyone, saying it was her maid-of-honor duty. According to rumor before they left, she'd hooked up with a surgeon from Palo Alto and was still having a blast. "That will take a few minutes, I know. Then she wanted to talk to your landscaper about trees."

"Trees? Never mind." Dav waved the answer away. "I hope she gets a satisfactory answer. I wouldn't like it if the gardener made her mad. When your lady gets mad, it is very impressive." He set down two of his china cups and joined Gates at the table. "It's also messy. I don't want to irritate her."

"You're right," Gates agreed, taking a cup, enjoying the warmth. It was cool in San Francisco after three weeks on Mykonos. "I also have to tell you, she's got a hell of a sharp eye for a house too."

"House? You looked for something in Greece?"

"No, not in Greece. Here. In the middle of the honeymoon she went online and looked at houses. Wouldn't be satisfied until we'd scanned through everything."

Dav was delighted. "I know a wonderful real estate agent," he began.

Gates shook a finger. "Uh-uh. I remember that woman. No way. Besides, we've already bought the old Henner place, a few miles away. She's now obsessed with the trees on the property, don't ask me why."

Delight suffused Dav's features, and he slapped the table, making the cups jump in their saucers. "That is cause for celebration, my friend. We will be neighbors as well as partners. Good. Wait here a moment." He moved to the desk, spoke to the chef. "We will have champagne."

"Champagne?" Ana said from the doorway, then laughed as Dav hurried to her and swung her off her feet, planting two smacking kisses on either cheek. "We about drowned in your wonderful champagne when we were in Greece." She kissed him back. "Thank you, Dav."

"There is no need for thanks among friends. Champagne is for celebrating, and you should drink a lot of it to celebrate when you are lucky enough to find someone you love. Celebrate it every day," Dav said, more serious now. "Truly, I am so pleased for you both, you know that, but I hope to never stop saying it."

Ana blushed a bit. "Thanks, Dav. If it weren't for you, for the case," she started, and had to stop. She still got emotional when it came to everything that had transpired. She pulled herself together when one of the men wheeled in a cart with the champagne.

"Here we are." Dav urged her to sit, popped the cork. "To celebrate your house, and being neighbors. When you finish with the incorporation papers for the new business, we will celebrate then as well."

He poured glasses for them all, and they raised them, let the crystal chime as they touched them together. "To a long and happy life together," he began, and Gates saw the emotion in his eyes, the mingled delight and sorrow. *"Stin eyia sou."*

"Cheers," Gates added in English as Ana echoed the Greek, *"Stin eyia sou."*

In the darkened house, Jurgens stood over the sleeping boy, Jeremiah. It had been difficult to get into the house, but his work was not yet done. There was a noise in the hall, and he slipped the Glock from its holster, the suppressor still faintly warm from its earlier task. He stood, waiting.

"Jurgens?" Caroline whispered, hurrying into the room. He turned a bit more, showing his face to her, and she gasped, seeing both his expression and the weapon in his hand.

She would know what it meant. It was the end.

Tears welled in her beautiful eyes and her lip quivered; fear shone there as well as she looked from man to child and back again.

"It's done? It's finally done?"

He nodded, a smile beginning to tug at his mouth. His cheeks were stiff with the long trial of keeping everything locked in, of staying silent.

"It's over. Only a year or so more to wait," he whispered back, careful of the sleeping child, his son, his Jeremiah. "Then I can court you properly, my love. Woo you and win the young widow's heart." His smile broadened as he reholstered the gun and opened his arms. She moved into them as if coming home.

Her sigh was long and heartfelt, and he echoed it. "You replaced the paintings as we agreed?" He murmured the words into her hair, breathing in the smell of her, of shampoo and the faint wild scent of her perfume. It was intoxicating.

She nodded into his chest, both answering his question and burrowing closer to him, a luxury they had been denied for far too long. Her arms banded around his taut waist to snug him close to her shapely body. "You are brilliant, my love, brilliant," he said. "I get down on my knees every night and bless the day that *mein Gott* led me to you. You are my heart, you and Jeremiah."

He kissed her then, a long, passionate kiss that brought them both to panting need.

"Can we—"

"I wish we could—" They both spoke at once.

He stroked a possessive hand down the lush length of her back. His, now. Always.

"Nothing of me must be in this house. They suspect Drake. If the worst happens and he's been foolish enough to leave evidence, they may come, inspect," he said, wishing he could stay, engulf himself in her love, her embrace.

Soon though, soon they would be together. A year wasn't very long, and by then, they could make a little brother or sister for Jeremiah. It would space the children well.

"I wish you could be here now. It will be hard," she whispered, still mindful of the boy, who slept undisturbed in his footie pajamas. "It's already been hard. The police, all the calls and questions."

"Soon," Jurgens murmured into her hair, "there will be the funeral."

"You think they will find him that quickly?" Caroline was concerned.

"It won't be long. You did your work well," he praised. She had timed everything perfectly. In the early hours of the morning, she'd arisen, called the warehouse, all of Drake's phones, every point of contact she could think of. There would be a record of her calling all the places, doing all she could to locate him. She'd called the hospitals next, then the police, just as any distraught young wife might do. She'd told them the baby had woken her and she'd realized Drake had not come home. He often worked late, she had gone on to bed.

The steps they'd planned, every move, she had executed with magnificent pathos. She was perfect, his beloved, his Caroline.

"You have courage now, for me, ja?"

"Ja," she echoed him with a watery smile. "But the waiting, the funeral," she murmured, ducking her head. "It will be hard to wait, to not know when it will all happen. How long it will be."

"You will be all the more convincing to them, because you will be shocked. You see this, ja?"

"Yes. Yes, I . . ." She wiped away her tears, took a bracing breath. "I know. I'll be patient."

He chuckled, feeling his heart swell. "I will send flowers. When the time comes. They will be for you, of course," he said, smiling with passion in his heart, knowing she would recognize them, the ones that came from him. "Something for our son as well. You will know."

She nodded, emotion suffusing her features. "I'll know. I always have."

"Sehr gut." Very good. "I must go." He hesitated, then spoke his mind. "I will miss you. Every moment, I'll miss you."

She hugged him again, even more tightly. "I'll miss you desperately, but I'll get through, knowing we'll be together in the end."

He smiled, relief coursing through him. She was so luminous, his Caroline. All his, now.

"You will be brilliant," he complimented, hugging her again, wishing he didn't have to release her now, let her go on with this part of their plan alone. Trust, though, was everything between them so he would step back, let her do her part.

Jurgens pressed an untraceable phone into her hand. He had learned much from Drake about keeping phones private and untrackable. "I'll call. It will be some time before they find him, but they will find him." He kissed her again, another long, magnificent kiss to hold him until he could claim her. "You'll see me. Here and there. When you do, know that I am wishing to be like this, with you. Always."

She buried her face in his chest once more, her strong arms holding him as if she would never release him. It swelled his heart with love for her.

She moved back, crossed her arms to hug herself as if bereft without him. "I'll be here. I know the steps, and I'll follow them, just as we planned."

"Ich liebe dich," he said, voicing it aloud for the very first time. *I love you.* It was like the sun breaking through the clouds, to see the joy on her face.

"Oh, darling." She nearly sobbed the words as she flung herself back into his arms. "I love you too."

The feel of her made it that much harder to leave, but go he must. He'd already spent too much time.

Jurgens slipped out the way he had come in, savoring her words, savoring the look, taste, and feel of her as he made his way through the underground passage that connected the mansion to its neighbor, half a mile away. Smiling, he changed his black watch cap for a ball cap, put on the heavy leather belt with its flashlight and nightstick that he'd left in the terminus of the passageway, and ghosted out of the simple garden shed.

Keys jingling, he got back into the small SUV and started the engine, making his rounds as the new hire by the neighborhood security company.

Did you miss Jeanne's other books?
Go back and read them all!

DARK AND DANGEROUS

Sizzling seduction and hair-raising suspense combine in Jeanne Adams's gripping new novel about a woman whose past returns—with a vengeance . . .

Nowhere to Hide

Dana Markham is up against a cold-blooded killer who knows her all too well: Donovan Walker. Wanted for drug trafficking, armed and dangerous—he's also her ex-husband. What she knows about him could land him behind bars forever . . . or put her and her young son in an early grave if Donovan finds them first. Dana's one chance lies with a man she barely knows at all. Tall and darkly sensual, Caine Bradley is an undercover FBI agent who's been posing as Walker's henchman. Compelled to work with Caine to lure her ex out of hiding, Dana must fight against her own raw, urgent needs. But is he who he says he is? Her passionate desire for him could be her salvation—or her greatest mistake . . .

The windchimes began to peal, a musical jangle. Dana had just set her book aside and turned out the bedside lights. Listening, she felt a twitch of intuition. For her, the tingle of unease was as good as a certified letter when it came to danger.

There had been no breeze, not even the barest hint of wind when she'd let their dog, Shadow, out for the last time at eleven. The cool spring air, redolent with the scent of new growth, had been still.

Getting out of bed, she flicked the television on for light. Tossing the remote on the bed, she walked to the inner hallway; continuing to listen, preparing to act.

The clanging of the chimes picked up speed. *Fools,* she thought, even as her heart raced, realizing what hovered outside her house.

Shadow began to growl. Everything seemed to slow down, separate into moments. They had come for her, for her son. She'd been dreading this and yet expecting it.

It had only been four hours since she'd sat with Xavier, reading from one of the *Harry Potter* books at bedtime. Now, she would have to wake him, to run.

They'd had to scurry away in the night before, or leave with bare minutes of leeway, but then they'd had help. The FBI or WitSec—the witness security program—had been there.

Donovan had found them again, and this time she was on her own.

As scared as she was, the clangor of the bells almost made her laugh. Almost. For all her ex-husband's cunning, for all the expensive black-market military hardware he bought with his drug money, he didn't have anyone smart enough to think about those windchimes.

Thank God.

Warned by the wind. If that's not cosmic justice, I don't know what is. How soon he forgot. He'd trained her well to take near-paranoid precautions. That hard-won expertise worked against him now, and ensured she knew trouble had arrived.

Being forewarned only helped her if she took action, she reminded herself, thinking furiously. There was no time to get to the van, and even if they did, the helicopter would be armed. They would be sitting ducks on the country roads. There was no time to go to the safe room in the basement, either.

Donovan's men would be on the ground by now.

She did have time to activate her other protective measures, pitiful though they were. Still growling, Shadow—one of her more traditional defenses—obviously sensed the peril, and stood ready for her commands.

DARK AND DEADLY

In Jeanne Adams's pulse-pounding thriller, a woman who's lost everything must turn to the man she considers her worst enemy. But he isn't the one who wants her dead . . .

No Escape

Cursed. Bad things happen to men who get close to Victoria Hagan. Now one of them has paid the ultimate price. Her ex-fiance, Todd, has been found murdered in the very church where he left her at the altar—and Torie is the prime suspect. Her only hope is the last person she wants to see . . .

Ever since he advised his best friend not to marry her and the bride-to-be walked in on the conversation, Paul Jameson has stayed far away from Torie—and resisted their dangerously hot mutual attraction. Still, Paul promised Todd he would take care of Torie. She certainly needs him now . . . almost as much as he wants her. And that's exactly what a killer is counting on . . .

"What do you mean we can't get married?" Torie's words were a panicked screech. "Todd, there are five hundred guests in the church. The music's started. They've seated our mothers, for God's sake." She gestured and rose petals flew from her bouquet, drifting to the floor like snow.

Panic filled her. Half of Philadelphia was waiting for her to walk down the aisle. Her sorority sisters were there. His fraternity brothers, mostly sober, were there. Even the lawyers from his new firm and her boss from the engineering firm were there to see her marry Todd.

"I know, I know. But, I can't do it Torie, I can't. Not now."

"What changed, Todd, between Monday, when I left the conference in Raleigh and today?" Torie's heart stuttered. "Oh, my God. You slept with someone. You had a fling."

"No, no, no," Todd protested, his face stricken, grabbing her waving hands, bouquet and all. "I didn't, I swear. What happened is—"

"Tell me," she insisted. "I have a right to know."

"I won the jackpot," he blurted. "Three hundred and sixty-eight million dollars. I never expected, I mean, you know, I always buy a ticket on special days."

He did. She knew that. They'd always talked about what they'd do if they won.

Her mind whirled. Oh good Lord, he'd won.

"You won?" she managed faintly. "All that money?"

They would never have to scrimp. Her mother's complaints about Todd's spendthrift habits and frat-boy ways would be nothing against that kind of income. They could—

Torie went very still as his words sank in. He was choosing the money over her, over the life they'd planned.

Devastation came first. Then hot anger boiled in her veins. He didn't want to share a new, financially prosperous life with her.

She wasn't good enough.

Oblivious to her reaction, he just shook his head. "I know, it's crazy. But you understand, right? This changes everything in my life."

"You son of a bitch," Torie snarled as she balled up her fist.

The door from the bride's room to the church opened, but Torie barely heard it, and didn't look around. The bouquet disintegrated and the best man gasped as Torie decked her groom.